GLORY IN DEATH

J. D. Robb

BERKLEY
New York

BERKLEY
An imprint of Penguin Random House LLC
penguinrandomhouse.com

Copyright © 1995 by Nora Roberts
Excerpt from *Judgment in Death* by J. D. Robb copyright © 2000 by Nora Roberts
Penguin Random House supports copyright. Copyright fuels creativity, encourages diverse voices,
promotes free speech, and creates a vibrant culture. Thank you for buying an authorized
edition of this book and for complying with copyright laws by not reproducing, scanning,
or distributing any part of it in any form without permission. You are supporting writers
and allowing Penguin Random House to continue to publish books for every reader.

BERKLEY and the BERKLEY & B colophon are registered trademarks of
Penguin Random House LLC.

ISBN: 9780593545645

Berkley mass-market edition / December 1995
Berkley trade paperback edition / March 2022

Printed in the United States of America
1st Printing

Fame then was cheap . . .
And they have kept it since, by being dead.

—DRYDEN

Chok'd with ambition of the meaner sort.

—SHAKESPEARE

chapter one

The dead were her business. She lived with them, worked with them, studied them. She dreamed of them. And because that didn't seem to be enough, in some deep, secret chamber of her heart, she mourned for them.

A decade as a cop had toughened her, given her a cold, clinical, and often cynical eye toward death and its many causes. It made scenes such as the one she viewed now, on a rainy night on a dark street nasty with litter, almost too usual. But still, she felt.

Murder no longer shocked, but it continued to repel.

The woman had been lovely once. Long trails of her golden hair spread out like rays on the dirty sidewalk. Her eyes, wide and still with that distressed expression death often left in them, were a deep purple against cheeks bloodlessly white and wet with rain.

She'd worn an expensive suit, the same rich color as her eyes. The jacket was neatly buttoned in contrast to the

jerked-up skirt that exposed her trim thighs. Jewels glittered on her fingers, at her ears, against the sleek lapel of
the jacket. A leather bag with a gold clasp lay near her
outstretched fingers.

Her throat had been viciously slashed.

Lieutenant Eve Dallas crouched down beside death and
studied it carefully. The sights and scents were familiar, but
each time, every time, there was something new. Both victim and killer left their own imprint, their own style, and
made murder personal.

The scene had already been recorded. Police sensors and
the more intimate touch of the privacy screen were in place
to keep the curious barricaded and to preserve the murder
site. Street traffic, such as it was in this area, had been
diverted. Air traffic was light at this hour of the night and
caused little distraction. The backbeat from the music of
the sex club across the street thrummed busily in the air,
punctuated by the occasional howl from the celebrants.
The colored lights from its revolving sign pulsed against the
screen, splashing garish colors over the victim's body.

Eve could have ordered it shut down for the night, but it
seemed an unnecessary hassle. Even in 2058 with the gun
ban, even though genetic testing often weeded out the
more violent hereditary traits before they could bloom,
murder happened. And it happened with enough regularity
that the fun seekers across the street would be miffed at the
idea of being moved along for such a minor inconvenience
as death.

A uniform stood by continuing video and audio. Beside
the screen a couple of forensics sweepers huddled against
the driving rain and talked shop and sports. They hadn't
bothered to look at the body yet, hadn't recognized her.

Was it worse, Eve wondered, and her eyes hardened as
she watched the rain wash through blood, *when you knew
the victim?*

She'd had only a professional relationship with Prosecuting Attorney Cicely Towers, but enough of one to have
formed a strong opinion of a strong woman. *A successful*

woman, Eve thought, *a fighter, one who had pursued justice doggedly.*

Had she been pursuing it here, in this miserable neighborhood?

With a sigh, Eve reached over and opened the elegant and expensive bag to corroborate her visual ID. "Cicely Towers," she said for the recorder. "Female, age forty-five, divorced. Resides twenty-one thirty-two East Eighty-third, number Sixty-one B. No robbery. Victim still wearing jewelry. Approximately . . ." She flipped through the wallet. "Twenty in hard bills, fifty credit tokens, six credit cards left at scene. No overt signs of struggle or sexual assault."

She looked back at the woman sprawled on the sidewalk. *What the hell were you doing out here, Towers?* she wondered. *Here, away from the power center, away from your classy home address?*

And dressed for business, she thought. Eve knew Cicely Towers's authoritative wardrobe well, had admired it in court and at City Hall. Strong colors—always camera ready —coordinated accessories, always with a feminine touch.

Eve rose, rubbed absently at the wet knees of her jeans.

"Homicide," she said briefly. "Bag her."

It was no surprise to Eve that the media had caught the scent of murder and were already hunting it down before she'd reached the glossy building where Cicely Towers had lived. Several remotes and eager reporters were camped on the pristine sidewalk. The fact that it was three A.M. and raining buckets didn't deter them. In their eyes, Eve saw the wolf gleam. The story was the prey, ratings the trophy.

She could ignore the cameras that swung in her direction, the questions shot out like stinging darts. She was almost used to the loss of her anonymity. The case she had investigated and closed during the past winter had catapulted her into the public eye. The case, she thought now as she aimed a steely glance at a reporter who had the nerve to block her path, and her relationship with Roarke.

The case had been murder. And violent death, however exciting, soon passed out of the public interest.

But Roarke was always news.

"What do you have, Lieutenant? Do you have a suspect? Is there a motive? Can you confirm that Prosecuting Attorney Towers was decapitated?"

Eve slowed her ground-eating stride briefly and swept her gaze over the huddle of soggy, feral-eyed reporters. She was wet, tired, and revolted, but she was careful. She'd learned that if you gave the media any part of yourself, it squeezed it, twisted it, and wrung it dry.

"The department has no comment at this time other than that the investigation into Prosecuting Attorney Towers's death is proceeding."

"Are you in charge of the case?"

"I'm primary," she said shortly, then swung between the two uniforms guarding the entrance to the building.

The lobby was full of flowers: long banks and flows of fragrant, colorful blooms that made her think of spring in some exotic place—the island where she had spent three dazzling days with Roarke while she'd recovered from a bullet wound and exhaustion.

She didn't take time to smile over the memory, as she would have under other circumstances, but flashed her badge and moved across the terra-cotta tiles to the first elevator.

There were more uniforms inside. Two were behind the lobby desk handling the computerized security, others watched the entrance, still others stood by the elevator tubes. It was more manpower than necessary, but as PA, Towers had been one of their own.

"Her apartment's secured?" Eve asked the closest cop.

"Yes, sir. No one's been in or out since your call at oh two ten."

"I'll want copies of the security discs." She stepped into the elevator. "For the last twenty-four hours, to start." She glanced down at the name on his uniform. "I want a detail of six, for door-to-doors beginning at seven hundred, Biggs.

Floor sixty-one," she ordered, and the elevator's clear doors closed silently.

She stepped out into the sixty-first's lush carpet and museum quiet. The halls were narrow, as they were in most multihabitation buildings erected within the last half century. The walls were a flawless creamy white with mirrors at rigid intervals to lend the illusion of space.

Space was no problem within the units, Eve mused. There were only three on the entire floor. She decoded the lock on 61-B using her Police and Security master card and stepped into quiet elegance.

Cicely Towers had done well for herself, Eve decided. And she liked to live well. As Eve took the pocket video from her field kit and clipped it onto her jacket, she scanned the living area. She recognized two paintings by a prominent twenty-first century artist hanging on the pale rose-toned wall above a wide U-shaped conversation area done in muted stripes of pinks and greens. It was her association with Roarke that had her identifying the paintings and the easy wealth in the simplicity of decor and selected pieces.

How much does a PA pull in per year? she wondered as the camera recorded the scene.

Everything was tidy, meticulously so. But then, Eve reflected, from what she knew of Towers, the woman had been meticulous. In her dress, in her work, in maintaining her privacy.

So, what had an elegant, smart, and meticulous woman been doing in a nasty neighborhood in the middle of a nasty night?

Eve walked through the room. The floor was white wood and shone like a mirror beneath lovely rugs that echoed the dominant colors of the room. On a table were framed holograms of children in varying stages of growth, from babyhood on through to the college years. A boy and girl, both pretty, both beaming.

Odd, Eve thought. She'd worked with Towers on countless cases over the years. Had she known the woman had children? With a shake of her head, she walked over to the small computer built into a stylish workstation in the corner of the room. Again she used her master card to engage it.

"List appointments for Cicely Towers, May two." Eve's lips pursed as she read the data. An hour at an upscale private health club prior to a full day in court followed by a six o'clock with a prominent defense attorney, then a dinner engagement. Eve's brow lifted. Dinner with George Hammett.

Roarke had dealings with Hammett, Eve remembered. She'd met him now twice and knew him to be a charming and canny man who made his rather exorbitant living with transportation.

And Hammett was Cicely Towers's final appointment of the day.

"Print," she murmured and tucked the hard copy in her bag.

She tried the tele-link next, requesting all incoming and outgoing calls for the past forty-eight hours. It was likely she would have to dig deeper, but for now she ordered a recording of the calls, tucked the disc away, and began a long, careful search of the apartment.

By five A.M., her eyes were gritty and her head ached. The single hour's sleep she had managed to tuck in between sex and murder was beginning to wear on her.

"According to known information," she said wearily for the recorder, "the victim lived alone. No indication from initial investigation to the contrary. No indication that the victim left her apartment other than voluntarily, and no record of an appointment that would explain why the victim traveled to the location of the murder. Primary has secured data from her computer and tele-link for further investigation. Door-to-doors will begin at oh seven hundred and building security discs will be confiscated. Primary is leaving victim's residence and will be en route to victim's offices in City Hall. Lieutenant Dallas, Eve. Oh five oh eight."

Eve switched off the audio and video, secured her field kit, and headed out.

It was past ten when she made it back to Cop Central. In concession to her hollow stomach, she zipped through the eatery, disappointed but not surprised to find most of the good stuff long gone by that hour. She settled for a soy muffin and what the eatery liked to pretend was coffee. As bad as it was, she downed everything before she settled in her office.

It was just as well, as her 'link beeped instantly.

"Lieutenant."

She bit back a sigh as she stared into Whitney's wide, grim-eyed face. "Commander."

"My office, now."

There wasn't time to close her mouth before the screen went blank.

The hell with it, she thought. She scrubbed her hands over her face, then through her short, choppy brown hair. There went any chance of checking her messages, of calling Roarke to let him know what she was into, or of the ten-minute catnap she'd been fantasizing about.

She rose again, worked out the kinks in her shoulders. She did take the time to remove her jacket. The leather had protected her shirt, but her jeans were still damp. Philosophically, she ignored the discomfort and gathered up what little data she had. If she was lucky, she might get another cup of cop coffee in the commander's office.

It only took Eve about ten seconds to realize the coffee would have to wait.

Whitney wasn't sitting behind his desk, as was his habit. He was standing, facing the single-wall window that gave him his personal view of the city he'd served and protected for more than thirty years. His hands were clasped behind his back, but the relaxed pose was negated by the white knuckles.

Eve briefly studied the broad shoulders, the grizzled dark hair, and the wide back of the man who had only months before refused the office of chief to remain in command here.

"Commander."

"It's stopped raining."

Her eyes narrowed in puzzlement before she carefully made them blank. "Yes, sir."

"It's a good city all in all, Dallas. It's easy to forget that from up here, but it's a good city all in all. I'm working to remember that right now."

She said nothing, had nothing to say. She waited.

"I made you primary on this. Technically, Deblinsky was up, so I want to know if she gives you any flak."

"Deblinsky's a good cop."

"Yes, she is. You're better."

Because her brows flew up, she was grateful he still had his back to her. "I appreciate your confidence, Commander."

"You've earned it. I overrode procedure to put you in control for personal reasons. I need the best, someone who'll go to the wall and over it."

"Most of us knew PA Towers, Commander. There isn't a cop in New York who wouldn't go to the wall and over it to find who killed her."

He sighed, and the deep inhalation of air rippled through his thick body before he turned. For a moment longer he said nothing, only studied the woman he'd put in charge. She was slim, deceptively so, for he had reason to know she had more stamina than was apparent in that long, slender body.

She was showing some fatigue now, in the shadows under her whiskey colored eyes, in the pallor of her bony face. He couldn't let that worry him, not now.

"Cicely Towers was a personal friend—a close personal friend."

"I see." Eve wondered if she did. "I'm sorry, Commander."

"I knew her for years. We started out together, a hotdog-ging cop and an eager-beaver criminal lawyer. My wife and

I are godparents to her son." He paused a moment and seemed to fight for control. "I've notified her children. My wife is meeting them. They'll stay with us until after the memorial."

He cleared his throat, pressed his lips together. "Cicely was one of my oldest friends, and above and beyond my professional respect and admiration for her, I loved her very much. My wife is devastated by this; Cicely's children are shattered. All I could tell them was that I would do everything, anything in my power to find the person who did this to her, to give her what she worked for most of her life: justice."

Now he did sit, not with authority but with weariness. "I'm telling you this, Dallas, so that you know up front I have no objectivity on this case. None. Because I don't, I'm depending on you."

"I appreciate you being frank, Commander." She hesitated only an instant. "As a personal friend of the victim's, it'll be necessary to interview you as soon as possible." She watched his eyes flicker and harden. "Your wife as well, Commander. If it's more comfortable, I can conduct the interviews at your home rather than here."

"I see." He drew another breath. "That's why you're primary, Dallas. There aren't many cops who'd have the nerve to zero in so directly. I'd appreciate it if you'd wait until tomorrow, perhaps even a day or two longer, to see my wife, and if you'd see her at home. I'll set it up."

"Yes, sir."

"What have you got so far?"

"I did a recon on the victim's residence and her office. I have files of the cases she had pending and those that she closed over the last five years. I need to cross-check names to see if anyone she sent up has been released recently, their families and associates. Particularly the violent offenders. Her batting average was very high."

"Cicely was a tiger in the courtroom, and I never knew her to miss a detail. Until now."

"Why was she there, Commander, in the middle of the

night? Prelim autopsy puts time of death at one sixteen. It's a rough neighborhood—shake-downs, muggings, sex joints. There's a known chemical trading center a couple of blocks from where she was found."

"I don't know. She was a careful woman, but she was also . . . arrogant." He smiled a little. "Admirably so. She'd go head to head with the worst this city's got to offer. But to put herself in deliberate jeopardy . . . I don't know."

"She was trying a case, Fluentes, murder two. Strangulation of a lady friend. His lawyer's using the passion defense, but word is Towers was going to send him away. I'm checking it out."

"Is he on the street or in a cage?"

"On the street. First violent offense, bail was dead low. Being it was murder, he was required to wear a homing bracelet, but that doesn't mean diddly if he knew anything about electronics. Would she have met with him?"

"Absolutely not. It would corrupt her case to meet a defendant out of the courtroom." Thinking of Cicely, remembering Cicely, Whitney shook his head. "That she'd never risk. But he could have used other means to lure her there."

"Like I said, I'm checking it out. She had a dinner appointment last night with George Hammett. Do you know him?"

"Socially. They saw each other occasionally. Nothing serious, according to my wife. She was always trying to find the perfect man for Cicely."

"Commander, it's best if I ask now, off the record. Were you sexually involved with the victim?"

A muscle in his cheek jerked, but his eyes stayed level. "No, I wasn't. We had a friendship, and that friendship was very valuable. In essence, she was family. You wouldn't understand family, Dallas."

"No." Her voice was flat. "I suppose not."

"I'm sorry for that." Squeezing his eyes shut, Whitney rubbed his hands over his face. "That was uncalled for, and unfair. And your question was relevant." He dropped his hands. "You've never lost anyone close to you, have you, Dallas?"

"Not that I remember."

"It shreds you to pieces," he murmured.

She supposed it would. In the decade she had known Whitney, she had seen him furious, impatient, even coldly cruel. But she had never seen him devastated.

If that was what being close, and losing, did to a strong man, Eve supposed she was better off as she was. She had no family to lose, and only vague, ugly flashes of her childhood. Her life as it was now had begun when she was eight years old and had been found, battered and abandoned, in Texas. What had happened before that day didn't matter. She told herself constantly that it didn't matter. She had made herself into what she was, who she was. For friendship she had precious few she cared enough for, trusted enough in. As for more than friendship, there was Roarke. He had whittled away at her until she'd given him more. Enough more to frighten her at odd moments—frighten her because she knew he wouldn't be satisfied until he had all.

If she gave him all, then lost him, would she be in shreds?

Rather than dwell on it, Eve dosed herself with coffee and the remains of a candy bar she unearthed in her desk. The prospect of lunch was a fantasy right up there with spending a week in the tropics. She sipped and munched while she scanned the final autopsy report on her monitor.

The time of death remained as issued in the prelim. The cause, a severed jugular and the resulting loss of blood and oxygen. The victim had enjoyed a meal of sea scallops and wild greens, wine, real coffee, and fresh fruit with whipped cream. Ingestion estimated at five hours before death.

The call had come in quickly. Cicely Towers had been dead only ten minutes before a cab driver, brave or desperate enough to work the neighborhood, had spotted the body and reported it. The first cruiser had arrived three minutes later.

Her killer had moved fast, Eve mused. Then again, it was easy to fade in a neighborhood like that, to slip into a car, a doorway, a club. There would have been blood; the jugular gushed and sprayed. But the rain would have been an asset, washing it from the murderer's hands.

She would have to comb the neighborhood, ask questions that were unlikely to receive any sort of viable answer. Still, bribes often worked where procedure or threats wouldn't.

She was studying the police photo of Cicely Towers with her necklace of blood when her 'link beeped.

"Dallas, Homicide."

A face flashed on her screen, young, beaming, and sly. "Lieutenant, what's the word?"

Eve didn't swear, though she wanted to. Her opinion of reporters wasn't terribly high, but C. J. Morse was on the lowest end of her scale. "You don't want to hear the word I've got for you, Morse."

His round face split with a smile. "Come on, Dallas, the public's right to know. Remember?"

"I've got nothing for you."

"Nothing? You want me to go on air saying that Lieutenant Eve Dallas, the finest of New York's finest, has come up empty in the investigation of the murder of one of the city's most respected, most prominent, and most visible public figures? I could do that, Dallas," he said, clicking his tongue. "I could, but it wouldn't look good for you."

"And you figure that matters to me." Her smile was thin and laser sharp, and her finger hovered over the disconnect. "You figure wrong."

"Maybe not to you personally, but it would reflect on the department." His girlishly long lashes fluttered. "On Commander Whitney for pulling strings to put you on as primary. And there's the backwash on Roarke."

Her finger twitched, then curled into her palm. "Cicely Towers's murder is a priority with the department, with Commander Whitney, and with me."

"I'll quote you."

Fucking little bastard. "And my work with the department has nothing to do with Roarke."

"Hey, brown-eyes, anything that touches you, touches Roarke now, and vice versa. And you know, the fact that your man had business dealings with the recently deceased, her ex-husband, and her current escort ties it up real pretty."

Her hands balled into fists of frustration. "Roarke has a lot of business dealings with a lot of people. I didn't know you were back on the gossip beat, C. J."

That wiped the smarmy little smile off his face. There was nothing C. J. Morse hated more than being reminded of his roots in gossip and society news. Especially now that he'd wormed his way onto the police beat. "I've got contacts, Dallas."

"Yeah, you've also got a pimple in the middle of your forehead. I'd have that taken care of." With that cheap but satisfying shot, Eve cut him off.

Springing up, she paced the small square of her office, jamming her hands into her pockets, pulling them out again. Goddamn it, why did Roarke's name have to come up in connection with the case? Just how closely was he involved with Towers's business dealings and her associates?

Eve dropped into her chair again and scowled at the reports on her desk. She'd have to find out, and quickly.

At least this time, with this murder, she knew he had an alibi. At the time Cicely Towers was having her throat slashed, Roarke had been fucking the hell out of the investigating officer.

chapter two

Eve would have preferred to have gone back to the apartment she continued to keep despite the fact that she spent most nights at Roarke's. There, she could have brooded, thought, slept, and walked herself back through the last day of Cicely Towers's life. Instead, she headed for Roarke's.

She was tired enough to give up the controls and let the auto program maneuver the car through late-evening traffic. Food was the first thing she needed, Eve decided. And if she could steal ten minutes to clear her mind, so much the better.

Spring had decided to come out and play, prettily. It tempted her to open the windows, ignore the sounds of bustling traffic, the hum of maxibuses, the griping of pedestrians, the overhead swish of air traffic.

To avoid the echoing bellow of the guides from the tourist blimps, she veered over toward Tenth. A shot through midtown and a quick zip up Park would have been quicker, but she would have been treated to the droning recitation of New York's attractions, the history and tradition of Broadway, the brilliance of museums, the variety of shops —and the plug for the blimp's own gift emporium.

As the blimp route skimmed over her apartment, she'd heard the spiel countless times. She didn't care to hear about the convenience of the people glides that connected the sparkling fashion shops from Fifth to Madison or the Empire State Building's newest sky walk.

A minor traffic snag at Fifty-second had her pondering a billboard where a stunning man and a stunning woman exchanged a passionate kiss, sweetened, they claimed each time they came up for air, by Mountain Stream Breath Freshener.

Their vehicles jammed flank to flank, a couple of cabbies shouted inventive insults at each other. A maxibus overflowing with passengers laid on its horn, adding an ear-stinging screech that had pedestrians on rampways and sidewalks shaking their heads or their fists.

A traffic hovercraft dipped low, blasted out the standard order to proceed or be cited. Traffic inched uptown, full of noise and temper.

The city changed as she moved from its core to its edges, where the wealthy and the privileged made their homes. Wider, cleaner streets, the sweep of trees from the islands of parks. Here the vehicles quieted to a whoosh of movement, and those who walked did so in tailored outfits and fine shoes.

She passed a dog walker who handled a brace of elegant gold hounds with the steady aplomb of a seasoned droid.

When she came to the gates of Roarke's estate, her car idled until the program cleared her through. His trees were blooming. White blossoms flowed along with pink, accented by deep, rich reds and blues, all carpeted by a long sweep of emerald grass.

The house itself towered up into the deepening sky, glass sparkling in the late sun, the stone grand and gray. It had been months since she had first seen it, yet she had never grown used to the grandeur, the sumptuousness, the simple, unadulterated wealth. She had yet to stop asking herself what she was doing here—here, with him.

She left her car at the base of the granite steps and climbed them. She wouldn't knock. That was pride, and it was ornery. Roarke's butler despised her and didn't trouble to hide it.

As expected, Summerset appeared in the hall like a puff of black smoke, his silver hair gleaming, a frown of disapproval ready on his long face.

"Lieutenant." His eyes scraped her, making her aware that she was wearing the same clothes she'd left in, and they were considerably rumpled. "We were unaware of the time of your return, or indeed, if you intended to return."

"Were we?" She shrugged, and because she knew it offended him, peeled off her scarred leather jacket and held it out to his elegant hands. "Is Roarke here?"

"He is engaged on an interspace transmission."

"The Olympus Resort?"

Summerset's mouth puckered like a prune. "I don't inquire as to Roarke's business."

You know exactly what he's doing and when, she thought, but turned out of the wide, glittery hall toward the curve of the stairs. "I'm going up. I need a bath." She tossed a glance over her shoulder. "You can let him know where I am when he's finished his transmission."

She climbed up to the master suite. Like Roarke, she rarely used the elevators. The moment she'd slammed the bedroom door behind her, she began to strip, leaving a trail of boots, jeans, shirt, and underwear in her wake on the way to the bath.

She ordered the water at 102 degrees Fahrenheit, and as an afterthought tossed in some of the salts Roarke had brought her back from Silas Three. They foamed into sea green froth that smelled of fairy tale woods.

She all but rolled into the oversized marble tub, all but wept when the heat seeped into her aching bones. Drawing one deep breath, she submerged, held herself down for a count of thirty seconds, and surfaced with a sigh of sheer sensual pleasure. She kept her eyes closed and drifted.

So he found her.

Most people would have said she was relaxed. But then, Roarke thought, most people didn't really know and certainly didn't understand Eve Dallas. He was more intimate with her, closer to her mind and heart than he had ever been with another. Yet there were still pockets of her he had yet to plumb.

She was, always, a fascinating learning experience.

She was naked, dipped to her chin in steamy water and perfumed bubbles. Her face was flushed from the heat, her eyes closed, but she wasn't relaxed. He could see the tension in the hand that was fisted on the wide ledge of the tub, in the faint frown between her eyes.

No, Eve was thinking, he mused. And worrying. And planning. He moved quietly, as he had grown up doing in the alleyways of Dublin, along wharves and the stinking streets of cities everywhere. When he sat on the ledge to watch her, she didn't stir for several minutes. He knew the instant she sensed him beside her.

Her eyes opened, the golden brown clear and alert as they latched onto his amused blue. As always, just the sight of him gave her a quick inner jolt. His face was like a painting, a depiction in perfect oils of some fallen angel. The sheer beauty of it, framed by all that rich black hair, was forever a surprise to her.

She cocked a brow, tilted her head. "Pervert."

"It's my tub." Watching her still, he slid an elegant hand through the bubbles into the water and along the side of her breast. "You'll boil in there."

"I like it hot. I needed it hot."

"You've had a difficult day."

He would know, she thought, struggling not to resent it. *He knew everything.* She only moved her shoulder as he rose and went to the automated bar built into the tiles. It hummed briefly as it served up two glasses of wine in faceted crystal.

He came back, sat on the ledge again, and handed her a glass. "You haven't slept; you haven't eaten."

"It goes with the territory." The wine tasted like liquid gold.

"Nonetheless, you worry me, Lieutenant."

"You worry too easily."

"I love you."

It flustered her to hear him say it in that lovely voice that hinted of Irish mists, to know that somehow, incredibly, it was true. Since she had no answer to give him, she frowned into her wine.

He said nothing until he'd managed to tuck away irritation at her lack of response. "Can you tell me what happened to Cicely Towers?"

"You knew her," Eve countered.

"Not well. A light social acquaintance, some business dealings, mostly through her former husband." He sipped his wine, watched the steam rise from her bath. "I found her admirable, wise, and dangerous."

Eve scooted up until the water lapped at the tops of her breasts. "Dangerous? To you?"

"Not directly." His lips curved slightly before he brought the wine to them. "To nefarious practices, to illegalities, small and large, to the criminal mind. She was very like you in that respect. It's fortunate I've mended my ways."

Eve wasn't entirely sure of that, but she let it slide. "Through your business dealings and your light social acquaintance, are you aware of anyone who would have wanted her dead?"

He sipped again, more deeply. "Is this an interrogation, Lieutenant?"

It was the smile in his voice that rubbed her wrong. "It can be," she said shortly.

"As you like." He rose, set his glass aside, and began to unbutton his shirt.

"What are you doing?"

"Getting into the swim, so to speak." He tossed the shirt aside, unhooked his trousers. "If I'm going to be questioned by a naked cop, in my own tub, the least I can do is join her."

"Damn it, Roarke, this is murder."

He winced as the hot water all but scalded him. "You're telling me." He faced her across the sea of froth. "What is it in me that is so perverse it thrives on ruffling you? And," he continued before she could give him her short, pithy opinion, "what is it about you that pulls at me, even when you're sitting there with an invisible badge pinned to your lovely breast?"

He skimmed a hand under, along her ankle, her calf, and to the spot on the back of her knee he knew weakened her. "I want you," he murmured. "Right now."

Her hand had gone limp on the stem of her glass before she managed to shift away. "Talk to me about Cicely Towers."

Philosophically, Roarke settled back. He had no intention of letting her out of the tub until he was finished, so he could afford patience. "She, her former husband, and George Hammett, were on the board of one of my divisions. Mercury, named after the god of speed. Import-export for the most part. Shipping, deliveries, rapid transports."

"I know what Mercury is," she said testily, dealing with the annoyance of not knowing that, too, was one of his companies.

"It was a poorly organized and failing business when I acquired it about ten years ago. Marco Angelini, Cicely's ex, invested, as did she. They were still married at the time, I believe, or just divorced. The termination of their marriage, apparently, was as amicable as such things can be. Hammett was also an investor. I don't believe he became personally involved with Cicely until some years later."

"And this triangle, Angelini, Towers, Hammett, was that amicable, too?"

"It seemed so." Idly he tapped a tile. When it flipped

open to reveal the hidden panel, he programmed in music. Something low and weepy. "If you're worried about my end of it, it was business, and successful business at that."

"How much smuggling does Mercury do?"

His grin flashed. "Really, Lieutenant."

Water lapped as she sat forward. "Don't play games with me, Roarke."

"Eve, it's my fondest wish to do just that."

She gritted her teeth, kicked at the hand that was sneaking up her leg. "Cicely Towers had a rep for being a no-nonsense prosecutor, dedicated, clean as they come. If she'd discovered any of Mercury's dealings skirted the law, she'd have gone after you with a vengeance."

"So, she discovered my perfidy, and I had her lured to a dangerous neighborhood and ordered her throat cut." His eyes were level and entirely too bland. "Is that what you think, Lieutenant?"

"No, damn it, you know it's not, but—"

"Others might," he finished. "Which would put you in a delicate position."

"I'm not worried about that." At the moment, she was worried only about him. "Roarke, I need to know. I need you to tell me if there's anything, anything at all, that might involve you in the investigation."

"And if there is?"

She went cold inside. "I'll have to turn it over to someone else."

"Haven't we been through this before?"

"It's not like the DeBlass case. Not anything like that. You're not a suspect." When he cocked a brow, she struggled to put reason rather than irritation in her voice. Why was everything so complicated when it touched on Roarke? "I don't think you had anything to do with Cicely Towers's murder. Is that simple enough?"

"You haven't finished the thought."

"All right. I'm a cop. There are questions I have to ask. I have to ask them of you, of anyone who's even remotely connected to the victim. I can't change that."

"How much do you trust me?"

"It has nothing to do with trusting you."

"That doesn't answer the question." His eyes went cool, remote, and she knew she'd taken the wrong step. "If you don't trust me by now, believe in me, then we have nothing but some rather intriguing sex."

"You're twisting this around." She was fighting to stay calm because he was scaring her. "I'm not accusing you of anything. If I had come into this case without knowing you or caring about you, I would have put you on the list on principle. But I do know you, and that's not what this is about. Hell."

She closed her eyes and rubbed wet hands over her face. It was miserable for her to try to explain her feelings. "I'm trying get answers that will help to keep you as far out of it as I can because I do care. And I can't stop trying to think of ways I can use you because of your connection with Towers. And your connections, period. It's hard for me to do both."

"It shouldn't have been so hard to simply say it," he murmured, then shook his head. "Mercury is completely legitimate—now—because there's no need for it to be otherwise. It runs well, makes an acceptable profit. And though you might think I'm arrogant enough to engage in criminal acts with a prosecuting attorney on my board of directors, you should know I'm not stupid enough to do so."

Because she believed him, the tightness that she'd carried in her chest for hours broke apart. "All right. There'll still be questions," she told him. "And the media has already made the connection."

"I know. I'm sorry for it. How difficult are they making it for you?"

"They haven't even started." In one of her rare shows of easy affection, she reached for his hand, squeezed it. "I'm sorry, too. Looks like we're in another one."

"I can help." He slid forward so that he could bring their joined hands to his lips. When she smiled, he knew she was, finally, ready to relax. "It isn't necessary for you to keep me out of anything. I can handle that myself. And there's no need to feel guilty or uncomfortable for considering that I could be useful to you in the investigation."

"I'll let you know when I figure out how you might be." This time she only arched her brows when his free hand snaked up her thigh. "If you try to pull that off in here, we're going to need diving equipment."

He levered himself to her, over her, so that water sloshed dangerously at the lip of the ledge. "Oh, I think we can manage just fine on our own."

And he covered her grinning mouth with his to prove it.

Late in the night when she slept beside him, Roarke lay awake watching the stars whirl through the sky window over the bed. Worry he hadn't let her see was in his eyes now. Their fates had intertwined, personally, professionally. It was murder that had brought them together, and murder that would continue to poke fingers into their lives. The woman beside him defended the dead.

As Cicely Towers had often done, he thought, and wondered if that representation is what had cost her her own life.

He made it a point not to worry too much or too often about how Eve made her living. Her career defined her. He was very much aware of that.

Both of them had made themselves—remade themselves —from the little or nothing they had been. He was a man who bought and sold, who controlled, and who enjoyed the power of it. And the profit.

But it occurred to him that there were pockets of his business that would cause her trouble, if the shadows came to light. It was perfectly true that Mercury was clean, but it hadn't always been true. He had other holdings, other interests that dealt in the gray areas. He had grown up in the darker portions of those gray areas, after all. He had a knack for them.

Smuggling, both terrestrial and interstellar, was a profitable and entertaining business. The truly excellent wines of Taurus Five, the stunning blue diamonds mined in the caves of Refini, the precious transparent porcelain manufactured in the Arts Colony of Mars.

True, he no longer had to bypass the law to live, and live well. But old habits die hard.

The problem remained: What if he hadn't yet converted Mercury into a legitimate operation? What he saw as a harmless business diversion would have weighed on Eve like a stone.

Added to that was the humbling fact that despite what they had begun to build together, she was far from sure of him.

She murmured something, shifted. Even in sleep, he mused, she hesitated before turning to him. He was having a very difficult time with that. Changes were going to be necessary, soon, for both of them.

For the moment, he would deal with what he could control. It would be very simple for him to make a few calls and ask a few questions relating to Cicely Towers. It would be less simple and take a bit more time to convert all of those gray areas of his concerns into the light.

He looked down to study her. She was sleeping well, her hand open and relaxed on the pillow. He knew sometimes she dreamed, badly. But tonight her mind was quiet. Trusting it would remain so, he slipped out of bed to begin.

Eve woke to the fragrance of coffee. Genuine, rich coffee ground from beans cultivated on Roarke's plantation in South America. The luxury of that was, Eve could admit, one of the first things she'd grown accustomed to, indeed come to depend on, when it came to staying at Roarke's.

Her lips were curved before her eyes opened.

"Christ, heaven couldn't be better than this."

"I'm glad you think so."

Her eyes might have still been bleary, but she managed to focus on him. He was fully dressed in one of the dark suits that made him look both capable and dangerous. In the sitting area below the raised platform where the bed stood, he seemed to be enjoying breakfast and his quick daily scan of the day's news on his monitor.

The gray cat she'd named Galahad lay like a fat slug on the arm of the chair and studied Roarke's plate with bicolored, avaricious eyes.

"What time is it?" she demanded, and the bedside clock murmured the answer: oh six hundred. "Jesus, how long have you been up?"

"Awhile. You didn't say when you had to be in."

She ran her hands over her face, up through her hair. "I've got a couple hours." A slow starter, she crawled out of bed and looked groggily around for something to wear.

Roarke watched her a moment. It was always a pleasure to watch Eve in the morning, when she was naked and glassy-eyed. He gestured toward the robe the bedroom droid had picked up from the floor and hung neatly over the foot of the bed. Eve groped into it, too sleepy yet to be baffled by the feel of silk against her skin.

Roarke poured her a cup of coffee and waited while she settled into the chair across from him and savored it. The cat, thinking his luck might change, thudded onto her lap with enough weight to make her grunt.

"You slept well."

"Yeah." She drew the coffee in like breath, winced only a little as Galahad circled her lap and kneaded her thighs with his needle claws. "I feel close to human again."

"Hungry?"

She grunted again. Eve already knew his kitchen was staffed with artists. She took a swan-shaped pastry from the silver tray and downed it in three enthusiastic bites. When she reached for the coffeepot herself, her eyes were fully open and clear. Feeling generous, she broke off a swan's head and gave it to Galahad.

"It's always a pleasure watching you wake up," he commented. "But sometimes I wonder if you want me only for my coffee."

"Well . . ." She grinned at him and sipped again. "I really like the food, too. And the sex isn't bad."

"You seemed to tolerate it fairly well last night. I have to be in Australia today. I may not make it back until tomorrow or the day after."

"Oh."

"I'd like you to stay here while I'm gone."

"We've been through that. I don't feel comfortable."

"Perhaps you would if you'd consider it your home as well as mine. Eve . . ." He laid a hand on hers before she could speak. "When are you going to accept what I feel for you?"

"Look, I'm just more comfortable in my own place when you're away. And I've got a lot of work right now."

"You didn't answer the question," he murmured. "Never mind. I'll let you know when I'll be back." His voice was clipped now, cool, and he turned the monitor toward her. "Speaking of your work, you might like to see what the media is saying."

Eve read the first headline with a kind of weary resignation. Mouth grim, she scanned from paper to paper. The banners were all similar enough. Renowned New York prosecutor murdered. Police baffled. There were images, of course, of Towers. Inside courtrooms, outside courthouses. Images of her children, comments and quotes.

Eve snarled a bit at her own image and the caption that labeled her the top homicide investigator in the city.

"I'm going to get grief on that," she muttered.

There was more, naturally. Several papers had printed a brief rundown of the case she'd closed the previous winter, involving a prominent U.S. senator and three dead whores. As expected, her relationship with Roarke was mentioned in every edition.

"What the hell does it matter who I am or who I'm with?"

"You've leaped into the public arena, Lieutenant. Your name now sells media chips."

"I'm a cop, not a socialite." Fuming, she swiveled to the

elaborate grillwork along the far wall. "Open viewing screen," she ordered. "Channel 75."

The grill slid open, revealing the screen. The sound of the early broadcast filled the room. Eve's eyes narrowed, her teeth clenched.

"There's that fang-toothed, dickless weasel."

Amused, Roarke sipped his coffee and watched C. J. Morse give his six o'clock report. He was well aware that Eve's disdain for the media had grown into a full-fledged disgust over the last couple of months. A disgust that stemmed from the simple fact that she now had to deal with them at every turn of her professional and personal life. Even without that, he didn't think he could blame her for despising Morse.

"And so, a great career has been cut off cruelly, violently. A woman of conviction, dedication, and integrity has been murdered on the streets of this great city, left there to bleed in the rain. Cicely Towers will not be forgotten, but will be remembered as a woman who fought for justice in a world where we struggle for it. Even death can't dim her legacy.

"But will her killer be brought to the justice she lived her entire life upholding? The Police and Security Department of New York as yet offers no hope. Primary investigating officer, Lieutenant Eve Dallas, a jewel of the department, is unable to answer that question."

Eve all but growled when her image filled the screen. Morse's voice continued.

"When reached by 'link, Lieutenant Dallas refused to comment on the murder and the progress of the investigation. No denial was issued as to the speculation that a cover-up is in process . . ."

"Why that smarmy-faced bastard. He never asked about a cover-up. What cover-up?" The slap of her hand on the arm of the chair made Galahad leap away to safer ground. "I've barely had the case for thirty hours."

"Ssh," Roarke said mildly and left her to spring up and stalk the room.

". . . the long list of prominent names that are linked

with Prosecutor Towers, among them Commander Whitney, Dallas's superior. The commander recently refused the offer of the position as Chief of Police and Security. A long-standing, intimate friend of the victim—"

"That's it!" Furious, Eve slapped the screen off manually. "I'm going to slice that worm into pieces. Where the hell is Nadine Furst? If we've got to have a reporter sniffing up our ass, at least she's got a mind."

"I believe she's on Penal Station Omega, a story on prison reform. You might consider a press conference, Eve. The simplest way to deal with this kind of heat is to toss a well-chosen log on the fire."

"Fuck that. What was that broadcast anyway, a report or an editorial?"

"There's little difference since the revised media bill passed thirty years ago. A reporter has the right to flavor a story with his opinion, as long as it's expressed as such."

"I know the damn law." The robe, brilliant with color, swirled around her legs as she turned. "He's not going to get away with insinuating a cover-up. Whitney runs a clean department. I run a clean investigation. And he's not going to get away with using your name to cloud it, either," she continued. "That's what he was leading up to with that excuse for news. That was next."

"He doesn't worry me, Eve. He shouldn't worry you."

"He doesn't worry me. He pisses me off." She closed her eyes and drew a deep breath to settle herself. Slowly, very slowly and very wickedly, she began to smile. "I've got the perfect payback." She opened her eyes again. "How do you think that little bastard would like it if I contacted Furst, gave her an exclusive?"

Roarke set aside his cup. "Come here."

"Why?"

"Never mind." He rose and went to her instead. Cupping her face in his hands, he kissed her hard. "I'm crazy about you."

"I take that to mean you think it's a pretty good idea."

"My late unlamented father taught me one valuable les-

son. 'Boy,' he would say to me in the thick brogue of a
champion drunk, 'the only way to fight is to fight dirty. The
only place to hit is below the belt.' I have a feeling you'll
have Morse nursing his balls before the day's out."

"No, he won't be nursing them." Delighted with herself,
Eve kissed him back. "Because I'll have sliced them right
off."

Roarke gave a mock shudder. "Vicious women are so
attractive. Did you say you had a couple of hours?"

"Not anymore."

"I was afraid of that." He stepped back, took a disc from
his pocket. "You might find this useful."

"What is it?"

"Some data I put together, on Towers's ex, on Hammett.
Files on Mercury."

Her fingers chilled as they closed over the disc. "I didn't
ask you to do this."

"No, you didn't. You'd have gotten access to it, but it
would have taken you longer. You know if you require my
equipment, it's available to you."

She understood he was talking about the room he had,
the unregistered equipment that the sensors of Com-
puguard couldn't detect. "I prefer going through proper
channels for the moment."

"As you like. If you change your mind while I'm gone,
Summerset's aware you have access."

"Summerset wishes I had access to hell," she muttered.

"Excuse me?"

"Nothing. I've got to get dressed." She turned away, then
stopped. "Roarke, I'm working on it."

"On what?"

"On accepting what you seem to feel for me."

He lifted a brow. "Work harder," he suggested.

chapter three

Eve didn't waste time. Her first order of business when she hit her office was to contact Nadine Furst. The 'link buzzed and crackled over the galactic channel. Sunspots, a satellite dink, or simply the aging equipment held up the transmission for several minutes. Finally, a picture wavered onto the screen, then popped into clear focus.

Eve had the pleasure of seeing Nadine's pale, groggy face. She hadn't considered the time difference.

"Dallas." Nadine's normally fluid voice was scratchy and weak. "Jesus, it's the middle of the night here."

"Sorry. You awake, Nadine?"

"Awake enough to hate you."

"Have you been getting Earth news up there?"

"I've been a little busy." Nadine pushed back her tumbled hair and reached for a cigarette.

"When did you start that?"

With a wince, Nadine drew in the first drag. "If you

terrestrial cops ever came up here, you'd give tobacco a shot. Even this dog shit you can buy in this rat hole. And anything else you could get your hands on. It's a fucking disgrace." She hitched in more smoke. "Three people to a cage, most of them zoned on smuggled chemicals. The medical facilities are like something out of the twentieth century. They're still sewing people up with string."

"And limited video privileges," Eve finished. "Imagine, treating murderers like criminals. My heart's breaking."

"You can't get a decent meal anywhere in the entire colony," Nadine griped. "What the hell do you want?"

"To make you smile, Nadine. How soon will you be finished up there and back on planet?"

"Depends." As she began to waken fully, Nadine's senses sharpened. "You have something for me."

"Prosecuting Attorney Cicely Towers was murdered about thirty hours ago." Ignoring Nadine's yelp, Eve continued briskly, "Her throat was slashed, and her body was discovered on the sidewalk of Hundred and forty-fourth between Ninth and Tenth."

"Towers. Jesus wept. I had a one-on-one with her two months ago after the DeBlass case. Hundred and forty-fourth?" The wheels were already turning. "Mugging?"

"No. She still had her jewelry and credit tokens. A mugging in that neighborhood wouldn't have left her shoes behind."

"No." Nadine closed her eyes a moment. "Damn. She was a hell of a woman. You're primary?"

"Right the first time."

"Okay." Nadine let out a long breath. "So, why is the primary on what has to be the top case in the country contacting me?"

"The devil you know, Nadine. Your illustrious associate Morse is drooling down my neck."

"Asshole," Nadine muttered, tamping out the cigarette in quick, jerky bumps. "That's why I didn't get word of it. He'd have blocked me out."

"You play square with me, Nadine, I play square with you."

Nadine's eyes sharpened, her nostrils all but quivered. "Exclusive?"

"We'll discuss terms when you get back. Make it fast."

"I'm practically on planet."

Eve smiled at the blank screen. *That ought to stick in your greedy craw, C. J.,* she mused. She was humming as she pushed away from her desk. She had people to see.

By nine A.M., Eve was cooling her heels in the plush living area of George Hammett's uptown apartment. His taste ran to the dramatic, she noted. Huge squares of crimson and white tiles were cool under her boots. The tinkling music of water striking rock sang from the audio of the hologram sweeping an entire wall with an image of the tropics. The silver cushions of the long, low sofa glittered, and when she pushed a finger into one, it gave like silken flesh.

She decided she'd continue to stand.

Objets d'art were placed selectively around the room. A carved tower that resembled the ruins of some ancient castle, the mask of a woman's face embedded in translucent rose-colored glass, what appeared to be a bottle that flashed with vivid, changing colors with the heat of her hand.

When Hammett entered from an adjoining room, Eve concluded that he was every bit as dramatic as his surroundings.

He looked pale, heavy eyed, but it only increased his stunning looks. He was tall and elegantly slim. His face was poetically hollowed at the cheeks. Unlike many of his contemporaries—Eve knew him to be in his sixties—he had opted to let his hair gray naturally. An excellent choice for him, she thought, as his thick lion's mane was as gleaming a silver as one of Roarke's Georgian candlesticks.

His eyes were the same striking color, though they were dulled now with what might have been grief or weariness.

He crossed to her, cupped her hand in both of his. "Eve." When his lips brushed her cheek, she winced. He was making the connection personal. She thought they both knew it.

"George," she began, subtly drawing back. "I appreciate your time."

"Nonsense. I'm sorry I had to keep you waiting. A call I had to complete." He gestured toward the sofa, the sleeves of his casual shirt billowing with the movement. Eve resigned herself to sitting on it. "What can I offer you?"

"Nothing, really."

"Coffee." He smiled a little. "I recall you're very fond of it. I have some of Roarke's blend." He pressed a button on the arm of the sofa. A small screen popped up. "A pot of Argentine Gold," he ordered, "two cups." Then, with that faint and sober smile still on his lips, he turned back to her. "It'll help me relax," he explained. "I'm not surprised to find you here this morning, Eve. Or perhaps I should be calling you Lieutenant Dallas, under the circumstances."

"Then you understand why I'm here."

"Of course. Cicely. I can't get used to it." His cream-over-cream voice shook a little. "I've heard it countless times on the news. I've spoken with her children and with Marco. But I can't seem to take in the fact that she's gone."

"You saw her the night she was killed."

A muscle in his cheek jerked. "Yes. We had dinner. We often did when our schedules allowed. Once a week at least. More, if we could manage it. We were close."

He paused as a small server droid glided in with the coffee. Hammett poured it himself, concentrating on the small task almost fiercely. "How close?" he murmured, and Eve saw his hand wasn't quite steady as he lifted his cup. "Intimate. We'd been lovers, exclusive lovers, for several years. I loved her very much."

"You maintained separate residences."

"Yes, she—we both preferred it that way. Our tastes, aesthetically speaking, were very different, and the simple truth was we both liked our independence and personal space. We enjoyed each other more, I think, by keeping a certain distance." He took a long breath. "But it was no secret that we had a relationship, at least not among our families and friends." He let the breath out. "Publicly, we both preferred to keep our private lives private. I don't expect that will be possible now."

"I doubt it."

He shook his head. "It doesn't matter. What should matter is finding out who did this to her. I just can't seem to work myself up about it. Nothing can change the fact that she's gone. Cicely was," he said slowly, "the most admirable woman I've ever known."

Every instinct, human and cop, told her this was a man in deep mourning, but she knew that even killers mourned their dead. "I need you to tell me what time you last saw her. George, I'm recording this."

"Yes, of course. It was about ten o'clock. We had dinner at Robert's on East Twelfth. We shared a cab after. I dropped her off first. About ten," he repeated. "I know I got in about quarter after because I had several messages waiting."

"Was that your usual routine?"

"What? Oh." He snapped himself back from some inner world. "We really didn't have one. Often we'd come back here, or go to her apartment. Now and again, when we felt adventurous, we'd take a suite at the Palace for a night." He broke off, and his eyes were suddenly blank and devastated as he shoved off the soft, silver sofa. "Oh God. My God."

"I'm sorry." Useless, she knew, against grief. "I'm so sorry."

"I'm starting to believe it," he said in a voice thick and low. "It's worse, I realize, when you begin to believe it. She laughed when she got out of the cab, and she blew me a kiss from her fingertips. She had such beautiful hands. And I went home, and forgot about her because I had messages waiting. I was in bed by midnight, took a mild tranq because I had an early meeting. While I was in bed, safe, she was lying dead in the rain. I don't know if I can bear that." He turned back, his already pale face bloodless now. "I don't know if I can bear it."

She couldn't help him. Even though his pain was so tangible she could feel it herself, she couldn't help him. "I wish I could do this later, give you time, but I just can't. As far as we know, you're the last person who saw her alive."

"Except her killer." He drew himself up. "Unless, of course, I killed her."

"It would be best for everyone if I ruled that out quickly."

"Yes, naturally, it would—Lieutenant."

She accepted the bitterness in his voice and did her job. "If you could give me the name of the cab company so that I can verify your movements."

"The restaurant called for one. I believe it was a Rapid."

"Did you see or speak with anyone between the hours of midnight and two A.M.?"

"I told you, I took a pill and was in bed by midnight. Alone."

She could verify that with the building security discs, though she had reason to know such things could be doctored. "Can you tell me her mood when you left her?"

"She was a bit distracted, the case she was prosecuting. Optimistic about it. We talked a bit about her children, her daughter in particular. Mirina's planning on getting married next fall. Cicely was pleased with the idea, and excited because Mirina wanted a big wedding with all the old-fashioned trimmings."

"Did she mention anything that was worrying her? Anything or anyone she was concerned about?"

"Nothing that would apply to this. The right wedding gown, flowers. Her hopes that she could swing the maximum sentence in the case."

"Did she mention any threats, any unusual transmissions, messages, contacts?"

"No." He put a hand over his eyes briefly, let it drop to

his side. "Don't you think I'd have told you if I had the slightest inkling of why this happened?"

"Why would she have gone to the Upper West Side at that time of night?"

"I have no idea."

"Was she in the habit of meeting snitches, sources?"

He opened his mouth then closed it again. "I don't know," he murmured, struck by it. "I wouldn't have thought . . . but she was so stubborn, so sure of herself."

"Her relationship with her former husband. How would you describe it?"

"Friendly. A bit reserved, but amiable. They were both devoted to the children and that united them. He was a little annoyed when we became intimate, but . . ." Hammett broke off, stared at Eve. "You can't possibly think . . ." With what might have been a laugh, he covered his face. "Marco Angelini skulking around that neighborhood with a knife, plotting to kill his ex? No, Lieutenant." He dropped his hands again. "Marco has his flaws, but he'd never hurt Cicely. And the sight of blood would offend his sense of propriety. He's much too cold, much too conservative to resort to violence. And he'd have no reason, no possible motive for wishing her harm."

That, Eve thought, was for her to decide.

She tripped from one world to another by leaving Hammett's apartment and going to the West End. Here she would find no silvery cushions, no tinkling waterfalls. Instead there were cracked sidewalks, ignored by the latest spruce-up-the-city campaign, graffiti-laced buildings that invited the onlookers to fuck all manner of man and beast. Storefronts were covered by security grills, which were so much cheaper and less effective than the force fields employed in the posher areas.

She wouldn't have been surprised to see a few rodents overlooked by the feline droids that roamed the alleyways.

Of the two-legged rodents, she saw plenty. One chemihead grinned at her toothily and rubbed his crotch proudly.

A street hawker sized her up quickly and accurately as cop, ducked his head under the wreath of feathers he sported around his magenta hair, and scurried off to safer pastures.

A selected list of drugs were still illegal. Some cops actually bothered to pay attention.

At the moment, Eve wasn't one of them. Unless a little arm twisting helped her get answers.

The rain had washed most of the blood away. The sweepers from the department would have sucked up anything in the immediate area that could be sifted through for evidence. But she stood for a moment over the spot where Towers had died, and she had no trouble envisioning the scene.

Now, she needed to work backward. *Had she stood here,* Eve wondered, *facing her killer? Most likely. Did she see the knife before it sliced across her throat? Possibly. But not quickly enough to react with anything more than a jerk, a gasp.*

Lifting her gaze, Eve scanned the street. Her skin prickled, but she ignored the stares of those leaning against the buildings or loitering around rusting cars.

Cicely Towers had come uptown. Not by cab. There was, to date, no record of a pickup or drop-off from any of the official companies. Eve doubted she would have been foolish enough to try a gypsy.

The subway, she deduced. It was fast and, with the scanners and droid cops, safe as a church, at least until you hit the street. Eve spotted the signal for the underground less than half a block away.

The subway, she decided. *Maybe she was in a hurry? Annoyed to be dragged out on a wet night. Sure of herself, as Hammett had said. She wouldn't have been afraid.*

She marched up the stairs to the street in her power suit, her expensive shoes. She—

Stopping, Eve narrowed her eyes. *No umbrella? Where was her damn umbrella? A meticulous woman, a practical, organized woman didn't go out in the rain without protection.*

Briskly, Eve pulled out her recorder and muttered a note to herself to check on it.

Was the killer waiting for her on the street? In a room? She studied the disintegrating brick of the unrehabbed buildings. *A bar? One of the flesh clubs?*

"Hey, white girl."

Brows knit, Eve turned at the interruption. The man was tall as a house and from the deepness of his complexion, a full black. He sported, as many did in this part of town, feathers in his hair. His cheek tattoo was vivid green and in the shape of a grinning human skull. He wore an open red vest and matching pants snug enough to show the bulge of his cock.

"Hey, black boy," she said in the same casually insulting tone.

He flashed a wide, dazzling grin at her from an unbelievably ugly face. "You looking for action?" He jerked his head toward the garish sign of the all-nude club across the street. "You a little skinny, but they be hiring. Don't get many white as you. Mostly mixed." He chucked her under the chin with fingers the width of soy wieners. "I be the bouncer, put in a word for you."

"Now why would you do that?"

"Out of the goodness of my heart, and five percent of your tips, honeypot. A long white girl like you make plenty jiggling her stuff."

"I appreciate the thought, but I've got a job." Almost with regret, she pulled out her badge.

He whistled through his teeth. "Now how come I don't be seeing that? White girl, you just don't smell like cop."

"Must be the new soap I'm using. Got a name?"

"They just call me Crack. That's the sound it makes when I bust heads." He grinned again, and illustrated by bringing his two huge hands together. "Crack! Get it?"

"I'm catching on. Were you on the door night before last, Crack?"

"Now, I'm sorry to say I was otherwise engaged, and

missed all the excitement. That be my night off, and I spent it catching up on cultural events."

"And those events were?"

"Vampire flick festival down to Grammercy, with my current young nibble. I sure do enjoy watching them bloodsuckers. But I hear we had ourselves a show right here. Got ourselves a dead lawyer. Big, important, fancy one, too. White girl, wasn't she? Just like you, honeypot."

"That's right. What else do you hear?"

"Me?" He trailed a finger down the front of his vest. The nail on his index finger was sharpened to a lethal point and painted black. "I'm too dignified to listen to street talk."

"I bet you are." Understanding the rules, Eve slipped a hundred-credit token from her pocket. "How about I buy a little of that dignity?"

"Well, the price, she looks right." His big hand enveloped the tokens and made them disappear. "I hear she was hanging around in the Five Moons 'long about midnight, give or take. Like she was hanging for somebody, somebody who don't show. Then she ditched."

He glanced down at the sidewalk. "Didn't go far though, did she?"

"No, she didn't. Did she ask for anyone?"

"Not so's I heard."

"Anyone see her with anyone?"

"Bad night. People stay off the street mostly. Some chemi-heads maybe wander, but business going to be slow."

"You know anyone around here who likes to cut?"

"Plenty carry blades and stickers, white girl." His eyes rolled in amusement. "Why you going to carry if you ain't going to use?"

"Anybody just likes to cut," she repeated. "Somebody who doesn't care about making a score."

His grin spread again. The skull on his cheek seemed to nod with the movement. "Everybody cares about making a score. Ain't you trying to?"

She accepted that. "Who do you know around here who's out of a cage recently?"

His laugh was like mortar fire. "Better if you ask don't I know anybody who ain't. And your money's done."

"All right." To his disappointment, she took a card rather than more tokens out of her pocket. "There may be more if you hear anything I can use."

"Keep it in mind. You decide you want to earn a little extra shaking those little white tits, you let Crack know." With this, he loped across the street with the surprising grace of an enormous black gazelle.

Eve turned and went in to try her luck at the Five Moons.

The dive might have seen better days, but she doubted it. It was strictly a drinking establishment: no dancers, no screens, no videos booths. The clientele who patronized the Five Moons weren't there to socialize. From the smell that slapped Eve the moment she stepped through the door, burning off stomach lining was the order of the day.

Even at this hour, the small, square room was well populated. Silent drinkers stood at stingy pedestals knocking back their poison of choice. Others huddled by the bar, closer to the bottles. Eve rated a few glances as she crossed the sticky floor, then people got back to the business of serious drinking.

The bartender was a droid, as most were, but she doubted this one had been programmed to listen cheerfully to the customers' hard luck stories. More likely an arm breaker, she mused, sizing it up as she sidled up to the bar. The manufacturers had given him the tilted eye, golden-skinned appearance of a mixed race. Unlike most of the drinkers, the droid didn't sport feathers or beads, but a plain white smock over a wrestler's body.

Droids couldn't be bribed, she thought with some regret. And threats had to be both clever and logical.

"Drink?" the droid demanded. His voice had a ping to it, a slight echo that indicated overdue maintenance problems.

"No." Eve wanted to keep her health. She showed her badge and had several customers shifting toward corners. "There was a murder two nights ago."

"Not in here."

"But the victim was."

"She was alive then." At some signal Eve didn't catch, the droid took a smudged glass from a drinker midbar, poured some noxious looking liquid into it, and slid it back.

"You were on duty."

"I'm a twenty-four/seven," he told her, indicating he was programmed for full operation without required rest or recharge periods.

"Did you ever see the victim before, in here, around the area?"

"No."

"Who did she meet here?"

"No one."

Eve drummed her fingers on the cloudy surface of the bar. "Okay, let's just make this simple. You tell me what time she came in, what she did, when she left, and how she left."

"I am not required to maintain surveillance on the customers."

"Right." Slowly, Eve rubbed a finger on the bar. When she lifted it, she pursed her lips at the smear of gunk staining the tip. "I'm Homicide, but I'm not required to overlook health violations. You know, I think if I called the Sensor Bugs in here, and they did a sweep, why they'd be shocked. So shocked they'd delete the liquor license."

As threats went, she didn't think it was particularly clever, but it was logical.

The droid took a moment to access the probabilities. "The woman came in at oh sixteen. She didn't drink. She left at one twelve. Alone."

"Did she speak to anyone?"

"She said nothing."

"Was she looking for someone?"

"I didn't ask."

Eve lifted a brow. "You observed her. Did it appear she was looking for someone?"

"It appeared, but she found no one."

"But she stayed nearly an hour. What did she do?"

"Stood, looked, frowned. Checked her watch often. Left."

"Did anyone follow her outside?"

"No."

Absently, Eve scrubbed her soiled finger on her jeans. "Did she have an umbrella?"

The droid looked as surprised by the question as droids were capable of looking. "Yes, a purple one, the same color as her suit."

"Did she leave with it?"

"Yes; it was raining."

Eve nodded, then worked her way through the bar, questioning unhappy customers.

All she really wanted when she returned to Cop Central was a long shower. An hour in the Five Moons had left what felt like a thin layer of muck on her skin. Even her teeth, she thought, running her tongue over them.

But the report came first. She swung into her office, then stopped, studying the wiry-haired man sitting at her desk plucking candied almonds from a bag.

"Nice work if you can get it."

Feeney crossed the feet he'd propped on the edge of her desk. "Good to see you, Dallas. You're a busy lady."

"Some of us cops actually work for a living. Others just play computer games all day."

"You should've taken my advice and worked on your comp skills."

With more affection than annoyance, she knocked his feet from the desk and plopped her butt down in the vacated space. "You just passing by?"

"I've come to offer my services, old pal." Generously, he held out the bag of nuts.

She munched and watched him. He had a hangdog face, one he had never bothered to have enhanced. Baggy eyes, the beginning of jowls, ears that were slightly too big for his head. She liked it just the way it was.

"Why?"

"Well, I got three reasons. First, the commander made an unofficial request; second, I had a lot of admiration for the prosecutor."

"Whitney called you?"

"Unofficially," Feeney explained again. "He thought that if you had someone with my outstanding skills working the data route with you, we'd tie this thing up faster. Never hurts to have a direct line to the Electronic Detection Division."

She considered it, and because she knew Feeney's skills were indeed outstanding, she approved. "Are you going to sign on the case officially or unofficially?"

"That's up to you."

"Then let's make it officially, Feeney."

He grinned and winked. "I figured you'd say that."

"The first thing I need you to do is run the victim's 'link. There's no record either on the log or on the security tapes that she had a visitor the night she was killed. So somebody called her, arranged a meet."

"Good as done."

"And I need a run on everybody she put away—"

"Everybody?" he interrupted, only slightly appalled.

"Everybody." Her face broke into sunny smiles. "I figure you can do it in about half the time I could. I need relatives, loved ones, associates, too. Also cases in progress and pending."

"Jesus, Dallas." But he rolled his shoulders, flexed his fingers like a pianist about to play a concert. "My wife's going to miss me."

"Being married to a cop sucks," she said, patting his shoulder.

"Is that what Roarke says?"

She dropped her hand. "We're not married."

Feeney merely hummed in his throat. He enjoyed seeing Eve's quick frown, quick nerves. "So how's he doing?"

"He's fine. He's in Australia." Her hands found their way into her pockets. "He's fine."

"Uh-huh. Caught the two of you on the news a few weeks ago. At some fancy do at the Palace. You look real sharp in a dress, Dallas."

She shifted uncomfortably, caught herself, and shrugged. "I didn't know you took in the gossip channels."

"Love them," he said unrepentantly. "Must be interesting, leading that high life."

"It has its moments," she muttered. "Are we going to discuss my social life, Feeney, or investigate a murder?"

"We'll have to make time to do both." He rose and stretched. "I'll go run the check on the victim's 'link before I get started on the years of perps she put away. I'll be in touch."

"Feeney." When he turned at her door, she cocked her head. "You said there were three reasons you wanted in. You only gave me two."

"Number three, I missed you, Dallas." He grinned. "Damn if I haven't missed you."

She was smiling when she sat down to work. Damn if she hadn't missed him, too.

chapter four

The Blue Squirrel was one teetering step up from the Five Moons. Eve had a cautious affection for it. There were times she even enjoyed the noise, the press of bodies, and the ever-changing costumes of the clientele. Most of the time she enjoyed the stage show.

The featured singer was one of the rare people Eve considered a genuine friend. The friendship might have had its roots in Eve's arrest of Mavis Freestone several years earlier, but it had flowered, nonetheless. Mavis might have gone straight, but she would never go ordinary.

Tonight, the slim, exuberant woman was screeching out her lyrics against the scream of trumpets, the brass waved by a three-piece female band on the holoscreen backdrop. That, and the quality of the single wine Eve had risked were enough to make her eyes water.

For tonight's show, Mavis's hair was a stunning emerald green. Eve knew Mavis preferred jewel colors. She continued the theme with the single swatch of glistening sapphire material she had somehow draped over herself to cover one generous breast and her crotch. Her other breast was decorated with shimmering stones, with a strategically placed silver star over the nipple.

One misplaced stud or swatch, and the Blue Squirrel could be fined for exceeding its license. The proprietors weren't willing to pay the hefty fee for nude class.

When Mavis whirled, Eve saw that the singer's heart-shaped butt was similarly decorated on each slim cheek. Just, she mused, within the limits of the law.

The crowd loved her. When she stepped from the stage after her set, it was to thunderous applause and drunken cheers. Patrons in the private smoking booths thumped fists enthusiastically on their tiny tables.

"How do you sit down in that?" Eve asked when Mavis arrived at her booth.

"Slowly, carefully, and with great discomfort." Mavis demonstrated, then let out a sigh. "What'd you think of the last number?"

"A real crowd pleaser."

"I wrote it."

"No shit?" Eve hadn't understood a single word, but pride swelled, nonetheless. "That's great, Mavis. I'm awed."

"I might have a shot at a recording contract." Beneath the glitter on her face, Mavis's cheeks flushed. "And I got a raise."

"Well, here's to it." In toast, Eve lifted her glass.

"I didn't know you were coming in tonight." Mavis punched her code into the menu and ordered bubble water. She had to baby her throat for the next set.

"I'm meeting someone."

"Roarke?" Mavis's eyes, currently green, shone. "Is he coming? I'll have to do that last number again."

"He's in Australia. I'm meeting Nadine Furst."

Mavis's disappointment at the opportunity to impress

Roarke shifted quickly to surprise. "You're meeting a reporter? On purpose?"

"I can trust her." Eve lifted a shoulder. "I can use her."

"If you say so. Hey, you think maybe she'd do a piece on
me?"

Not for worlds would Eve have extinguished the light in
Mavis's eyes. "I'll mention it."

"Decent. Listen, tomorrow's my night off. Want to catch
some dinner or hang someplace?"

"If I can manage it. But I thought you were seeing that
performance artist—the one with the pet monkey."

"Flicked him off." Mavis illustrated by brushing a finger
over her bare shoulder. "He was just too static. Gotta go."
She slid out of the booth, her butt decor making little
scraping sounds. Her emerald hair gleamed in the swirling
lights as she edged through the crowd.

Eve decided she didn't want to know what Mavis considered too static.

When her communicator hummed, Eve pulled it out and
punched in her code. Roarke's face filled the miniscreen.
Her first reaction, unbidden, was a huge, delighted smile.

"Lieutenant, I've tracked you down."

"Apparently so." She worked on dimming the smile.
"This is an official channel, Roarke."

"Is it?" His brow lifted. "It doesn't sound like official
surroundings. The Blue Squirrel."

"I'm meeting someone. How's Australia?"

"Crowded. With luck I'll be back within thirty-six hours.
I'll find you."

"I'm not hard to find." She smiled again. "Obviously.
Listen." To amuse them both, she tilted the unit as Mavis
roared into her next set.

"She's unique," Roarke managed after several bars.
"Give her my best."

"I will. I'll—ah—see you when you get back."

"Count on it. You'll think of me."

"Sure. Safe trip, Roarke."

"Eve, I love you."

She let out a baffled breath when his image dissolved.

"Well, well." Nadine Furst moved from her position behind Eve's shoulder and slid into the booth opposite.
"Wasn't that sweet?"

Torn between annoyance and embarrassment, Eve
jammed her communicator back in her pocket. "I thought
you had more class than to eavesdrop."

"Any reporter worth her salary eavesdrops, Lieutenant.
Just like a good cop." Nadine stretched back in the booth.
"So, what does it feel like to have a man like Roarke in love
with you?"

Even if she could have explained it, Eve wouldn't have.
"Thinking of switching from hard news to the romance
channel, Nadine?"

Nadine merely held up a hand, then let out a sigh when
she scanned the club. "I can't believe you wanted to meet
here again. The food's terrible."

"But the atmosphere, Nadine, the atmosphere."

Mavis hit a piercing note and Nadine shuddered. "Fine,
it's your deal."

"You got back on planet quickly."

"I managed to catch a flash transport. One of your boy-
friend's."

"Roarke's not a boy."

"You're telling me. Anyway . . ." Nadine waved that
away. She was obviously tired and a little lagged. "I've got
to eat, even if it kills me." She scanned the menu and
settled dubiously on the stuffed shells supreme. "What are
you drinking?"

"Number fifty-four; it's supposed to be a chardonnay."
Experimentally, Eve sipped again. "It's at least three steps
up from horse piss. I recommend it."

"Fine." Nadine programmed her order and sat back
again. "I was able to access all the data available on the
Towers's homicide on the trip back. Everything the media
has broadcast so far."

"Morse know you're back?"

Nadine's smile was thin and feral. "Oh, he knows. I've

got seniority on the crime beat. I'm in, he's out. And is he pissed!"

"Then my mission is a success."

"But it's not complete. You promised an exclusive."

"And I'll deliver." Eve studied the noodle dish that slid through the serving slot. It didn't look half bad. "Under my terms, Nadine. What I feed you, you broadcast when I give you the light."

"What else is new?" Nadine sampled the first shell, decided it was nearly palatable.

"I'll see that you get more data, and that you get it ahead of the pack."

"And when you've got a suspect."

"You'll get the name first."

Trusting Eve's word, Nadine nodded as she forked up another shell. "Plus a one-on-one with the suspect and another with you."

"I can't guarantee the suspect. You know I can't," Eve continued before Nadine could interrupt. "The perp has rights to choose his own media, or to refuse it all. The best I can do is suggest, maybe even encourage."

"I want pictures. Don't tell me you can't guarantee. You can find a way to see that I get video of the arrest. I want to be on the scene."

"I'll weigh that in when the time comes. In exchange, I want everything you have, every tip that comes in, every rumor, every story lead. No broadcast surprises."

Nadine slipped pasta between her lips. "I can't guarantee," she said sweetly. "My associates have their own agenda."

"What you know, when you know it," Eve said flatly. "And anything that comes out of intramedia espionage." At Nadine's innocent expression, Eve snorted. "Stations spy on stations, reporters spy on reporters. Getting the story on air first is the name of the game. You've got a good batting average, Nadine, or I wouldn't be bothering with you."

"I'll say the same." Nadine sipped her wine. "And for the

most part, I trust you, even if you have no taste in wine. This is barely one step up from horse piss."

Eve sat back and laughed. It felt good, it felt easy, and when Nadine grinned in return, they had a deal.

"Let me see yours," Nadine requested. "And I'll let you see mine."

"The biggest thing I've got," Eve began, "is a missing umbrella."

Eve met Feeney at Cicely Towers's apartment at ten the following morning. One look at his hangdog expression and she knew the news wasn't going to be sunny.

"What wall did you hit?"

"On the 'link." He waited while Eve disarmed the police security on the door, then followed her inside. "She had plenty of transmissions, kept the unit on auto record. Your tag was on the disc."

"That's right, I took it into evidence. Are you trying to tell me no one contacted her to arrange a meet at the Five Moons?"

"I'm trying to tell you I can't tell you." In disgust, Feeney ran a hand through his wiry hair. "Her last call came in at eleven thirty, the transmission ended at eleven forty-three."

"And?"

"She erased the recording. I can get the times, but that's it. The communication, audio, video, are zapped. She zapped them," he continued. "From this unit."

"She erased the call," Eve murmured and began to pace. "Why would she do that? She had the unit on auto; that's standard for law enforcers, even for personal calls. But she erased this one. Because she didn't want any record of who called and why."

She turned back. "You're sure nobody tampered with the disc after it was in evidence?"

Feeney looked pained, then insulted. "Dallas," was all he said.

"Okay, okay, so she zapped it before she went out. That tells me she wasn't afraid, personally, but was protecting herself—or somebody else. If it had to do with a case, she'd have wanted it on record. She'd have made damn sure it was on record."

"I'd say so. If it was a snitch, she could have put a lock on it under her private code, but it doesn't make sense to zap it."

"We'll check her cases anyway, all the way back." She didn't have to see his face to know Feeney was rolling his eyes. "Let me think," she muttered. "She left City Hall at nineteen twenty-six. That's on her log. And several witnesses saw her. Her last stop was the women's lounge where she freshened up for the evening and chatted with an associate. The associate tells me her mood was calm but upbeat. She'd had a good day in court."

"Fluentes is going up. She laid the groundwork. Taking her out won't change that."

"He might have thought different. We'll see about that. She didn't come back here." Frowning, Eve scanned the room. "She didn't have time, so she went straight to the restaurant and met Hammett. I've been by there. His story and his time frame check out with the staff."

"You've been busy."

"Time's passing. The maître d' called them a cab, a Rapid. They were picked up at a twenty-one forty-eight. It was starting to rain."

In her mind, Eve pictured it. The handsome couple in the back of the cab, chatting, maybe brushing fingertips while the cab zipped uptown with raindrops pattering on the roof. She'd been wearing a red dress and matching jacket, according to their server. Power colors for court that she'd dressed up with good pearls and silver heels for the evening.

"The cab dropped her off first," Eve continued. "She told Hammett not to get out, why get wet? She was laughing when she ran for the building, then turned and blew him a kiss."

"Your report said they were tight."

"He loved her." More from habit than hunger, she

dipped a hand into the bag Feeney held out. "Doesn't mean he didn't kill her, but he loved her. According to him, they were both happy with their arrangement, but . . ." She lifted her shoulders. "If he wasn't, and was looking to set up a good alibi, he set a nice romantic, cozy stage. It doesn't work for me, but it's early yet. So, she came up," Eve continued, moving to the door. "Her dress is a little damp, so she goes to the bedroom to hang it up."

As she spoke, Eve followed the projected route, walking over the lovely rugs into the spacious bedroom with its quiet colors and lovely antique bed.

She ordered lights to brighten the area. The police shields on the windows not only frustrated the fly-bys, but blocked most of the sunlight.

"To the closet," she said and pressed the button that opened the long, mirrored sliding doors. "She hangs up the suit." Eve pointed to the red dress and jacket, neatly arranged in a wardrobe ordered in sweeps of color. "Puts away her shoes, puts on a robe."

Eve turned to the bed. A long flow of ivory was spread there. Not folded, not neatly arranged as was the rest of the room, but rumpled, as though it had been impatiently tossed.

"She puts her jewelry in the safe in the side wall of the closet, but she doesn't go to bed. Maybe she goes out to catch the news, to have a nightcap."

With Feeney following, Eve went back to the living area. A briefcase, neatly closed, sat on the table in front of the sofa with a single empty glass beside it.

"She's relaxing, maybe thinking over the evening, rehearsing her court strategy for the next day or her planning her daughter's wedding. Her 'link beeps. Whoever it was, whatever they tell her, gets her moving. She's settled in for the night, but she goes back to the bedroom, after she's zapped the record. She dresses again. Another power suit. She's going to the West End. She doesn't want to blend, she wants to exude authority, confidence. She doesn't call a cab. That's another record. She decides she'll take the subway. It's raining."

Eve moved to a closet tucked into the wall near the front door and pressed it to open. Inside were jackets, wraps, a man's overcoat she suspected was Hammett's, and a fleet of umbrellas in varying colors.

"She takes out the umbrella she bought to match the suit. It's automatic, her mind is on her meet. She doesn't take a lot of money, so it's not a payoff. She doesn't call anyone, because she wants to handle it herself. But when she gets to the Five Moons, nobody meets her. She waits nearly an hour, impatient, checking her watch. She leaves a few minutes after one, back into the rain. She's got her umbrella and starts to walk back to the subway. I figure she's steamed."

"Classy woman, kicking in a dive for an hour for a no show." Feeney popped another nut. "Yeah, steamed would be my take."

"So, she heads out. It's raining pretty hard. Her umbrella's up. She only gets a few feet. Someone's there, probably been close by all along, waiting for her to come out."

"Doesn't want to see her inside," Feeney put in. "Doesn't want to be seen."

"Right. They have to talk a couple of minutes according to the time frame. Maybe they argue—not much of an argument, there isn't time. Nobody's on the street—nobody who'd pay attention, anyway. A couple of minutes later, her throat's slashed, she's bleeding on the sidewalk. Did he plan to do her all along?"

"Lotsa people carry stickers in that area." Thoughtful, Feeney rubbed his chin. "Couldn't get premeditated on that by itself. But the timing, the setup. Yeah, that's how it shakes down to me."

"Me, too. One slice. No defensive wounds, so she didn't have time to feel threatened. The killer doesn't take her jewelry, the leather bag, her shoes, or her credits. He just takes her umbrella, and he walks away."

"Why the umbrella?" Feeney wondered.

"Hell, it's raining. I don't know, an impulse, a souvenir. As far as I can see, it's the only mistake he made. I've got grunts out checking a ten-block area to see if he ditched it."

"If he ditched it in that area, some chemi-head's walking around with a purple parasol."

"Yeah." A visual of that almost made her smile. "How could he be sure she'd zap the recording, Feeney? He had to be sure."

"Threat?"

"A PA lives with threats. One like Towers would shake them off like lint."

"If they were aimed at her," he agreed. "She's got kids." He nodded toward the framed holograms. "She wasn't just a lawyer. She was a mother."

With a frown, Eve walked over to the holograms. Curious, she picked up one of the boy and girl together as young teenagers. A flick of her finger over the back had the audio bubbling out.

Hey, big shot. Happy Mother's Day. This will last longer than the flowers. We love you.

Oddly disturbed, Eve set the frame down again. "They're adults now. They're not kids anymore."

"Dallas, once a parent, always a parent. You never finish the job."

Hers had, she thought. A long time finished.

"Then I guess my next stop is Marco Angelini."

Angelini had offices in Roarke's building on Fifth. Eve stepped into the now familiar lobby with its huge tiles and pricey boutiques. The cooing voices of computer guides offered assistance to various locations. She scanned one of the moving maps and ignoring the glides, hiked her way to the elevators along the south end.

The glass tube shot her to the fifty-eighth floor, then opened onto solemn gray carpet and blinding white walls.

Angelini Exports claimed a suite of five offices in this

location. After one quick scan, Eve noted that the company was small potatoes in relation to Roarke Industries.

Then again, she thought with a tight smile, *what isn't?*

The receptionist in the greeting area showed great respect and not a little nerves at the sight of Eve's badge. She fumbled and swallowed so much Eve wondered if the woman had a cache of illegal substances in her desk drawer.

But the fear of cop had her all but shoving Eve into Angelini's office after less than ninety seconds of lag time.

"Mr. Angelini, I appreciate your time. My sympathies for your loss."

"Thank you, Lieutenant Dallas, please sit."

He wasn't elegant, as Hammett was, but he was powerful. A small man, solidly built with jet hair combed slickly back from a prominent widow's peak. His skin was a pale, dusky gold, his eyes bright, hard marbles of azure under thick brows. He had a long nose, thin lips, and the glitter of a diamond on his hand.

If he was grieving, the former husband of the victim hid it better than her lover had.

He sat behind a console-style desk that was smooth as satin. It was absolutely clear but for his still and folded hands. Behind him was a tinted window that blocked the UV rays while letting in the view of New York.

"You've come about Cicely."

"Yes, I was hoping you could spare some time now to answer some questions."

"You have my full cooperation, Lieutenant. Cicely and I were divorced, but we remained partners, in business and in parenthood. I admired and respected her."

There was a hint of his native country in his voice. Just a whisper of it. It reminded her that, according to his dossier, Marco Angelini spent a large part of his time in Italy.

"Mr. Angelini, can you tell me the last time you saw or spoke with Prosecutor Towers?"

"I saw her on March eighteenth, at my home on Long Island."

"She came to your home."

"Yes, for my son's twenty-fifth birthday. We gave him a party together, using my estate there, as it was most convenient. David, our son, often stays there when he is on the East Coast."

"You hadn't seen her since that date."

"No, we were both busy, but we had planned to meet in the next week or two to discuss plans for Mirina's wedding. Our daughter." He cleared his throat gently. "I was in Europe for most of April."

"You called Prosecutor Towers on the night of her death."

"Yes, I left a message to see if we could meet for lunch or drinks at her convenience."

"About the wedding," Eve prompted.

"Yes, about Mirina's wedding."

"Had you spoken with Prosecutor Towers since the day of March eighteenth and the night of her death?"

"Several times." He pulled his fingers apart, linked them again. "As I said, we considered ourselves partners. We had the children, and there were a few business interests."

"Including Mercury."

"Yes." His lips curved ever so slightly. "You are an . . . acquaintance of Roarke's."

"That's right. Did you and your former wife disagree on any of your partnerships, personally or professionally?"

"Naturally we did, on both. But we'd learned, as we had been unable to learn during our marriage, the value of compromise."

"Mr. Angelini, who inherits Prosecutor Towers's interest in Mercury after her death?"

His brow lifted. "I do, Lieutenant, according to the terms of our business contract. There are also a few holdings in some real estate that will revert to me. This was an arrangement of our divorce settlement. I would guide the interests, advise her on investments. Upon the death of one of us, the interests and profits or losses would revert to the other. We both agreed, you see, and trusted that in the end, all either of us had of value would go to our children."

"And the rest of her estate. Her apartment, her jewelry, whatever possessions that weren't part of your agreement?"

"Would, I assume, be left to our children. I imagine there would be a few bequests to personal friends or charities."

Eve was going to dig quickly to learn just how much Towers had tucked away. "Mr. Angelini, you were aware that your ex-wife was intimately involved with George Hammett."

"Naturally."

"And this was . . . not a problem?"

"A problem? Do you mean, Lieutenant, did I, after nearly twelve years of divorce, harbor homicidal jealousy for my ex-wife? And did I slice the throat of the mother of my children and leave her dead on the street?"

"In words to that effect, Mr. Angelini."

He said something in Italian under his breath. Something, Eve suspected, uncomplimentary. "No, I did not kill Cicely."

"Can you tell me your whereabouts on the night of her death?"

She could see his jaw tense and noticed the control it took for him to relax it again, but his eyes never flickered. She imagined he could stare a hole through steel.

"I was at home in my townhouse from eight o'clock on."

"Alone?"

"Yes."

"Did you see or speak with anyone who can verify that?"

"No. I have two domestics, and both were out on their night off, which was why I was home. I wanted quiet and privacy for an evening."

"You made no calls, received none during the evening?"

"I received a call at about three A.M. from Commander Whitney informing me of my wife's death. I was in bed, alone, when the call came in."

"Mr. Angelini, your ex-wife was in a West End dive at one o'clock in the morning. Why?"

"I haven't any idea. No idea at all."

Later, when Eve stepped into the glass tube to descend, she beeped Feeney. "I want to know if Marco Angelini was in any kind of financial squeeze, and how much that squeeze would have loosened at his ex-wife's sudden death."

"You smell something, Dallas?"

"Something," she muttered. "I just don't know what."

chapter five

Eve stumbled into her apartment at nearly one A.M. Her head was ringing. Mavis's idea of dinner on her night off had been to take in a rival club. Already aware she would pay for the evening's entertainment in the morning, Eve stripped on the way to the bedroom.

At least the evening out with Mavis had pushed the Towers case out of her mind. Eve might have worried she had no mind left, but she was too exhausted to think about it.

She fell naked and facedown on the bed and was asleep in seconds.

Eve woke, violently aroused.

It was Roarke's hands on her. She knew their texture, their rhythm. Her heart tripped against her ribs, then bounded into her throat as his mouth covered hers. His was greedy, hot, giving her no choice, really no choice at all but to respond in kind. Even as she fumbled for him, those long, clever fingers pierced her, diving into her so that she bowed up into the frenzy of orgasm.

His mouth on her breast, sucking, teeth scraping. His elegant hands relentless so that her cries came out in whimpers of shock and gratitude. Another staggering climax to layer thick over the first.

Her hands sought purchase in the tangled sheets, but nothing could anchor her. As she flew up again, she gripped him, nails scraping down his back, up to grab handfuls of his hair.

"God!" It was the single coherent word she managed as he plunged into her, so hard, so deep she was amazed she didn't die from the pleasure of it. Her body bucked helplessly, frantically, continued to shudder even after he'd collapsed on her.

He let out a long, satisfied sigh and lazily nuzzled her ear. "Sorry to wake you."

"Roarke? Oh, was that you?"

He bit her.

She smiled quietly in the dark. "I didn't think you'd be back until tomorrow."

"I got lucky. Then I followed your trail into the bedroom."

"I was out with Mavis. We went to a place called Armageddon. My hearing's starting to come back." She stroked his back, yawned hugely. "It's not morning, is it?"

"No." Recognizing the weariness in her voice, he shifted, gathered her close against him, and kissed her temple. "Go to sleep, Eve."

"Okay." She obliged him in less than ten seconds.

He woke at first light and left her curled in the middle of the bed. In the kitchen, he programmed the AutoChef for coffee and a toasted bagel. The bagel was stale, but that was to be expected. Making himself at home, he sat by the kitchen monitor and skimmed through the paper to the financial section.

He couldn't concentrate.

He was trying not to resent the fact that she'd chosen her bed over their bed. Or what he wanted her to think of as their bed. He didn't begrudge her the need for personal space; he understood well the need for privacy. But his house was large enough that she could have appropriated an entire wing for herself if she wanted it.

Pushing away from the monitor, he paced to the window. He wasn't used to this struggle, this war to balance his needs with someone else's. He'd grown up thinking of himself first and last. He'd had to, in order to survive and then to succeed. One was every bit as important to him as the other.

The habit was difficult to break—or had been, until Eve.

It was humiliating to admit, even to himself, that every time he went away to see to business, a seed of fear rooted in his heart that she would have shaken herself loose of him by the time he returned.

The simple fact was, he needed the one thing she had refused him. A commitment.

Turning from the window, he went back to the monitor and forced himself to read.

"Good morning," Eve said from the doorway. Her smile was quick and bright, as much from the pleasure of seeing him as from the fact that her trip to Armageddon didn't have the consequences she'd feared. She felt terrific.

"Your bagels are stale."

"Mmm." She tested by trying a bite of the one on the table. "You're right." Coffee was always a better bet. "Anything in the news I should worry about?"

"Are you concerned with the Treegro takeover?"

Eve knuckled one eye as she sipped her first cup of coffee. "What's Treegro and who's taking it over?"

"Treegro's a reforestry company, hence the overly adorable name. I'm taking it over."

She grunted. "Figures. I was thinking more of the Towers case."

"Cicely's memorial service is scheduled for tomorrow.

She was important enough, and Catholic enough, to warrant St. Patrick's Cathedral."

"Will you go?"

"If I can reschedule a few appointments. Will you?"

"Yeah." Thinking, Eve leaned back on the counter. "Maybe her killer will be there."

She studied him as he scanned the monitor. He should have looked out of place in her kitchen, she mused, in his expensive, meticulously tailored linen shirt and with the luxurious mane of hair swept back from that remarkable face.

She kept waiting for him to look out of place there, with her.

"Problem?" he murmured, well aware that she was staring at him.

"No. Things on my mind. How well do you know Angelini?"

"Marco?" Roarke frowned over something he saw on the monitor, took out his notebook, entered a memo. "Our paths cross often enough. Normally a careful businessman, always a devoted father. Prefers spending his time in Italy, but his power base is here in New York. Contributes generously to the Catholic Church."

"He stands to gain financially from Towers's death. Maybe it's just a drop in the bucket, but Feeney's checking it out."

"You could have asked me," Roarke murmured. "I would have told you Marco's in trouble. Not desperate trouble," he amended when Eve's eyes sharpened. "He's made some ill-advised acquisitions over the past year or so."

"You said he was careful."

"I said he was normally careful. He bought several religious artifacts without having them thoroughly authenticated. His zeal got in the way of his business sense. They were forgeries, and he's taken a hard loss."

"How hard?"

"In excess of three million. I can get you exact figures, if necessary. He'll recover," Roarke added with a shrug for three million dollars Eve knew she would never get used to. "He needs to focus and downsize a bit here and there. I'd say his pride was hurt more than his portfolio."

"How much was Towers's share of Mercury worth?"

"On today's market?" He took out his pocket diary, jiggled some numbers. "Somewhere between five and seven."

"Million?"

"Yes," Roarke said with the faintest hint of a smile. "Of course."

"Good Christ. No wonder she could live like a queen."

"Marco made very good investments for her. He would have wanted the mother of his children to live comfortably."

"You and I have dramatically different ideas about comfort."

"Apparently." Roarke tucked the diary away and rose to refill his coffee and hers. An airbus rumbled by the window, chased by a fleet of private shuttles. "You suspect that Marco killed her to recoup his losses?"

"Money's a motive that never goes out of style. I interviewed him yesterday. I knew something didn't quite fit. Now it's beginning to."

She took the fresh coffee he offered, paced to the window where the noise level was rising, then away again. Her robe was slipping off her shoulder. Casually, Roarke tucked it back into place. Bored commuters often carried long-range viewers for just such an opportunity.

"Then there's the friendly divorce," she went on, "but whose idea was it? Divorce is complicated for Catholics when there are children involved. Don't they have to get some sort of clearance?"

"Dispensation," Roarke corrected. "A complex business, but both Cicely and Marco had connections with the hierarchy."

"He's never remarried," Eve pointed out, setting her coffee aside. "I haven't been able to find even a whiff of a steady or serious companion. But Towers was having a long-term intimate relationship with Hammett. Just how did Angelini feel about the mother of his children snuggling with a business partner?"

"If it were me, I'd kill the business partner."

"That's you," Eve said with a quick glance. "And I imagine you'd kill both of them."

"You know me so well." He stepped toward her, put his hands on her shoulders. "On the financial end, you may want to consider that whatever Cicely's share of Mercury was, Angelini's matches it. They held equal shares."

"Fuck." She struggled with it. "Still, money's money. I have to follow that scent until I get a new one." He continued to stand there, his hands cupping her shoulders, his eyes on hers. "What are you looking at?"

"The gleam in your eye." He touched his lips to hers once, then again. "I have some sympathy for Marco, you see, because I remember what it's like to be on the receiving end of that look, and that tenacity."

"You hadn't killed anyone," she reminded him. "Lately."

"Ah, but you weren't sure of that for a time, and still you were . . . drawn. Now we're—" The beeper on his watch pinged. "Hell." He kissed her again, quick and distracted. "We'll have to reminisce later. I have a meeting."

Just as well, Eve thought. Hot blood interfered with a clear head. "I'll see you later then."

"At home?"

She fiddled with her coffee cup. "At your place, sure."

Impatience flickered in his eyes as he shrugged into his jacket. The slight bulge in the pocket reminded him. "I'd nearly forgotten. I bought you a present in Australia."

With some reluctance, Eve took the slim gold box. When she opened it, reluctance scattered. There was no room for it in shocked panic. "Jesus bleeding Christ, Roarke. Are you insane?"

It was a diamond. She knew enough to be sure of that. The stone graced a twisted gold chain and glinted fire. Shaped like a tear, it was as long and wide as the first joint of a man's thumb.

"They call it the Giant's Tear," he said as he casually took it from the box and draped the chain over her head. "It was mined about a hundred and fifty years ago. It happened to come up for auction while I was in Sydney." He stepped back and studied its shooting sparks against the plain blue robe she wore. "Yes, it suits you. I thought it would." Then he looked at her face and smiled. "Oh, I see you were counting on kiwi. Well, perhaps next time." When he leaned in to kiss her good-bye, he was brought up short by the slap of her hand against his chest. "Problem?"

"This is crazy. You can't expect me to take something like this."

"You do occasionally wear jewelry." To prove his point, he flicked a finger at the gold dangling from her ear.

"Yeah, and I buy it from the street stall on Lex."

"I don't," he said easily.

"You take this back."

She started to pull at the chain, but he closed his hands over hers. "It doesn't go with my suit. Eve, a gift is not supposed to make the blood drain out of your cheeks." Suddenly exasperated, he gave her a quick shake. "It caught my eye, and I was thinking of you. Damn you, I always am. I bought it because I love you. Christ Jesus, when are you going to swallow that?"

"You're not going to do this to me." She told herself she was calm, very calm. Because she was right, very right. His temper didn't worry her, she'd seen it flare before. But the stone weighed around her neck, and what she feared it represented worried her very much.

"Do what to you, Eve? Exactly what?"

"You're not going to give me diamonds." Terrified and furious, she shoved away from him. "You're not going to pressure me into taking what I don't want, or being what I can't be. You think I don't know what you've been doing these past few months. Do you think I'm stupid?"

His eyes flashed, hard as the stone between her breasts. "No, I don't think you're stupid. I think you're a coward."

Her fist came up automatically. Oh, how she would have

loved to have used it to wipe that self-righteous sneer from his face. If he hadn't been right, she could have. So she used other weapons.

"You think you can make me depend on you, get used to living in that glorified fortress of yours and wearing silk. Well, I don't give a damn about any of that."

"I'm well aware of that."

"I don't need your fancy food or your fancy gifts or your fancy words. I see the pattern, Roarke. Say I love you at regular intervals until she learns to respond. Like a well-trained pet."

"Like a pet," he repeated as his fury froze into ice. "I see I'm wrong. You are stupid. You really think this is about power and control? Have it your way. I'm tired of having you toss my feelings back in my face. My mistake for allowing it, but that can be rectified."

"I never—"

"No, you never," he interrupted coolly. "Never once risked your pride by saying those words back to me. You keep this place as your escape hatch rather than commit to staying with me. I let you draw the line, Eve, and now I'm moving it." It wasn't just temper pushing him now, nor was it just pain. It was the truth. "I want all," he said flatly. "Or I want nothing."

She wouldn't panic. He wouldn't make her panic like a first-time rookie on a night run. "What exactly does that mean?"

"It means sex isn't enough."

"It's not just sex. You know—"

"No, I don't. The choice is yours now—it always was. But now you'll have to come to me."

"Ultimatums just piss me off."

"That's a pity." He gave her one long last look. "Good-bye, Eve."

"You can't just walk—"

"Oh yes." And he didn't look back. "I can."

Her mouth dropped open when she heard the door slam. For a moment she simply stood, rigid, the sun glinting off the jewel around her neck. Then she began to vibrate. With fury, of course, she told herself and ripped the precious diamond off to toss it on the counter.

He thought she would go crawling after him, begging him to stay. Well, he could go on thinking that into the next millennium. Eve Dallas didn't crawl, and she didn't beg.

She closed her eyes against a pain more shocking than a laser strike. *Who the hell is Eve Dallas?* she wondered. *And isn't that the core of it all?*

She blocked it out. What choice did she have? The job came first. Had to come first. If she wasn't a good cop, she was nothing. She was as empty and as helpless as the child she had been, lying broken and traumatized in a dark alley in Dallas.

She could bury herself in work. The demands and pressures of it. When she was standing in Commander Whitney's office, she was only a cop with murder on her hands.

"She had plenty of enemies, Commander."

"Don't we all." His eyes were clear again, sharp. Grief could never outweigh responsibility.

"Feeney's run a list of her convictions. We're breaking them down, concentrating on the lifers first—family and known associates. Someone she put in a cage for the duration would have the strongest revenge ratio. Next down the line are the uncorrected deviants. UDs sometimes slip through the cracks. She put plenty away on mental, and some of them are bound to have crawled their way out."

"That's a lot of computer time, Dallas."

It was a subtle warning about budgets, which she chose to ignore. "I appreciate you putting Feeney on this with me. I couldn't get through it without him. Commander, these checks are SOP, but I don't think this was an attack on the prosecutor."

He sat back, inclined his head, waiting.

"I think it was personal. She was covering something. For herself, for somebody else. She zapped the 'link recording."

"I read your report, Lieutenant. Are you telling me you

believe Prosecuting Attorney Towers was involved in something illegal?"

"Are you asking me as my friend or as my commander?"

He bared his teeth before he could control himself. After a short internal struggle, he nodded. "Well put, Lieutenant. As your commander."

"I don't know if it was illegal. It's my opinion at this stage of the investigation that there was something on that recording the victim wanted kept private. It was important enough to have her get dressed and go out again into the rain to meet someone. Whoever that was, was certain she would come alone and that she would leave no record of the contact. Commander, I need to speak with the rest of the victim's family, her close friends, your wife."

He'd accepted that, or tried to. Throughout his career he had worked hard to keep his loved ones out of the often nasty air of his job. Now he had to expose them.

"You have my address, Lieutenant. I'll contact my wife now and tell her to expect you."

"Yes, sir. Thank you."

Anna Whitney had made a fine home from the two-level house in the quiet street in the suburbs of White Plains. She had raised her children there, and raised them well, choosing the profession of mother over a teaching career. It wasn't the state salary for full-time parents that had swayed her. It had been the thrill of being in on each and every stage of childhood development.

She'd earned her salary. Now, with her children grown, she earned her retirement stipend by putting the same dedication into nurturing her home, her husband, and her reputation as a hostess. Whenever she could, she filled the house with her grandchildren. In the evenings, she filled it with dinner parties.

Anna Whitney hated solitude.

But she was alone when Eve arrived. As always, she was perfectly groomed: her cosmetics were carefully and expertly applied, and her pale blond hair was coiffed in a swept-back style that suited her attractive face.

She wore a one-piece suit of good American cotton, and held out a hand adorned only with a wedding ring to welcome Eve.

"Lieutenant Dallas, my husband said you would come."

"I'm sorry to intrude, Mrs. Whitney."

"Don't apologize. I'm a cop's wife. Come in. I've made some lemonade. It's tablet, I'm afraid. Fresh or frozen is so monstrously hard to come by. It's a little early for lemonade, but I had a yen for it today."

Eve let Anna chatter as they walked into the formal living area with its stiff-backed chairs and straight-edged sofa.

The lemonade was fine, and Eve said so after the first sip.

"You know the memorial service is at ten tomorrow."

"Yes, ma'am. I'll be there."

"There are so many flowers already. We've made arrangements to have them distributed after . . . but that's not why you're here."

"Prosecutor Towers was a good friend to you."

"She was a very good friend to me and my husband."

"Her children are staying with you?"

"Yes, they're . . . they've gone with Marco just now to speak with the archbishop about the service."

"They're close to their father."

"Yes."

"Mrs. Whitney, why are they staying here, rather than with their father?"

"We all thought it best. The house—Marco's house—holds so many memories. Cicely lived there when the children were young. Then there's the media. They don't have our address, and we wanted to keep the children from dealing with reporters. They've swamped poor Marco. It'll be different tomorrow, of course."

Her pretty hands plucked at the knee of her suit, then calmed and lay still again. "They'll have to face it. They're still in shock. Even Randall. Randall Slade, Mirina's fiancé. He'd gotten very close to Cicely."

"He's here as well."

"He'd never leave Mirina alone at such a time. She's a strong young woman, Lieutenant, but even strong women need an arm to lean on now and then."

Eve blocked out the quick image of Roarke that popped into her brain. As a result of the effort, her voice was a bit more formal than usual as she led Anna through the routine questions.

"I've asked myself over and over what could have possessed her to go to that neighborhood," Anna concluded. "Cicely could be stubborn, and certainly strong willed, but she was rarely impulsive and never foolish."

"She talked to you, confided in you."

"We were like sisters."

"Would she have told you if she was in trouble of some kind? If someone close to her was in trouble?"

"I would have thought so. She would have handled it herself, or tried to first." Her eyes swam, but the tears didn't fall. "But sooner or later she would have blown off steam with me."

If she'd had time, Eve thought. "You can think of nothing she was concerned about before her death?"

"Nothing major. Her daughter's wedding—getting older. We joked about her becoming a grandmother. No," Anna said with a laugh as she recognized Eve's look. "Mirina isn't pregnant, though that would have only pleased her mother. She was always concerned for David as well: Would he settle down? Was he happy?"

"And is he?"

Another cloud came into her eyes before she lowered them. "David is a great deal like his father. He likes to wheel and deal. He does a great deal of traveling for the business, always looking for new arenas, new opportunities. There's no doubt he'll take the helm if and when Marco decided to turn it over."

She hesitated, as if about to add something, then smoothly switched gears. "Mirina, on the other hand, prefers to live in one spot. She manages a boutique in Rome.

That's where she met Randall. He's a designer. Her shop handles his line exclusively now. He's quite talented. This is his," she said, indicating the slim suit she wore.

"It's lovely. So as far as you know, Prosecutor Towers had no reason to be concerned for her children. Nothing she would have felt obliged to smooth out or cover over?"

"Cover over? No, of course not. They're both bright, successful people."

"And her ex-husband. He's having some business difficulties?"

"Marco? Is he?" Anna shrugged that off. "I'm sure he'll straighten them out. I never shared Cicely's interest in business."

"She was involved then, in business. Directly?"

"Of course. Cicely insisted on knowing exactly what was going on and having a say in it. I never knew how she could keep so many things in her head. If Marco was having difficulties, she'd have known, and probably have suggested a half dozen ways to right things. She was quite brilliant." When her voice broke, Anna pressed a hand to her lips.

"I'm sorry, Mrs. Whitney."

"No, it's all right. I'm better. Having her children with me helped so much. I feel I can stand for her with them. I can't do what you do, and look for her killer. But I can stand for her with her children."

"They're very lucky to have you," Eve murmured, surprised to hear herself say it and mean it. Odd, she'd always considered Anna Whitney a mild pain in the ass. "Mrs. Whitney, can you tell me about Prosecutor Towers's relationship with George Hammett?"

Anna pokered up. "They were dear, good friends."

"Mr. Hammett has told me they were lovers."

Anna huffed out a breath. She was a traditionalist, and unashamed of it. "Very well, that's true. But he wasn't the right man for her."

"Why?"

"Set in his ways. I'm very fond of George, and he made an excellent escort for Cicely. But a woman can hardly be completely happy when she goes home to an empty apartment most nights, to an empty bed. She needed a mate. George wanted it both ways, and Cicely deluded herself into thinking she wanted that, too."

"And she didn't."

"She shouldn't have," Anna snapped, obviously going over an old argument. "Work isn't enough, as I pointed out to her many times. She simply wasn't serious enough about George to risk."

"Risk?"

"I'm speaking of emotional risk," Anna said impatiently. "You cops are so literal-minded. She wanted her life tidy more than she wanted the mess of a full-time relationship."

"I had the impression that Mr. Hammett regretted that, that he loved her very much."

"If he did, why didn't he push?" Anna demanded, and tears threatened. "She wouldn't have died alone then, would she? She wouldn't have been alone."

Eve drove out of the quiet suburbs, and on impulse she pulled her car over to the curb and slumped down in the seat. She needed to think. Not about Roarke, she assured herself. There was nothing to think about there. That was settled.

On a hunch, she called up her computer at her office and had it get to work on David Angelini. If he was like his father, maybe he had also made a few poor investments. While she was at it, she ordered a run on Randall Slade and the boutique in Rome.

If anything popped up, she would have a scan on the flights from Europe to New York.

Damn it, a woman who had nothing to worry about didn't leave her warm, dry apartment in the middle of the night.

Stubbornly, Eve retraced all the steps in her head. As she thought it through, she studied the neighborhood. Nice old trees spreading shade, neat postcard-sized yards with one- and two-story fully detached houses.

What would it have been like to have been raised in a pretty, settled community? Would it make you secure, confident, the way being dragged from filthy room to filthy room, from stinking street to stinking street made her jittery, moody?

Maybe there were fathers here who snuck into their little girls' bedrooms, too. But it was hard to believe it. The fathers here couldn't smell of bad liquor and sour sweat and have thick fingers that pushed themselves into innocent flesh.

Eve caught herself rocking in the seat and choked back a sob.

She wouldn't do it. She wouldn't remember. She wouldn't let herself conjure up that face looming over her in the dark, or the taste of that hand clamping over her mouth to smother her screams.

She wouldn't do it. It had all happened to someone else, some little girl whose name she couldn't even remember. If she tried to, if she let herself remember it all, she would become that helpless child again and lose Eve.

She laid her head back on the seat and concentrated on calming herself. If she hadn't been wallowing in self-pity, she would have seen the woman breaking the window at the side of the modified rancher across the street before the first shard fell.

As it was, Eve scowled, asked herself why she'd had to pull over at just this spot. And did she really want the hassle of dealing with intra-jurisdiction paperwork?

Then she thought about the nice family who would come home that night and find their valuables gone.

With a long-suffering sigh, she got out of the car.

The woman was half in and half out of the window when Eve reached her. The security shield had been deactivated by a cheap jammer, available at any electronic outlet. With a shake of her head for the naïveté of suburbanites, Eve tapped the thief smartly on the butt that was struggling to wiggle through the opening.

"Forget your code, ma'am?"

Her answer was a hard donkey-style kick to the left shoulder. Eve considered herself lucky it had missed her face. Still, she went down, crushing some early tulips. The perp popped out of the window like a cork and bolted across the lawn.

If her shoulder hadn't been aching, Eve might have let her go. She caught her quarry in a flying tackle that sent them both sprawling into a bed of sunny-faced pansies.

"Get your fucking hands off me, or I'll kill you."

Eve thought briefly that it was a possibility. The woman outweighed her by a good twenty pounds. To ensure it didn't happen, she jammed an elbow against the woman's windpipe and dug for her badge.

"You're busted."

The woman's dark eyes rolled in disgust. "What the hell's a city cop doing here? Don't you know where Manhattan is, asshole?"

"Looks like I'm lost." Eve kept her elbow in place, adding just a little more pressure for her own satisfaction while she pulled out her communicator and requested the closest 'burb cruiser.

chapter six

By the next morning, her shoulder was singing as fiercely as Mavis on a final set. Eve admitted the extra hours she'd put in with Feeney and a night tossing alone in bed hadn't helped it any. She was leery of anything but the mildest painkillers, and took a single stingy dose before she dressed for the memorial service.

She and Feeney had come across one tasty little tidbit. David Angelini had withdrawn three large payments from his accounts over the last six months, to a grand total of one million six hundred and thirty-two dollars, American.

That was more than three-quarters of his personal savings, and he'd drawn it in anonymous credit tokens and cash.

They were still digging on Randall Slade and Mirina, but so far, they were both clean. Just a happy young couple on the brink of matrimony.

God knew how anybody could be happy on the brink, Eve thought as she located her gray suit.

The damn button on the jacket was still missing, she realized as she started to fasten it. And she remembered Roarke had it, carried it like some sort of superstitious talisman. She'd been wearing the suit the first time she'd seen him—at a memorial for the dead.

She ran a hasty comb through her hair and escaped the apartment and the memories.

St. Patrick's was bulging by the time she arrived. Uniforms in the best dress blues flanked the perimeter for a full three blocks on Fifth. A kind of honor guard, Eve mused, for a lawyer who cops had respected. Both street and air traffic had been diverted from the usually choked avenue, and the media was thronged like a busy parade across the wide street.

After the third uniform stopped her, Eve attached her badge to her jacket and moved unhampered into the ancient cathedral and the sounds of the dirge.

She didn't care for churches much. They made her feel guilty for reasons she didn't care to explore. The scent of candle wax and incense was ripe. Some rituals, she thought as she slipped into a side pew, were as timeless as the moon. She gave up any hope of speaking directly with Cicely Towers's family that morning and settled down to watch the show.

Catholic rites had gone back to Latin some time in the last decade. Eve supposed it added a kind of mysticism and a unity. The ancient language certainly seemed appropriate to her in the Mass for the Dead.

The priest's voice boomed out, reaching to the lofty ceilings, and the congregation's responses echoed after. Silent and watchful, Eve scanned the crowd. Dignitaries and politicians sat with bowed heads. She'd positioned herself just close enough to catch glimpses of the family. When Feeney slipped in beside her, she inclined her head.

"Angelini," she murmured. "That would be the daughter beside him."

"With her fiancé on her right."

"Um-hmm." Eve studied the couple: young, attractive. The woman was of slight build with golden hair, like her mother. The unrelieved black she wore swept down from a high neck, covered her arms to the wrists, and skimmed her ankles. She wore no veil or shaded glasses to shield her red-rimmed, puffy eyes. Grief, simple, basic, and undiluted, seemed to shimmer around her.

Beside her, Randall Slade stood tall, one long arm supporting her shoulders. He had a striking, almost brutally handsome face, which Eve remembered well from the image she'd generated on her computer screen: large jaw, long nose, hooded eyes. He looked big and tough, but the arm around the woman lay gently.

Flanking Angelini's other side was his son. David stood just a space apart. That sort of body language hinted at friction. He stared straight ahead, his face a blank. He stood slightly shorter than his father, as dark as his sister was fair. And he was alone, Eve thought. Very much alone.

The family pew was completed by George Hammett.

Directly behind were the commander, his wife, and his family.

She knew Roarke was there. She had already glimpsed him once at the end of an aisle beside a teary-eyed blond. Now, when Eve skimmed a glance his way, she saw him lean down to the woman and murmur something that had her turning her face into his shoulder.

Furious at the quick pang of jealousy, Eve scanned the crowd again. Her eyes met C. J. Morse's.

"How'd that little bastard manage to get in?"

Feeney, a good Catholic, winced at the use of profanity in church. "Who?"

"Morse—at eight o'clock."

Shifting his eyes, Feeney spotted the reporter. "A crowd like this, I guess some of the slippery ones could slide through security."

Eve debated hauling him out just for the satisfaction of it, then decided the scuffle would give him just the kind of attention he craved.

"Fuck him."

Feeney made a sound like a man who'd been pinched. "Christ Jesus, Dallas, you're in St. Pat's."

"If God's going to make little weasels like him, she's going to have to listen to complaints."

"Have some respect."

Eve looked back to Mirina, who lifted a hand to her face. "I've got plenty of respect," she murmured. "Plenty." With this she stepped around Feeney and strode down the side to the exit.

By the time he caught up with her, she was just finishing issuing instructions to one of the uniforms.

"What's the problem?"

"I needed some air." Churches always smelled like the dying or the dead to her. "And I wanted to get a jump on the weasel." Smiling now, she turned to Feeney. "I've got the uniforms looking out for him. They'll confiscate any communication or recording devices he's got on him. Privacy law."

"You're just going to steam him."

"Good. He steams me." She let out a long breath, studying the media horde across the avenue. "I'll be damned if the public has a right to know everything. But at least those reporters are playing by the rules and showing some of that respect you were talking about for the family."

"I take it you're done in there."

"There's nothing I can do in there."

"I figured you'd be sitting with Roarke."

"No."

Feeney nodded slowly and nearly dug into his pocket for his bag of nuts before he remembered the occasion. "Is that the burr up your butt, kid?"

"I don't know what you're talking about." She started to walk without any destination in mind, stopped, and turned around. "Who the hell was that blonde he was wrapped around?"

"I couldn't say." He sucked air through his teeth. "She was a looker though. Want me to rough him up for you?"

"Just shut up." She jammed her hands in her pockets. "The commander's wife said they were having a small, private memorial at their home. How long do you figure this sideshow will take?"

"Another hour, minimum."

"I'm heading back to Cop Central. I'll meet you at the commander's in two hours."

"You're the boss."

Small and private meant there were more than a hundred people packed into the commander's suburban home. There was food to comfort the living, liquor to dull the grieving. The perfect hostess, Anna Whitney hurried over the moment she spotted Eve. She kept her voice down and a carefully pleasant expression on her face.

"Lieutenant, must you do this now, here and now?"

"Mrs. Whitney, I'll be as discreet as I possibly can. The sooner I complete the interview stage, the sooner we'll find Prosecutor Towers's killer."

"Her children are devastated. Poor Mirina can barely function. It would be more appropriate if you'd—"

"Anna." Commander Whitney laid a hand on his wife's shoulder. "Let Lieutenant Dallas do her job."

Anna said nothing, merely turned and walked stiffly away.

"We said good-bye to a very dear friend today."

"I understand, Commander. I'll finish here as quickly as I can."

"Be careful with Mirina, Dallas. She's very fragile at the moment."

"Yes, sir. Perhaps I could speak to her first, privately."

"I'll see to it."

When he left her alone, Eve backed up toward the foyer and turned directly into Roarke.

"Lieutenant."

"Roarke." She glanced at the glass of wine in his hand. "I'm on duty."

"So I see. This wasn't for you."

Eve followed his gaze to the blonde sitting in the corner. "Right." She could all but feel the marrow of her bones turn green. "You move fast."

Before she could step aside, he put a hand on her arm. His voice, like his eyes, was carefully neutral. "Suzanna is a mutual friend of mine and Cicely's. The widow of a cop, killed in the line of duty. Cicely put his murderer away."

"Suzanna Kimball," Eve said, battling back shame. "Her husband was a good cop."

"So I'm told." With the faintest trace of amusement shadowing his mouth, he skimmed a glance down her suit. "I'd hoped you'd burned that thing. Gray's not your color, Lieutenant."

"I'm not making a fashion statement. Now, if you'll excuse me—"

The fingers on her arm tightened. "You might look into Randall Slade's gambling problem. He owes considerable sums to several people. As does David Angelini."

"Is that right?"

"That's quite right. I'm one of the several."

Her eyes hardened. "And you've just decided I might be interested."

"I've just discovered my own interest. He's worked up a rather impressive debt at one of my casinos on Vegas II. Then there's a matter of a little scandal some years back involving roulette, a redhead, and a fatality on an obscure gaming satellite in Sector 38."

"What scandal?"

"You're the cop," he said and smiled. "Find out."

He left Eve to go to the cop's widow and hold her hand.

"I have Mirina in my office," Whitney murmured at Eve's ear. "I promised you wouldn't keep her long."

"I won't." Struggling to smooth the feathers Roarke had

ruffled, she followed the commander's broad back down the hall.

Though his home office wasn't quite as spartan as the one at Cop Central, it was obvious that Whitney kept his wife's lush feminine taste at bay here. The walls were a plain beige, the carpet a deeper tone, and the chairs were wide and a practical brown.

His work counter and console were in the center of the room. In the corner by the window, Mirina Angelini waited in her long sweep of mourning black. Whitney went to her first, spoke quietly, and squeezed her hand. With one warning glance at Eve, he left them alone.

"Ms. Angelini," Eve began. "I knew your mother, worked with her, admired her. I'm very sorry for your loss."

"Everyone is," Mirina responded in a voice as fragile and pale as her white cheeks. Her eyes were dark, nearly black, and glassy. "Except the person who killed her, I suppose. I'll apologize ahead of time if I'm of little help to you, Lieutenant Dallas. I bowed to pressure and let myself be tranq'ed. I am, as anyone will tell you, taking this rather hard."

"You and your mother were close."

"She was the most wonderful woman I've ever known. Why should I have to be calm and composed when I've lost her like this?"

Eve came closer, sat in one of the wide brown chairs. "I can't think of any reason why you should be."

"My father wants a public show of strength." Mirina turned her face to the window. "I'm letting him down. Appearances are important to my father."

"Was your mother important to him?"

"Yes. Their personal and professional lives were twined together. The divorce didn't change that. He's hurting." She drew in a shaky breath. "He won't show it because he's too proud, but he's hurting. He loved her. We all loved her."

"Ms. Angelini, tell me about your mother's mood, what

you spoke of, who you spoke of, the last time you had contact."

"The day before she died we were on the 'link for an hour, maybe more. Wedding plans." Tears dripped out and spilled over the pale cheeks. "We were both so full of wedding plans. I'd send her transmissions of dresses: wedding dresses, mother-of-the-bride ensembles. Randall was designing them. We talked about clothes. Doesn't that seem shallow, Lieutenant, that the last time I'll ever speak with my mother, I spoke of fashion?"

"No, it doesn't seem shallow. It seems friendly. Loving."

Mirina pressed a hand to her lips. "Do you think?"

"Yes, I do."

"What do you talk to your mother about?"

"I don't have a mother. I never did."

Mirina blinked, focused again. "How odd. What does it feel like?"

"I . . ." There was no way to describe what simply was. "It wouldn't be the same for you, Ms. Angelini," Eve said gently. "When you were speaking to your mother, did she mention anything, anyone who was concerning her?"

"No. If you're thinking about her work, we rarely talked of it. I wasn't very interested in the law. She was happy, excited that I was coming over for a few days. We laughed a lot. I know she had this image, her professional image, but with me, with the family she was . . . softer, looser. I teased her about George, saying that Randy could design her wedding dress while he was doing mine."

"Her reaction?"

"We just laughed. Mama liked to laugh," she said, a little dreamy now as the tranq began to work. "She said she was having too much fun being mother of the bride to spoil it with the headaches of being a bride herself. She was very fond of George, and I think they were good together. But I don't suppose she loved him."

"Don't you?"

"Why, no." There was a faint smile on her lips, a glassy gleam to her eyes. "When you love someone, you have to be with them, don't you? To be part of their life, to have them be part of yours. She wasn't looking for that with George. With anyone."

"Was Mr. Hammett looking for that with her?"

"I don't know. If he was, he was happy enough to let their relationship drift. I'm drifting now," she murmured. "I don't feel as though I'm here at all."

Because she needed Mirina to hold off on the float a bit longer, Eve rose to request water from the console. Carrying the glass back, she pushed it into Mirina's hands.

"Did that relationship cause problems between him and your father? Between your mother and father?"

"It . . . was awkward, but not uncomfortable." Mirina smiled again. She was sleepy now, so relaxed she could have folded her arms on the window ledge and slipped away. "That sounds contradictory. You'd have to know my father. He would refuse to let it bother him, or at least to let it affect him. He's still friendly with George."

She blinked down at the glass in her hand as if she'd just realized it was there, and took a delicate sip. "I don't know how he might have felt if they had decided to marry, but well, that isn't an issue now."

"Are you involved in your father's business, Ms. Angelini?"

"In the fashion arm. I do all the buying for the shops in Rome and Milan, have the final say as to what's exported to our shops in Paris and New York and so forth. Travel a bit to attend shows, though I don't care much for traveling. I hate going off planet, don't you?"

Eve realized she was losing her. "I haven't done it."

"Oh, it's horrid. Randy likes it. Says it's an adventure. What was I saying?" She pushed a hand through her lovely golden hair, and Eve rescued the glass before it could tumble to the floor. "About the buying. I like to buy clothes. Other aspects of the business never interested me."

"Your parents and Mr. Hammett were all stockholders in a company called Mercury."

"Of course. We use Mercury exclusively for our shipping needs." Her eyelids drooped. "It's fast, dependable."

"There were no problems that you know of, in that or any other of your family holdings?"

"No, none at all."

It was time to try a different tack. "Was your mother aware of Randall Slade's gambling debts?"

For the first time Mirina showed a spark of life, and the life was anger, flashing in the pale eyes. She seemed to snap awake. "Randall's debts were not my mother's concern, but his, and mine. We're dealing with them."

"You didn't tell her?"

"There was no reason to worry her about something that was being handled. Randall has a problem with gambling, but he's gotten help. He doesn't wager anymore."

"The debts are considerable?"

"They're being paid," Mirina said hollowly. "Arrangements have been made."

"Your mother was a wealthy woman in her own right. You'll inherit a large portion of her estate."

Either the tranqs or grief dulled Mirina's wits. She seemed oblivious to the implication. "Yes, but I won't have my mother, will I? I won't have Mama. When I marry Randall, she won't be there. She won't be there," she repeated, and began to weep quietly.

David Angelini wasn't fragile. His emotions showed themselves in stiff impatience with undercurrents of chained rage. For all appearances, this was a man insulted at the very idea that he would be expected to speak to a cop.

When Eve sat across from him in Whitney's office, he answered her questions briefly in a clipped, cultured voice.

"Obviously it was some maniac she'd prosecuted who did this to her," he stated. "Her work brought her entirely too close to violence."

"Did you object to her work?"

"I didn't understand why she loved it. Why she needed

it." He lifted the glass he'd brought with him and drank. "But she did, and in the end, it killed her."

"When did you see her last?"

"On March eighteenth. My birthday."

"Did you have contact with her since then?"

"I spoke with her about a week before she died. Just a family call. We never went more than a week without speaking."

"How would you describe her mood?"

"Obsessed—with Mirina's wedding. My mother never did things by halves. She was planning the wedding as meticulously as she did any of her criminal cases. She was hoping it would rub off on me."

"What would?"

"The wedding fever. My mother was a romantic woman under the prosecutor's armor. She hoped I would find the right mate and make a family. I told her I'd leave that to Mirina and Randy and stay married to business awhile."

"You're actively involved in Angelini Exports. You'd be aware of the financial difficulties."

His face tightened. "They're blips, Lieutenant. Bumps. Nothing more."

"My information indicates there are more serious difficulties than blips and bumps."

"Angelini is solid. There's simply a need for some reorganization, some diversification, which is being done." He flicked a hand, elegant fingers, a sparkle of gold. "A few key people have made unfortunate mistakes that can and will be rectified. And that has nothing to do with my mother's case."

"It's my job to explore all angles, Mr. Angelini. Your mother's estate is substantial. Your father will come into a number of holdings, as will you."

David got to his feet. "You're speaking of my mother. If you suspect that anyone in the family would cause her harm, then Commander Whitney has made a monstrous error in judgment putting you in charge of the investigation."

"You're entitled to your opinion. Do you gamble, Mr. Angelini?"

"What business is that of yours?"

Since he was going to stand, Eve rose to face him. "It's a simple question."

"Yes, I gamble on occasion, as do countless others. I find it relaxing."

"How much do you owe?"

His fingers tightened on the glass. "I believe at this point, my mother would have advised me to consult counsel."

"That's certainly your right. I'm not accusing you of anything, Mr. Angelini. I'm fully aware that you were in Paris on the night of your mother's death." Just as she was fully aware that shuttles skimmed across the Atlantic hourly. "It's my job to get a clear picture, a full and clear picture. You're under no obligation to answer my question. But I can, with very little trouble, access that information."

The muscles in his jaw worked a moment. "Eight hundred thousand, give or take a few dollars."

"Are you unable to settle the debt?"

"I am neither a welsher nor a pauper, Lieutenant Dallas," he said stiffly. "It can and will be settled shortly."

"Was your mother aware of it?"

"Neither am I a child, Lieutenant, who needs to run to his mother for help whenever he skins a knuckle."

"You and Randall Slade gambled together?"

"We did. My sister disapproves, so Randy has given up the hobby."

"Not before he incurred debts of his own."

His eyes, very like his father's, chilled. "I wouldn't know about that, nor would I discuss his business with you."

Oh yes, you would, Eve thought, but let it slide for the moment. "And the trouble in Sector 38 a few years ago? You were there?"

"Sector 38?" He looked convincingly blank.

"A gambling satellite."

"I often go to Vegas II for a quick weekend, but I don't

recall patronizing a casino in that sector. I don't know what trouble you're referring to."

"Do you play roulette?"

"No, it's a fool's game. Randy's fond of it. I prefer black-jack."

Randall Slade didn't look like a fool. He looked to Eve like a man who could knock anything out of his path without breaking stride. Nor was he her image of a fashion de-signer. He dressed simply, his black suit unadorned by any of the studs or braids currently in fashion. And his wide hands had the look of a laborer rather than an artist.

"I hope you'll be brief," he said in the tone of a man used to giving orders. "Mirina is upstairs lying down. I don't want to leave her for long."

"Then I'll be brief." Eve didn't object when he took out a gold case containing ten slim black cigarettes. Technically, she could have, but she waited until he'd lighted one. "What was your relationship with Prosecutor Towers?"

"We were friendly. She was soon to become my mother-in-law. We shared a deep love for Mirina."

"She approved of you."

"I have no reason to believe otherwise."

"Your career has benefited quite a lot through your asso-ciation with Angelini Exports."

"True." He blew out smoke that smelled lightly of lemon mint. "I like to think Angelini has also benefited quite a lot through their association with me." He surveyed Eve's gray suit. "That cut and color are both incredibly unflattering. You might want to take a look at my on-the-rack line here in New York."

"I'll keep it in mind, thanks."

"I dislike seeing attractive women in unattractive clothes." He smiled and surprised Eve with a flare of charm. "You should wear bolder colors, sleeker lines. A woman with your build would carry them well."

"So I'm told," she muttered, thinking of Roarke. "You're about to marry a very wealthy woman."

"I'm about to marry the woman I love."

"It's a happy coincidence that she's wealthy."

"It is."

"And money is something you have a need for."

"Don't we all?" Smooth, unoffended, again amused.

"You have debts, Mr. Slade. Large, outstanding debts in an area that can cause considerable pain in the collecting process."

"That's accurate." He drew smoke in again. "I'm a gambling addict, Lieutenant. Recovering. With Mirina's help and support, I've undergone treatment. I haven't made a wager in two months, five days."

"Roulette, wasn't it?"

"I'm afraid so."

"And the amount you owe, in round figures?"

"Five hundred thousand."

"And the amount of your fiancée's inheritance?"

"Probably triple that, in round figures. More, considering the stocks and holdings that wouldn't be converted into credit or cash. Killing my fiancée's mother would certainly have been one way to solve my financial difficulties." He stubbed his cigarette out thoughtfully. "Then again, so would the contract I've just signed for my fall line. Money isn't important enough to me to kill for it."

"But gambling was important enough?"

"Gambling was like a beautiful woman. Desirable, exciting, capricious. I had a choice between her and Mirina. There was nothing I wouldn't do to keep Mirina."

"Nothing?"

He understood, and inclined his head. "Nothing at all."

"Does she know about the scandal in Sector 38?"

His amused, faintly smug expression froze, and he paled. "That was nearly ten years ago. That has nothing to do with Mirina. Nothing to do with anything."

"You haven't told her."

"I didn't know her. I was young, foolish, and I paid for my mistake."

"Why don't you explain to me, Mr. Slade, how you came to make that mistake?"

"It has nothing to do with this."

"Indulge me."

"Damn it, it was one night out of my life. One night. I'd had too much to drink, was stupid enough to mix the liquor with chemicals. The woman killed herself. It was proven the overdose was self-inflicted."

Interesting, Eve thought. "But you were there," she hazarded.

"I was zoned. I'd lost more heavily than I could afford at roulette, and between us we made a scene. I told you I was young. I blamed my bad luck on her. Maybe I did threaten her. I just don't remember. Yes, we argued publicly, she struck me, and I struck her back. I'm not proud of it. Then I just don't remember."

"Don't remember, Mr. Slade?"

"As I testified, the next thing I remember is waking up in some filthy little room. We were in bed, naked. And she was dead. I was still groggy. Security came in. I must have called them. They took pictures. I was assured the pictures were destroyed after the case was closed and I was exonerated. I barely knew the woman," he continued, heating up. "I'd picked her up in the bar—or thought I had. My attorney discovered she was a professional companion, unlicensed, working the casinos."

He closed his eyes. "Do you think I want Mirina to know that I was, however briefly, accused of murdering an unlicensed whore?"

"No," Eve said quietly. "I don't imagine you do. And as you said, Mr. Slade, you'd do anything to keep her. Anything at all."

Hammett was waiting for her the moment she stepped out of the commander's office. The hollows in his cheeks seemed deeper, his skin grayer.

"I'd hoped to have a moment, Lieutenant—Eve."

She gestured behind her, let him slip into the room first, then closed the door on the murmurs of conversation.

"This is a difficult day for you, George."

"Yes, very difficult. I wanted to ask, needed to know . . . Is there anything more? Anything at all?"

"The investigation's proceeding. There's nothing I can tell you that you wouldn't have heard through the media."

"There must be more." His voice rose before he could control it. "Something."

She could feel pity, even when there was suspicion. "Everything that can be done is being done."

"You've interviewed Marco, her children, even Randy. If there is anything they knew, anything they told you that might help, I have a right to be told."

Nerves? she wondered. *Or grief?* "No," she said quietly, "you don't. I can't give you any information acquired during an interview or through investigative procedure."

"We're talking about the murder of the woman I loved!" He exploded with it, his pale face flushing dark. "We might have been married."

"Were you planning to be married, George?"

"We'd discussed it." He passed a hand over his face, a hand that shook slightly. "We'd discussed it," he repeated, and the flush washed away from his skin. "There was always another case, another summation to prepare. There was supposed to be plenty of time."

With his hands balled into fists, he turned away from her. "I apologize for shouting at you. I'm not myself."

"It's all right, George. I'm very sorry."

"She's gone." He said it quietly, brokenly. "She's gone."

There was nothing left for her to do but give him privacy. She closed the door behind her, then rubbed a hand at the back of her neck where tension was lodged.

On her way out, Eve signaled to Feeney. "Need you to do some digging," she told him as they headed outside. "Old case, about ten years past, on one of the gambling hells in Sector 38."

"What you got, Dallas?"

"Sex, scandal, and probable suicide. Accidental."

"Hot damn," Feeney said mournfully. "And I was hoping to catch a ball game on the screen tonight."

"This should be just as entertaining." She spied Roarke helping the blonde into his car, hesitated, then detoured past him. "Thanks for the tip, Roarke."

"Any time, Lieutenant. Feeney," he added with a brief nod before he slipped into the car.

"Hey," Feeney said when the car glided away. "He's really pissed at you."

"He seemed fine to me," Eve muttered and wrenched open her car door.

Feeney snorted. "Some detective you are, pal."

"Just dig up the case, Feeney. Randall Slade's the accused." She slammed her door and sulked.

chapter seven

Feeney knew Eve wasn't going to like the data he'd unearthed. Anticipating her reaction, and being a wise man, he sent it through computer rather than delivering it in person.

"I've got the goods on the Slade incident," he said when his droopy face blipped onto her monitor. "I'm going to send it through. I'm—ah—going to be stuck here for awhile. I've got about twenty percent of Tower's conviction list eliminated. It's slow going."

"Try to speed it up, Feeney. We've got to narrow the field."

"Right. Ready for transmission." His face blinked off. In its place was the police report from Sector 38.

Eve frowned over it as the data scrolled. There was little more information above what Randal Slade had already told her. Suspicious death, overdose. The victim's name was Carolle Lee, age 24, birthplace New Chicago Colony, unemployed. The image showed a young, black-haired woman of mixed heritage with exotic eyes and coffee-toned skin. Randall looked pale, his eyes glazed, in his mug shot.

She skimmed through, searching for any detail Randall might have left out. It was bad enough as it was, Eve mused. The murder charges had been dropped, but he'd copped to soliciting an unlicensed companion, possession of illegal chemicals, and contributing to a fatality.

He'd been lucky, she decided, very lucky that the incident had occurred on such an obscure sector, in a hellhole that didn't garner much attention. But if someone—anyone —had come across the details, had threatened to take them to his pretty, fragile fiancée, it would have been a real mess.

Had Towers known? Eve wondered. That was the big question. And if she had, how would she have handled it? The attorney might have looked at the facts, weighed them, and dismissed the case as resolved.

But the mother? Would the loving mother who chatted about fashion for an hour with her daughter, the devoted parent who carved out time to help plan the perfect wedding, have accepted the scandal as the wild oats of a young, foolish man? Or would she have stood like a barricade between the older, less foolish man and what he wanted most?

Eve narrowed her eyes and continued to scan the documents. Then she stopped cold when Roarke's name jumped out at her.

"Son of a bitch," she muttered, slamming a fist on the desk. "Son of a bitch."

Within fifteen minutes, she was striding across the glossy tiles of the lobby of Roarke's building in midtown. Her jaw was set as she accessed the code, then slapped her palm onto the handplate of his private elevator. She hadn't bothered to call, but let righteous fury zip her up to the top floor.

The receptionist in his elegant outer office started to smile in greeting. One look at Eve's face had her blinking. "Lieutenant Dallas."

"Tell him I'm here, and that I see him now, or down at Cop Central."

"He's—he's in a meeting."

"Now."

"I'll call through." She swiveled and punched a button for private communication. She murmured the message and apologies while Eve stood fuming.

"If you would wait in his office for a moment, Lieutenant—" the receptionist began and rose.

"I know the way," Eve snapped, striding across the plush carpet through the towering double doors and into Roarke's New York sanctum.

There had been a time when she would have helped herself to a cup of coffee or wandered over to admire his view from a hundred fifty stories up. Today she stood, every nerve quivering with temper. And beneath that was fear.

The panel on the east wall slid open silently, and he walked through. He still wore the dark suit he'd chosen for the memorial service. As the panel closed behind him, he fingered the button in his pocket that belonged on Eve's gray jacket.

"You were quick," he said easily. "I thought I would finish my board meeting before you came by."

"You think you're clever," she shot back. "Giving me just enough to start digging with. Damn it, Roarke, you're right in the middle of this."

"Am I?" Unconcerned, he walked to a chair, sat, stretched out his legs. "And how is that, Lieutenant?"

"You owned the damn casino where Slade was gambling. You owned the fucking fleabag hotel where the woman died. You had an unlicensed hooker working your hellhole."

"Unlicensed companions in Sector 38?" He smiled a little. "Why, I'm shocked."

"Don't get cute with me. It connects you. Mercury was bad enough, but this is deeper. Your statement's on record."

"Naturally."

"Why are you making it so hard for me to keep your name out of this?"

"I'm not interested in making it hard or easy for you, Lieutenant."

"Fine, then. Just fine." If he could be cold, so could she. "Then we'll just get the questions and answers out of the way and move on. You knew Slade."

"Actually, I didn't. Not personally. Actually, I'd forgotten all about it, and him, until I did some research of my own. Wouldn't you like some coffee?"

"You forgot you were involved in a murder investigation?"

"Yes." Idly, he steepled his hands. "It wasn't the first brush I'd had with the police, nor apparently, is it the last. In the grand scheme of things, Lieutenant, it really didn't concern me."

"Didn't concern you," she repeated. "You had Slade tossed out of your casino."

"I believe the manager of the casino handled that."

"You were there."

"Yes, I was there, somewhere on the premises, in any case. Dissatisfied clients often become rowdy. I didn't pay much attention at that time."

She took a deep breath. "If it meant so little, and the entire matter slipped your mind, why did you sell the casino, the hotel, everything you owned in Sector 38 within forty-eight hours of Cicely Towers's murder?"

He said nothing for a moment, his eyes on hers. "For personal reasons."

"Roarke, just tell me so I can put this whole connection to bed. I know the sale didn't have anything to do with Towers's murder, but it looks dicey. 'For personal reasons' isn't good enough."

"It was for me. At the time. Tell me, Lieutenant Dallas, are you thinking I decided to blackmail Cicely over her future son-in-law's youthful indiscretion, had some henchman in my employ lure her to the West End, and when she didn't cooperate, slit her throat?"

She wanted to hate him for putting her in the position of having to answer. "I told you I didn't believe you had anything to do with her death, and I meant it. You've put me in a position where it's a scenario we'll have to work with. One that will take time and manpower away from finding the killer."

"Damn you, Eve." He said it quietly; so quietly, so calmly, her throat burned in reaction.

"What do you want from me, Roarke? You said you'd help, that I could use your connections. Now, because you're pissed about something else, you're blocking me."

"I changed my mind." His tone was dismissive as he rose and walked behind his desk. "About several things," he added, watching her with eyes that sliced at her heart.

"If you would just tell me why you sold. The coincidence of that can't be ignored."

He considered for a moment his decision to reorganize some of his less-than-legal enterprises and shake loose of what couldn't be changed. "No," he murmured. "I don't believe I will."

"Why are you putting me in this position?" she demanded. "Is this some sort of punishment?"

He sat, leaned back, steepled his fingers. "If you like."

"You're going to be pulled into this, just like the last time. There's just no need for it." Driven by frustration, she slapped her hands on his desk. "Can't you see that?"

He looked at her face, the dark, worried eyes, the ridiculously chopped hair. "I know what I'm doing." He hoped he did.

"Roarke, don't you understand, it's not enough for me to know you had nothing to do with it. Now I have to prove it."

He wanted to touch her, so much that his fingers ached from it. More than anything at that moment, he wished he could hate her for it. "Do you know, Eve?"

She straightened, dropped her hands to her sides. "It doesn't matter," she said and turned and left him.

But it did matter, he thought. At the moment, it was all

that really mattered. Shaken, he shifted forward. He could curse her now, now that those big, whiskey-colored eyes were no longer staring into him. He could curse her for bringing him so low he was nearly ready to beg for whatever scraps of her life she was willing to share with him.

And if he begged, if he settled, he would probably grow to hate her almost as much as he would hate himself.

He knew how to outwait a rival, how to outmanuever an opponent. He certainly knew how to fight for what he wanted or intended to have. But he was no longer sure he could outwait, outmanuever, or fight Eve.

Taking the button out of his pocket, he toyed with it, studied it as though it were some intriguing puzzle to be solved.

He was an idiot, Roarke realized. It was humiliating to admit what an incredible fool love could make of a man. He stood, slipped the button back in his pocket. He had a board meeting to complete, business to take care of.

And, he thought, some research to do on whether any details of the Slade arrest had left Sector 38. And if they had, how and why.

Eve couldn't put off her appointment with Nadine. The necessity of it irritated, as did the fact she had to schedule the time between Nadine's evening and late live broadcasts.

She plopped down at a table at a small café near Channel 75 called Images. It was, with its quiet corners and leafy trees, several large steps away from the Blue Squirrel. Eve winced at the prices on the menu—broadcasters were paid a great deal more than cops—and settled on a Classic Pepsi.

"You ought to try the muffins," Nadine told her. "The place is famous for them."

"I bet it is." At about five bucks a rehydrated blueberry, Eve thought. "I don't have a lot of time."

"Neither do I." Nadine's on-camera makeup was still perfectly in place. Eve could only wonder how anyone could stand having their pores gunked for hours at a time.

"You go first."

"Fine." Nadine broke open her muffin and it steamed fragrantly. "Obviously the memorial is the big news of the day. Who came, who said what. Lots of side stories about the family, focus is tight on the grieving daughter and her fiancé."

"Why?"

"Human interest, Dallas. Big splashy wedding plans interrupted by violent murder. Word's leaked that the ceremony will be postponed until the first part of next year."

Nadine took a bite of muffin. Eve ignored the envious reaction of her stomach juices. "Gossip isn't what I'm after, Nadine."

"But it adds color. Look, it was more like a plant than a leak. Somebody wanted the media to know the wedding's been postponed. So I wonder if this means there'll be a wedding after all. What I smell is the scent of trouble in paradise. Why would Mirina turn away from Slade at a time like this? Seems to me they'd have a nice quiet private ceremony so he'd be there to comfort her."

"Maybe that's the plan exactly, and they're throwing you off the scent."

"It's possible. Anyway, without Towers as buffer, speculation's running that Angelini and Hammett will dissolve their business associations. They were very cool to each other, never spoke during the service—before or after it, either."

"How do you know?"

Nadine smiled, feline and pleased. "I have my sources. Angelini needs income, and fast. Roarke's made him an offer for his shares, which now include Towers's interest, in Mercury."

"Has he?"

"You didn't know. Interesting." Sly as a cat, Nadine licked crumbs from her fingertips. "I thought it was interesting, too, that you didn't attend the service with Roarke."

"I was there in an official capacity," Eve said shortly. "Let's stick to the point."

"More trouble in paradise," Nadine murmured, then her eyes sobered. "Look, Dallas, I like you. I don't know why, but I do. If you and Roarke are having problems, I'm sorry for it."

Buddy-to-buddy confidences were something Eve was never comfortable with. She shifted, surprised that she was tempted, even for an instant, to share. Then she set it down to Nadine's skill as a reporter. "The point," she repeated.

"Okay." Nadine moved a shoulder and took another bite of muffin. "Nobody knows dick," she said briefly. "We've got speculation. Angelini's financial difficulties, the son's gambling habits, the Fluentes case."

"You can forget the Fluentes case," Eve interrupted. "He's going down. Both he and his lawyer know it. The evidence is clean. Taking Towers out won't change a thing."

"He might have been pissed."

"Maybe. But he's small time. He doesn't have the contacts or the money to buy a hit the size of Towers. It doesn't check out. We're running everybody she ever put away. So far we've got zip."

"You've cooled off on the revenge theory, haven't you?"

"Yeah. I think it was closer to home."

"Anyone in particular?"

"No." Eve shook her head when Nadine studied her. "No," she repeated. "I don't have anything solid yet. Here's what I want you to look into, and I need you to hold it off the air until I clear it."

"That was the deal."

Briefly, Eve told her of the incident in Sector 38.

"Holy shit, that's hot. And it's public record, Dallas."

"That may be, but you wouldn't know where to look unless I'd tipped you. Stick with the deal, Nadine. You hold it off air, and you poke around. See if you can find out if anyone know, or cares. If there's a connection to the murder, I'll hand it to you. If not, I guess it'll be up to your conscience whether you want to broadcast something that could ruin the reputation of a man and his relationship with his fiancée."

"Low blow, Dallas."

"Depends on where you're standing. Keep the cover on it, Nadine."

"Um-hmm." Her mind was humming. "Slade was in San Francisco the night of the murder." She waited a beat. "Wasn't he?"

"So the record shows."

"And there are dozens of coast-to-coast shuttles, public and private, running every hour, back and forth."

"That's right. You keep in touch, Nadine," Eve said as she rose. "And you keep the cover on."

Eve made it an early night. When her 'link beeped at one, she was screaming her way out of a nightmare. Sweating, shaking, she tore off the covers that wrapped around her, fought off the hands that were groping over her body.

She choked back another scream, pressed her fingers against her eyes, and ordered herself not to be sick. She answered the call without turning the lights on, and blocked video.

"Dallas."

"Dispatch. Voice print verified. Probable homicide, female. Report Five thirty-two Central Park South, rear of building. Code yellow."

"Acknowledged." Eve ended the transmission and, still trembling from the aftershocks of the dream, crawled out of bed.

It took her twenty minutes. She'd needed the comfort of a hot shower, even if it had only been for thirty seconds.

It was a trendy neighborhood, peopled by residents who patronized fashionable shops and private clubs, and who aspired to move just another notch up the social and ecomonic ladder.

The streets were quiet here, though it wasn't quite out of the realm of public taxis and into private transpo-cars. Upper middle class all the way, she mused as she made her way around to the back of a sleek steel building with its pleasant view of the park.

Then again, murder happened everywhere.

It had certainly happened here.

The rear of the building couldn't boast a view of the park, but the developers had made up for it with a nice plot of green. Beyond the trim trees was a security wall that separated one building from the next.

On the narrow stone path through a border of gold petunias, the body sprawled, facedown.

Female, Eve noted, flashing her badge at the waiting uniforms. Dark hair, dark skin, well dressed. She studied the stylish red-and-white-striped heel that lay point up on the path.

Death had knocked her out of her shoes.

"Pictures?"

"Yes, sir, Lieutenant. ME on the way."

"Who reported it?"

"Neighbor. Came out to let his dog use the facilities. We've got him inside."

"Do we have a name on her?"

"Yvonne Metcalf, Lieutenant. She lives in eleven twenty-six."

"Actress," Eve murmured as the name struck a cord. "Up and coming."

"Yes, sir." One of the uniforms looked down at the body. "She won an Emmy last year. Been doing the talk show rounds. She's pretty famous."

"Now she's pretty dead. Keep the camera running. I need to turn her over."

Even before she used the protective spray to seal her hands, before she crouched down to turn the body, Eve knew. Blood was everywhere. Someone hissed sharply as the body rolled faceup, but it wasn't Eve. She'd been braced for it.

The throat was cut, and the cut was deep. Yvonne's lovely green eyes stared up at Eve: two blank questions.

"What the hell did you have to do with Cicely Towers?" she murmured. "Same MO: one wound to the throat, severed jugular. No robbery, no signs of sexual assault or struggle." Gently, Eve lifted one of Yvonne's limp hands, shone her light at the nails, under them. They were painted a sparkling scarlet with tiny white stripes. And they were perfect. No chips, no snags, no scrapes of flesh or stains of blood under them.

"All dressed up and no place to go," Eve commented, studying the victim's flashy red-and-white-striped bodysuit. "Let's find out where she'd been or where she was going," Eve began. Her head came around as she heard the sound of approaching feet.

But it wasn't the medical examiner and his team, nor was it the sweepers. It was, she saw with disgust, C. J. Morse and a crew from Channel 75.

"Get that camera out of here." Temper vibrating, she sprang to her feet, instinctively shielding the body. "This is a crime scene."

"You haven't posted it," Morse said, smiling sweetly. "Until you do, it's public access. Sherry, get a shot of that shoe."

"Post the goddamn scene," Eve ordered a uniform. "Confiscate that camera, the recorders."

"You can't confiscate media equipment until the scene's posted," C. J. reminded her, as he tried to rubberneck around her to get a good look. "Sherry, get me a nice pan, then focus on the lieutenant's pretty face."

"I'm going to kick your ass, Morse."

"Oh, I wish you'd try, Dallas." Some of his bubbling resentment simmered into his eyes. "I'd love to bring you up on charges, and broadcast it, after that stunt you pulled on me."

"If you're still on this scene when it's posted, you'll be the one facing charges."

He only smiled again, backing off. He calculated he had another fifteen seconds of video time before he ran into trouble. "Channel 75 has a fine team of lawyers."

"Detain him and his crew." Eve flashed a snarl at a uniform. "Off scene, until I'm through."

"Interfering with media—"

"Kiss ass, Morse."

"I bet yours is tasty." He continued to grin as he was escorted away.

When Eve came around the building, he was doing a sober stand-up report on the recent homicide. Without missing a beat, he angled himself toward her. "Lieutenant Dallas, will you confirm that Yvonne Metcalf, the star of *Tune In* has been murdered?"

"The department has no comment to make at this time."

"Isn't it true that Ms. Metcalf was a resident of this building, and that her body was discovered this morning on the rear patio? Hadn't her throat been cut?"

"No comment."

"Our viewing audience is waiting, Lieutenant. Two prominent women have been violently murdered by the same method, and in all likelihood by the same person, barely a week apart. And you have no comment?"

"Unlike certain irresponsible reporters, the police are more careful, and more concerned with facts than speculation."

"Or is it that the police are simply unable to solve these crimes?" Quick on his feet, he sidestepped, came up in her face again. "Aren't you concerned about your reputation, Lieutenant, and the connection between the two victims and your close friend Roarke?"

"My reputation isn't at issue here. The investigation is."

Morse turned back to the camera. "At this hour, the investigation, headed by Lieutenant Eve Dallas, is at an apparent deadlock. Another murder has taken place less than a hundred yards from where I stand. A young woman, talented, beautiful, and full of promise has had her life sliced off by a violent sweep of a knife. Just as only one week ago, the respected and dedicated defender of justice, Cicely Towers had her life brought to an end. Perhaps the question is not when will the killer be caught, but what prominent woman will be next? This is C. J. Morse for Channel 75, reporting live from Central Park South."

He nodded to the camera operator before turning to

beam at Eve. "See, if you'd cooperate, Dallas, I might be able to help you out with public opinion."

"Fuck you, Morse."

"Oh, well, maybe if you asked nice." His grin never wavered when she grabbed him by the shirtfront. "Now, now, don't touch unless you mean it."

She was a full head taller than he, and gave serious thought to pounding him into the sidewalk. "Here's what I want to know, Morse. I want to know how a third-rate reporter ends up on a crime scene, with a crew, ten minutes after the primary."

He smoothed down the front of his shirt. "Sources, Lieutenant, which, as you know I'm under no obligation to share with you." His smile dimmed into a sneer. "And at this stage, I'd say we're talking third-rate primary. You'd have been better off hooking up with me instead of Nadine. That was a nasty turn you served, helping her bump me off the Towers story."

"Was it? Well, I'm glad to hear that, C. J., because I just plain hate your guts. It didn't bother you at all, did it, to go back there, camera running, and broadcast pictures of that woman? You didn't think about her right to a little dignity or the fact that someone who cared about her might not have been notified. Her family, for instance."

"Hey, you do your job, I do mine. You didn't look too bothered poking at her."

"What time did you get the tip?" Eve asked briefly.

He hesitated, stringing it out. "I guess it wouldn't hurt to tell you that. It came in on my private line at twelve thirty."

"From?"

"Nope. I protect my sources. I called the station, drummed up a crew. Right, Sherry?"

"Right." The camera operator moved a shoulder. "The night desk sent us out to meet C. J. here. That's show biz."

"I'm going to do whatever I can to confiscate your logs, Morse, to bring you in for questioning, to make your life hell."

"Oh, I hope you do." His round face gleamed. "You'll

give me double my usual airtime and put my popularity quotient through the roof. And you know what's going to be fun? The side story I'm going to work up on Roarke and his cozy relationship with Yvonne Metcalf."

Her stomach shuddered, but she kept her voice bland. "Watch your step there, C. J., Roarke's not nearly as nice as I am. Keep your crew off scene," she warned. "Put one toe on, and I confiscate your equipment."

She turned, and when she was far enough away, pulled out her communicator. She was going outside of procedure, risking a reprimand or worse. But it had to be done.

She could tell when Roarke answered that he hadn't yet been to bed.

"Well, Lieutenant, this is a surprise."

"I've only got a minute. Tell me what your relationship was with Yvonne Metcalf."

He lifted a brow. "We're friends, were close at one time."

"You were lovers."

"Yes, briefly. Why?"

"Because she's dead, Roarke."

His faint smile faded. "Oh Christ, how?"

"She had her throat cut. Stay available."

"Is that an official request, Lieutenant?" he asked, and his voice was hard as rock.

"It has to be. Roarke . . ." She hesitated. "I'm sorry."

"So am I." He ended the transmission.

chapter eight

Eve had no problem listing several connections between Cicely Towers and Yvonne Metcalf. Number one was murder. The method and the perpetrator. They had both been women in the public eye, well respected, and held in great affection. They were successful in their chosen fields and were dedicated to that field. They both had families who loved and who mourned.

Yet they had worked and played in dramatically different social and professional circles. Yvonne's friends had been artists, actors, and musicians, while Cicely had socialized with law enforcers, businesspeople, and politicians.

Cicely had been an organized career woman of impeccable taste who had guarded her privacy fiercely.

Yvonne had been a cheerfully disorganized, borderline messy actor who courted the public eye.

But someone had known them both well enough and felt strongly enough about both to kill them.

The only name Eve found in Cicely's tidy address book and Yvonne's disordered one that matched was Roarke.

For the third time in an hour, Eve ran the lists through her computer, pushing for a connection. A name that clicked with another name, an address, a profession, a personal interest. The few connections that came through were so loosely linked she could barely justify taking the next step toward the interview.

But she would do it, because the alternative was Roarke.

While the computer handled the short list, she took another pass through Yvonne's electronic diary.

"Why the hell didn't the woman put in names?" Eve muttered. There were times, dates, occasionally initials, often little side notes or symbols of Yvonne's mood.

1:00—lunch at the Crown Room with B. C. Yippee! Don't be late, Yvonne, and wear the green number with the short skirt. He likes prompt women with legs.

Beauty day at Paradise. Thank God. 10:00. Should try to hit Fitness Palace at 8 for workout. Ugh.

Fancy lunches, Eve mused. Pampering in the top salon in the city. Sweating a little in a luxury gym. Not a bad life, all in all. Who had wanted to end it?

She flipped through to the day of the murder.

8:00—Power breakfast—little blue suit with matching shoes. LOOK PROFESSIONAL FOR CHRIST'S SAKE, YVONNE!!

11:00—P. P.'s office to discuss contract negotiations. Maybe sneak in some shopping first. SHOE SALE AT SAKS. Hot damn.

Lunch—skip dessert. Maybe. Tell cutie he was wonderful in show. No penalty for lying to pals about their acting. God, wasn't he awful?

Call home.

Hit Saks if you missed it earlier.

5ish. Drinks. Stick with spring water, babe. You talk too much when you're loose. Be bright, sparkle. Push Tune In. *$$$***. Don't forget photo layout in morning and stay away from that wine. Go home, take a nap.*

Midnight meeting. Could be hot stuff. Wear the red-and-white-striped number, and smile, smile, smile. Bygones are bygones, right? Never close that door. Small world, and so on. What a dumb ass.

So she'd documented the meeting at midnight. Not who, not where, not what, but she'd wanted to be well dressed for it. Someone she'd known, had a history with. Bygones. A past problem with?

Lover? Eve mused. She didn't think so. Yvonne hadn't put little hearts around the notation or told herself to be sexy, sexy, sexy. Eve thought she was beginning to understand the woman. Yvonne had been amused at herself, ready for fun, enjoying her lifestyle. And she'd been ambitious.

Wouldn't she have told herself to smile, smile, smile, for a career opportunity? A part, good press, a new script, an influential fan.

What would she have said about Roarke? Eve wondered. *Most likely she'd have noted him down with a big, bold-faced capital R. She would have put hearts around the date, or dollar signs, or smiles. As she had eighteen months before she died.*

Eve didn't have to look at Yvonne's previous diaries. She remembered perfectly the woman's last notation on Roarke.

*Dinner with **R**—8:30. YUM-YUM. Wear the white satin —matching teddy. Be prepared, might get lucky. The man's body is awesome—wish I could figure out his head. Oh well, just think sexy and see what happens.*

Eve didn't particularly want to know if Yvonne had gotten lucky. Obviously they'd been lovers—Roarke had said so himself. So why hadn't she put down any more dates with him after the white satin?

It was something, she supposed, she'd have to find out— for investigative purposes only.

Meanwhile, she would make another trip to Yvonne's apartment, try again to reconstruct the last day of her life. She had interviews to schedule. And, as Yvonne's parents called her at least once a day, Eve knew she would have to talk with them again, steel herself against their horrible grief and disbelief.

She didn't mind the fourteen- and sixteen-hour days. In fact, at this stage of her life she welcomed them.

Four days after Yvonne Metcalf's murder, Eve was running on empty. She had questioned over three dozen people extensively, exhaustively. Not only had she been unable to discover a single viable motive, she'd found no one who hadn't adored the victim.

There wasn't a hint of an obsessed fan. Yvonne's mail had been mountainous, and Feeney and his computer were still scanning the correspondence. But among the first section, there had been no threats, veiled or overt, no weird or unsavory offers or suggestions.

There had been a hefty percentage of marriage proposals and other propositions. Eve culled them out with little hope or enthusiasm. There was still a chance that someone who had written to Yvonne had written or contacted Cicely. As time passed, the chance became a long shot.

Eve did what was expected in unsolved multiple homicides, what departmental procedure called for at this stage of an investigation. She made an appointment with the shrink.

While she waited, Eve struggled with her mixed feelings for Dr. Mira. The woman was brilliant, insightful, quietly efficient, and compassionate.

Those were the precise reasons Eve dragged her feet. She had to remind herself again that she hadn't come to Mira for personal reasons or because the department was sending her for therapy. She wasn't going through Testing, they weren't going to discuss her thoughts, her feelings—or her memory.

They were going to dissect the mind of a killer.

Still, she had to concentrate on keeping her heart rate level, her hands still and dry. When she was gestured into

Mira's office, Eve told herself her legs were shaky because she was tired, nothing more.

"Lieutenant Dallas." Mira's pale blue eyes skimmed over Eve's face, noted the fatigue. "I'm sorry you had to wait."

"No problem." Though she would have preferred standing, Eve took the blue scoop chair beside Mira's. "I appreciate you getting to the case so quickly."

"We all do our jobs as best we can," Mira said in her soothing voice. "And I had a great deal of respect and affection for Cicely Towers."

"You knew her?"

"We were contemporaries, and she consulted me on many cases. I often testified for the prosecution—as well as the defense," she added, smiling a little. "But you knew that."

"Just making conversation."

"I also admired Yvonne Metcalf's talent. She brought a lot of happiness to the world. She'll be missed."

"Someone isn't going to miss either of them."

"True enough." In her smooth, graceful way, Mira programmed her AutoChef for tea. "I realize you might be a bit pressed for time, but I work better with a little stimulation. And you look as though you could use some."

"I'm fine."

Recognizing the tightly controlled hostility in the tone, Mira only lifted a brow. "Overworked, as usual. It happens to those who are particularly good at their jobs." She handed Eve a cup of tea in one of the pretty china cups. "Now, I've read over your reports, the evidence you've gathered, and your theories. My psychiatric profile," she said, tapping a sealed disc on the table between them.

"You've completed it." Eve didn't trouble to mask the irritation. "You could have transmitted the data and saved me a trip."

"I could have, but I preferred to discuss this with you, face to face. Eve, you're dealing with something, someone, very dangerous."

"I think I picked up on that, Doctor. Two women have had their throats slashed."

"Two women, thus far," Mira said quietly and sat back. "I'm very much afraid there will be more. And soon."

Because she believed the same, Eve ignored the quick chill that sprinted up her spine. "Why?"

"It was so easy, you see. And so simple. A job well done. There's a satisfaction in that. There's also the attention factor. Whoever accomplished the murders can now sit back in his or her home and watch the show. The reports, the editorials, the grieving, the services, the public arena of the investigation."

She paused to savor her tea. "You have your theory, Eve. You're here so that I can corroborate it or argue against it."

"I have several theories."

"Only one you believe in." Mira smiled her wise smile, aware that it made Eve bristle. "Fame. What else did these two women have in common but their public prominence? They didn't share the same social circle or professional one. Knew few of the same people, even on a casual level. They didn't patronize the same shops, health centers, or cosmetic experts. What they did share was fame, public interest, and a kind of power."

"Which the killer envied."

"I would say exactly that. Resented as well and wished, by killing them, to bask in the reflected attention. The murders themselves were both vicious and uncommonly clean. Their faces weren't marred, nor their bodies. One quick slice across the throat, according to the ME, from the front. Face to face. A blade is a personal weapon, an extension of the hand. It isn't distant like a laser, or aloof like poison. Your murderer wanted the feel of killing, the sight of blood, the smell of it. The full experience that makes him or her one who appreciates having control, following through on a plan."

"You don't believe it was a hired hit."

"There's always that possibility, Eve, but I'm more inclined to see the killer as an active participant rather than a hireling. Then there are the souvenirs."

"Towers's umbrella."

"And Metcalf's right shoe. You've managed to keep that out of the press."

"Barely." Eve scowled over the memory of Morse and his crew invading the murder scene. "A pro wouldn't have taken a souvenir, and the killings were too well thought out to have been planned by a street hit."

"I agree. You have an organized mind, an ambitious one. Your murderer is enjoying his work, which is why there'll be another."

"Or hers," Eve put in. "The envy factor can be leaned toward a female. These two women were what she wanted to be. Beautiful, successful, admired, famous, strong. It's often the weak who kill."

"Yes, quite often. No, it isn't possible to determine gender from the data we have at this point, only to access the probability factor that the killer targets females who have reached a high level of public attention."

"What am I supposed to do about that, Dr. Mira? Put a security beeper on every prominent, well-known, or successful woman in the city? Including yourself?"

"Odd, I was thinking more about you."

"Me?" Eve jiggled the tea she hadn't touched, then set it on the table with a snap. "That's ridiculous."

"I don't think so. You've become a familiar face, Eve. For your work, certainly, and most particularly since the case last winter. You're very respected in your field. And," she continued before Eve could interrupt, "you also have one more important connection to both victims. All of you have had a relationship with Roarke."

Eve knew her blood drained from her face. That wasn't something she could control. But she could keep her voice level and hard. "Roarke had a business partnership, a relatively minor one, with Towers. With Metcalf, the intimate side of their relationship has been over for quite some time."

"Yet you feel the need to defend him to me."

"I'm not defending him," Eve snapped. "I'm stating facts. Roarke's more than capable of defending himself."

"Undoubtedly. He's a strong, vital, and clever man. Still, you worry for him."

"In your professional opinion, is Roarke the killer?"

"Absolutely not. I have no doubt that were I to analyze him, I would find his killer instinct well developed." The fact was, Mira would have loved the opportunity to study Roarke's mind. "But his motive would have to be very defined. Great love or great hate. I doubt there is much else that would push him over the line. Relax, Eve," Mira said quietly. "You're not in love with a murderer."

"I'm not in love with anyone. And my personal feelings aren't at issue here."

"On the contrary, the investigator's state of mind is always an issue. And, if I'm required to give my opinion on yours, I'll have to say I found you near exhaustion, emotionally torn, and deeply troubled."

Eve picked up the profile disc and rose. "Then it's fortunate you're not going to be required to give your opinion. I'm perfectly capable of doing my job."

"I don't doubt it for a moment. But at what cost to yourself?"

"The cost would be higher if I didn't do it. I'm going to find who killed these women. Then it'll be up to someone like Cicely Towers to put them away." Eve tucked the disk in her bag. "There's a connection you left out, Dr. Mira. Something these two women had in common." Eve's eyes were hard and cold. "Family. Both of them had close family that was a large and important part of their lives. I'd say that lets me out as a possible target. Wouldn't you?"

"Perhaps. Have you been thinking of your family, Eve?"

"Don't play with me."

"You mentioned it," Mira pointed out. "You're always careful in what you say to me, so I must assume family is on your mind."

"I don't have family," Eve shot back. "And I've got murder on my mind. If you want to report to the commander that I'm unfit for duty, that's just fine."

"When are you going to trust me?" There was impatience, for the first time in Eve's memory, in the careful voice. "Is it so impossible for you to believe that I care about you? Yes, I care," Mira said when Eve blinked in surprise. "And I understand you better than you wish to admit."

"I don't need for you to understand me." But there were nerves in Eve's voice now. She heard them herself. "I'm not in Testing or here for a therapy session."

"There are no recorders on here." Mira set her tea down with a snap that had Eve jamming her hands in her pockets. "Do you think you're the only child who lived with horror and abuse? The only woman who's struggled to overcome it?"

"I don't have to overcome anything. I don't remember—"

"My stepfather raped me repeatedly from the time I was twelve until I was fifteen," Mira said calmly, and stopped Eve's protest cold. "For those three years I lived never knowing when it would happen, only that it would. And no one would listen to me."

Shaken, sick, Eve wrapped her arms around her body. "I don't want to know this. Why are you telling me this?"

"Because I look in your eyes and see myself. But you have someone who'll listen to you, Eve."

Eve stood where she was, moistened her dry lips. "Why did it stop?"

"Because I finally found the courage to go to an abuse center, tell the counselor everything, to submit to the examinations, both physical and psychiatric. The terror of that, the humiliation of that, was no longer as huge as the alternative."

"Why should I have to remember it?" Eve demanded. "It's over."

"Why aren't you sleeping?"

"The investigation—"

"Eve."

The gentle tone had Eve closing her eyes. It was so hard, so trying, to fight that quiet compassion. "Flashbacks," she murmured, hating herself for the weakness. "Nightmares."

"Of before you were found in Texas?"

"Just blips, just pieces."

"I can help you put them together."

"Why should I want to put them together?"

"Haven't you already started to?" Now Mira rose. "You can work with this haunting your subconscious. I've watched you do so for years. But happiness eludes you, and will continue to do so until you've convinced yourself you deserve it."

"It wasn't my fault."

"No." Mira touched a gentle hand to Eve's arm. "No, it wasn't your fault."

Tears were threatening, and that was a shock and an embarrassment. "I can't talk about this."

"My dear, you've already begun to. I'll be here when you're ready to do so again." She waited until Eve had reached the door. "Can I ask you a question?"

"You always ask questions."

"Why stop now?" Mira said and smiled. "Does Roarke make you happy?"

"Sometimes." Eve squeezed her eyes shut and swore. "Yes, yes, he makes me happy. Unless he's making me miserable."

"That's lovely. I'm very pleased for both of you. Try to get some sleep, Eve. If you won't take chemicals, you might use simple visualization."

"I'll keep it in mind." Eve opened the door, kept her back to the room. "Thank you."

"You're welcome."

Visualization wouldn't be much help, Eve decided. Not after a rescan of autopsy reports.

The apartment was too quiet, too empty. She was sorry

she'd left the cat with Roarke. At least Galahad would have been company.

Because her eyes burned from studying data, she pushed away from her desk. She didn't have the energy to seek out Mavis, and she was bored senseless with the video offerings on her screen.

She ordered music, listened for thirty seconds, then switched it off.

Food usually worked, but when she poked into the kitchen, she was reminded she hadn't restocked her AutoChef in weeks. The pickings were slim, and she didn't have enough of an appetite to order in.

Determined to relax, she tried out the virtual reality goggles Mavis had given her for Christmas. Because Mavis had used them last, they were set for Nightclub, at full volume. After a hurried adjustment and a great deal of swearing, Eve programmed Tropics, Beach.

She could feel the grit of hot, white sand under her bare feet, the punch of the sun on her skin, the soft, ocean breeze. It was lovely to stand in the gentle surf, watch the swoop of gulls, and sip from an icy drink that carried the zing of rum and fruit.

There were hands on her bare shoulders, rubbing. Sighing, she leaned back into them, felt the firm length of male against her back. Far out on the blue sea a white ship sailed toward the horizon.

It was easy to turn into the arms that waited for her, to lift her mouth to the mouth she wanted. And to lie on the hot sand with the body that fit so perfectly with hers.

The excitement was as sweet as the peace. The rhythm as old as the waves that lapped over her skin. She let herself be taken, shivered as the needs built toward fulfillment. His breath was on her face, his body linked with her when she groaned out his name.

Roarke.

Furious with herself, Eve tore off the goggles and heaved them aside. He had no right to intrude, even here, inside her head. No right to bring her pain and pleasure when all she wanted was privacy.

Oh, he knew what he was doing, she thought as she sprang up to pace. He knew exactly what he was doing. And they were going to settle it, once and for all.

She slammed the apartment door behind her. It didn't occur to her until she was speeding through his gates that he might not be alone.

The idea of that was so infuriating, so devastating, that she took the stone steps two at a time, hit the door with a fresh burst of violent energy.

Summerset was waiting for her. "Lieutenant, it's one twenty in the morning."

"I know what time it is." She bared her teeth when he stepped in front of her to block the staircase. "Let's understand each other, pal. I hate you, you hate me. The difference is I've got a badge. Now get the hell out of my way or I'll haul your bony ass in for obstructing an officer."

Dignity coated him like silk. "Do I take that to mean you're here, at this hour, in an official capacity, Lieutenant?"

"Take it any way you want. Where is he?"

"If you'll state your business, I'll be happy to determine Roarke's current whereabouts and see if he's available to you."

Out of patience, Eve jammed an elbow in his gut and skirted his wheezing form. "I'll find him myself," she stated as she bounded up the stairs.

He wasn't in bed, alone or otherwise. She wasn't entirely sure how she felt about that, or what she would have done if she'd found him twined around some blonde. Refusing to think about it, she turned on her heel and marched away toward his office, with Summerset hot on her trail.

"I intend to file a complaint."

"File away," she shot back over her shoulder.

"You have no right to intrude on private property, in the middle of the night. You will not disturb Roarke." He slapped a hand on the door as she reached it. "I will not allow it."

To Eve's surprise, he was out of breath and red-faced. His eyes were all but jittering in their sockets. It was, she decided, more emotion than she'd believed him capable of.

"This really puts your jocks in a twist, doesn't it?" Before he could prevent it, she hit the mechanism and the door slid open.

He made a grab for her, and Roarke, who turned from his study of the city, had the curious surprise of watching them grapple.

"Put a hand on me again, you tight-assed son of a bitch, and I'll deck you." She lifted a fist to demonstrate. "The satisfaction would be worth my badge."

"Summerset," Roarke said mildly. "I believe she means it. Leave us alone."

"She's exceeded her authority—"

"Leave us alone," Roarke repeated. "I'll deal with this."

"As you wish." Summerset jerked his starched jacket back into place and strode out—with only the slightest of limps.

"If you want to keep me out," Eve snapped on her march toward the desk, "you're going to have to do better than that flat-assed guard dog."

Roarke merely folded his hands on the desktop. "If I'd wanted to keep you out, you would no longer be cleared through gate security." Deliberately, he flicked a glance at his watch. "It's a bit late for official interviews."

"I'm tired of people telling me what time it is."

"Well then." He leaned back in the chair. "What can I do for you?"

chapter nine

Attack was the emotional choice. Eve could justify it as the logical one as well.

"You were involved with Yvonne Metcalf."

"As I told you, we were friends." He opened an antique silver box on the desk and took out a cigarette. "At one time, intimate friends."

"Who changed the aspect of your relationship, and when?"

"Who? Hmmm." Roarke thought it over as he lighted the cigarette, blew out a thin haze of smoke. "I believe it was a mutual decision. Her career was rising quickly, causing numerous demands on her time and energy. You could say we drifted apart."

"You quarreled?"

"I don't believe we did. Yvonne was rarely quarrelsome. She found life too . . . amusing. Would you like a brandy?"

"I'm on duty."

"Yes, of course you are. I'm not."

When he rose, Eve saw the cat spring from his lap. Galahad examined her with his bicolored eyes before plunking down to wash. She was too busy scowling at the cat to note that Roarke's hands weren't quite steady as he stood at the carved liquor cabinet pouring brandy from decanter to snifter.

"Well," he said, swirling the glass with half the width of the room between them. "Is that all?"

No, she thought, *that was far from all.* If he wouldn't help her voluntarily, she would poke and prod and use his canny brain without mercy and without a qualm. "The last time you're noted in her diary was a year and a half ago."

"So long," Roarke murmured. He had regret, a great deal of it, for Yvonne. But he had his own problems at the moment, the biggest of which was standing across the room, watching him with turbulent eyes. "I didn't realize."

"Was that the last time you saw her?"

"No, I'm sure it wasn't." He stared into his brandy, remembering her. "I recall dancing with her at a party, last New Year's Eve. She came back here with me."

"You slept with her," Eve said evenly.

"Technically, no." His voice took on a clip of annoyance. "I had sex with her, conversation, brunch."

"You resumed your former relationship?"

"No." He chose a chair and ordered himself to enjoy his brandy and cigarette. Casually, he crossed his feet at the ankles. "We might have, but we were both quite busy with our own projects. I didn't hear from her again for six weeks, maybe seven."

"And?"

He'd brushed her off, he recalled. Casually, easily. Perhaps thoughtlessly. "I told her I was . . . involved." He examined the bright tip of his cigarette. "At that time I was falling in love with someone else."

Her heartbeat hitched. She stared at him, jammed her hands in her pockets. "I can't eliminate you from the list unless you help me."

"Can't you? Well, then."

"Damn it, Roarke, you're the only one who was involved with both victims."

"And what's my motive, Lieutenant?"

"Don't use that tone with me. I hate it when you do that. Cold, controlled, superior." Giving up, she began to pace. "I know you didn't have anything to do with the murders, and there's no evidence to support your involvement. But that doesn't break the link."

"And that makes it difficult for you, because your name is, in turn, linked with mine. Or was."

"I can handle that."

"Then why have you lost weight?" he demanded. "Why are there shadows under your eyes? Why do you look so unhappy?"

She yanked out her recorder, slapped it on his desk. A barrier between them. "I need you to tell me everything you know about these women. Every small, insignificant detail. Damn it, damn it, damn it, I need help. I have to know why Towers would go to the West End in the middle of the night. Why Metcalf would dress herself up and go out to the patio at midnight."

He tapped out his cigarette, then rose slowly. "You're giving me more credit than I deserve, Eve. I didn't know Cicely that well. We did business, socialized in the most distant of fashions. Remember my background and her position. As to Yvonne, we were lovers. I enjoyed her, her energy, her zest. I know she had ambition. She wanted stardom and she earned it, deserved it. But I can't tell you the minds of either of these women."

"You know people," she argued. "You have a way of getting inside their heads. Nothing ever surprises you."

"You do," he murmured. "Continually."

She only shook her head. "Tell me why you think Yvonne Metcalf went out to meet someone on the patio."

He sipped brandy, shrugged. "For advancement, glory, excitement, love. Probably in that order. She would have dressed carefully because she was vain, admirably so. The time of the meeting wouldn't have meant anything to her. She was impulsive, entertainingly so."

She let out a little breath. This was what she needed. He could help her see the victims. "Were there other men?"

He was brooding, he realized, and forced himself to stop. "She was lovely, entertaining, bright, excellent in bed. I imagine there were a great many men in her life."

"Jealous men, angry men?"

He lifted a brow. "Do you mean someone might have killed her because she wouldn't give him what he wanted? Needed?" His eyes stayed steady on hers. "It's a thought. A man could do a great deal of damage to a woman for that, if he wanted or needed badly enough. Then again, I haven't killed you. Yet."

"This is a murder investigation, Roarke. Don't get cute with me."

"Cute?" He stunned them both by flinging the half-empty snifter across the room. Glass shattered on the wall, liquor sprayed. "You come bursting in here, without warning, without invitation, and expect me to sit cooperatively, like a trained dog, while you interrogate me? You ask me questions about Yvonne, a woman I cared for, and expect me to cheerfully answer them while you imagine me in bed with her."

She'd seen his temper spurt and flash before. She usually preferred it to his icy control. But at the moment her nerves had shattered along with the glass. "It's not personal, and it's not an interrogation. It's a consultation with a useful source. I'm doing my job."

"This has nothing to do with your job, and we both know it. If there's even a germ of belief in you that I had anything to do with slitting the throats of those two women, then I've made even a bigger mistake than I'd imagined. If you want to poke holes in me, Lieutenant, do it on your own time, not mine." He scooped her recorder off the desk and tossed it to her. "Next time, bring a warrant."

"I'm trying to eliminate you completely."

"Haven't you done that already?" He moved back behind his desk and sat wearily. "Get out. I'm done with this."

She was surprised she didn't stumble on her way to the door, the way her heart was pounding and her knees were shaking. She fought for breath as she reached for it. At the desk, Roarke cursed himself for a fool and hit the button to engage the locks. Damn her, and damn himself, but she wasn't walking out on him.

He was opening his mouth to speak when she turned, inches from the door. There was fury on her face now. "All right. Goddamn it, all right, you win. I'm miserable. Isn't that what you want? I can't sleep, I can't eat. It's like something's broken inside me, and I can barely do my job. Happy now?"

He felt the first tingle of relief loosen the fist around his heart. "Should I be?"

"I'm here, aren't I? I'm here because I couldn't stay away anymore." Dragging at the chain under her shirt, she strode to him. "I'm wearing the damn thing."

He glanced at the diamond she thrust in his face. It flashed at him, full of fire and secrets. "As I said, it suits you."

"A lot you know," she muttered and swung around. "It makes me feel like an idiot. This whole thing makes me feel like an idiot. So fine; I'll be an idiot. I'll move in here. I'll tolerate that insulting robot you call a butler. I'll wear diamonds. Just don't—" She broke, covering her face as the sobs took over. "I can't take this anymore."

"Don't. For Christ's sake, don't cry."

"I'm just tired." She rocked herself for comfort. "I'm just tired, that's all."

"Call me names." He rose, shaken and more than a little terrified by the storm of weeping. "Throw something. Take a swing at me."

She jerked back when he reached for her. "Don't. I need a minute when I'm making a fool of myself."

Ignoring her, he gathered her close. She pulled back twice, was brought back firmly against him. Then, in a desperate move, her arms came around him, clutched. "Don't go away." She pressed her face to his shoulder. "Don't go away."

"I'm not going anywhere." Gently, he stroked her back, cradled her head. Was there anything more astounding or more frightening to a man, he wondered, than a strong woman in tears? "I've been right here all along. I love you, Eve, almost more than I can stand."

"I need you. I can't help it. I don't want to."

"I know." He eased back, tucking a hand under her chin to lift her face to his. "We're going to have to deal with it." He kissed one wet cheek, then the other. "I really can't do without you."

"You told me to go."

"I locked the door." His lips curved a little before they brushed over hers. "If you'd waited a few more hours, I would have come to you. I was sitting here tonight, trying to talk myself out of it and not having any luck. Then you stalked in. I was perilously close to getting on my knees."

"Why?" She touched his face. "You could have anyone. You probably have."

"Why?" He tilted his head. "That's a tricky one. Could it be your serenity, your quiet manner, your flawless fashion sense?" It did his heart good to see her quick, amused grin. "No, I must be thinking of someone else. It must be your courage, your absolute dedication to balancing scales, that restless mind, and that sweet corner of your heart that pushes you to care so much about so many."

"That's not me."

"Oh, but it is you, darling Eve." He touched his lips to hers. "Just as that taste is you, the smell, the look, the sound. You've undone me. We'll talk," he murmured, brushing his thumbs over drying tears. "We'll figure out a way to make this work for both of us."

She drew in a shuddering breath. "I love you." And let it out. "God."

The emotion that swept through him was like a summer

storm, quick, violent, then clean. Swamped with it, he rested his brow on hers. "You didn't choke on it."

"I guess not. Maybe I'll get used to it." And maybe her stomach wouldn't jump like a pond of frogs next time. Angling her face up, she found his mouth.

In an instant the kiss was hot, greedy, and full of edgy need. The blood was roaring in her head, so loud and fierce she didn't hear herself say the words again, but she felt them, in the way her heart stuttered and swelled.

Breathless and already wet, she tugged at his slacks. "Now. Right now."

"Absolutely now." He'd dragged her shirt over her head before they hit the floor.

They rolled, groping for each other. Limbs tangled. Giddy with hunger, she sank her teeth into his shoulder as he yanked down her jeans. He had a moment to register the feel of her skin under his hands, the shape of her, the heat of her, then it was a morass of the senses, a clash of scents and textures abrading against the urgent need to mate.

Finesse would have to wait, as would tenderness. The beast clawed at them both, devouring even when he was deep inside her, pumping wildly. He could feel her body clutch and tense, heard her long, low moan of staggering release. And let himself empty, heart, soul, and seed.

She awoke in his bed with soft sunlight creeping through the window filters. With her eyes closed, she reached out and found the space beside her warm but empty.

"How the hell did I get here?" she wondered.

"I carried you."

Her eyes sprang open and focused on Roarke. He sat naked, cross-legged at her knees, watching her. "Carried me?"

"You fell asleep on the floor." He leaned over to rub a thumb over her cheek. "You shouldn't work yourself into exhaustion, Eve."

"You carried me," she said again, too groggy to decide if she was embarrassed or not. "I guess I'm sorry I missed it."

"We have plenty of time for repeat performances. You worry me."

"I'm fine. I'm just—" She caught the time on the bedside clock. "Holy Christ, ten. Ten A.M.?"

He used one hand to shove her back when she started to scramble out of bed. "It's Sunday."

"Sunday?" Completely disoriented now, she rubbed her eyes clear. "I lost track." She wasn't on duty, she remembered, but regardless—

"You needed sleep," he said, reading her mind. "And you need fuel, something other than caffeine." He reached for the glass on the nightstand and held it out.

Eve studied the pale pink liquid dubiously. "What is it?"

"Good for you. Drink it." To make sure she did, he held the glass to her lips. He could have given her the energy booster in pill form, but he knew well her dislike for anything resembling drugs. "It's a little something one of my labs has been working on. We should have it on the market in about six months."

Her eyes narrowed. "Experimental?"

"It's quite safe." He smiled and set the empty glass aside. "Hardly anyone's died."

"Ha-ha." She sat back again, feeling amazingly relaxed, amazingly alert. "I have to go in to Cop Central, do some work on the other cases on my desk."

"You need some time off." He held up a hand before she could argue. "A day. Even an afternoon. I'd like you to spend it with me, but even if you spend it alone, you need it."

"I guess I could take a couple of hours." She sat up, linked her arms around his neck. "What did you have in mind?"

Grinning, he rolled her back onto the bed. This time there was finesse, and there was tenderness.

Eve wasn't surprised to find a pile of messages waiting. Sunday had stopped being a day of rest decades before. Her message disc beeped along, recounting transmissions from

Nadine Furst, the arrogant weasel Morse, another from
Yvonne Metcalf's parents that had her rubbing her temples, and a short message from Mirina Angelini.

"You can't take on their grief, Eve," Roarke said from
behind her.

"What?"

"The Metcalfs. I can see it in your face."

"I'm all they've got to hold onto." She initialed the messages to document her receipt. "They have to know someone's looking after her."

"I'd like to say something."

Eve rolled her eyes, prepared for him to lecture her
about rest, objectivity, or professional distance. "Spit it out
then so I can get to work."

"I've dealt with a lot of cops in my time. Evaded them,
bribed them, outmaneuvered them, or simply outran
them."

Amused, she nudged a hip onto the corner of her desk.
"I'm not sure you should be telling me that. Your record's
suspiciously clean."

"Of course it is." On impulse he kissed the tip of her
nose. "I paid for it."

She winced. "Really, Roarke, what I don't know can't
hurt you."

"The point is," he continued blandly, "I've dealt with a
lot of cops over the years. You're the best."

Caught completely off guard, she blinked. "Well."

"You'll stand, Eve, for the dead and the grieving. I'm
staggered by you."

"Cut it out." Miserably embarrassed, she shifted. "I
mean it."

"You can use that when you call Morse back and run up
against his irritating whine."

"I'm not calling him back."

"You initialed the transmissions."

"I zapped his first." She smiled. "Oops."

With a laugh he picked her up off the desk. "I like your
style."

She indulged herself by combing her fingers through his hair before she tried to wriggle free. "Right now you're cramping it. So back off while I see what Mirina Angelini wants." Brushing him off, she engaged the number, waited.

It was Mirina herself who answered, her pale, tense face on-screen. "Yes, oh, Lieutenant Dallas. Thank you for getting back to me so quickly. I was afraid I wouldn't hear from you until tomorrow."

"What can I do for you, Ms. Angelini?"

"I need to speak with you as soon as possible. I don't want to go through the commander, Lieutenant. He's done enough for me and my family."

"Is this regarding the investigation?"

"Yes, at least, I suppose it is."

Eve signaled to Roarke to leave the office. He merely leaned against the wall. She snarled at him, then looked back at the screen. "I'll be happy to meet with you at your convenience."

"That's just it, Lieutenant, it's going to have to be at my convenience. My doctors don't want me to travel again just now. I need you to come to me."

"You want me to come to Rome? Ms. Angelini, even if the department would clear the trip, I need something concrete to justify the time and expense."

"I'll take you," Roarke said easily.

"Keep quiet."

"Who else is there? Is someone else there?" Mirina's voice trembled.

"Roarke is with me," Eve said between her teeth. "Ms. Angelini—"

"Oh, that's fine. I've been trying to reach him. Could you come together? I realize this is an imposition, Lieutenant. I hesitate to pull strings, but I will, if necessary. The commander will clear it."

"I'm sure he will," Eve muttered. "I'll leave as soon as he does. I'll be in touch." She broke transmission. "The spoiled rich irritate the hell out of me."

"Grief and worry don't have economic boundaries," Roarke said.

"Oh shut up." She huffed, kicked bad-temperedly at the desk.

"You'll like Rome, darling," Roarke said and smiled.

Eve did like Rome. At least she thought she did from the brief blur she caught of it on the zooming trip from the airport to Angelini's flat overlooking the Spanish Steps: fountains and traffic and ruins too ancient to be believed.

From the rear of the private limo, Eve watched the fashionable pedestrians with a kind of baffled awe. Sweeping robes were in this season, apparently. Clingy, sheer, voluminous, in colors from the palest white to the deepest bronze. Jeweled belts hung from waists, coordinating with crusted gems on flat-soled shoes and little jeweled bags carried by men and women alike. Everyone looked like royalty.

Roarke hadn't known she could gawk. It pleased him enormously to see that she could forget her mission long enough to stare and wonder. It was a shame, he thought, that they couldn't take a day or two so that he could show her the city, the grandeur of it, and its impossible continuity.

He was sorry when the car pulled jerkily to the curb and yanked her back to reality.

"This better be good." Without waiting for the driver, she slammed out of the car. When Roarke took her elbow to lead her inside the apartment building, she turned her head and frowned at him. "Aren't you even the least bit annoyed at being summoned across a damn ocean for a conversation?"

"Darling, I often go a great deal farther for less. And without such charming company."

She snorted and had nearly taken out her badge to flash at the security droid before she remembered herself. "Eve Dallas and Roarke for Mirina Angelini."

"You're expected, Eve Dallas and Roarke." The droid glided to a gilt-barred elevator and keyed in a code.

"You could get one of those," Eve nodded toward the droid before the elevator's doors closed, "and ditch Summerset."

"Summerset has his own charm."

She snorted again, louder. "Yeah. You bet."

The doors slid open into a gold and ivory foyer with a small, tinkling fountain in the shape of a mermaid.

"Jesus," Eve whispered, scanning the palm trees and paintings. "I didn't think anybody but you really lived like this."

"Welcome to Rome." Randall Slade stepped forward. "Thank you for coming. Please come in. Mirina's in the sitting room."

"She didn't mention you'd be here, Mr. Slade."

"We made the decision to call you together."

Biding her time for questions, Eve walked passed him. The sitting room was sided on the front wall in sheer glass. One-way glass, Eve assumed, as the building was only six stories high. Despite the relatively short height, it afforded an eye-popping view of the city.

Mirina sat daintily on a curved chair, sipping tea from a hand that shook slightly.

She seemed paler, if possible, and even more fragile in her trendy robe of ice blue. Her feet were bare, the nails painted to match her robe. She'd dressed her hair up in a severe knot, secured with a jeweled comb. Eve thought she looked like one of the ancient Roman goddesses, but her mythology was too sketchy to choose which one.

Mirina didn't rise, nor did she smile, but set her cup aside to pick up a slim white pot and pour two more.

"I hope you'll join me for tea."

"I didn't come for a party, Ms. Angelini."

"No, but you've come, and I'm grateful."

"Here, let me do that." With a smooth grace that almost masked the way the cups rattled in Mirina's hands, Slade took them from her. "Please sit down," he invited. "We won't keep you any longer than necessary, but you might as well be comfortable."

"I don't have any jurisdiction here," Eve began as she took a cushioned chair with a low back, "but I'd like to record this meeting, with your permission."

Mirina looked at Slade, bit her lip. "Yes, of course." She cleared her throat when Eve took out her recorder and set it on the table between them. "You know about the . . . difficulties Randy had several years ago in Sector 38."

"I know," Eve confirmed. "I was told you didn't."

"Randy told me yesterday." Mirina reached up blindly, and his hand was there. "You're a strong, confident woman, Lieutenant. It may be difficult for you to understand those of us who aren't so strong. Randy didn't tell me before because he was afraid I wouldn't handle it well. My nerves." She moved her thin shoulders. "Business crises energize me. Personal crises devastate me. The doctors call it an avoidance tendency. I'd rather not face trouble."

"You're delicate," Slade stated, squeezing her hand. "It's nothing to be ashamed of."

"In any case, this is something I have to face. You were there," she said to Roarke, "during the incident."

"I was on the station, probably in the casino."

"And the security at the hotel, the security Randy called, they were yours."

"That's right. Everyone has private security. Criminal cases are transferred to the magistrate—unless they can be dealt with privately."

"You mean through bribes."

"Naturally."

"Randy could have bribed security. He didn't."

"Mirina." He hushed her with another squeeze of his hand. "I didn't bribe them because I wasn't thinking clearly enough to bribe them. If I had, there wouldn't have been a record, and we wouldn't be discussing it now."

"The heavy charges were dropped," Eve pointed out. "You were given the minimum penalty for the ones that stood."

"And I was assured that the entire matter would remain

buried. It didn't. I prefer something stronger than tea. Roarke?"

"Whiskey if you have it, two fingers."

"Tell them, Randy," Mirina whispered while he programmed two whiskeys from the recessed bar.

He nodded, brought Roarke his glass, then knocked back the contents of his own. "Cicely called me on the night she was murdered."

Eve's head jerked up like a hound scenting blood. "There was no record of that on her 'link. No record of an outgoing call."

"She called from a public phone. I don't know where. It was just after midnight, your time. She was agitated, angry."

"Mr. Slade, you told me in our official interview that you had not had contact with Prosecutor Towers on that night."

"I lied. I was afraid."

"You now choose to recant your earlier statement."

"I wish to revise it. Without benefit of counsel, Lieutenant, and fully aware of the penalty for giving a false statement during a police investigation. I'm telling you now that she contacted me shortly before she was killed. That, of course, gives me an alibi, if you like. It would have been very close to impossible for me to have traveled cross-country and killed her in the amount of time I had. You can, of course, check my transmission records."

"Be sure that I will. What did she want?"

"She asked me if it was true. Just that, at first. I was distracted, working. It took me a moment to realize how upset she was, and then when she was more definite, to understand she was referring to Sector 38. I panicked, made some excuses. But you couldn't lie to Cicely. She pinned me to the wall. I was angry, too, and we argued."

He paused, his eyes going to Mirina. He watched her, Eve thought, as if he waited for her to shatter like glass.

"You argued, Mr. Slade?" Eve prompted.

"Yes. About what had happened, why. I wanted to know how she had found out about it, but she cut me off. Lieutenant, she was furious. She told me she was going to deal with it for her daughter's sake. Then she would deal with me. She ended transmission abruptly, and I settled down to brood and to drink."

He walked back to Mirina, laid a hand on her shoulder, stroked. "It was early in the morning, just before dawn, when I heard the news report and knew she was dead."

"She had never spoken to you about the incident before."

"No. We had an excellent relationship. She knew about the gambling, disapproved, but in a mild way. She was used to David. I don't think she understood how deeply we were both involved."

"She did," Roarke corrected. "She asked me to cut you both off."

"Ah." Slade smiled into his empty glass. "That's why I couldn't get through the door of your place in Vegas II."

"That's why."

"Why now?" Eve asked. "Why have you decided to revise your previous statement?"

"I felt it was closing in on me. I knew how hurt Mirina would be if she heard it from someone else. I needed to tell her. It was her decision to contact you."

"Our decision." Mirina reached for his hand again. "I can't bring my mother back, and I know how it will affect my father when we tell him Randy was used to hurt her. Those are things I have to learn to live with. I can do that, if I know that whoever used Randy, and me, will pay for it. She would never have gone out there, she would never have gone, but to protect me."

When they were flying west, Eve paced the comfortable cabin. "Families." She tucked her thumbs into her back pockets. "Do you ever think about them, Roarke?"

"Occasionally." Since she was going to talk, he switched the business news off his personal monitor.

"If we follow one theory, Cicely Towers went out on that rainy night as a mother. Someone was threatening her child's happiness. She was going to fix it. Even if she gave Slade the heave-ho, she was going to fix it first."

"That's what we assume is the natural instinct of a parent."

She slanted him a glance. "We both know better."

"I wouldn't claim that either of our experiences are the norm, Eve."

"Okay." Thoughtful, she sat on the arm of his chair. "So, if it's normal for a mother to jump to shield her child against any trouble, Towers did exactly as her killer expected. He understood her, judged her character well."

"Perfectly, I'd say."

"She was also a servant of the court. It was her duty, and certainly should have been her instinct, to call the authorities, report any threats or blackmail attempts."

"A mother's love is stronger than the law."

"Hers was, and whoever killed her knew it. Who knew her? Her lover, her ex-husband, her son, her daughter, Slade."

"And others, Eve. She was a strong, vocal supporter of professional motherhood, of family rights. There have been dozens of stories about her over the years highlighting her personal commitment to her family."

"That's risking a lot, going by press. Media can be—and is—biased, or it slants a story to suit its own ends. I say her killer knew, not assumed, but knew. There'd been personal contact or extensive research."

"That hardly narrows the field."

Eve brushed that aside with a flick of the hand. "And the same goes for Metcalf. A meeting's set, but it isn't going to be specifically documented in her diary. How does the killer know that? Because he knows her habits. My job is to figure out his or hers. Because there'll be another one."

"You're so sure?"

"I'm sure, and Mira confirmed it."

"You've spoken to her then."

Restless, she rose again. "He—it's just easier to say he—envies, resents, is fascinated by powerful women. Women in the public eye, women who make a mark. Mira thinks the killings may be motivated by control, but I wonder. Maybe that's giving him too much credit. Maybe it's just the thrill. The stalking, the luring, the planning. Who is he stalking now?"

"Have you looked in the mirror?"

"Hmm?"

"Do you realize how often your face is on the screen, in the papers?" Fighting back fear, he rose and put his hands on her shoulders, and read her face. "You've thought of it already?"

"I've wished for it," she corrected, "because I'd be ready."

"You terrify me," he managed.

"You said I was the best." She grinned, patted his cheek. "Relax, Roarke, I'm not going to do anything stupid."

"Oh, I'll sleep easy now."

"How much longer before we land?" Impatient, she turned to walk to the viewscreen.

"Thirty minutes or so, I imagine."

"I need Nadine."

"What are you planning, Eve?"

"Me? Oh, I'm planning on getting lots of press." She shoveled her fingers through her untidy hair. "Haven't you got some ritzy affairs, the kind the media just love to cover, that we can go to?"

He let out a sigh. "I suppose I could come up with a few."

"Great. Let's set some up." She plopped down in a seat and tapped her fingers on her knee. "I guess I can even push it to getting a couple of new outfits."

"Above and beyond." He scooped her up and sat her on his lap. "But I'm sticking close, Lieutenant."

"I don't work with civilians."

"I was talking about the shopping."

Her eyes narrowed as his hand snaked under her shirt. "Is that a dig?"

"Yes."

"Okay." She swiveled around to straddle him. "Just checking."

chapter ten

"I'm going to do my lead-in first." Nadine looked around Eve's office and cocked a brow. "Not much of a sanctum."

"Excuse me?"

Casually, Nadine adjusted the angle of Eve's monitor. It squeaked. "Up till now, you've guarded this room like holy ground. I expected something more than a closet with a desk and a couple of ratty chairs."

"Home's where the heart is," Eve said mildly, and leaned back in one of those ratty chairs.

Nadine had never considered herself claustrophobic, but the industrial beige walls were awfully close together, making her rethink the notion. And the single, stingy window, though undoubtedly blast treated, was unshaded and offered a narrow view of an air traffic snarl over a local transport station.

The little room, Nadine mused, was full of crowds.

"I'd have thought after you broke the DeBlass case last

winter, you'd have rated a snazzier office. With a real window and maybe a little carpet."

"Are you here to decorate or to do a story?"

"And your equipment's pathetic." Enjoying herself, Nadine clucked her tongue over Eve's work units. "At the station, relics like this would be delegated to some low-level drone, or more likely, kicked to a charity rehab center."

She would not scowl, Eve told herself. She would not scowl. "Remember that, the next time you're tagged for a donation to the Police and Security Fund."

Nadine smiled, leaned back on the desk. "At Channel 75, even drones have their own AutoChef."

"I'm learning to hate you, Nadine."

"Just trying to get you pumped for the interview. You know what I'd like, Dallas, since you're in the mood for exposure? A one-on-one, an in-depth interview with the woman behind the badge. The life and loves of Eve Dallas, NYPSD. The personal side of the public servant."

Eve couldn't stop it. She scowled. "Don't push your luck, Nadine."

"Pushing my luck's what I do best." Nadine dropped down into a chair, shifted it. "How's the angle, Pete?"

The operator held his palm-sized remote up to his face. "Yo."

"Pete's a man of few words," Nadine commented. "Just how I like them. Want to fix your hair?"

Eve caught herself before she tunneled her fingers through it. She hated being on camera, hated it a lot. "No."

"Suit yourself." Nadine took a small, mirrored compact out of her oversized bag, patted something under her eyes, checked her teeth for lipstick smears. "Okay." She dropped the compact back in her bag, crossed her legs smoothly with the faintest whisper of silk against silk, and turned toward camera. "Roll."

"Rolling."

Her face changed. Eve found it interesting to watch. The minute the red light glowed, her features became glossier, more intense. Her voice, which had been brisk and light, slowed and deepened, demanding attention.

"This is Nadine Furst, reporting direct from Lieutenant Eve Dallas's office in the Homicide Division of Cop Central. This exclusive interview centers on the violent and as yet unsolved murders of Prosecutor Cicely Towers and award-winning actor Yvonne Metcalf. Lieutenant, are these murders linked?"

"The evidence indicates that probability. We can confirm from the medical examiner's report that both victims were killed by the same weapon, and by the same hand."

"There's no doubt of that?"

"None. Both women were killed by a thin, smooth-edged blade, nine inches in length, tapered from point to hilt. The point was honed to a V. In both cases, the victims were frontally attacked with one swipe of the weapon across the throat from right to left, and at a slight angle."

Eve picked up a signature pen from her desk, causing Nadine to jerk and blink when she slashed it a fraction of an inch from Nadine's throat. "Like that."

"I see."

"This would have severed the jugular, causing instant and dramatic blood loss, disabling the victim immediately, preventing her from calling for help or defending herself in any way. Death would have occurred within seconds."

"In other words, the killer needed very little time. A frontal attack, Lieutenant. Doesn't that indicate that the victims knew their attacker?"

"Not necessarily, but there is other evidence that leads to the conclusion that the victims knew their attacker, or were expecting to meet someone. The absence of any defense wounds for example. If I came at you . . ." Eve thrust out with the pen again, and Nadine threw a hand in front of her throat. "You see, it's automatic defense."

"That's interesting," Nadine said and had to school her face before it scowled. "We have the details on the murders themselves, but not on the motive behind them, or the killer. What is it that connects Prosecutor Towers to Yvonne Metcalf?"

"We're investigating several lines of inquiry."

"Prosecutor Towers was killed three weeks ago, Lieutenant, yet you have no suspects?"

"We have no evidence to support an arrest at this time."

"Then you do have suspects?"

"The investigation is proceeding with all possible speed."

"And motive?"

"People kill people, Ms. Furst, for all manner of reasons. They've done so since we crawled out of the muck."

"Biblically speaking," Nadine put in, "murder is the oldest crime."

"You could say it has a long tradition. We may be able to filter out certain undesirable tendencies through genetics, chemical treatments, beta scans, we deter with penal colonies and the absence of freedom. But human nature remains human nature."

"Those basic motives for violence that science is unable to filter: love, hate, greed, envy, anger."

"They separate us from the droids, don't they?"

"And make us susceptible to joy, sorrow, and passion. That's a debate for the scientists and the intellectuals. But which of those motives killed Cicely Towers and Yvonne Metcalf?"

"A person killed them, Ms. Furst. His or her purpose remains unknown."

"You have a psychiatric profile, of course."

"We do," Eve confirmed. "And we will use it and all of the tools at our disposal to find the murderer. I'll find him," Eve said deliberately flicking her eyes toward the camera. "And once the cage door is closed, motive won't matter. Only justice."

"That sounds like a promise, Lieutenant. A personal promise."

"It is."

"The people of New York will depend on you keeping that promise. This is Nadine Furst, reporting for Channel

75." She waited a beat, then nodded. "Not bad, Dallas. Not bad at all. We'll run it again at six and eleven, with the recap at midnight."

"Good. Take a walk, Pete."

The operator shrugged and wandered out of the room.

"Off the record," Eve began. "How much airtime can you give me?"

"For?"

"Exposure. I want plenty of it."

"I figured there was something behind this little gift." Nadine let out a little breath that was nearly a sigh. "I have to say I'm disappointed, Dallas. I never figured you for a camera hound."

"I've got to testify on the Mondell case in a couple of hours. Can you get a camera there?"

"Sure. The Mondell case is small ratings, but it's worth a couple zips." She pulled her diary out and noted it.

"I've got this thing tonight, too, at the New Astoria. One of those gold plate dinners."

"The Astoria dinner ball, sure." Her smile turned derisive. "I don't work the social beat, Dallas, but I can tell the assignment desk to cue on you. You and Roarke are always good for the gossip eaters. It is you and Roarke, isn't it?"

"I'll let you know where you can catch me over the next couple of days," Eve continued, ignoring the insult. "I'll feed you regular updates to air."

"Fine." Nadine rose. "Maybe you'll trip over the killer on your way to fame and fortune. Got an agent yet?"

For a moment, Eve said nothing, just tapped her fingertips together. "I thought it was your job to fill airtime and guard the public's right to know, not to moralize."

"And I thought it was yours to serve and protect, not to cash in." Nadine snagged up her bag by the strap. "Catch you on the screen, Lieutenant."

"Nadine." Pleased, Eve tipped back in her chair. "You left out one of those basic human motives for violence before. Thrill."

"I'll make a note of it." Nadine wrenched at the door,

then let it slip out of her hands. When she turned back, her face was white and shocked under its sheen of camera makeup. "Are you out of your mind? You're bait? You're fucking bait?"

"Pissed you off, didn't it?" Smiling, Eve allowed herself the luxury of propping her feet on the desk. Nadine's reaction had brought the reporter up several notches on Eve's opinion scale. "Thinking about me wanting all that airtime, and getting it, really steamed you. It's going to steam him, too. Can't you hear him, Nadine? 'Look at that lousy cop getting all my press.' "

Nadine came back in and sat down carefully. "You had me. Dallas, I'm not about to tell you how to do your job—"

"Then don't."

"Let me see if I'm figuring this right. You deduce the motive was, at least partially, for the thrill, for the attention in the media. Kill a couple of ordinary citizens, you get press, sure, but not so intense, not so complete."

"Kill two prominent citizens, familiar faces, and the sky's the limit."

"So you make yourself a target."

"It's just a hunch." Thoughtfully, Eve scratched a vague itch on her knee. "It could be that all I'll end up with is a lot of idiotic blips of me on screen."

"Or a knife at your throat."

"Gee, Nadine, I'm going to start to think you care."

"I think I do." She spent a moment studying Eve's face. "I've worked with, around, and through cops for a long time now. You get instincts on who's putting in time and who gives a damn. You know what worries me, Dallas? You give too much of a damn."

"I carry a badge," Eve said soberly and made Nadine laugh.

"Obviously you've been watching too many old videos, too. Well, it's your neck—literally. I'll see to it that you get it exposed."

"Thanks. One more thing," she added when Nadine stood again. "If this theory has weight, then future targets would fall into the well-known, media-hyped female variety. Keep an eye on your own neck, Nadine."

"Jesus." Shuddering, Nadine rubbed fingers over her throat. "Thanks for sharing that, Dallas."

"My pleasure—literally." Eve had time to chuckle between the time the door closed and the call came through from the commander's office.

Obviously, he'd heard about the broadcast.

She was still stinging a bit when she bolted up the steps of the courthouse. The cameras were there, as Nadine had promised. They were there in the evening at the New Astoria when she stepped out of Roarke's limo and tried to pretend she was enjoying herself.

After two days of tripping over a camera every time she took three steps, she was surprised she didn't find one zooming over her in bed, and she said as much to Roarke.

"You asked for it, darling."

She was straddling him, in what was left of the three-piece cocktail suit he'd chosen for her to wear to the governor's mansion. The glittering black and gold vest skimmed her hips and was already unbuttoned to her navel.

"I don't have to like it. How do you stand it? You live with this stuff all the time. Isn't it creepy?"

"You just ignore it." He flipped open another button. "And go on. I liked the way you looked tonight." Idly he toyed with the diamond that hung between her breasts. "Of course, I'm enjoying the way you look right now more."

"I'm never going to get used to it. All the fancy work. Small talk, big hair. And I don't fit the clothes, either."

"They might not suit the lieutenant, but they suit Eve. You can be both." He watched her pupils dilate when he spread his hands over her breasts, cupped them. "You liked the food."

"Well, sure, but . . ." She shivered into a moan as he scraped his thumbs over her nipples. "I think I was trying to make a point. I should never talk to you in bed."

"Excellent deduction." He reared up and replaced his thumbs with his teeth.

She was sleeping deeply, dreamlessly, when he woke her. The cop surfaced first, alert and braced.

"What?" Despite being naked, she reached for her weapon. "What is it?"

"I'm sorry." When he leaned over the bed to kiss her, she could tell from the vibrations of his body that he was laughing.

"It's not funny. If I'd been armed, you'd have been on your ass."

"Lucky me."

Absently, she shoved at Galahad who'd decided to sit on her head. "Why are you dressed? What's going on?"

"I've had a call. I'm needed on FreeStar One."

"The Olympus Resort. Lights, dim," she ordered and blinked to focus as they highlighted his face. God, she thought, he looked like an angel. A fallen one. A dangerous one. "Is there a problem?"

"Apparently. Nothing that can't be handled." Roarke picked up the cat himself, stroked it, then set Galahad on the floor. "But I have to handle it personally. It may take a couple of days."

"Oh." It was because she was groggy, she told herself, that this awful sense of deflation snuck in. "Well, I'll see you when you get back."

He skimmed a finger over the dent in her chin. "You'll miss me."

"Maybe. Some." It was his quick smile that defeated her. "Yes."

"Here, put this on." He shoved a robe in her hands. "There's something I want to show you before I go."

"You're going now?"

"The transport's waiting. It can wait."

"I guess I'm supposed to come down and kiss you good-bye," she muttered as she fumbled into the robe.

"That would be nice, but first things first." He took her

hand and pulled her from the platform to the elevator. "There isn't any need for you to be uncomfortable here while I'm gone."

"Right."

He put his hands on her shoulders as the car began to glide. "Eve, it's your home now."

"I'm going to be busy, anyway." She felt the slight shift as the car veered to horizontal mode. "Aren't we going all the way down?"

"Not just yet." He slipped an arm around her shoulders when the doors opened.

It was a room she hadn't seen. Then again, she mused, there were probably dozens of rooms she'd yet to tour in the labyrinth of the building. But it took only one quick glimpse for her to realize it was hers.

The few things she considered of any value from her apartment were here, with new pieces added to fill it out into a pleasant, workable space. Stepping away from Roarke, she wandered in.

The floors were wood and smooth, and there was a carpet woven in slate blue and mossy green, probably from one of his factories in the East. Her desk, battered as it was, stood on the priceless wool and held her equipment.

A frosted-glass wall separated a small kitchen area, fully equipped, that led to a terrace.

There was more, of course. With Roarke there was always more. A communications board would allow her to call up any room in the house. The entertainment center offered music, video, a hologram screen with dozens of visualization options. A small indoor garden bloomed riotously below an arching window where dawn was breaking.

"You can replace what you don't like," he said as she ran her hand over the soft back of a sleep chair. "Everything's been programmed for your voice and your palm print."

"Very efficient," she said and cleared her throat. "Very nice."

Surprised to find himself riddled with nerves, he tucked his hands in his pockets. "Your work requires your own space. I understand that. You require your own space and privacy. My office is through there, the west panel. But it locks on either side."

"I see."

Now he felt temper snapping at the nerves. "If you can't be comfortable in the house while I'm not here, you can barricade yourself in this apartment. You can damn well barricade yourself in it while I am here. It's up to you."

"Yes, it is." She took a deep breath and turned to him. "You did this for me."

Annoyed, he inclined his head. "There doesn't seem to be much I wouldn't do for you."

"I think that's starting to sink in." No one had ever given her anything quite so perfect. No one, she realized, understood her quite so well. "That makes me a lucky woman, doesn't it?"

He opened his mouth, bit back something particularly nasty. "The hell with it," he decided. "I have to go."

"Roarke, one thing." She walked to him, well aware he was all but snarling with temper. "I haven't kissed you good-bye," she murmured and did so with a thoroughness that rocked him back on his heels. "Thank you." Before he could speak, she kissed him again. "For always knowing what matters to me."

"You're welcome." Possessively, he ran a hand over her tousled hair. "Miss me."

"I already am."

"Don't take any unnecessary chances." His hands gripped in her hair hard, briefly. "There's no use asking you not to take the necessary ones."

"Then don't." Her heart stuttered when he kissed her hand. "Safe trip," she told him when he stepped into the elevator. She was new at it, so waited until the doors were almost shut. "I love you."

The last thing she saw was the flash of his grin.

"What have you got, Feeney?"

"Maybe something, maybe nothing."

It was early, just eight o'clock on the morning after Roarke left for FreeStar One, but Feeney already looked haggard. Eve punched two coffees, double strength, from her AutoChef.

"You're in here at this hour, looking like you've been up all night, and in that suit, I have to deduce it's something. And I'm a gold-star detective."

"Yeah. I've been noodling the computer, going down another level on the families and personal relations of the victims like you wanted."

"And?"

Stalling, he drank his coffee, dug out his bag of candied nuts, scratched his ear. "Saw you on the news last night. The wife did, actually. Said you looked flash. That's one of the kid's expressions. We try to keep up."

"In that case, you're rocking me, Feeney. That's one of the kid's expressions, too. Translation, you're not coming clear."

"I know what it means. Shit. This one cuts close to home, Dallas. Too close."

"Which is why you're here instead of trasmitting what you've got over a channel. So let's have it."

"Okay." He puffed out a breath. "I was dicking around with David Angelini's records. Financial stuff mostly. We knew he was into some spine twisters for gambling debts. He's been holding them off, giving them a little trickle here and there. Could be he's dipped into the company till, but I can't get a lock on that. He's covered his ass."

"So, we'll uncover it. I can get the name of the spine twisters," she mused, thinking of Roarke. "Let's see if he made them any promises—like he'd be coming into an inheritance." Her brows knit. "If it wasn't for Metcalf, I'd think hard about somebody he owed hurrying up on the IOUs by taking out Towers."

"Might be that simple, even with Metcalf. She had a nice nest egg set aside. I haven't found anybody among the beneficiaries who needed quick money, but that doesn't mean I won't."

"Okay, you keep working that angle. But that isn't why you're here playing with your nuts."

He nearly managed a laugh. "Cute. Okay, here it is. I turned up the commander's wife."

"Run that by slow, Feeney. Real slow."

He couldn't sit, so he sprang up to pace the small space. "David Angelini made some healthy deposits into his personal credit account. Four deposits of fifty K over the last four months. The final one was keyed in two weeks before his mother got terminated."

"All right, he got his hands on two hundred K in four months, and banked it like a good boy. Where'd he get it? Fuck." She already knew.

"Yeah. I accessed the E-transactions. Backtracked. She transferred it to his New York bank, and he flipped it over into his personal account in Milan. Then he withdraws it, in cash, hard bills, at an AutoTell on Vegas II."

"Jesus Christ, why didn't she tell me?" Eve pressed her balled fists to her temples. "Why the hell did she make us look for it?"

"It wasn't like she tried to hide it," Feeney said quickly. "When I clicked over to her records, it was all out front. She has an account of her own, just like the commander." He cleared his throat at Eve's level stare. "I had to look, Dallas. He hasn't made any unusual transactions out of his, or out of their joint. But she's cut her principal in half doling out to Angelini. Christ, he was bleeding her."

"Blackmail," Eve speculated, struggling to think coolly. "Maybe they had an affair. Maybe she was stuck on the bastard."

"Oh man, oh Jesus." Feeney's stomach did a long sickening roll. "The commander."

"I know. We have to go to him with this."

"I knew you were going to say that." Mournfully, Feeney took a disc out of his pocket. "I got it all. How do you want to play it?"

"What I want to do is go out to White Plains and knock

Mrs. Whitney on her perfect ass. Barring that, we go to the commander's office and lay it out for him."

"They've still got some of that old body armor down in storage," Feeney suggested as Eve rose.

"Good thinking."

They could have used it. Whitney didn't climb over his desk and body slam them, nor did he pull out his stunner. He did all the damage necessary with the lethal glare of his eyes.

"You accessed my wife's personal accounts, Feeney."

"Yes, sir, I did."

"And took this information to Lieutenant Dallas."

"As per procedure."

"As per procedure," Whitney repeated. "Now you're bringing it to me."

"To the commanding officer," Feeney began, then drooped. "Oh hell, Jack, was I supposed to bury it?"

"You could have come to me first. But then . . ." Whitney trailed off, shifted his hard eyes to Eve's. "Your stand on this, Lieutenant?"

"Mrs. Whitney paid David Angelini a sum of two hundred thousand dollars over a four-month period. This fact was not volunteered during either primary or follow-up interviews. It's necessary to the investigation that—" She broke off. "We have to know why, Commander." The apology was in her eyes, lurking just behind the cop. "We have to know why the money was paid, why there have been no more payments since the death of Cicely Towers. And I have to ask, Commander, as primary, if you were aware of the transactions and the reason behind them."

There was a clutching in his stomach, a burning that warned of untreated stress. "I'll answer that after I've spoken with my wife."

"Sir." Eve's voice was a quiet plea. "You know we can't allow you to consult with Mrs. Whitney before we question her. This meeting has already risked contaminating the investigation. I'm sorry, Commander."

"You're not bringing my wife in to interview."

"Jack—"

"Fuck this, Feeney, she's not going to be dragged down here like a criminal." He clutched his hands into fists under the desk and struggled to remain in control. "Question her at home, with our attorney present. That doesn't violate procedure, does it, Lieutenant Dallas?"

"No, sir. With respect, Commander, will you come with us?"

"With respect, Lieutenant," he said bitterly. "You couldn't stop me."

chapter eleven

Anna Whitney met them at the door. Her hands fluttered, then gripped together at her waist. "Jack, what's happening? Linda's here. She said you called her and told her I needed counsel." Her gaze darted from Eve to Feeney, then back to her husband. "Why would I need counsel?"

"It's all right." He put a tense but protective hand on her shoulder. "Let's go inside, Anna."

"But I haven't done anything." She managed one nervous laugh. "I haven't even gotten a traffic ticket lately."

"Just sit down, honey. Linda, thanks for coming so quickly."

"No problem."

The Whitneys' attorney was young, sharp-eyed, and polished to a gleam. It took Eve several moments to remember she was also their daughter.

"Lieutenant Dallas, isn't it?" Linda scanned and

summed up quickly. "I recognize you." She gestured to a chair before either of her parents thought of it. "Please sit."

"Captain Feeney, EDD."

"Yes, my father's mentioned you many times, Captain Feeney. Now." She laid a hand over her mother's. "What's this all about?"

"Information has just come to light that needs clarification." Eve took out her recorder, offered it to Linda for examination. She tried not to think that Linda favored her father, the caramel-colored skin, the cool eyes. Genes and family traits both fascinated and frightened her.

"I take it this is going to be a formal interview." With careful calm, Linda set the recorder on the table and took out her own.

"That's right." Eve recited the date and time. "Interviewing officer Dallas, Lieutenant Eve. Also present, Whitney, Commander Jack, and Feeney, Captain Ryan. Interviewee Whitney, Anna, represented by counsel."

"Whitney, Linda. My client is aware of all rights and agrees to this time and place of interview. Counsel reserves the right to terminate at her discretion. Proceed, Lieutenant."

"Mrs. Whitney," Eve began. "You were acquainted with Cicely Towers, deceased."

"Yes, of course. Is this about Cicely? Jack—"

He only shook his head and kept his hand on her shoulder.

"You are also acquainted with the deceased's family. Her former husband Marco Angelini, her son, David Angelini, and her daughter, Mirina."

"I'm more than acquainted. Her children are like family. Why, Linda even dated—"

"Mom." With a bolstering smile, Linda interrupted. "Just answer the question. Don't elaborate."

"But this is ridiculous." Some of Anna's puzzlement edged over into irritation. It was her home, after all, her family. "Lieutenant Dallas already knows the answers."

"I'm sorry to go over the same ground, Mrs. Whitney. Would you describe your relationship with David Angelini?"

"David? Why I'm his godmother. I watched him grow up."

"You're aware that David Angelini was in financial distress prior to the death of his mother."

"Yes, he was . . ." Her eyes went huge. "You don't seriously believe that David . . . That's hideous." She snapped it out before her mouth compressed into a thin red line. "I'm not going to dignify this with an answer."

"I understand you feel protective toward your godson, Mrs. Whitney. I understand you would go to some lengths to protect him—and to some expense. Two hundred thousand dollars."

Anna's face whitened under her careful cosmetics. "I don't know what you mean."

"Mrs. Whitney, do you deny paying to David Angelini the sum of two hundred thousand dollars, in installments of fifty thousand dollars over a four-month period, beginning in February of this year and ending in May?"

"I . . ." She clutched at her daughter's hand, avoided her husband's. "Do I have to answer that, Linda?"

"A moment please, to confer with my client." Briskly, Linda scooped an arm around her mother and led her into the next room.

"You're very good, Lieutenant," Whitney said tightly. "It's been some time since I observed one of your interviews."

"Jack." Feeney sighed, hurting for everyone. "She's doing her job."

"Yes, she is. It's what she's best at." He looked over as his wife came back into the room.

She was pale, trembling a little. The burning in his gut flared.

"We'll continue," Linda said. There was a warrior glint in her eye when she focused on Eve. "My client wishes to make a statement. Go ahead, Mom, it's all right."

"I'm sorry." Tears starred on her lashes. "Jack, I'm sorry. I couldn't help it. He was in trouble. I know what you said, but I couldn't help it."

"It's all right." Resigned, he took the hand that reached out for his and stood beside her. "Tell the lieutenant the truth, and we'll deal with it."

"I gave him the money."

"Did he threaten you, Mrs. Whitney?"

"What?" Shock seemed to dry up the tears swimming in her eyes. "Oh my goodness. Of course he didn't threaten me. He was in trouble," she repeated, as if that should be enough for anyone. "He owed a very great deal of money to the wrong kind of people. His business—that portion of his father's business that he oversaw—was in some temporary upheaval. And he had a new project he was trying to get off the ground. He explained it," she added with a wave of her free hand. "I don't remember precisely. I don't bother overmuch with business."

"Mrs. Whitney, you gave him four payments of fifty thousand. You didn't relay this information to me in our other interviews."

"What business of yours was it?" Her spine was back, snapped hard and cold so that she sat like a statue. "It was my money, and a personal loan to my godchild."

"A godchild," Eve said with straining patience, "who was being questioned in a murder investigation."

"His mother's murder. You might as well accuse me of killing her as David."

"You didn't inherit a sizable portion of her estate."

"Now, you listen to me." Anger suited her. Anna's face glowed as she leaned forward. "That boy adored his mother, and she him. He was devastated by her death. I know. I sat with him, I comforted him."

"You gave him two hundred thousand dollars."

"It was my money to do with as I chose." She bit her lip. "No one would help him. His parents refused. They'd agreed to refuse this time. I spoke with Cicely about it months ago. She was a wonderful mother, and she loved her children, but she was a very strong believer in discipline. She was determined that he had to handle his problem on his own, without her help. Without mine. But when he came to me, desperate, what was I to do? What was I to do?" she demanded, turning to her husband. "Jack, I know you told me to stay out of it, but he was terrified, afraid they would cripple him, even kill him. What if it had been Linda, or Steven? Wouldn't you have wanted someone to help?"

"Anna, feeding his problem isn't help."

"He was going to pay me back," she insisted. "He wasn't going to gamble with it. He promised. He only needed to buy some time. I couldn't turn him away."

"Lieutenant Dallas," Linda began. "My client lent her own money to a family member in good faith. There is no crime in that."

"Your client hasn't been charged with a crime, counselor."

"Did you, in any of your previous interviews, ask my client directly about disposition of funds? Did you ask my client if she had any financial dealings with David Angelini?"

"No, I did not."

"Then she is not required to volunteer such information, which would appear to be personal and unconnected to your investigation. To the best of her knowledge."

"She's a cop's wife," Eve said wearily. "Her knowledge ought to be better than most. Mrs. Whitney, did Cicely Towers argue with her son over money, over his gambling, over his debts and the settlement thereof?"

"She was upset. Naturally they argued. Families argue. They don't hurt each other."

Maybe not in your cozy little world, Eve thought. "Your last contact with Angelini?"

"A week ago. He called to make sure I was all right, that Jack was all right. We discussed plans for setting up a memorial scholarship fund in his mother's name. His idea,

Lieutenant," she said with swimming eyes. "He wanted her to be remembered."

"What can you tell me about his relationship with Yvonne Metcalf?"

"The actress." Anna's eyes went blank before she dabbed at them. "Did he know her? He never mentioned it."

It had been a shot in the dark, and hadn't found a target. "Thank you." Eve picked up her recorder, logged in the end of the interview. "Counselor, you should advise your client that it would be in her best interest not to mention this interview or any portion of it to anyone outside this room."

"I'm a cop's wife." Anna neatly tossed Eve's words back in her face. "I understand the drill."

The last glimpse Eve had of the commander as she stepped outside, he was holding his wife and daughter.

Eve wanted a drink. By the time she'd logged out for the day, she had spent the better part of the afternoon chasing after David Angelini's tail. He was in a meeting, he was out of contact, he was anywhere but where she looked. Without any other choice, she'd left messages at every possible point on the planet and figured she'd be lucky to hear from him before the following day.

Meanwhile, she was faced with an enormous, empty house and a butler who hated the air she breathed. The impulse struck as she zipped through the gates. She grabbed her car 'link and ordered Mavis's number.

"Your night off, right?" she asked the instant Mavis's face blipped on screen.

"You bet. Gotta rest those vocal chords."

"Plans?"

"Nothing that can't be tossed out for better. What do you have in mind?"

"Roarke's off planet. You want to come over here and hang, stay over, get drunk?"

"Hang at Roarke's, stay over at Roarke's, get drunk at Roarke's? I'm on my way."

"Wait, wait. Let's do it up big. I'll send a car for you."

"A limo?" Mavis forgot her vocal chords and squealed. "Jesus, Dallas, make sure the driver wears, like, a uniform. The people in my building will be hanging out the windows with their eyes popped out."

"Fifteen minutes." Eve broke transmission and all but danced up the steps to the door. Summerset was there, just as expected, and she sent him a haughty nod. She'd been practicing. "I'm having a friend over for the evening. Send a car and driver to 28 Avenue C."

"A friend." His voice was ripe with suspicion.

"That's right, Summerset." She glided up the stairs. "A very good, very close friend. Be sure and tell the cook there'll be two for dinner."

She managed to get out of earshot before doubling over with laughter. Summerset was expecting a tryst, she was sure. But it was going to be even more of a scandal when he got a load of Mavis.

Mavis didn't disappoint her. Though for Mavis, she was conservatively dressed. Her hair de jour was rather tame, a glittery gold fashioned in what was called a half-swing. One glistening side curved to her ear while the other half skimmed her shoulder.

She'd only worn perhaps a half dozen varied earrings— and all in her ears. A distinguished look for Mavis Freestone.

She stepped out of a torrential spring downpour, handing a speechless Summerset her transparent cloak strung with tiny lights, and turned three circles. More, Eve thought, in awe of the hallway than to show off her skin-hugging red body suit.

"Wow."

"My thoughts exactly," Eve said. She'd hovered near the hallway waiting, not wanting Mavis to face Summerset alone. The strategy was obviously unnecessary, as the usually disdainful butler was struck dumb.

"It's just mag," Mavis said in reverent tones. "Really mag. And you've got the whole digs to yourself."

Eve sent Summerset a cool, sidelong glance. "Just about."

"Decent." With a flutter of inch-long lashes, Mavis held out a hand with interlinking hearts tattooed on the back. "And you must be Summerset. I've heard so much about you."

Summerset took the hand, so staggered he nearly lifted it to his lips before he remembered himself. "Madam," he said stiffly.

"Oh, you just call me Mavis. Great place to work, huh? You must get a hard charge out of it."

Unsure if he was appalled or enchanted, Summerset stepped back, managed a half bow, and disappeared down the hall with her dripping cloak.

"A man of few words." Mavis winked, giggled, then clattered down the hall on six-inch inflatable platforms. And let out a sensual groan at the first doorway. "You've got a real fireplace."

"A couple dozen of them, I think."

"Jesus, do you do it in front of the fire? Like in the old flicks?"

"I'll leave that up to your imagination."

"I can imagine good. Christ, Dallas, that car you sent. A real limo, a classic. It just had to be raining." She whirled back, sending her earrings dancing. "Only about half the people I wanted to impress saw me. What are we going to do first?"

"We can eat."

"I'm starving, but I've got to see the place first. Show me something."

Eve pondered. The roof terrace was incredible, but it was raining furiously. The weapon room was out, as was the target range. Eve considered those areas off limits to guests without Roarke's presence. There was plenty more, of course. Dubiously Eve studied Mavis's shoes.

"Can you really walk in those?"

"They're air glided. I hardly know I've got them on."

"All right then, we'll take the stairs. You'll see more that way."

She took Mavis to the solarium first, amused by her friend's dropped-jaw reaction to the exotic plants and trees, the sparkling waterfalls, and chattering birds. The curved glass wall was battered with rain, but through it the lights of New York gleamed.

In the music room, Eve programmed a trash band and let Mavis entertain her with a glass-shattering short set of current favorites.

They spent an hour in the game room, competing with the computer, each other, and hologram opponents at Free Zone and Apocalypse.

Mavis did a lot of oohing and ahing over the bedrooms, and finally chose the suite for her overnight stay.

"I can have a fire if I want?" Mavis ran a possessive hand over the rich lapis lazuli of the hearth.

"Sure, but it is nearly June."

"I don't care if I roast." Arms out, she took long swinging steps over the floor, gazed up through the sky dome, and plopped down on the lake-sized bed with its thick silver cushions. "I feel like a queen. No, no, an empress." She rolled over and over while the floating mattress undulated beneath her. "How do you stay normal in a place like this?"

"I don't know. I haven't lived here very long."

Still rolling lavishly from one side of the air cushions to the other, Mavis laughed. "It would only take me one night. I'm never going to be the same." Scooting up to the padded headboard, she punched buttons. Lights flickered on and off, revolved, sparkled. Music throbbed, pulsed. Water began to run in the next room.

"What's that?"

"You programmed your bath," Eve informed her.

"Oops. Not yet." Mavis flicked it off, tried another, and

had the panel on the far wall sliding open to reveal a ten-foot video screen. "Definitely decent. Wanna eat?"

While Eve settled in the dining room with Mavis, enjoying her first full evening off in weeks, Nadine Furst scowled over the editing of her next broadcast.

"I want to enhance that, freeze on Dallas," she ordered the tech. "Yeah, yeah, bring her up. She looks damn good on camera."

Sitting back, she studied the five screens while the tech worked the panel. Editing Room One was quiet, but for the murmuring clash of voices from the screen. For Nadine, putting images together seamlessly was as exciting as sex. The majority of broadcasters left the process to their techs, but Nadine wanted her hand in here. Everywhere.

In the newsroom one level down, it would be bedlam. She enjoyed that, too. The scurry to beat the competition to the latest sound bite, the latest picture, the most immediate angle. Reporters manning their 'links for one more quote, bumping their computers for that last bit of data.

The competition wasn't all outside on Broadcast Avenue. There was plenty of it right in the Channel 75 newsroom.

Everybody wanted the big story, the big picture, the big ratings. Right now, she had it all. And Nadine didn't intend to lose it.

"There, hold it there, when I'm standing on Metcalf's patio. Yeah, now try a split screen, use the shot of me on the sidewalk where Towers bought it. Um-hmm." Eyes narrowed, she studied the image. She looked good, she decided. Dignified, sober-eyed. Our intrepid, clear-sighted reporter, revisiting the scenes of the crimes.

"Okay." She folded her hands and rested her chin on them. "Cue in the voice-over."

Two women, talented, dedicated, innocent. Two lives brutally ended. The city reels, looks over its shoulder, and asks why. Loving families mourn, bury their dead, and ask for justice. There is one person working to answer that question, to meet that demand.

"Freeze," Nadine ordered, "Bleed to Dallas, exterior courtroom shot. Bring up audio."

Eve's image filled the screens, full length, with Nadine beside her. That was good, Nadine, thought. The visual lent the impression they were a team, working together. Couldn't hurt. There had been the faintest of breezes, ruffling their hair. Behind them, the courthouse speared up, a monument to justice, its elevators busily gliding up and down, its glass walkway crowded with people.

My job is to find a killer, and I take my job seriously. When I finish mine, the courts begin theirs.

"Perfect." Nadine fisted her hand. "Oh yes, just perfect. Fade it there, and I'll pick it up on live. Time?"

"Three forty-five."

"Louise, I'm a genius, and you're not so bad yourself. Print it."

"Printed." Louise swiveled away from the console and stretched. They'd worked together for three years and were friends. "It's a good piece, Nadine."

"Damn right it is." Nadine angled her head. "But."

"Okay." Louise released her stubby ponytail and ran a hand through her thick, dark curls. "We're getting close to retreading here. We've had nothing new in a couple of days."

"Neither has anybody else. And I've got Dallas."

"And that's a big one." Louise was a pretty woman, soft-featured, bright-eyed. She'd come to Channel 75 direct from college. After less than a month on the job, Nadine had scooped her up as her main tech. The arrangement suited them both. "She's got a solid visual and an excellent throat. The Roarke factor adds a gold edge. That's not including the fact she's got a rep as a good cop."

"So?"

"So, I'm thinking," continued Louise, "until you get some new bites on this, you might want to splice in some of the business from the DeBlass case. Remind people our lieutenant broke one of the big ones, took a hit in the line of duty. Build up confidence."

"I don't want to take the focus off the current investigation."

"Maybe you do," Louise disagreed. "At least until there's a new lead. Or a new victim."

Nadine grinned. "A little more blood would heat things up. Another couple of days, we'll be out of the sweeps and into the June doldrums. Okay, I'll keep it in mind. You might want to put something together."

Louise cocked a brow. "I might?"

"And if I use it, you get full on-air credit, you greedy bitch."

"Deal." Louise tapped the pocket of her editing vest, winced. "Out of smokes."

"You've got to stop that. You know how the brass feel about employees taking health risks."

"I'm sticking with the herb shit."

"Shit's right. Get me a couple while you're at it." Nadine had the grace to look sheepish. "And keep it to yourself. They're tougher on the on-air talent than you techs."

"You've got some time before the midnight recap. Aren't you going to take your break?"

"No, I've got a couple of calls to make. Besides, it's pouring out." Nadine patted her perfectly coiffed hair. "You go." She reached into her bag. "I'll pay."

"Good deal—since I have to go all the way to Second to find a store that's licensed to sell smokes." Resigned, she rose. "I'm using your raincoat."

"Go ahead." Nadine passed her a handful of credits. "Just put my share in the pocket, okay? I'll be in the newsroom."

They walked out together, with Louise bundling into the stylish blue coat. "Nice material."

"Sheds water like a duck."

They crossed the rampway, passed a series of editing and production rooms, and walked toward a descending people glide. Noise began to filter through, so Nadine pitched her voice over it.

"Are you and Bongo still thinking of taking the big step?"

"Thinking hard enough that we've started looking at apartments. We're going the traditional route. We'll give living together a try for a year. If it works, we'll make it legal."

"Better you than me," Nadine said with feeling. "I can't think of a single reason why a rational person would lock themselves to another rational person."

"Love." Louise put a dramatic hand to her heart. "It makes reason and rationality fly out the old window."

"You're young and free, Louise."

"And if I'm lucky, I'm going to be old and chained to Bongo."

"Who the hell wants to be chained to anybody named Bongo?" Nadine muttered.

"Me. Catch you later." With a quick salute, Louise continued on the descent while Nadine stepped off toward the newsroom.

And thinking of Bongo, Louise wondered if she'd be able to get home before one A.M. It was their night at her place. That was a little inconvenience that would end once they found one suitable apartment rather than shifting back and forth between his rooms and hers.

Idly, she glanced over at one of the many monitors lining the walls, playing Channel 75's current broadcast. Right now it was a popular sitcom, a dead medium that had been revived over the past couple years by talent such as Yvonne Metcalf's.

Louise shook her head over that thought, then chuckled a little as the life-sized actor on screen mugged outrageously for the viewing audience.

Nadine might have been married to the news, but Louise liked sheer entertainment. She looked forward to those rare evenings when she and Bongo could cuddle up in front of the screen.

In Channel 75's wide lobby there were more monitors, security stations, and a pleasant sitting area ringed with holograms of the station's stars. And, of course, a gift shop stocked with souvenir T-shirts, hats, signed mugs, and holograms of the station's biggest stars.

Twice a day, between the hours of ten and four, tours were guided through the station. Louise had taken one herself as a child, had gawked with the best of them, and had, she remembered with a smug smile, decided then and there on her career.

She waved to the guard at the front entrance, detoured to the east end, which was the shortest route to Second. At the side door for employees, she passed her palm over the handplate to deactivate the lock. As the door swung open, she winced at the heavy sound of drumming rain. She almost changed her mind.

Was one sneaky smoke worth a two-block sprint through the cold and damp? Damn right, she thought and flipped up the hood. The good, expensive raincoat would keep her dry enough, and she'd been stuck in Editing with Nadine for more than an hour.

Hunching her shoulders, she bolted outside.

The wind kicked so that she broke her stride just long enough to secure the coat at the waist. Her shoes were soaked before she reached the bottom of the steps, and looking down at them, she swore under her breath.

"Well, shit."

They were the last words she spoke.

A movement caught her attention and she looked up, blinking once to clear the rain from her eyes. She never saw the knife, already in an arching slash, glint wetly in the rain then slice viciously across her throat.

The killer studied her for only a moment, watched the blood fountain, the body collapse like a puppet cut from its strings. There was shock, then anger, then a quick, jittering fear. The gored knife hurried back into a deep pocket before the darkly clad figure ran off into the shadows.

"I think I could live like this." After a meal of rare Montana beef accented with lobsters harvested from Icelandic waters, washed down with French champagne, Mavis lounged in the lush indoor lagoon off the solarium. She yawned, blissfully naked and just a little drunk. "You are living like this."

"Sort of." Not quite as free-spirited as Mavis, Eve wore a snug one-piece tank suit. She'd cozied herself on a smooth seat made of stone, and was still drinking. She hadn't allowed herself to relax to this extent in too long to remember. "I don't really have a lot of time for this part of it."

"Make time, babe." Mavis submerged, popped up again, perfect round breasts gleaming in the showy blue lights she'd programmed. Lazily, she paddled over to a water lily, gave a sniff. "Christ, this is the real thing. Do you know what you've got here, Dallas?"

"Indoor swimming?"

"What you've got," Mavis began as she frog kicked her way over to the float that held her glass, "is a grade one fantasy. The kind you can't get from the top-line VR goggles." She took a long sip of icy champagne. "You're not going to get all weirded out and blow it, are you?"

"What are you talking about?"

"I know you. You'll pick it apart, question everything, analyze." Noting Eve's glass was empty, Mavis did the honors. "Well, I'm telling you, pal. Don't."

"I don't pick things apart."

"You're the champion picked—pick it part—damn it, pick it aparter. Whew. Try saying that five times fast when your tongue's numb." She used a bare hip to nudge Eve over and squeezed in next to her. "He's crazy about you, isn't he?"

Eve jerked her shoulders and drank.

"He's rich, I mean mag rich, gorgeous as a god, and that body—"

"What d'you know about his body?"

"I got eyes. I use 'em. I've got a pretty good idea of what he looks like naked." Amused by the glint in Eve's eyes, Mavis licked her lips. "Of course, any time you want to fill in the missing details, I'm here for you."

"What a pal."

"That's me. Anyway, he's all that stuff. Then there's that power trip. He's got all that power, sort of shoots out from him." She highlighted the statement by splashing up water. "And he looks at you like he could eat you alive. In big . . . greedy . . . bites. Shit, I'm getting hot."

"Keep your hands off me."

Mavis snorted. "Maybe I'll go seduce Summerset."

"I don't think he has a dick."

"Bet I could find out." But she was just too lazy at the moment. "You're in love with him, aren't you?"

"Summerset? I've had a hell of a time controlling myself around him."

"Look me dead in the eye. Come on." To ensure obedience, Mavis snagged Eve's chin, swiveled until they were face to face, glassy eye to glassy eye. "You're in love with Roarke."

"It looks that way. I don't want to think about it."

"Good. Don't. Always said you thought too damn much." Holding the glass over her head, Mavis pushed off into the lagoon. "Can we use the jets?"

"Sure." Impaired with wine, Eve fumbled a bit for the correct control. Once the water started to bubble and spew, Mavis let out a laughing moan.

"Christ Jesus, who needs a man when you've got one of these? Come on, Eve, bump up the music. Let's party."

Obliging, Eve doubled the volume on the controls so that the music screamed off the walls and water. The Rolling Stones, Mavis's favorite classic artists, wailed. Lounged back, Eve laughed as Mavis improvised dance steps and started to send the server droid after another bottle.

"I beg your pardon."

"Huh?" Bleary-eyed, Eve studied the glossy black shoes

at the lip of the lagoon. Slowly, and with mild curiosity, she let her gaze travel up the smoke-colored, pipe-stemmed pants, the short, stiff jacket, and into Summerset's stony face. "Hey, you wanna take a little dip?"

"Come on in, Summerset." Water lapped around Mavis's waist and dripped cheerfully from her classy breasts as she waved. "The more the merrier."

He sniffed, his lips curled. Sheer habit had the words dropping out of his mouth like knife-edged ice cubes, but his gaze kept wandering back to Mavis's swirling body.

"There's a transmission for you, Lieutenant. Apparently you were unable to hear my attempts to inform you."

"What? Okay, okay." She sniggered, paddled toward the 'link set in the side of the lagoon. "Is it Roarke?"

"It is not." It affronted his dignity to shout, but it would have offended his pride to order the music lower. "It is Dispatch from Cop Central."

Even as Eve reached for the 'link, she stopped, swore. Then slicked the hair back from her face. "Music off," she snapped, and had Mick and his pals echoing into silence. "Mavis, stay out of video range, please." Eve sucked in a deep breath, then opened the 'link. "Dallas."

"Dispatch, Dallas, Lieutenant Eve. Voice print verified. Report immediately to Broadcast Avenue, Channel 75. Confirmed Homicide. Code Yellow."

Eve's blood ran cold. Her fingers gripped on the edge of the pool. "Victim's name?"

"That information is not cleared for transmission at this time. Confirm receipt of orders, Dallas, Lieutenant Eve."

"Confirmed. ETA twenty minutes. Request Feeney, Captain, EDD on scene."

"Request verified. Dispatch out."

"Oh God. Oh God." Weak with guilt and liquor, Eve laid her head on the edge of the pool. "I fucking killed her."

"Stop it." Mavis swam over, laid a hand on Eve's shoulder. "Cut it out, Eve," she said briskly.

"He took the wrong bait, the wrong bait, Mavis, and she's dead. It was supposed to be me."

"I said stop it." Confused by the words, but not by the sentiment, Mavis pulled her back and gave Eve a quick shake. "Snap out of it, Dallas."

Helpless, Eve pressed a hand to her spinning head. "Oh my Christ, I'm drunk. That's perfect."

"I can fix that. I've got some Sober Up in my bag." At Eve's moan, Mavis gave her another shake. "I know you hate pills, but they'll clean the alcohol out of your bloodstream in ten minutes flat. Come on, we'll get some into you."

"Fine. Dandy. I'll be sober when I have to look at her."

She started up the steps, slipped, was surprised to find her arm taken firmly. "Lieutenant." Summerset's voice was still cool, but he held out a towel and helped her up onto the stone skirt of the pool. "I'll see that your car's ready."

"Yeah, thanks."

chapter twelve

Mavis's handy antidote worked like a charm. Eve had a foul taste in the back of her throat, but she was stone-cold sober when she reached Channel 75's sleek silver building.

It had been constructed in the mid-twenties when the media boom had hit such astronomical proportions as to generate more profits than a small country. One of the loftier buildings on Broadcast Avenue, it towered up from a wide, flat hilt, housed several thousand employees, five elaborate studios, including the most lavish new set on the East Coast, and enough power to beam transmissions to every pocket of the planet and its orbiting stations.

The east wing, where Eve was directed, faced Third with its tony mutiplexes and apartment buildings designed for the convenience of the broadcast industry.

Due to the thick air traffic, Eve realized word had already hit. Control was going to be a problem. Even as she rounded the building, she called Dispatch and requested air barricades as well as ground security. A homicide right in the lap of the media was going to be hard enough to deal with, without the vultures flying.

Steady now, she locked away guilt and stepped from her car to approach the scene. The uniforms had been busy, she saw with some relief. They'd cleared the area and had the outside door sealed off. Reporters and their teams were there, naturally. There would be no keeping them away. But she'd have room to breathe.

She'd already attached her badge to her jacket and moved through the rain to the porta-tarp some wise soul had tossed over the crime scene. Raindrops pinged musically against the strong, clear plastic.

She recognized the raincoat, dealt viciously with the quick, instinctive lurch of her stomach. She asked if the immediate scene had been scanned and recorded, and receiving the affirmative, crouched down.

Her hands were rock steady as they reached for the hood that had fallen forward over the victim's face. She ignored the blood that pooled in a sticky puddle at the toes of her boots and managed to smother the gasp and the shudder as she tossed the hood away from a stranger's face.

"Who the hell is this?" she demanded.

"Victim's been preliminarily identified as Louise Kirski, editorial tech for Channel 75." The uniform pulled a log out of the pocket of her slick black raincoat. "She was found at approximately eleven fifteen by C. J. Morse. He tossed his cookies just over there," she went on with light disdain for civilian delicacy. "Went inside through this door, screaming his head off. Building security verified his story, such as it was, called it in. Dispatch logged the call at eleven twenty-two. I arrived on scene at eleven twenty-seven."

"You made good time, Officer . . . ?"

"Peabody, Lieutenant. I was on a swing of First Avenue. I verified homicide, secured the outer door, called for additional uniforms and a primary."

Eve nodded toward the building. "They get any of this on camera?"

"Sir." Peabody's mouth thinned. "I ordered a news team off scene when I arrived. I'd say they got plenty before we secured."

"Okay." With fingertips encased in clear seal, Eve did a search of the body. A few credits, a little jingling change, a pricey mini 'link attached to the belt. No defense wounds, no signs of struggle or assault.

She recorded it all dutifully, her mind working fast. Yes, she recognized the raincoat, she thought, and her initial exam complete, she straightened.

"I'm going in. I'm expecting Captain Feeney. Pass him through. She can go with the ME."

"Yes, sir."

"You stand, Peabody," Eve decided. The cop had a good, firm style. "Keep those reporters in line." Eve glanced over her shoulder, ignoring the shouted questions, the glint of lenses. "Give no comment, no statement."

"I've got nothing to say to them."

"Good. Keep it that way."

Eve unsealed the door, passed through, resealed it. The lobby was nearly empty. Peabody, or someone like her, had cleared it of all but essential personnel. Eve shot a look at the security behind the main console. "C. J. Morse. Where?"

"His station's on level six, section eight. Some of your people took him up that way."

"I'm expecting another cop. Send him after me." Eve turned and stepped onto the ascent.

There were people here and there, some huddled together, others standing against video backdrops talking furiously to cameras. She caught the scent of coffee, the stale just-burned fragrance so similar to a cop's bull pen. Another time, it might have made her smile.

The noise level was climbing, even as she did. She stepped off on level six into the frantic buzz of the newsroom.

Consoles were set back to back, with traffic areas snaking through. Like police work, broadcasting was a twenty-four-hour business. Even at this hour, there were more than a dozen stations manned.

The difference, Eve noted, was that cops looked over-worked, rumpled, even sweaty. This crew was video perfect. Clothes were streamlined, jewelry camera friendly, faces carefully polished.

Everyone seemed to have a job to do. Some were talking quickly to their 'link screens—feeding their satellites up-dates, Eve imagined. Others barked at their computers or were barked at by them as data was requested, accessed, and transmitted to the desired source.

It all looked perfectly normal, except mixed with the stale scent of bad coffee was the sticky odor of fear.

One or two noticed her, started to rise, questions in their eyes. Her brutally cold stare was as effective as a steel shield.

She turned to the wall where screens hugged against each other. Roarke had a similar setup, and she knew each screen could be used for a separate image, or in any combi-nation. Now the wall was filled with a huge picture of Na-dine Furst on the news set. The familiar three-dimensional view of New York's skyline rose behind her.

She, too, looked polished, perfect. Her eyes seemed to meet and hold on Eve's as Eve stepped closer to listen to the audio.

"And again tonight, a senseless killing. Louise Kirski, an employee of this station, was murdered only a few steps away from the building where I am now broadcasting this report."

Eve didn't bother to curse as Nadine added a few more details and segued to Morse. She'd expected this.

"An ordinary evening," Morse said in a clear reporter's voice. "A rainy night in the city. But once again, despite the best offered by our police force, murder happens. This re-porter is now able to give you a first-hand view of the horror, the shock, and the waste."

He paused, timing perfect, as the camera zoomed in on his face. "I found Louise Kirski's body, crumpled, bleeding, at the bottom of the steps of this building where both she and I have worked many nights. Her throat had been slashed, her blood pouring out on the wet pavement. I'm not ashamed to say that I froze, that I was revolted, that the smell of death clogged in my lungs. I stood, looking down at her, unable to believe what I saw with my own eyes. How could this be? A woman I knew, a woman who I had often shared a friendly word with, a woman I had occasionally had the privilege of working with. How could she be lying there, lifeless?"

The screen dissolved from his pale, serious face, to a gruesomely graphic shot of the body.

They hadn't missed a beat, Eve thought in disgust, and whirled on the closest manned console. "Where's the studio?"

"Excuse me?"

"I said, where's the goddamn studio?" She jerked a thumb toward the screen.

"Well, ah . . ."

Furious, she leaned over, caged him between her stiffened arms. "You want to see how fast I can shut this place down?"

"Level twelve, Studio A."

She whirled away just as Feeney stepped off the ascent. "Took your sweet time."

"Hey, I was in New Jersey visiting my folks." He didn't bother to ask, but fell into step with her.

"I need a gag on the broadcast."

"Well." He scratched his head as they headed up. "We can probably finagle an order to confiscate the pictures of the scene." He moved his shoulders at Eve's glance. "I caught some of it on the screen in the car on the way here. They'll get it back, but we can hang them up for a few hours, anyway."

"Get to work on it. I need all the data available on the victim. They should have records here."

"That's simple enough."

"Feed them to my office, will you, Feeney? I'll be on my way there shortly."

"No problem. Anything else?"

Eve stepped off, scowled at the thick white doors of Studio A. "I might need some backup in here."

"That'd be my pleasure."

The doors were locked, the On Air sign glowing. Eve struggled with a desperate urge to draw her weapon and blow the security panel apart. Instead, she jabbed the emergency button and waited for response.

"Channel 75 News now in progress, live," came the soothing electronic voice. "What is the nature of your problem?"

"Police emergency." She held her ID up to the small scanner.

"One moment, Lieutenant Dallas, while your request is accessed."

"It's not a request," Eve said evenly. "I want these doors open now, or I'll be forced to break in under Code 83B, subsection J."

There was a quiet hum, an electronic hiss, as if the computer were considering, then expressing annoyance. "Clearing doors. Please remain quiet and do not pass the white line. Thank you."

Inside the studio, the temperature dropped ten degrees. Eve stalked directly toward a glass partition facing the set and rapped hard enough to have the news director go white with worry. He held a desperate finger to his lips. Eve held up her badge.

With obvious reluctance, he clicked open the door and gestured them in. "We're live," he snapped and turned back to his view of the set. "Camera Three on Nadine. Back image of Louise. Mark."

The robotics on set obeyed smoothly. Eve watched the small suspended camera shift. On the control monitor, Louise Kirski smiled cheerily.

"Slow down, Nadine. Don't rush it. C. J., ready in ten."

"Go to commercial," Eve told him.

"We're running without ads on this broadcast."

"Go to commercial," she repeated, "or you're going to go to black."

He screwed up his forehead, puffed out his chest. "Now listen here—"

"You listen." She poked him none too gently in that expanded chest. "You've got my eyewitness out there. You do what you're told, or your competitors are going to have ratings through the roof with the story I'm going to give them on how Channel 75 interfered with a police investigation on the murder of one of its own people." She lifted a brow while he considered. "And maybe I'm going to start to think you look like a suspect. He strike you as the cold-blooded killer type, Feeney?"

"I was just thinking that. Maybe we need to take him in, have a nice long chat. After a strip search."

"Just hold on. Hold on." He wiped a hand across his mouth. What could a quick ninety-second commercial break hurt? "Go to Zippy spot in ten. C. J., wind it up. Cue music. Camera One pan back. Mark."

He let out a long breath. "I'm calling legal on this."

"You do that." Eve stepped out of the booth and stalked to the long black console Morse and Nadine shared.

"We've got a right to—"

"I'm going to tell you all about your rights," Eve interrupted Morse. "You've got a right to call your lawyer and have him meet you at Cop Central."

He went dead white. "You're arresting me. Jesus Christ, are you nuts?"

"You're a witness, asshole. And you're not going to make any further statements until you've made one to me. Officially." She flicked a scathing gaze in Nadine's direction. "You'll just have to muddle through the rest on your own."

"I want to go with you." On shaky legs, Nadine rose. To dispense with the frantic shouts from the control booth, she tugged her earpiece free and tossed it down. "I was probably the last person to speak to her."

"Fine. We'll talk about that." Eve led them out, pausing only to grin nastily toward control. "You could fill in with some old reruns of *NYPD Blue.* It's a classic."

"Well, well, C. J." However miserable she was, Eve could appreciate the moment. "I've finally got you where I want you. Comfy?"

He looked a little green around the gills, but managed to sneer as he took a long scan of the interview room. "You guys could use a decorator."

"We're trying to work that into the budget." She settled back at the single table in the room. "Record," she requested. "June 1—Jeez, where did May go?—Subject C. J. Morse, position Interview Room C, Interview conducted by Dallas, Lieutenant Eve, re Homicide, victim Louise Kirsky. Time oh oh forty-five. Mr. Morse, you've been advised of your rights. Do you want your attorney present during this interview?"

He reached for his glass of water and took a sip. "Am I being charged with anything?"

"Not at this time."

"Then get on with it."

"Take me back, C. J. Tell me exactly what happened."

"Fine." He drank again, as if his throat was parched. "I was coming into the station. I had the coanchor on the midnight report."

"What time did you arrive?"

"About quarter after eleven. I went to the east side entrance, most of us use that end because it's more direct to the newsroom. It was raining, so I made a quick dash from the car. I saw something at the base of the steps. I couldn't tell what it was, at first."

He stopped speaking, covered his face with his hands, and rubbed hard. "I couldn't tell," he continued, "until I was practically on top of her. I thought—I don't know what I thought, really. Somebody took a hell of a spill."

"You didn't recognize the victim?"

"The—the hood." he gestured vaguely, helplessly with

his hands. "It was over her face. I reached down, and I started to move it away from her face." He gave one violent shudder. "Then I saw the blood—her throat. The blood," he repeated, and covered his eyes.

"Did you touch the body?"

"No, I don't think—no. She was just lying there, and her throat was wide open. Her eyes. No, I didn't touch her." He dropped his hand again, made what appeared to be a herculean effort for control. "I got sick. You probably don't understand that, Dallas. Some people have basic human reactions. All that blood, her eyes. God. I got sick, and I got scared and I ran inside. The guard on the desk. I told him."

"You knew the victim?"

"Sure, I knew her. Louise had edited a few pieces for me. Mostly she worked with Nadine, but she did some pieces for me and for some others. She was good, real good. Quick, a sharp eye. One of the best. Christ." He reached for the pitcher on the table. Water sloshed as he poured it. "There was no reason to kill her. No reason at all."

"Was it her habit to go out that exit at that time?"

"I don't know. I don't think—she should have been in Editing," he said fiercely.

"Were you close, personally?"

His head came up, and his eyes narrowed. "You're trying to pin this on me, aren't you? You'd really like that."

"Just answer the questions, C. J. Were you involved with her?"

"She had a relationship, talked about some guy named Bongo. We worked together, Dallas. That's all."

"You arrived at Channel 75 at eleven fifteen. Before that?"

"Before that I was at home. When I have the midnight shift, I catch a couple hours' sleep. I didn't have a feature running, so I didn't have much prep. It was supposed to be just a read, a recap of the day. I had dinner with some friends about seven, headed home around eight, and took a nap."

He propped his elbows on the table and lowered his head

into his hands. "I had my wake-up at ten, then headed out just before eleven. Gave myself a little extra travel time because of the weather. Jesus, Jesus, Jesus."

If Eve hadn't watched him report on camera minutes after his discovery of the body, she might have felt sorry for him. "Did you see anyone at or near the scene?"

"Just Louise. There's not a lot of people going in and out that time of night. I didn't see anybody. Just Louise. Just Louise."

"Okay, C. J., that's about it this time around."

He set down the glass he'd guzzled from again. "I can go?"

"Keep in mind you're a witness. If you're holding back, or if you remember anything not revealed in this interview, I'll charge you with withholding evidence and impeding an investigation." She smiled pleasantly. "Oh, and give me the names of your friends, C. J. I didn't think you had any."

She let him go and brooded while she waited for Nadine to be brought in. The scenario was all too clear. And the guilt came with it. To keep both fresh, she flipped open the file and studied the hard copy photos of Louise Kirski's body. She turned them facedown when the door opened.

Nadine didn't look polished now. The professional gloss of the on-air personality had given way to a pale, shaken woman with swollen eyes and a trembling mouth. Saying nothing, Eve gestured to the chair and poured water in a fresh glass.

"You were quick," she said coolly, "getting your report on the air."

"That's my job." Nadine didn't touch the glass, but gripped her hands in her lap. "You do yours, I do mine."

"Right. Just serving the public, aren't we?"

"I'm not very interested in what you think of me right now, Dallas."

"Just as well, because I don't think very much of you right now." For the second time, she started the recorder, fed in the necessary information. "When did you last see Louise Kirski alive?"

"We were working in Editing, refining and timing a piece for the midnight spot. It didn't take as much time as we'd scheduled to finish. Louise was good, really good." Nadine drew a deep breath and continued to stare at a spot an inch above Eve's left shoulder. "We talked for a few minutes. She and the man she'd been seeing for the last several months were looking for an apartment together. She was happy. Louise was a happy person, easy to get along with, bright."

She had to stop again, had to. Her breath was backing up. Carefully, firmly, she ordered herself to inhale, exhale. Twice. "Anyway, she was out of cigarettes. She liked to catch a quick smoke between assignments. Everybody looked the other way, even though she'd sneak off into a closet somewhere and light up. I told her to pick me up a couple while she was at it, gave her some credits. We went down together, and I got off at the newsroom. I had some calls to make. Otherwise, I'd have gone with her. I'd have been with her."

"Did you usually go out together before the broadcast?"

"No. Normally, I take a short break, head out, have a quiet cup of coffee in this little café on Third. I like to—get away from the station, especially before the midnight. We've got a restaurant, lounges, a coffee shop in house, but I like to break off and take ten on my own."

"Habitually?"

"Yeah." Nadine met Eve's eyes, veered away. "Habitually. But I wanted to make those calls, and it was raining, so . . . so I didn't go. I lent her my raincoat, and she went out." Her eyes shifted back, straight to Eve's. And were devastated. "She's dead instead of me. You know that, and I know that. Don't we, Dallas?"

"I recognized your coat," Eve said briefly. "I thought it was you."

"She didn't do anything but run out for a few cigarettes. Wrong place, wrong time. Wrong coat."

Wrong bait, Eve thought, but didn't say it. "Let's take this a step at a time, Nadine. An editor has a certain amount of power, of control."

"No." Slowly, methodically, Nadine shook her head. The sickness in her stomach had snuck into her throat, and tasted foul. "It's the story, Dallas, and the on-air personality. Nobody appreciates, or even thinks of an editor but the reporter. She wasn't the target, Dallas. Let's not pretend otherwise."

"What I think and what I know are handled in different ways, Nadine. But let's go with what I think for now. I think you were the target, and I think the killer mistook Louise for you. You've got different builds, but it was raining, she was wearing your coat, had the hood on. There either wasn't time, or there wasn't a choice once the mistake was realized."

"What?" Dazed at having it all said so flatly, Nadine struggled to focus. "What did you say?"

"It was over quickly. I've got the time she left from the security desk. She waved to the guard. We've got Morse stumbling over her ten minutes later. Either it was timed extremely well, or our killer was cocky. And you can bet your ass he wanted to see it on the news before she'd gotten cold."

"We accommodated him, didn't we?"

"Yeah." Eve nodded. "You did."

"You think it was easy for me?" Nadine's voice, raspy and thick, burst out. "You think it was easy to sit there and give a report knowing she was still lying outside?"

"I don't know," Eve said mildly. "Was it?"

"She was my friend." Nadine began to weep, tears rushing out, pouring down her cheeks and leaving trails in her camera makeup. "I cared about her. Damn it, she mattered to me, not just a story. She isn't just a fucking story."

Struggling to carry her own guilt, Eve nudged the glass toward Nadine. "Drink," she ordered. "Take a minute."

Nadine had to use both hands to keep the glass even partially steady. She would, she realized, have preferred brandy, but that would have to wait. "I see this kind of thing all the time, not so different from you."

"You saw the body," Eve snapped. "You went out on the scene."

"I had to see." With eyes still swimming, she looked back at Eve. "That was personal, Dallas. I had to see. I didn't want to believe it when word came up."

"How did word come up?"

"Somebody heard Morse yelling to the guard that somebody was dead, that somebody had been murdered right outside. That drew a lot of attention," she said, rubbing her temples. "Word travels. I hadn't finished my second call before I caught the buzz. I hung up on my source and went down. And I saw her." Her smile was grim and humorless. "I beat the cameras—and the cops."

"And you and your pals risked contaminating a crime scene." Eve swiped a hand through the air. "That's done. Did anybody touch her? Did you see anybody touch her?"

"No, nobody was that stupid. It was obvious she was dead. You could see—you could see the wound, the blood. We sent for an ambulance anyway. The first police unit was there within minutes, ordered us back inside, sealed the door. I talked to somebody. Peabody." She rubbed fingers over her temples. Not because they hurt; because they were numb. "I told her it was Louise, then I went up to prep for broadcast. And the whole time I was thinking, *It was supposed to be me.* I was alive, facing the camera, and she was dead. It was supposed to be me."

"It wasn't supposed to be anyone."

"We killed her, Dallas." Nadine's voice was steady again. "You and me."

"I guess we'll have to live with that." Eve drew a breath and leaned forward. "Let's go over the timing again, Nadine. Step by step."

chapter thirteen

Sometimes, Eve thought, the drudge of routine police work payed off. Like a slot machine, fed habitually, mindlessly, monotonously, so that you're almost shocked when the jackpot falls in your lap.

That's just the way it was when David Angelini fell into hers.

She'd had several questions on small details of the Kirski case. The timing was one of them.

Nadine skips her usual break, Kirksi goes out instead, passing the lobby desk at approximately 23:04. She steps out into the rain, and into a knife. Minutes later, running late, Morse arrives at the station lot, stumbles over the body, vomits, and runs inside to report a murder.

All of it, she mused, quick, fast, and in a hurry.

As a matter of course, she ran the discs from the security gate at Channel 75. It wasn't possible to know if the killer had driven through them, parked a car on the station's lot, strolled over to wait for Nadine, sliced Louise by mistake, then driven off again.

An assailant could just as easily have cut across the property from Third on foot, just as Louise had intended to do. Gate security was to make sure that there were parking facilities for station employees and that guests weren't infringed upon by every frustrated driver looking for a place to stick his car or minishuttle off the street.

Eve reviewed the discs because it was a matter of routine, and because, she admitted to herself, she hoped Morse's story wouldn't gel. He'd have recognized Nadine's raincoat, and he'd have known her habit of cutting out for some solo time before the midnight broadcast.

There was nothing she'd have enjoyed more, on a basic, even primal personal level, than nailing his skinny butt to the wall.

And that's when she saw the sleek little two-passenger Italian model cruise like a shiny cat to the gate. She'd seen that car before, parked outside of the commander's home after the memorial service.

"Stop," she ordered, and the image on screen froze. "Enhance sector twenty-three through thirty, full screen." The machine clicked, then clunked, wobbling the image. With an impatient snarl, Eve smacked the screen with the heel of her hand, jarring it back on course. "Goddamn budget cuts," she muttered, and then her smile began, slow and savoring. "Well, well, Mr. Angelini."

She took a deep breath as David's face filled her screen. He looked impatient, she thought. Distracted. Nervous.

"What were you doing there?" she murmured, flicking her glance down to the digital time frozen at the bottom left corner. "At twenty-three oh two and five seconds?"

She leaned back in her chair, rifling through a drawer with one hand as she continued to study the screen. Absently, she bit into a candy bar that was going to pass for breakfast. She'd yet to go home.

"Hard copy," she ordered. "Then go back to original view and hard copy." She waited patiently while her machine wheezed its way through the process. "Continue disc run, normal speed."

Nibbling on her breakfast, she watched the pricey sports car whiz past camera range. The image blinked. Channel 75 could afford the latest in motion-activated security cameras. Eleven minutes had passed on the counter when Morse's car approached.

"Interesting," she murmured. "Copy disc, transfer copy to file 47833-K, Kirski, Louise. Homicide. Cross reference to case file 47801-T, Towers, Cicely and 47815-M, Metcalf, Yvonne. Homicides."

Turning from the screen, she engaged her 'link. "Feeney."

"Dallas." He stuffed the last of a danish into his mouth. "I'm working on it. Christ, it's barely seven A.M."

"I know what time it is. I've got a sensitive matter here, Feeney."

"Hell." His already rumpled face grew more wrinkles. "I hate when you say that."

"I've got David Angelini on the gate security disc at Channel 75, coming in about ten minutes before Louise Kirski's body was discovered."

"Shit, shit, shit. Who's going to tell the commander?"

"I am—after I've had a talk with Angelini. I need you to cover for me, Feeney. I'm going to transmit what I've got, excluding Angelini. You take it in to the commander. Tell him I'm hooking a couple hours of personal time."

"Yeah, like he'll buy that one."

"Feeney, tell me I need some sleep. Tell me you'll report to the commander, and to go home and catch a couple hours of sleep."

Feeney heaved a long sigh. "Dallas, you need some sleep. I'll report to the commander. Go home and catch a couple hours."

"Now you can tell him you told me," she said, and flicked off.

•   •   •

Like routine police work, a cop's gut often paid off. Eve's told her that David Angelini would close himself in with family. Her first stop was the Angelini pied-à-terre, cozied in an affluent East Side neighborhood.

Here the brownstones had been constructed barely thirty years before, reproductions of those designed during the nineteenth, and destroyed during the dawn of the twenty-first when most of New York's infrastructure had failed. A large portion of New York's posher homes in this area had been condemned and razed. After much debate, this area had been rebuilt in the old tradition—a tradition only the very wealthy had been able to afford.

After a ten-minute search, Eve managed to find a spot among the expensive European and American cars. Overhead, a trio of private minishuttles jockeyed for air space, circling as they looked for a clear landing.

Apparently, public transportation wasn't high on the list in the neighborhood, and property was too dear to waste on garage facilities.

Still, New York was New York, and she locked the doors on her battered police issue before heading up the sidewalk. She watched a teenager skim by on an airboard. He took the opportunity to impress his small audience with a few complicated maneuvers, ending with a long, looping flip. Rather than disappoint him, Eve flashed him an appreciative grin.

"Nice moves."

"I got the groove," he claimed in a voice that was hovering between puberty and manhood with less security than he hovered over the sidewalk. "You board?"

"No. Too risky for me." When she continued to walk, he circled around her, pivoting on the board with quick footwork.

"I could show you some of the easy scoots in five minutes."

"I'll keep it in mind. You know who lives there, in twenty-one?"

"Twenty-one? Sure, Mr. Angelini. You're not one of his nibbles."

She stopped. "I'm not?"

"Come on." The boy cocked a grin, showing perfect teeth. "He goes for the dignified type. Older, too." He did a quick vertical rock, side to side. "You don't look like a domestic, either. Anyway, he mostly does the droid thing for that."

"Does he have a lot of nibbles?"

"Only seen a few around here. Always come up in a private car. Sometimes they'll stay till morning, but mostly not."

"And how would you know?"

He grinned, unabashed. "I live right over there." He pointed to a townhouse across the street. "I like to keep my eye on what's doing."

"Okay, why don't you tell me if anybody came around last night?"

He swiveled his board, spun. "How come?"

"'Cause I'm a cop."

His eyes widened as he studied her badge. "Wow. Decent. Hey, you think he popped his old lady? Gotta keep up with current events and shit for school."

"This isn't a quiz. Were you keeping your eye out last night? What's your name?"

"It's Barry. I was kind of hanging loose last night, watching some screen, listening to some tune. Supposed to be studying for this monster final in Comp Tech."

"Why aren't you in school today?"

"Hey, you're not with the Truant Division?" His grin turned a little nervous. "It's too early for class. Anyway, I got the three-day thing, E-school at home."

"Okay. Last night?"

"While I was hanging, I saw Mr. Angelini go out. About eight, I guess. Then, late, probably closing on midnight, this other dude, flash car pulls up. He didn't get out for awhile, just kinda sat there like he couldn't make up his mind."

Barry did a quick whirl-a-loop, dancing up the length of

the board. "Then he went in. Walking funny. I figured he'd been dousing a few. Went right on in, so he knew the code. Didn't see Mr. Angelini come back. I was probably zeeing by then. You know, catching winks."

"Sleeping, yeah. I get it. Did you see anybody leave this morning?"

"Nope, but the flash car's still there."

"I see. Thanks."

"Hey." He scooted behind her. "Is being a cop a rocking thing?"

"Sometimes it rocks, sometimes it doesn't." She climbed the short steps to the Angelini home and identified herself to the cool tones of the greeting scanner.

"I'm sorry, Lieutenant, there is no one at home. If you would like to leave a message, it will be returned at the first opportunity."

Eve looked directly at the scanner. "Process this. If there's no one at home, I'm going to walk back to my car, request an entry and search warrant. That should take about ten minutes."

She stood her ground and waited less than two before David Angelini opened the door.

"Lieutenant."

"Mr. Angelini. Here or Cop Central? Your choice."

"Come in." He stepped back. "I just arrived in New York last night. I'm still a bit disorganized this morning."

He led her into a dark-toned, high-ceilinged sitting room and offered her coffee politely, which she declined with equal politeness. He wore the slim, narrow cuffed slacks she'd seen on the streets of Rome with a wide-sleeved silk shirt of the same neutral cream color. His shoes matched the tone and looked soft enough to dent with a fingertip.

But his eyes were restless, and his hands tapped rhythmically on the arms of his chair when he sat.

"You have more information about my mother's case."

"You know why I'm here."

He flicked his tongue over his lips, shifted. Eve thought

she understood why he did so poorly at gaming. "Excuse me?"

She set her recorder on the table in full view. "David Angelini, your rights are as follows. You are under no obligation to make a statement. If you do make a statement, it will be logged into record and can and will be used against you in court or any legal proceeding. You have a right to the presence and advice of an attorney or representative."

She continued the brisk recitation of his rights while his breathing quickened and grew more audible. "The charges?"

"You are not yet charged. Do you understand your rights?"

"Of course I understand them."

"Do you wish to call your attorney?"

His mouth opened, a breath shuddered out. "Not yet. I assume you're going to make the purpose of this interrogation clear, Lieutenant."

"I think it's going to be crystal. Mr. Angelini, where were you between the hours of eleven P.M., May 31 and twelve A.M., June 1?"

"I told you I'd just gotten into the city. I drove in from the airport and came here."

"You came here, directly from the airport?"

"That's right. I had a late meeting, but I—I canceled it." He flicked open the top hook of his shirt, as if he needed air. "Rescheduled it."

"What time did you arrive at the airport?"

"My flight got in around ten-thirty, I believe."

"You came here."

"I've said so."

"Yes, you did." Eve angled her head. "And you're a liar. A bad liar. You sweat when you bluff."

Aware of the damp line running down his back, he rose. His voice tried for outrage but ended on fear. "I believe I'll contact my attorney after all, Lieutenant. And your superior. Is it standard police procedure to harass innocent people in their own homes?"

"Whatever works," she murmured. "Then again, you're not innocent. Go ahead and call your attorney, and we'll all go down to Cop Central."

But he didn't move toward his 'link. "I haven't done anything."

"For starters, you've lied on record to an investigating officer. Call your attorney."

"Wait, wait." Rubbing a hand over his mouth, David paced the room. "It isn't necessary. It isn't necessary to take this that far."

"That's your choice. Would you care to revise your previous statement?"

"This is a delicate matter, Lieutenant."

"Funny, I've always thought of murder as a crude matter, myself."

He continued to pace, working his hands together. "You have to understand the business is in a tenuous position at the moment. The wrong kind of publicity will influence certain transactions. In a week, two at the most, it will all be resolved."

"And you think I should hold off on all this until you get your financial ducks in a row?"

"I'd be willing to compensate you for your time and your discretion."

"Would you?" Eve widened her eyes. "What sort of compensation are you suggesting, Mr. Angelini?"

"I can swing ten thousand." He struggled for a smile. "Double that if you simply bury all of this for good."

Eve crossed her arms. "Let the record show that David Angelini offered a monetary bribe to investigating primary Lieutenant Eve Dallas, and the aforesaid bribe was refused."

"Bitch," he said softly.

"You bet. Why were you at Channel 75 last night?"

"I've never said I was."

"Let's cut the dreck. You were recorded by gate security entering the property." To emphasize, she opened her bag, took out the hard copy of his face, tossed it on the table.

"Gate security." His legs seemed to fold from under him and he groped into a chair. "I never thought—never considered. I panicked."

"Slicing someone's jugular can do that to you."

"I never touched her. I never went near her. Good God, do I look like a murderer?"

"They come in all styles. You were there. I have documentation. Hands!" she said sharply as her own jumped to her shoulder harness. "Keep your hands out of your pockets."

"Name of God, do you think I'm carrying a knife?" Slowly he drew out a handkerchief, wiped his brow. "I didn't even know Louise Kirski."

"But you know her name."

"I saw it on the news." He closed his eyes. "I saw it on the news. And I saw him kill her."

The muscles in Eve's shoulders bunched, but unlike David she was good at the game. Both her face and voice were bland. "Well then, why don't you tell me all about it?"

He worked his hands together again, linking fingers, twisting. He wore two rings, one diamond, one ruby, both set in heavy gold. They clinked together musically.

"You have to keep my name out of this."

"No," she said evenly, "I don't. I don't make deals. Your mother was a PA, Mr. Angelini. You should know if there are going to be any deals, they're going to come through that office, not me. You've already lied on the record." She kept her tone flat, easy. It was best when working with a nervous suspect to ease them in. "I'm giving you a chance to revise your previous statement, and again reminding you that you have the right to contact your attorney at any time during this interview. But if you want to talk to me, talk now. And I'll start, to make it easy for you. What were you doing at Channel 75 last night?"

"I had a late meeting. I told you that I had one and canceled. That's the truth. We've been—I've been working on an expansion deal. Angelini has some interest in the entertainment industry. We've been developing projects, programs, features for in-home viewing. Carlson Young, the head of the entertainment division of the channel, had done quite a bit to bring these projects to fruition. I was to meet him in his office there."

"A little after business hours, wasn't it?"

"The entertainment field doesn't have what you might call normal business hours. Both of our schedules were tight, and this was a time that suited us both."

"Why not handle it over the 'link?"

"A great deal of our business was done that way. But we both felt it was time for a personal meeting. We'd hoped—still hope—to have the first project on air by fall. We have the script," he continued, almost talking to himself now. "The production team's in place. We've already signed some of the cast."

"So, you had a late night meeting with Carlson Young of Channel 75."

"Yes. The weather held me up a bit. I was running late." His head came up. "I called him from my car. You can check that, too. You can check. I called him a few minutes before eleven when I realized I would be late."

"We'll check everything, Mr. Angelini. Count on it."

"I arrived at the main gate. I was distracted, thinking of . . . of some casting problems. I turned. I should have gone straight to the main entrance, but I was thinking of something else. I stopped the car, realized I'd have to backtrack. Then I saw—" He used his handkerchief, rubbed at his mouth. "I saw someone come out of a door. Then there was someone else, he must have been standing there watching, waiting. He moved so fast. It all moved so fast. She turned, and I saw her face. Just for a second, I saw her face in the light. His hand jerked up. Fast, very fast. And . . . dear God. The blood. It gushed, like a fountain. I didn't understand. I couldn't believe—it just spurted out of her. She fell, and he was running, running away."

"What did you do?"

"I—I just sat there. I don't know how long. I was driving away. I don't even remember. I was driving and everything was like a dream. The rain, and the lights from other cars. Then I was here. I can't even remember how I got here. But I was outside in the car. I called Young, and told him I'd been delayed again, that we needed to reschedule. I came inside, there was no one here. I took a sedative and went to bed."

Eve let the silence hum a moment. "Let's see if I've got this. You were on your way to a meeting, took a wrong turn, and saw a woman brutally murdered. Then you drove away, canceled your meeting, and went to bed. Is that accurate?"

"Yes. Yes, I suppose it is."

"It didn't occur to you to get out of your car, to see if she could be helped? Or perhaps to use your 'link to notify the authorities, the MTs?"

"I wasn't thinking. I was shaken."

"You were shaken. So you came here, took a pill, and went to bed."

"That's what I said," he snapped out. "I need a drink." With sweaty fingers, he fumbled for a control. "Vodka," he ordered. "Bring the bottle."

Eve let him stew until the server droid arrived with a bottle of Stoli and a short thick glass on its tray. She let him drink.

"There was nothing I could do," he mumbled, goaded, as she'd intended, by her silence. "I wasn't involved."

"Your mother was murdered a few weeks ago by the method you've just described to me. And this didn't involve you?"

"That was part of the problem." He poured again, drank again. Shuddered. "I was shocked, and—and afraid. Violence isn't part of my life, Lieutenant. It was part of my mother's, a part I could never understand. She understood violence," he said quietly. "She understood it."

"And did you resent that, Mr. Angelini? That she understood violence, was strong enough to face it? Fight against it?"

His breathing was shallow. "I loved my mother. When I

saw this other woman murdered, as my mother had been murdered, all I could think of to do was run."

He paused, took a last quick swallow of vodka. "Do you think I don't know you've been checking on me, asking questions, digging into my personal and professional lives? I'm a suspect already. How much worse would it have been for me to be there, right there, at the scene of another murder?"

Eve rose. "You're about to find out."

chapter fourteen

Eve questioned him again, in the less comforting sur-roundings of Interview Room C. He'd finally taken up his right for counsel, and three pinstriped, cold-eyed lawyers ranged beside their client at the conference table.

Eve had privately dubbed them Moe, Larry, and Curly.

Moe apparently was in charge. She was a tough-voiced woman with a severe bowl-cut hairstyle that had inspired Eve to christen her. Her associates said little but looked sober and occasionally made important-looking notations on the yellow legal pads that lawyers never seemed to tire of.

Now and again Curly, his wide forehead creased, would tap a few buttons on his log book and murmur conspiratori-ally in Larry's ear.

"Lieutenant Dallas." Moe folded her hands, which were tipped with wicked looking inch-long scarlet nails, on the table. "My client is eager to cooperate."

"He wasn't," Eve stated, "as you've seen for yourself from the first interview. After recanting his original story, your client admitted to leaving the scene of a crime and failing to report said crime to the proper authorities."

Moe sighed. It was a windy, disappointed sound. "You can, of course, charge Mr. Angelini with those lapses. We will, in turn, claim diminished capacity, shock, and the emotional trauma of his mother's recent murder. This would all be a waste of the court's time, and the taxpayer's dollar."

"I haven't charged your client with those . . . lapses as yet. We're dealing with a larger theme here."

Curly scribbled something, tilted his pad for Larry to read. The two of them murmured together and looked grave.

"You have confirmed my client's appointment at Channel 75."

"Yeah, he had an appointment, which he canceled at eleven thirty-five. Odd that his diminished capacity and his emotional trauma eased off enough for him to take care of business." Before Moe could speak again, Eve turned and pinned Angelini with one hard stare. "You know Nadine Furst?"

"I know who she is. I've seen her on the news." He hesitated, leaned over to consult Moe. After a moment, he nodded. "I'd met her a few times socially, and spoke with her briefly after my mother's death."

Eve already knew all of that, and circled her quarry. "I'm sure you've seen her reports. You'd have a vested interest, as she's been covering the recent murders. Your mother's murder."

"Lieutenant, what does my client's interest in the news coverage of his mother's death have to do with the murder of Ms. Kirski?"

"I'm wondering. You have seen Nadine Furst's reports over the last couple weeks, Mr. Angelini."

"Of course." He'd recovered enough to sneer. "You've gotten a lot of airtime out of it, Lieutenant."

"Does that bother you?"

"I think it's appalling that a public servant, paid by the city, would seek notoriety through tragedy."

"Sounds like it pissed you off," Eve said with an easy shrug. "Ms. Furst has been getting plenty of notoriety out of it, too."

"One learns to expect someone like her to use someone else's pain for her own advancement."

"You didn't like the coverage?"

"Lieutenant," Moe said with her patience obviously straining. "Where's the point in this?"

"This isn't a trial, yet. I don't need a point. Were you annoyed by the coverage, Mr. Angelini? Angry?"

"I—" He broke off at a sharp look from Moe. "I come from a prominent family," he said more carefully. "We're accustomed to such things."

"If we could get back to the business at hand," Moe requested.

"This is the business at hand. Louise Kirski was wearing Nadine Furst's raincoat when she was killed. You know what I think, Mr. Angelini? I think the killer hit the wrong target. I think he was waiting for Nadine and Louise just happened to choose the wrong time to go out in the rain for cigarettes."

"It doesn't have anything to do with me." His eyes darted toward his attorneys. "It still doesn't have anything to do with me. I saw it. That's all."

"You said it was a man. What did he look like?"

"I don't know. I didn't see him clearly, his back was to me. It happened so fast."

"But you saw enough to know it was a man."

"I assumed." He broke off, struggling to control his breathing while Moe whispered in his ear. "It was raining," he began. "I was several meters away, in my car."

"You said you saw the victim's face."

"The light, she turned her head toward the light when he—or when the killer—went toward her."

"And this killer, who might have been a man, and who came out of nowhere. Was he tall, short, old, young?"

"I don't know. It was dark."

"You said there was light."

"Just that circle of light. He'd been in the shadows. He was wearing black," David said on a burst of inspiration. "A long black coat—and a hat, a hat that drooped down low."

"That's convenient. He was wearing black. It's so original."

"Lieutenant, I can't advise my client to continue to cooperate if you persist in sarcasm."

"Your client's in hip deep. My sarcasm's the least of his worries. We've got the three big ones. Means, motive, opportunity."

"You have nothing but my client's admission that he witnessed a crime. Further," Moe went on, tapping those dangerous nails on the conference table, "you have absolutely nothing to link him with the other murders. What you've got, Lieutenant, is a maniac on the loose, and a desperate need to appease your superiors and the public with an arrest. It's not going to be my client."

"We'll have to see about that. Now—" Her communicator beeped, twice, a signal from Feeney. Her adrenaline surged, and she masked it with a bland smile. "Excuse me, I'll only be a moment."

She stepped out of the room into the hallway. Behind her through the one-way glass, a huddle was in progress. "Give me good news, Feeney. I want to nail this son of a bitch."

"Good news?" Feeney rubbed his chin. "Well, you might like this. Yvonne Metcalf was in negotiations with our pal in there. Covert negotiations."

"For?"

"The lead in some flick. It was all on the Q.T. because her contract for *Tune In* was coming up. I finally pinned her agent down. If she snagged the part, she was willing to ditch the sitcom. But they were going to have to up the ante, guarantee a three-feature deal, international distribution, and twenty hours' straight promo."

"Sounds like she wanted a lot."

"She was squeezing him some. My take from what the agent said is he needed Metcalf to guarantee some of the financial backing, but they wanted a chunk on the front end. He was scrambling to come up with it and save his project."

"He knew her. And she had the controls."

"According to the agent, he came in to meet Metcalf personally, several times. They had a couple of tête-à-têtes at her apartment. He got a little hot, but Metcalf laughed it off. She was banking that he'd come around."

"I love when it falls into place, don't you?" She turned, studying Angelini through the glass. "We've got a connection, Feeney. He knew them all."

"He was supposed to be on the coast when Metcalf got whacked."

"How much do you want to bet he's got a private plane? You know something I've learned since Roarke, Feeney? Flight plans don't mean squat if you've got money, and your own transpo. No, unless he comes up with ten witnesses who were kissing his ass when Metcalf went down, I've got him. Watch him sweat," she muttered as she swung back into the interview room.

She sat, crossed her arms on the table, and met Angelini's eyes. "You knew Yvonne Metcalf."

"I—" Off balance, David reached up, tugged at the collar of his shirt. "Certainly, I . . . everyone did."

"You had business with her, met her personally, you'd been to her apartment."

This was obviously news to Moe, who bared her teeth, tossed up a hand. "One moment, Lieutenant. I'd like to speak to my client privately."

"All right." Obliging, Eve rose. Outside, she watched the show through the glass, and thought it a pity that the law prevented her from turning on the audio.

Still, she could see Moe fire questions at David and could

gauge his stuttering responses while Larry and Curly looked grim and scribbled furiously on their pads.

Moe shook her head at one of David's answers, stabbed him with one of her lethal red nails. Eve was smiling when Moe lifted a hand and signaled her back into the room.

"My client is prepared to state that he was acquainted with Yvonne Metcalf, on a professional level."

"Uh-huh." This time Eve leaned a hip on the table. "Yvonne Metcalf was giving you some grief, wasn't she, Mr. Angelini?"

"We were in negotiations." His hands linked together again, twisted. "It's standard for the talent side of a project to demand the moon. We were . . . coming to terms."

"You met her in her apartment. Argued?"

"We—I—we had meetings at several locations. Her home was one of them. We discussed terms and options."

"Where were you, Mr. Angelini, on the night Yvonne Metcalf was murdered?"

"I'd have to check my diary," he said with surprising control. "But I believe I was in New Los Angeles, the Planet Hollywood complex. I stay there whenever I'm in town."

"And where might you have been between oh, seven and midnight, West Coast time?"

"I couldn't say."

"You're going to want to say, Mr. Angelini."

"Most likely in my room. I had a great deal of business to see to. The script needed reworking."

"The script you were tailoring for Ms. Metcalf."

"Yes, actually."

"And you were working alone?"

"I prefer to be alone when I write. I wrote the script, you see." He flushed a little, the color rising from the collar of his shirt. "I put a great deal of time and effort into preparing it."

"You keep a plane?"

"A plane. Naturally, the way I travel, I—"

"Was your plane in New Los Angeles?"

"Yes, I—" His eyes went wide and blank as he realized the implication. "You can't seriously believe this!"

"David, sit down," Moe said firmly when he lurched to his feet. "You have nothing more to say at this time."

"She thinks I killed them. That's insane. My own mother, for God's sake. What reason? What possible reason could there be for that?"

"Oh, I've got a few ideas on that. We'll see if the shrink agrees with me."

"My client is under no obligation to submit to psychiatric testing."

"I think you're going to advise him to do just that."

"This interview," Moe said in snippy tones, "is terminated."

"Fine." Eve straightened, enjoyed the moment when her eyes met David's. "David Angelini, you're under arrest. You are charged with leaving the scene of a crime, obstruction of justice, and attempted bribery of a police officer."

He lunged at her, going ironically, Eve thought, for the throat. She waited until his hands had closed over it, his eyes bulging with fury, before she knocked him down.

Ignoring the snapping orders of his attorney, Eve leaned over him. "We won't bother with adding assaulting an officer and resisting arrest. I don't think we're going to need it. Book him," she snapped at the uniforms who had charged the door.

"Nice work, Dallas," Feeney congratulated as they watched David being led away.

"Let's hope the PA's office thinks so, enough to block bail. We have to hold him and sweat him. I want him on murder one, Feeney. I want him bad."

"We're close to it, kid."

"We need the physical evidence. We need the damn weapon, blood, the souvenirs. Mira's psychiatric will help, but I can't bump up the charges without some physical." Impatient, she consulted her watch. "Shouldn't take too long to get a search warrant, even with the lawyers trying to block."

"How long you been up?" he wondered. "I can count the circles under your eyes."

"Long enough that another couple of hours won't matter. How about I buy you a drink while we wait for the warrant?"

He put a paternal hand on her shoulder. "I think we're both going to need one. The commander got wind of it. He wants us, Dallas. Now."

She dug a finger along the center of her brow. "Let's get it together then. And make it two drinks after we're done."

Whitney didn't waste time. The moment Eve and Feeney stepped into his office, he scalded them both with one long look. "You brought David in to Interview."

"I did, yes, sir." Eve took an extra step forward to take the heat. "We have video of him on the gate security at Channel 75 at the time of Louise Kirski's murder." She didn't pause, but streamed through her report, her voice brisk, her eyes level.

"David says he saw the murder."

"He claims he saw someone, possibly male, in a long black coat and a hat, attack Kirski, then run toward Third."

"And he panicked," Whitney added, still in control. His hands were quiet on his desk. "Left the scene without reporting the incident." Whitney may have been cursing inwardly, his stomach might have been in greasy knots of tension, but his eyes were cool, hard, and steady. "It's not an atypical reaction from a witness to a violent crime."

"He denied he was on scene," Eve said calmly. "Tried to cover, offered a bribe. He had the opportunity, Commander. And he's linked to all three victims. He knew Metcalf, was working with her on a project, had been to her apartment."

Whitney's only reaction was to curl his fingers, then uncurl them. "Motive, Lieutenant?"

"Money first," she said. "He's having financial difficulties that will be eased after his mother's will is probated. The victims, or in the third case, the intended victim, were all strong women in the public eye. Were all, in some manner, causing him distress. Unless his lawyers try to block it, Doctor Mira will test him, determine his emotional and mental state, the probability factor of his aptitude toward violence."

She thought of the press of his hands around her throat and figured the probability was going to be nice and high.

"He wasn't in New York for the first two murders."

"Sir." She felt a bolt of pity, but suppressed it. "He has a private plane. He can shuttle anywhere he likes. It's pathetically simple to doctor flight plans. I can't book him for the murders yet, but I want him held until we gather more evidence."

"You're holding him on leaving the scene and the bribery charge?"

"It's a good arrest, Commander. I'm requesting search warrants. When we find any physical evidence—"

"If," Whitney interrupted. He rose now, no longer able to sit behind his desk. "That's a very big difference, Dallas. Without physical evidence, your murder case can't hold."

"Which is why he has yet to be charged for murder." She laid a hard copy on his desk. She and Feeney had taken the time to swing past her office and use her computer for the probability ratio. "He knew the first two victims and Nadine Furst, had contact with them, was on the scene of the last murder. We suspect that Towers was covering for someone when she zapped the last call on her 'link. She would have covered for her son. And their relationship was strained due to his gambling problem and her refusal to bail him out. With known data, the probability factor of guilt is eighty-three point one percent."

"You haven't taken into account that he's incapable of that kind of violence." Whitney laid his hands on the edge of his desk and leaned forward. "You didn't factor that in to the mix, did you, Lieutenant? I know David Angelini, Dallas. I know him as well as I know my own children. He isn't a killer. He's a fool, perhaps. He's weak, perhaps. But he isn't a cold-blooded killer."

"Sometimes the weak and the foolish strike out. Commander, I'm sorry. I can't kick him loose."

"Do you have any idea what it would do to a man like him to be penned? To know he's suspected of killing his own mother?" There was no choice left for him, in Whitney's mind, but a plea. "I can't deny that he was spoiled. His father wanted the best for him and for Mirina, and saw that they got it. From childhood he was accustomed to asking for something and having it fall into his lap. Yes, his life has been easy, privileged, even indulgent. He's made mistakes, errors in judgment, and they've been fixed for him. But there's no malice in him, Dallas. No violence. I know him."

Whitney's voice didn't rise, but it reverberated with emotion. "You'll never convince me that David took a knife and ripped it across his mother's throat. I'm asking you to consider that, and to delay the paperwork on the yellow sheet and recommend his release on his own recognizance."

Feeney started to speak, but Eve shook her head. He may have outranked her, but she was primary. She was in charge. "Three women are dead, Commander. We have a suspect in custody. I can't do what you're asking. You put me on as primary because you knew I wouldn't."

He turned and stared hard out of the window. "Compassion's not your strong suit, is it, Dallas?"

She winced, but said nothing.

"That's a wrong swing, Jack," Feeney said, with heat. "And if you're going to take one at her, then you'll have to take one at me, 'cause I'm with Dallas on this. We've got enough to book him on the small shit, to take him off the street, and that's what we're doing."

"You'll ruin him." Whitney turned back. "But that's not your problem. You get your warrants, and you do your search. But as your commanding officer, I'm ordering you to keep the case open. You keep looking. Have your reports on my desk by fourteen hundred." He flicked a last glance at Dallas. "You're dismissed."

She walked out, surprised that her legs felt like glass: the thin, fragile kind that could be shattered with a careless brush of the hand.

"He was out of line, Dallas," Feeney said, catching at her arm. "He's hurting, and he took a bad shot at you."

"Not so bad." Her voice was rough and raw. "Compassion's not my strong suit, is it? I don't know shit about family ties and loyalties, do I?"

Uncomfortable, Feeney shifted his feet. "Come on, Dallas, you don't want to take it personal."

"Don't I? He's stood behind me plenty of times. Now he's asking me to stand behind him, and I have to say sorry, no chance. That's pretty fucking personal, Feeney." She shook off his hand. "Let's take a rain check on the drinks. I'm not feeling sociable."

At a loss, Feeney dumped his hands in his pockets. Eve strode off in one direction, the commander remained behind closed doors in the other. Feeney stood unhappily between them.

Eve supervised the search of Marco Angelini's brownstone personally. She wasn't needed there. The sweepers knew their job, and their equipment was as good as the budget allowed. Still, she sprayed her hands, coated her boots, and moved through the three-story home looking for anything that would tie up the case, or, thinking of Whitney's face, break it.

Marco Angelini remained on the premises. That was his right as owner of the property, and as the father of the prime suspect. Eve blocked out his presence, the cold azure eyes that followed her moves, the haggard look to his face, the quick muscle twitch in his jaw.

One of the sweepers did a thorough check of David's wardrobe with a porta-sensor, looking for bloodstains. While he worked, Eve meticulously searched the rest of the room.

"Coulda ditched the weapon," the sweeper commented. He was an old, buck-toothed vet nicknamed Beaver. He traced the sensor, the arm of it wrapped over his left shoulder, down a thousand-dollar sport coat.

"He used the same one on all three women," Eve answered, speaking more to herself than Beaver. "The lab confirms it. Why would he ditch it now?"

"Maybe he was done." The sensor switched from its muted hum to a quick beep. "Just a little salad oil," Beaver announced. "Extra virgin olive. Spotted his pretty tie. Maybe he was done," Beaver said again.

He admired detectives, had once had ambitions to become one. The closest he'd managed to get was as a field tech. But he read every detective story available on disc.

"See, three's like a magic number. An important number." His eyes sharpened behind his tinted glasses as the treated lenses picked up a minute spot of talc on a cuff. He moved on, warming to the theme. "So this guy, see, he fixes on three women, women he knows, sees all the time on the screen. Maybe he's hot for them."

"The first victim was his mother."

"Hey." Beaver paused long enough to swivel a look toward Eve. "You never heard of Oedipus? That Greek guy, you know, had the hots for his mama. Anyhow, he does the three, then ditches the weapon and the clothes he was wearing when he did them. This guy's got enough clothes for six people, anyway."

Frowning, Eve walked over to the spacious closet, scanned the automatic racks, the motorized shelves. "He doesn't even live here."

"Dude's rich, right?" To Beaver that explained everything. "He's got a couple suits in here ain't never been worn. Shoes, too." He reached down, picked up one of a pair of leather half boots, turned them over. "Nothing, see?" He skimmed the sensor over the unscuffed bottom. "No dirt, no dust, no sidewalk scrapes, no fibers."

"That only makes him guilty of self-indulgence. Goddamn it, Beaver, get me some blood."

"I'm working on it. Probably tossed what he was wearing, though."

"You're a real optimist, Beaver."

In disgust, she turned toward a U-shaped lacquered desk and began to rifle through the drawers. The discs she would bag and run through her own computer. They could get lucky and find some correspondence between David Angelini and his mother or Metcalf. Or luckier yet, she mused, and find some rambling confessional diary that described the murders.

Where the hell had he put the umbrella? she wondered. *The shoe?* She wondered if the sweepers in N.L.A. or the ones in Europe were having any better luck. The thought of backtracking and searching all the cozy little homes and luxury hideaways of David Angelini was giving her a bad case of indigestion.

Then she found the knife.

It was so simple. Open the middle drawer of the work console, and there it was. Long, slim, and lethal. It had a fancy handle, carved out of what might have been genuine ivory, which would have made it an antique—or an international crime. Harvesting ivory, or purchasing it in any form had been outlawed planetwide for more than half a century after the near extinction of African elephants.

Eve wasn't an antique buff, nor was she an expert on environmental crime, but she'd studied forensics enough to know that the shape and length of the blade were right.

"Well, well." Her indigestion was gone, like a bad guest. In its place was the clear, clean high of success. "Maybe three wasn't his magic number after all."

"He kept it? Son of a bitch." Disappointed in the foolishness of a murderer, Beaver shook his head. "Guy's an idiot."

"Scan it," she ordered, crossing to him.

Beaver shifted the bulk of the scanner, changed the program from clothing. After a quick adjustment of his lenses, he ran the funnel of the arm up the knife. The scanner beeped helpfully.

"Got some shit on it," Beaver muttered, his thick fingertips playing over controls like a concert pianist's over keys.

"Fiber—maybe paper. Some kind of adhesive. Prints on the handle. Want a hard copy of 'em?"

"Yeah."

"'Kay." The scanner spit out a square of paper dotted with fingerprints. "Turn her over. And bingo. There's your blood. Not much of it." He frowned, skimming the funnel along the edge of the blade. "Going to be lucky if it's enough for typing, much less DNA."

"You keep that positive outlook, Beaver. How old's the blood?"

"Come on, Lieutenant." Behind the sensor lenses, his eyes were huge and cynical. "You know I can't give you that from one of the portables. Gotta take it in. All this little girl does is identify. No skin," he announced. "Be better if you had some skin."

"I'll take the blood." As she sealed the knife into evidence, a movement caught her eyes. She looked up and into the dark, damning eyes of Marco Angelini.

He glanced down at the knife, then back into her face. Something moved across his, something wrenching that had the muscle jerking in his jaw.

"I'd like a moment of your time, Lieutenant Dallas."

"I can't give you much more than that."

"It won't take long." His eyes flicked to Beaver, then back to the knife as Dallas slipped it into her bag. "In private, please."

"All right." She nodded to the uniform who stood at Angelini's shoulder. "Tell one of the team to come up and finish the hands-on search in here," she ordered Beaver, then followed Angelini out of the room.

He turned toward a set of narrow, carpeted steps, his hand trailing along a glossy banister as he climbed. At the top, he shifted right and stepped into a room.

An office, Eve discovered. Sunwashed now in the brilliant afternoon. Light beamed and glinted off the surfaces of communication equipment, struck and bounced from the smooth semi-circular console of sober black, flashed and pooled on the surface of the gleaming floor.

As if annoyed with the strength of the sunlight, Angelini hit a switch that had the windows tinted to a soft amber. Now the room had shadows around pale gold edges.

Angelini walked directly to a wall unit and ordered a bourbon on the rocks. He held the square glass in his hand, took one careful sip.

"You believe my son murdered his mother and two other women."

"Your son has been questioned on those charges, Mr. Angelini. He is a suspect. If you have any questions about the procedure, you should speak with his counsel."

"I've spoken with them." He took another sip. "They believe there's a good chance you will charge him, but that he won't be indicted."

"That's up to the grand jury."

"But you think he will."

"Mr. Angelini, if and when I have arrested your son and charged him with three counts of first-degree murder, it will be because I believe he will be indicted, tried, and convicted on those charges, and that I have the evidence to ensure that conviction."

He looked at her field bag where she'd put some of that evidence. "I've done some research on you, Lieutenant Dallas."

"Have you?"

"I like to know the odds," he said with a humorless smile that came and went in a blink. "Commander Whitney respects you. And I respect him. My former wife admired your tenacity and your thoroughness, and she was not a fool. She spoke of you, did you know that?"

"No, I didn't."

"She was impressed by your mind. A clean cop's mind she called it. You're good at your job, aren't you, Lieutenant?"

"Yeah, I'm good at it."

"But you make mistakes."

"I try to keep them to a minimum."

"A mistake in your profession, however minimal, can

cause incredible pain to the innocent." His eyes stayed on hers, relentlessly. "You found a knife in my son's room."

"I can't discuss that with you."

"He rarely uses this house," Angelini said carefully. "Three or four times a year perhaps. He prefers the Long Island estate when he's in the area."

"That may be, Mr. Angelini, but he used this house on the night Louise Kirski was killed." Impatient now, eager to get the evidence to the lab, Eve moved a shoulder. "Mr. Angelini, I can't debate the state's case with you—"

"But you're very confident that the state has a good case," he interrupted. When she didn't answer, he took another long study of her face. Then he finished the drink in one swallow, set the glass aside. "But you're wrong, Lieutenant. You've got the wrong man."

"You believe in your son's innocence, Mr. Angelini. I understand that."

"Not believe, Lieutenant, know. My son didn't kill those women." He took a breath, like a diver about to plunge under the surface. "I did."

chapter fifteen

Eve had no choice. She took him in and grilled him. After a full hour, she had a vicious headache and the calm, unshakable statement from Marco Angelini that he had killed three women.

He refused counsel, and refused to or was unable to elaborate.

Each time Eve asked him why he had killed, he stared straight into her eyes and claimed it had been impulse. He'd been annoyed with his wife, he stated. Personally embarrassed by her continued intimacy with a business partner. He'd killed her because he couldn't have her back. Then he'd gotten a taste for it.

It was all very simple, and to Eve's mind, very rehearsed. She could picture him repeating and refining the lines in his head before he spoke them.

"This is bullshit," she said abruptly and pushed back from the conference table. "You didn't kill anybody."

"I say I did." His voice was eerily calm. "You have my confession on record."

"Then tell me again." Leaning forward, she slapped her hands on the table. "Why did you ask your wife to meet you at the Five Moons?"

"I wanted it to happen somewhere out of our milieu. I thought I could get away with it, you see. I told her there was trouble with Randy. She didn't know the full problem of his gambling. I did. So, of course, she came."

"And you slit her throat."

"Yes." His skin whitened slightly. "It was very quick."

"What did you do then?"

"I went home."

"How?"

He blinked. "I drove. I'd parked my car a couple of blocks away."

"What about the blood?" She peered into his eyes, watching his pupils. "There'd have been a lot of it. She'd have gushed all over you."

The pupils dilated, but his voice remained steady. "I was wearing a top coat, rain resistant. I discarded it along the way." He smiled a little. "I imagine some itinerant found it and made use of it."

"What did you take from the scene?"

"The knife, of course."

"Nothing of hers?" She waited a beat. "Nothing to make it look like a robbery, a mugging?"

He hesitated. She could almost see his mind working behind his eyes. "I was shaken. I hadn't expected it to be so unpleasant. I had planned to take her bag, the jewelry, but I forgot, and just ran."

"You ran, taking nothing, but were smart enough to ditch your blood-splattered coat."

"That's right."

"Then you went after Metcalf."

"She was an impulse. I kept dreaming about what it had been like, and I wanted to do it again. She was easy." His breathing leveled and his hands lay still on the table. "She was ambitious and rather naive. I knew David had written a screenplay with her in mind. He was determined to complete this entertainment project—it was something we disagreed over. It annoyed me, and it would have cost the company resources that are, at the moment, a bit strained. I decided to kill her, and I contacted her. Of course she agreed to meet me."

"What was she wearing?"

"Wearing?" He fumbled for a moment. "I didn't pay attention. It wasn't important. She smiled, held out both of her hands as I walked toward her. And I did it."

"Why are you coming forward now?"

"As I said, I thought I could get away with it. Perhaps I could have. I never expected my son to be arrested in my place."

"So, you're protecting him?"

"I killed them, Lieutenant. What more do you want?"

"Why did you leave the knife in his drawer, in his room?"

His eyes slid away, slid back. "As I said, he rarely stays there. I thought it was safe. Then I was contacted about the search warrant. I didn't have time to remove it."

"You expect me to buy this? You think you're helping him by clouding the case, by coming forward with this lame confession. You think he's guilty." She lowered her voice, bit off each word. "You're so terrified that your son is a murderer that you're willing to take the rap rather than see him face the consequences. Are you going to let another woman die, Angelini? Or two, or three before you swallow reality?"

His lips trembled once, then firmed. "I've given you my statement."

"You've given me bullshit." Turning on her heel, Eve left the room. Struggling to calm herself, she stood outside, watched with a jaundiced eye as Angelini pressed his face into his hands.

She could break him, eventually. But there was always a chance that word would leak and the media would scream that there was a confession from someone other than the prime.

She looked over at the sound of footsteps, and her body stiffened like steel. "Commander."

"Lieutenant. Progress?"

"He's sticking to his story. It's got holes you could drive a shuttle through. I've given him the opening to bring up the souvenirs from the first two hits. He didn't bite."

"I'd like to talk to him. Privately, Lieutenant, and off the record." Before she could speak, he held up a hand. "I realize it's not procedure. I'm asking you for a favor."

"And if he incriminates himself or his son?"

Whitney's jaw tightened. "I'm still a cop, Dallas. God-damn it."

"Yes, sir." She unlocked the door, then after only a faint hesitation, darkened the two-way glass and shut off audio. "I'll be in my office."

"Thank you." He stepped inside. He gave her one last look before shutting the door and turning to the man slumped at the table. "Marco," Whitney said on a long sigh. "What the fuck do you think you're doing?"

"Jack." Marco offered a thin smile. "I wondered if you'd be along. We never did make that golf date."

"Talk to me." Whitney sat down heavily.

"Hasn't your efficient and dogged lieutenant filled you in?"

"The recorder's off," Whitney said sharply. "We're alone. Talk to me, Marco. We both know you didn't kill Cicely or anyone else."

For a moment, Marco stared up at the ceiling, as if pondering. "People never know each other as well as they believe. Not even the people they care for. I loved her, Jack. I never stopped loving her. But she stopped loving me. Part of me was always waiting for her to start loving me again. But she never would have."

"Damn it, Marco, do you expect me to believe that you slit her throat because she divorced you twelve years ago?"

"Maybe I thought she might have married Hammett. He

wanted that," Marco said quietly. "I could see that he wanted that. Cicely was reluctant." His voice remained calm, quiet, faintly nostalgic. "She enjoyed her independence, but she was sorry to disappoint Hammett. Sorry enough that she might have given in eventually. Married him. It would have really been over then, wouldn't it?"

"You killed Cicely because she might have married another man?"

"She was my wife, Jack. Whatever the courts and the Church said."

Whitney sat a moment, silent. "I've played poker with you too many times over the years, Marco. You've got tells." Folding his arms on the table, he leaned forward. "When you bluff, you tap your finger on your knee."

The finger stopped tapping. "This is a long way from poker, Jack."

"You can't help David this way. You've got to let the system work."

"David and I . . . there's been a lot of friction between us in the last several months. Business disagreements and personal ones." For the first time he sighed, deep and long and wearily. "There shouldn't be distance between father and son over such foolishness."

"This is hardly the way to mend fences, Marco."

The steel came back into Angelini's eyes. There would be no more sighs. "Let me ask you something, Jack, just between us. If it was one of yours, and there was the slightest chance—just the slightest—that they'd be convicted of murder, would anything stop you from protecting them?"

"You can't protect David by stepping in with some bullshit confession."

"Who said it was bullshit?" The word sounded like cream in Angelini's cultured voice. "I did it, and I'm confessing because I can't live with myself if my own child pays for my crime. Now tell me, Jack, would you stand behind your son, or in front of him?"

"Ah, hell, Marco," was all Whitney could say.

He stayed for twenty minutes, but got nothing more. For

a time he guided the conversation into casual lines, golf scores, the standings of the baseball team Marco had a piece of. Then, quick and sleek as a snake, he'd toss out a hard, leading question on the murders.

But Marco Angelini was an expert negotiator, and had already given his bottom line. He wouldn't budge.

Guilt, grief, and the beginnings of real fear made an unsettling stew in Whitney's stomach as he stepped into Eve's office. She was hunched over her computer, scanning data, calling up more.

For the first time in days, his eyes cleared of their own fatigue and saw hers. She was pale, her eyes shadowed, her mouth grim. Her hair stood up in spikes as if she'd dragged her hands through it countless times. Even as he watched, she did so again, then pressed her fingers to her eyes as if they burned.

He remembered the morning in his office, the morning after Cicely had been murdered. And the responsibility he'd hung around Eve's neck.

"Lieutenant."

Her shoulders straightened as if she'd slammed steel poles into them. Her head came up, her eyes carefully blank.

"Commander." She got to her feet. *Got to attention,* Whitney thought, annoyed by the stiff and impersonal formality.

"Marco's in holding. We can keep him for forty-eight hours without charging him. I thought it best to let him think behind bars for a while. He still refuses counsel."

Whitney stepped in while she stood there, and he looked around. He wasn't often in this sector of the complex. His officers came to him. Another weight of command.

She could have had a bigger office. She'd earned one. But she seemed to prefer to work in a room so small that if three people crowded into it, they'd be in sin.

"Good thing you're not claustrophobic," he commented. She gave no response, didn't so much as twitch an eyebrow. Whitney muttered an oath. "Listen, Dallas—"

"Sir." Her interruption was fast and brittle. "Forensics has the weapon retrieved from David Angelini's room. I'm informed that there will be some delay on the results as the blood traces detected by the sweeper are of an amount borderline for typing and DNA."

"So noted, Lieutenant."

"The fingerprints on the weapon in evidence have been matched to those of David Angelini. My report—"

"We'll get to your report momentarily."

Her chin jutted up. "Yes, sir."

"Goddamn it, Dallas, yank that stick out of your butt and sit down."

"Is that an order, Commander?"

"Ah, hell," he began.

Mirina Angelini burst through the doorway in a clatter of high heels and a crackle of silk. "Why are you trying to destroy my family?" she demanded, shaking off the restraining hand of Slade who had come in behind her.

"Mirina, this isn't going to help."

She jerked away and crowded into Eve. "Isn't it enough that my mother was murdered on the street? Murdered because American cops are too busy chasing shadows and filling out useless reports to protect the innocent?"

"Mirina," Whitney said, "come on to my office. We'll talk."

"Talk?" She turned on him like a cat, gold and sleek, teeth bared for blood. "How can I talk to you? I trusted you. I thought you cared about me, about David, about all of us. You've let her lock David in a cell. And now my father."

"Mirina, Marco came in voluntarily. We'll talk about this. I'll explain it all to you."

"There's nothing to explain." She turned her back on him and aimed her scorching fury at Eve. "I went to my father's house. He wanted me to stay in Rome, but I couldn't. Not when every report in the media is smearing my brother's name. When we arrived, a neighbor was more than happy, even gleeful, to tell me that my father had been taken away by the police."

"I can arrange for you to speak with your father, Ms. Angelini," Eve said coolly. "And your brother."

"You're damn right you'll arrange it. And now. Where is my father?" She used both hands to shove Eve back a pace before Whitney or Slade could stop her. "What have you done with him, you bitch!"

"You want to keep your hands off me," Eve warned. "I've just about had my fill of Angelinis. Your father's in holding, here. Your brother's in the tower at Riker's. You can see your father now. If you want to see your brother, you'll be shuttled over." Her gaze flicked to Whitney, and stung. "Or since you've got some pull around here, you can probably have him transported to Visitation for an hour."

"I know what you're doing." This was no fragile flower now. Mirina fairly vibrated with power. "You need a scapegoat. You need an arrest so that the media will get out of your face. You're playing politics, using my brother, even my murdered mother, so that you won't lose your job."

"Yeah, some cushy job." She smiled sourly. "I toss innocent people in a cage every day so I can keep all the benefits."

"It keeps your face on the screen, doesn't it?" Mirina tossed her glorious hair. "How much publicity have you traded over my mother's dead body?"

"That's enough, Mirina." Whitney's voice lashed like a whip, in one vicious snap. "Go to my office and wait." He looked over her shoulder at Slade. "Take her out of here."

"Mirina, this is useless," Slade murmured, trying to tuck her under his arm. "Let's go now."

"Don't hold me." She bit off each word as if they were stringy meat, then shrugged away from him. "I'll go. But you're going to pay for the grief you've brought my family, Lieutenant. You're going to pay for every bit of it."

She stalked out, giving Slade time for only a muttered apology before he followed after her.

Whitney stepped quietly into the silence. "You okay?"

"I've dealt with worse." Eve jerked a shoulder. Inside she was sick with anger and guilt. Sick enough that she wanted badly to be alone behind closed doors. "If you'll excuse me, Commander, I want to finish going over this report."

"Dallas—Eve." It was the weariness in his tone that had her gaze lifting warily to his. "Mirina's upset, understandably so. But she was out of line, way out of line."

"She was entitled to a couple of shots at me." Because she wanted to press her hands to her throbbing head, she tucked them negligently into her pockets. "I've just put what's left of her family in a cage. Who else is she going to be pissed at? I can take it." Her gaze remained cool, steely. "Feelings aren't my strong suit."

He nodded slowly. "I had that coming. I put you on this case, Dallas, because you're the best I've got. Your mind's good, your gut's good. And you care. You care about the victim." Letting out a long breath, he dragged a hand over his hair. "I was off base this morning, Dallas, in my office. I've been off base a number of times with you since this whole mess began. I apologize for it."

"It doesn't matter."

"I wish it didn't." He searched her face, saw the stiff restraint. "But I see it does. I'll take care of Mirina, arrange the visitations."

"Yes, sir. I'd like to continue my interview with Marco Angelini."

"Tomorrow," Whitney said and set his teeth when she didn't quite mask the sneer. "You're tired, Lieutenant, and tired cops make mistakes and miss details. You'll pick it up tomorrow." He headed for the door, swore again, and stopped without looking back at her. "Get some sleep, and for Christ's sake, take a painkiller for that headache. You look like hell."

She resisted slamming the door after him. Resisted because it would be petty and unprofessional. But she sat down, stared at the screen, and pretended her head wasn't shuddering with pain.

When a shadow fell over her desk moments later, she looked up, eyes fired for battle.

"Well," Roarke said mildly and leaned over to kiss her snarling mouth. "That's quite a welcome." He patted his chest. "Am I bleeding?"

"Ha-ha."

"There's that sparkling wit I missed." He sat on the edge of the desk where he could look at her and catch a glimpse of the data on the screen to see if that was what had put the miserable anger in her eyes. "Well, Lieutenant, and how was your day?"

"Let's see. I booked my superior's favorite godson on obstruction and other assorted charges, found what may be the murder weapon in his console drawer in the family town house, took a confession from the prime suspect's father, who claims he did it, and just took a couple of shots between the eyes from the sister, who thinks I'm a media grabbing bitch." She tried on a small smile. "Other than that, it's been pretty quiet. How about you?"

"Fortunes won, fortunes lost," he said mildly, worried about her. "Nothing nearly as exciting as police work."

"I wasn't sure you were coming back tonight."

"Neither was I. The construction on the resort's moving ahead well enough. I should be able to handle things from here for a time."

She tried not to be so relieved. It irritated her that in a few short months she'd gotten so used to his being there. Even dependent upon it. "That's good, I guess."

"Mmm." He read her well. "What can you tell me about the case?"

"It's all over the media. Pick a channel."

"I'd rather hear it from you."

She brought him up to date in much the way she would file a report: in quick, efficient terms, heavy on facts, light on personal comments. And, she discovered, she felt better for it afterward. Roarke had a way of listening that made her hear herself more clearly.

"You believe it's the younger Angelini."

"We've got means and opportunity, and a good handle on motive. If the knife matches . . . Anyway, I'll be meeting with Dr. Mira tomorrow to discuss his psych testing."

"And Marco," Roarke continued. "What do you think of his confession?"

"It's a handy way to confuse things, tie up the investigation. He's a clever man, and he'll find a way to leak it to the media." She scowled over Roarke's shoulder. "It'll jerk everything around for a while, cost us some time and trouble. But we'll smooth it out."

"You think he confessed to the murders to complicate the investigation?"

"That's right." She shifted her gaze to his, lifted a brow. "You've got another theory."

"The drowning child," Roarke murmured. "The father believes his son is about to go under for the third time, jumps into the torrent. His life for his child's. Love, Eve." He cupped her chin in his hand. "Love stops at nothing. Marco believes his son is guilty, and would rather sacrifice himself than see his child pay the price."

"If he knows, or even believes, that David killed those women, it would be insane to protect him."

"No, it would be love. There's probably none stronger than a parent's for a child. You and I don't have any experience with that, but it exists."

She shook her head. "Even when the child's defective?"

"Perhaps especially then. When I was a boy in Dublin, there was a woman whose daughter had lost an arm in an accident. There was no money for a replacement. She had five children, and loved them all. But four were whole, and one was damaged. She built a shield around that girl, to protect her from the stares and the whispers and the pity. It was the damaged child she pushed to excel, who they all devoted themselves to. The others didn't need her as much, you see, as the one who was flawed."

"There's a difference between a physical defect and a mental one," Eve insisted.

"I wonder if there is, to a parent."

"Whatever Marco Angelini's motive, we'll cut through to the truth in the end."

"No doubt you will. When's your shift over?"

"What?"

"Your shift," he repeated. "When is it over?"

She glanced at the screen, noted the time in the bottom corner. "About an hour ago."

"Good." He rose and held out a hand. "Come with me."

"Roarke, there are some things I should tie up here. I want to review the interview with Marco Angelini. I may find a hole."

He was patient because he had no doubt he'd have his own way. "Eve, you're so tired you wouldn't see a hundred-meter hole until you'd fallen into it." Determined, he took her hand and pulled her to her feet. "Come with me."

"All right, maybe I could use a break." Grumbling a bit, she ordered her computer off and locked. "I'm going to have to goose the techs at the lab. They're taking forever on the knife." Her hand felt good in his. She didn't even worry about the ribbing she'd take from the other cops who might see them in the hall or elevator. "Where are we going?"

He brought their linked hands to his lips and smiled at her over them. "I haven't decided."

He opted for Mexico. It was a quick, easy flight, and his villa there on the turbulent west coast was always prepared. Unlike his home in New York, he kept it fully automated, calling in domestics only for lengthy stays.

In Roarke's mind, droids and computers were convenient but impersonal. For the purposes of this visit, however, he was content to rely on them. He wanted Eve alone, he wanted her relaxed, and he wanted her happy.

"Jesus, Roarke."

She took one look at the towering, multilayered building on the brink of a cliff and goggled. It looked like a extension of the rock, as if the sheer glass walls had been polished from it. Gardens tumbled over terraces in vivid colors, shapes, and fragrances.

Above, the deepening sky was devoid of any traffic. Just blue, the swirl of white clouds, the flashing wings of birds. It looked like another world.

She'd slept like a stone on the plane, barely surfacing when the pilot had executed a snazzy drop landing that had placed them neatly at the foot of zigzagging stone steps that climbed the towering cliff. She was groggy enough to reach up to be certain he hadn't slipped VR goggles on her while she'd slept.

"Where are we?"

"Mexico," he said simply.

"Mexico?" Stunned, she tried to rub the sleep and the shock from her eyes. Roarke thought, with affection, that she looked like a cranky child awakened from a nap. "But I can't be in Mexico. I have to—"

"Ride or walk?" he asked, pulling her along like a stubborn puppy.

"I have to—"

"Ride," he decided. "You're still groggy."

She could enjoy the climb later, he thought, and its many views of sea and cliffs. Instead, he nudged her into a sleek little air cart, taking the controls himself and shooting them up to vertical with a speed that knocked the rest of sleep out of her system.

"Christ, not so fast." Her instinct for survival had her clutching the side, wincing as rocks, flowers, and water whizzed by. He was roaring with laughter when he slipped the little cart into place at the front patio.

"Awake now, darling?"

She had her breath back, barely. "I'm going to kill you as soon as I make sure all my internal organs are in place. What the hell are we doing in Mexico?"

"Taking a break. I need one." He stepped out of the cart and came around to her side. "There's no doubt you do." Since she was still holding onto the side, knuckles white, he reached in, plucked her up, and carried her over the irregularly shaped stones toward the door.

"Cut it out. I can walk."

"Stop complaining." He turned his head, expertly finding her mouth, deepening the kiss until her hand stopped pushing at his shoulder and began to knead it.

"Damn it," she murmured. "How come you can always do that to me?"

"Just lucky, I guess. Roarke, disengage," he said, and the decorative bars across the entrance slid apart. Behind them, doors ornate with carving and etched glass clicked open and swung back in welcome. He stepped inside. "Secure," he ordered, and the doors efficiently closed while Eve stared.

One wall of the entrance level was glass, and through it she could see the ocean. She'd never seen the Pacific, and she wondered now how it had earned its serene name when it looked so alive, so ready to boil.

They were in time for sunset, and as she watched, speechless, the sky exploded and shimmered with bolts and streams of wild color. And the fat red globe of the sun sank slowly, inevitably, toward the blue line of water.

"You'll like it here," he murmured.

She was staggered by the beauty of an ending day. It seemed that nature had waited for her, held the show. "It's wonderful. I can't stay."

"A few hours." He pressed a kiss to her temple. "Just overnight for now. We'll come back and spend a few days when we have more time."

Still carrying her, he walked closer to the glass wall until it seemed to Eve that the entire world was made of frantic color and shifting shapes.

"I love you, Eve."

She looked away from the sun, the ocean, and into his eyes. And it was wonderful, and for the moment, it was simple. "I missed you." She pressed her cheek to his and held him tightly. "I really missed you. I wore one of your shirts." She could laugh at herself now because he was here. She could smell him, touch him. "I actually went into your closet and stole one of your shirts—one of the black silk ones you have dozens of. I put it on, then snuck out of the house like a thief so Summerset wouldn't catch me."

Absurdly touched, he nuzzled her neck. "At night, I'd play your transmissions over, just so I could look at you, hear your voice."

"Really?" She giggled, a rare sound from her. "God, Roarke, we've gotten so sappy."

"We'll keep it our little secret."

"Deal." She leaned back to look at his face. "I have to ask you something. It's so lame, but I have to."

"What?"

"Was it ever . . ." She winced, wished she could muffle the need to ask. "Before, with anyone else—"

"No." He touched his lips to her brow, her nose, the dip in her chin. "It was never, with no one else."

"Not for me, either." She simply breathed him in. "Put your hands on me. I want your hands on me."

"I can do that."

He did, tumbling with her to a spread of floor cushions while the sun died brilliantly in the ocean.

chapter sixteen

Taking a break with Roarke wasn't quite like stopping off at the deli for a quick veggie hash salad and soy coffee. She wasn't sure how he managed it all, but then, great quantities of money talk, and talk big.

They dined on succulent grilled lobster, drenched in real, creamy, rich butter. They sipped champagne so cold it frosted Eve's throat. A symphony of fruit was there for the sampling, exotic hybrids that sprinkled harmonized flavors on the tongue.

Long before she could admit that she loved him, Eve had accepted the fact that she was addicted to the food he could summon up with the flick of a wrist.

She soaked naked in a small whirling lagoon cupped under palm trees and moonlight, her muscles slack from the heated water and thorough sex. She listened to the song of night birds—no simulation, but the real thing—that hung on the fragrant air like tears.

For now, for one night, the pressures of the job were light-years away.

He could do that to her, and for her, she realized. He could open little pockets of peace.

Roarke watched her, pleased at the way the tension had melted from her face with a bit of pampering. He loved seeing her this way, unwound, limp with pleasuring her senses, too lax to remember to be guilty for indulging herself. Just as he loved seeing her revved, her mind racing, her body braced for action.

No, it had never been like this for him before, with anyone. Of all the women he'd known, she was the only one he was compelled to be with, driven to touch. Beyond the physical, the basic and apparently unsatiable lust she inspired in him, was a constant fascination. Her mind, her heart, her secrets, her scars.

He had told her once they were two lost souls. He thought now he'd spoken no more than the truth. But with each other, they'd found something that rooted them.

For a man who had been wary of cops all of his life, it was staggering to know his happiness now depended on one.

Amused at himself, he slipped into the water with her. Eve managed to drum up enough energy to open her eyes to slits.

"I don't think I can move."

"Then don't." He handed her another flute of champagne, wrapping her fingers around the stem.

"I'm too relaxed to be drunk." But she managed to find her mouth with the glass. "It's such a weird life. Yours," she elaborated. "I mean you can have anything you want, go anywhere, do anything. You want to take a night off, you zip over to Mexico and nibble on lobster and—what was that stuff again, the stuff you spread on crackers?"

"Goose liver."

She winced and shuddered. "That's not what you called it when you shoved it in my mouth. It sounded nicer."

"Foie gras. Same thing."

"That's better." She shifted her legs, tangled them with

his. "Anyway, most people program a video or take a quick trip with their VR goggles, maybe plug a few credits into a simulation booth down at Times Square. But you do the real thing."

"I prefer the real thing."

"I know. That's another odd piece of you. You like old stuff. You'd rather read a book than scan a disc, rather go to the trouble to come out here when you could have programmed a simulation in your holoroom." Her lips curved a little, dreamily. "I like that about you."

"That's handy."

"When you were a kid, and things were bad for you, is this what you dreamed about?"

"I dreamed about surviving, getting out. Having control. Didn't you?"

"I guess I did." Too many of her dreams were jumbled and dark. "After I was in the system, anyway. Then what I wanted most was to be a cop. A good cop. A smart cop. What did you want?"

"To be rich. Not to be hungry."

"We both got what we wanted, more or less."

"You had nightmares while I was gone."

She didn't have to open her eyes to see the concern in his. She could hear it in his voice. "They aren't too bad. They're just more regular."

"Eve, if you'd work with Doctor Mira—"

"I'm not ready to remember it. Not all of it. Do you ever feel the scars, from what your father did to you?"

Restless with the memories, he shifted and sank deeper in the hot, frothy water. "A few beatings, careless cruelty. Why should it matter now?"

"You shrug it off." Now she opened her eyes, looked at him, saw he was brooding. "But it made you, didn't it? What happened then made you."

"I suppose it did, roughly."

She nodded, tried to speak casually. "Roarke, do you think if some people lack something, and that lack lets them brutalize their kids—the way we were—do you think it passes on? Do you think—"

"No."

"But—"

"No." He cupped a hand over her calf and squeezed. "We make ourselves, in the long run. You and I did. If that wasn't true, I'd be drunk in some Dublin slum, looking for something weaker to pummel. And you, Eve, would be cold and brittle and without pity."

She closed her eyes again. "Sometimes I am."

"No, that you never are. You're strong, and you're moral, and sometimes you make yourself ill with compassion for the innocent."

Her eyes stung behind her closed lids. "Someone I admire and respect asked me for help, asked me for a favor. I turned him down flat. What does that make me?"

"A woman who had a choice to make."

"Roarke, the last woman who was killed. Louise Kirski. That's on my head. She was twenty-four, talented, eager, in love with a second-rate musician. She had a cluttered one-room apartment on West Twenty-sixth and liked Chinese food. She had a family in Texas that will never be the same. She was innocent, Roarke, and she's haunting me."

Relieved, Eve let out a long breath. "I haven't been able to tell anyone that. I wasn't sure I could say it out loud."

"I'm glad you could say it to me. Now, listen." He set his glass down, scooted forward to take her face in his hands. Her skin was soft, her eyes a narrow slant of dark amber. "Fate rules, Eve. You follow the steps, and you plan and you work, then fate slips in laughing and makes fools of us. Sometimes we can trick it or outguess it, but most often it's already written. For some, it's written in blood. That doesn't mean we stop, but it does mean we can't always comfort ourselves with blame."

"Is that what you think I'm doing? Comforting myself?"

"It's easier to take the blame than it is to admit there was nothing you could do to stop what happened. You're an arrogant woman, Eve. Just one more aspect of you that I find attractive. It's arrogant to assume responsibility for events beyond our control."

"I should have controlled it."

"Ah, yes." He smiled. "Of course."

"It's not arrogance," she insisted, miffed. "It's my job."

"You taunted him, assuming he'd come after you." Because the thought of that still twisted in his gut like hissing snakes, Roarke tightened his grip on her face. "Now you're insulted, annoyed that he didn't follow your rules."

"That's a hideous thing to say. Goddamn you, I don't—" She broke off, sucked in her breath. "You're pissing me off so I'll stop feeling sorry for myself."

"It seems to have worked."

"All right." She let her eyes close again. "All right. I'm not going to think about it anymore right now. Maybe by tomorrow I'll have a better shot at sorting it out. You're pretty good, Roarke," she said with a ghost of a smile.

"Thousands concur," he murmured and caught her nipple lightly between his thumb and forefinger.

The ripple effect made it all the way down to her toes. "That's not what I meant."

"It's what I meant." He tugged gently, listened to her breath catch.

"Maybe if I can manage to crawl out of here, I can take you up on your interesting offer."

"Just relax." Watching her face, he slid his hand between her legs, cupped her. "Let me." He managed to catch her glass as it slipped from her hand, and he set it aside. "Let me have you, Eve."

Before she could answer, he shot her to a fast, wracking orgasm. Her hips arched up, pumped against his busy hand, then went lax.

She wouldn't think now, he knew. She would be wrapped in layered sensations. She never seemed to expect it. And her surprise, her sweet and naive response was, as always, murderously arousing. He could have pleasured her endlessly, for the simple delight of watching her absorb every touch, every jolt.

So he indulged himself, exploring that long, lean body, suckling the small, hot breasts, wet with perfumed water, gulping in the rapid breath that gasped from her lips.

She felt drugged, helpless, her mind and body burdened with pleasure. Part of her was shocked, or tried to be. Not so much at what she let him do, but at the fact that she allowed him complete and total control of her. She couldn't have stopped him, wouldn't have, even when he held her near to screaming on the edge before shoving her over into another shuddering climax.

"Again." Greedy, he dragged her head back by the hair and stabbed his fingers inside her, worked her ruthlessly until her hands splashed bonelessly in the water. "I'm all there is tonight. We're all there is." He savaged her throat on the way to her mouth, and his eyes were like fierce blue suns. "Tell me you love me. Say it."

"I do. I do love you." A moan ripped from her throat when he plunged himself into her, jerked her hips high, and plunged deeper.

"Tell me again." He felt her muscles squeeze him like a fist and gritted his teeth to keep from exploding. "Tell me again."

"I love you." Trembling from it, she wrapped her legs around him and let him batter her past delirium.

She did have to crawl out of the pool. Her head was spinning, her body limp. "I don't have any bones left."

Roarke chuckled and gave her a friendly slap on the butt. "I'm not carrying you this time, darling. We'd both end up on our faces."

"Maybe I'll just lie down right here." It was a struggle to remain on her hands and knees on the smooth tiles.

"You'll get cold." With an effort, he summoned the strength to drag her to her feet where they rocked together like drunks.

She began to snicker, teetering. "What the hell did you do to me? I feel like I've downed a couple of Freebirds."

He managed to grip her waist. "Since when did you play with illegals?"

"Standard police training." She bit experimentally at her bottom lip and found that it was, indeed, numb. "We have to take a course in illegals at the academy. I palmed most of mine and flushed them. Is your head spinning?"

"I'll let you know when I regain feeling above the waist." He tipped her head back and kissed her lightly. "Why don't we see if we can make it inside. We can . . ." He trailed off, eyes narrowing over her shoulder.

She might have been impaired, but she was still a cop. Instinctively, she whirled and braced, unconsciously shielding his body with hers. "What? What is it?"

"Nothing." He cleared his throat, patted her shoulder. "Nothing," he repeated. "Go on in, I'll be right along."

"What?" She stood her ground, scanning for trouble.

"It's nothing, really. I just . . . I neglected to disengage the security camera. It's, ah, activated by motion or voice." Naked, he strode over toward a low stone wall, flicked a switch and palmed a disc.

"Camera." Eve held up a finger. "There was a recording on the entire time we've been out here?" She flicked a narrow-eyed stare at the lagoon. "The entire time."

"Which is why I generally prefer people to automations."

"We're on there? All on there?"

"I'll take care of it."

She started to speak again, then got a good look at his face. The devil took over. "I'll be damned, Roarke. You're embarrassed."

"Certainly not." If he'd been wearing anything but skin, he would have pushed his hands into his pockets. "It was simply an oversight. I said I'd take care of it."

"Let's play it back."

He stopped short, and gave Eve the rare pleasure of seeing him goggle. "I beg your pardon?"

"You are embarrassed." She leaned over to kiss him, and while he was distracted, snatched the disc. "That's cute. Really cute."

"Shut up. Give me that."

"I don't think so." Delighted, she danced back a step and held the disc out of reach. "I bet this is very hot. Aren't you curious?"

"No." He made a grab, but she was very quick. "Eve, give me the damn thing."

"This is fascinating." She edged back toward the open patio doors. "The sophisticated, seen-it-all Roarke is blushing."

"I am not." He hoped to Christ he wasn't. That would top it. "I simply see no reason to document lovemaking. It's private."

"I'm not going to pass it on to Nadine Furst for broadcast. I'm just going to review it. Right now." She dashed inside while he swore and ran after her.

She walked into her office at nine A.M. sharp with a spring to her step. Her eyes were clear and unshadowed, her system toned and her shoulders free of tension. She was all but humming.

"Somebody got lucky," Feeney said mournfully and kept his feet planted on her desk. "Roarke's back on planet, I take it."

"I got a good night's sleep," she retorted and shoved his feet aside.

He grunted. "Be grateful, 'cause you're not going to find much peace today. Lab report's in. The fucking knife doesn't match."

Her sunny mood vanished. "What do you mean, the knife doesn't match?"

"The blade's too thick. A centimeter. Might as well be a meter, goddamn it."

"That could be the angle of the wounds, the thrust of the blow." Mexico vanished like a bubble of air. Thinking fast, she began to pace. "What about the blood?"

"They managed to scrape off enough to get type, DNA." His already gloomy face sagged. "It matches our boy. It's David Angelini's blood, Dallas. Lab says it's old, six months minimum. From the fibers they got, it looks like he used it to open packages, probably nicked himself somewhere along the line. It's not our weapon."

"Screw it." She heaved a breath, refused to be discouraged. "If he had one knife, he could have had two. We'll wait to hear from the other sweepers." Taking a moment, she scrubbed her face with her hands. "Listen to me, Feeney, if we go with Marco's confession as bogus, we have to ask why. He's not a crank or a loony calling in trying to take credit. He's saving his son's ass is what he's doing. So we work on him, and we work hard. I'll bring him in to interview, try to crack him."

"I'm with you there."

"I've got a session with Mira in a couple hours. We'll just let our main boy stew for awhile."

"While we pray one of the teams turns up something."

"Praying can't hurt. Here's the big one, Feeney, our boy's lawyers get a hold of Marco's confession, it's going to corrupt the hearing on the minor charges. We'll whistle for an indictment."

"With that, and without physical evidence, he's going back out, Dallas."

"Yeah. Son of a bitch."

Marco Angelini was like a boulder cemented to concrete. He wasn't going to budge. Two hours of intense interrogation didn't shake his story. Though, Eve consoled herself, he hadn't shored up any of the holes in it, either. At the moment, she had little choice but to pin her hopes on Mira's report.

"I can tell you," Mira said in her usual unruffled fashion, "that David Angelini is a troubled young man with a highly developed sense of self-indulgence and protection."

"Tell me he's capable of slicing his mother's throat."

"Ah." Mira sat back and folded her neat hands. "What I can tell you is, in my opinion, he is more capable of running from trouble than confronting it, on any level. When combining and averaging his placements on the Murdock-Lowell and the Synergy Evaluations—"

"Can we skip over the psych buzz, Doctor? I can read that in the report."

"All right." Mira shifted away from the screen where she had been about to bring up the evaluations. "We'll keep this in simple terms for the time being. Your man is a liar, one who convinces himself with little effort that his lies are truth in order to maintain his self-esteem. He requires good opinion, even praise, and is accustomed to having it. And having his own way."

"And if he doesn't get his own way?"

"He casts blame elsewhere. It is not his fault, nor his responsibility. His world is insular, Lieutenant, comprised for the most part of himself alone. He considers himself successful and talented, and when he fails, it's because someone else made a mistake. He gambles because he doesn't believe he can lose, and he enjoys the thrill of risk. He loses because he believes himself above the game."

"How would he react at the risk of having his bones snapped over gambling debts?"

"He would run and he would hide, and being abnormally dependent on his parents, he would expect them to clean up the mess."

"And if they refused?"

Mira was silent for a moment. "You want me to tell you that he would strike out, react violently, even murderously. I can't do that. It is, of course, a possibility that can't be ruled out in any of us. No test, no evaluation can absolutely conclude the reaction of an individual under certain circumstances. But in those tests and those evaluations, the subject reacted consistently by covering, by running, by shifting blame rather than by attacking the source of his problem."

"And he could be covering his reaction, to skew the evaluation."

"It's possible, but unlikely. I'm sorry."

Eve stopped pacing and sank into a chair. "You're saying that in your opinion, the murderer may still be out there."

"I'm afraid so. It makes your job more difficult."

"If I'm looking in the wrong place," Eve said to herself, "where's the right place? And who's next?"

"Unfortunately, neither science nor technology is yet able to forecast the future. You can program possibilities, even probabilities, but they can't take into account impulse or emotion. Do you have Nadine Furst under protection?"

"As much as possible." Eve tapped a finger on her knee. "She's difficult, and she's torn up about Louise Kirski."

"And so are you."

Eve slid her gaze over, nodded stiffly. "Yeah, you could say that."

"Yet you look uncommonly rested this morning."

"I got a good night's sleep."

"Untroubled?"

Eve moved a shoulder, tucked Angelini and the case into a corner of her mind where she hoped it would simmer into something fresh. "What would you say about a woman who can't seem to sleep well unless this man's in bed with her?"

"I'd say she may be in love with him, is certainly growing used to him."

"You wouldn't say she's overly dependent?"

"Can you function without him? Do you feel able to make a decision without asking his advice, opinion, or direction?"

"Well, sure, but . . ." She trailed off, feeling foolish. Well, if one was to feel foolish, what better place than a shrink's office? "The other day, when he was off planet, I wore one of his shirts to work. That's—"

"Lovely," Mira said with a slow, easy smile. "Romantic. Why does romance worry you?"

"It doesn't. I— Okay, it scares the shit out of me, and I don't know why. I'm not used to having someone there, having someone look at me like—the way he does. Sometimes it's unnerving."

"Why is that?"

"Because I haven't done anything to make him care about me as much as he does. I know he does."

"Eve, your self-worth has always been focused on your job. Now a relationship has forced you to begin evaluating yourself as a woman. Are you afraid of what you'll find?"

"I haven't figured that out. It's always been the job. The highs and lows, the rush, the monotony. Everything I needed to be was there. I busted my ass to make lieutenant, and I figure I can sweat my way up to captain, maybe more. Doing the job was it, all of it. It was important to be the best, to make a mark. It's still important, but it's not all anymore."

"I would say, Eve, that you'll be a better cop, and a better woman because of it. Single focus limits us, and can too often obsess us. A healthy life needs more than one goal, one passion."

"Then I guess my life's getting healthier."

Eve's communicator beeped, reminding her that she was on the clock, a cop first. "Dallas."

"You're going to want to switch over to public broadcast, Channel 75," Feeney announced. "Then get your butt back here to the Tower. The new chief wants to fry our asses."

Eve cut him off, and Mira had already opened her viewing screen. They came in on C. J. Morse's noon update.

". . . continuing problems with the investigation of the murders. A Cop Central source has confirmed that while David Angelini has been charged with obstruction of justice, and remains prime suspect for the three murders, Marco Angelini, the accused's father, has confessed to those murders. The senior Angelini, president of Angelini Exports and former husband of the first victim, Prosecuting Attorney Cicely Towers, surrendered to the police yesterday. Though he has confessed to all three murders, he has not been charged, and the police continue to hold David Angelini."

Morse paused, shifted slightly to face a new camera angle. His pleasant, youthful face radiated concern. "In other developments, a knife taken from the Angelini home during a police search has proven through testing not to be the murder weapon. Mirina Angelini, daughter of the late Cicely Towers, spoke to this reporter in an exclusive interview this morning."

The screen snapped to a new video and filled with Mirina's lovely, outraged face. "The police are persecuting my family. It isn't enough that my mother is dead, murdered on the street. Now, in a desperate attempt to cover their own ineptitude, they've arrested my brother and they're holding my father. It wouldn't surprise me to find myself taken away in restraints at any moment."

Eve ground her teeth while Morse led Mirina through questions, prodded her to make accusations, tears gleaming in her eyes. When the broadcast switched back to the news desk, he was frowning seriously.

"A family under siege? There are rumors of cover-ups clouding the investigation. Primary investigating officer, Lieutenant Eve Dallas could not be reached for comment."

"Little bastard. Little bastard," Eve muttered and swung away from the screen. "He never tried to reach me for comment. I'd give him a comment." Furious, she snatched up her bag and shot Mira one last look. "You ought to analyze that one," she said jerking her head toward the screen. "That little prick has delusions of grandeur."

chapter seventeen

Harrison Tibble was a thirty-five-year vet on the police force. He'd plodded his way up from beat cop, working the West Side barrios when cops and their quarries still carried guns. He'd even taken a hit once: three nasty rounds in the abdomen that might have killed a lesser man and would certainly have given most ordinary cops cause to consider their career choices. Tibble had been back on full duty within six weeks.

He was an enormous man, a full six foot six and two hundred sixty pounds of solid muscle. After the gun ban, he'd used his bulk and cold, terrifying grin to intimidate his quarries. He still had the mind of a street cop, and his record was clean enough to serve tea on.

He had a large, square face, skin the color of polished onyx, hands the size of steamship rounds, and no patience for bullshit.

Eve liked him and could privately admit she was a little afraid of him.

"What is this pile of shit we've got ourselves into, Lieutenant?"

"Sir." Eve faced him, flanked by Feeney and Whitney. But at the moment, she knew she was very much alone. "David Angelini was on scene the night Louise Kirski was killed. We have that locked. He has no solid alibi for the times of the other two murders. He's in debt big time to the spine twisters, and with his mother's death, he comes into a nice, healthy inheritance. It's been confirmed that she had refused to bail him out this time."

"Look for the money's a tried and true investigative tool, Lieutenant. But what about the other two?"

He knew all of this, Eve thought and struggled not to squirm. Every word of every report had passed by him. "He knew Metcalf, had been to her apartment, was working with her on a project. He needed her to commit, but she was playing coy, covering her bases. The third victim was a mistake. We believe strongly that the intended victim was Nadine Furst, who at my suggestion and with my cooperation was putting a great deal of pressure on the story. He also knew her personally."

"That's real good so far." His chair creaked under his weight as he shifted back. "Real good. You've placed him at one of the scenes, established motives, dug up the links. Now we run into the hard place. You don't have a weapon, you don't have any blood. You don't have diddly as far as physical evidence."

"Not at this time."

"You've also got a confession, but not from the accused."

"That confession's nothing more than a smoke screen," Whitney put in. "An attempt by a father to protect his son."

"So you believe," Tibble said mildly. "But the fact is, it's now on record and is public knowledge. The psych profile doesn't fit, the weapon doesn't fit, and in my opinion, the PA's office was too eager to put the spotlight on. It happens when it's one of your own."

He held up a plate-sized hand before Eve could speak. "I'll tell you what we've got, what it looks like to all those fine people watching their screens. A grieving family hammered by cops, circumstantial evidence, and three women with their throats cut open."

"No one's throat's been cut open since David Angelini's been locked up. And the charges filed against him are clean."

"True enough, but that handy fact won't get an indictment on the lessers—not when the jury's going to feel sorry for him, and the counsel starts hawking diminished capacity."

He waited, scanning faces, tapped his fingers when no one disagreed with him. "You're the number whiz, Feeney, the electronic genius. What are the odds on the grand jury if we send our boy over tomorrow on the obstruction and bribery charges?"

Feeney hunched his shoulders. "Fifty-fifty," he said mournfully. "At the outside, considering that idiot Morse's latest news flash."

"That's not good enough. Spring him."

"Spring him? Chief Tibble—"

"All we're going to get if we push those charges is bad press and public sympathy for the son of a martyred public servant. Cut him loose, Lieutenant, and dig deeper. Put someone on him," he ordered Whitney. "And on his daddy. I don't want them to fart without hearing about it. And find the fucking leak," he added, his eyes going hard. "I want to know what asshole fed that idiot Morse data." His grin spread suddenly, terrifyingly. "Then I want to talk to him, personally. Keep your distance from the Angelinis, Jack. This isn't any time for friendship."

"I'd hoped to talk to Mirina. I might be able to persuade her not to give any more interviews."

"It's a little late for damage control there," Tibble considered. "Hold off on that. I've worked hard to get the stink of the word *cover-up* out of this office. I want to keep it that way. Get me a weapon. Get me some blood. And for Christ's sake do it before somebody else gets sliced."

His voice boomed out, fingers jabbing, as he snapped orders. "Feeney, work some of your magic. Go over the names from the victims' diaries again, cross them with Furst's. Find me somebody else who had an interest in those ladies. That'll be all, gentlemen." He got to his feet. "Lieutenant Dallas, another moment of your time."

"Chief Tibble," Whitney began formally. "I want it on record that as Lieutenant Dallas's commanding officer, I consider her pursuit of this investigation to be exemplary. Her work has been top rate despite difficult circumstances, both professional and personal, some of which I have caused."

Tibble cocked a bushy brow. "I'm sure the lieutenant appreciates your review, Jack." He said nothing more, waiting until the men left. "Me and Jack, we go back a ways," he began conversationally. "Now he thinks since I'm sitting here where that corrupt pie-faced fucker Simpson used to rest his sorry ass, I'm going to use you as a handy scapegoat and feed you to the media dogs." He held Eve's eyes steadily. "Is that what you think, Dallas?"

"No, sir. But you could."

"Yeah." He scratched the side of his neck. "I could. Have you bumbled this investigation, Lieutenant?"

"Maybe I have." It was a hard one to swallow. "If David Angelini is innocent—"

"The courts decide innocence or guilt," he interrupted. "You gather evidence. You gathered some nice evidence, and the jerk was there for Kirski. If he didn't kill her, the bastard watched some woman get slaughtered and walked away. He don't win any prizes in my book."

Tibble steepled his fingers and peered over them. "You know what would make me take you off this case, Dallas? If I thought you were carrying around too much baggage about Kirski." When she opened her mouth, then shut it again, he gave her a thin-lipped smile. "Yeah, best to keep it shut. You laid out some bait, took a chance. There was a pretty good shot he'd come after you. I'd have done the same thing in my glory days," he added with some wistful regret that they were over. "Problem is, he didn't, and some poor woman with a tobacco habit gets hit instead. You figure you're responsible for that?"

She struggled with the lie, gave up to the truth. "Yes."

"Get over it," he said with a snap. "The trouble with this case is, there's too much emotion. Jack can't get past his grief, you can't get past your guilt. That makes the two of you useless. You want to be guilty, you want to be pissed, wait till you nail him. Clear?"

"Yes, sir."

Satisfied, he leaned back again. "You walk out of here, the media's going to be all over you like lice."

"I can handle the media."

"I'm sure you can." He blew out a breath. "So can I. I've got a fucking press conference. Clear out."

There was only one place to go, and that was back to the beginning. Eve stood on the sidewalk outside the Five Moons and stared down. Playing the route back in her mind, she strode to the subway entrance.

It was raining, she remembered. *I'd have a hand on my umbrella, my purse over my shoulder with a good grip on that, too. Bad neighborhood. I'm pissed. I walk fast, but I keep an eye shifting for anybody who wants my purse as much as I do.*

She walked into the Five Moons, ignoring the quick glances and the bland face of the droid behind the bar as she tried to read Cicely Towers's thoughts.

Disgusting place. Dirty. I'm not going to drink, not even going to sit down. God knows what I'd pick up on my suit. Check the watch. Where the hell is he? Let's get this over with. Why the hell did I meet him here? Stupid, stupid. Should have used my office, my turf.

Why didn't I?

Because it's private, Eve thought, closing her eyes. *It's personal. Too many people there, too many questions. Not city business. Her business.*

Why not her apartment?

Didn't want him there. Too angry—upset—eager—to argue when he named the time and place.

No, it's just angry, impatient, Eve decided, remembering the droid's statement. *She'd checked her watch again and again, she'd frowned, she'd given up, and walked out.*

Eve followed the route, remembering the umbrella, the purse. *Quick steps, heels clicking. Someone there. She stops. Does she see him, recognize him? Has to, it's face to face. Maybe she speaks to him: "You're late."*

He does it quick. It's a bad neighborhood. Not much cruising traffic, but you can never tell. Security lights are dinky, always are around here. Nobody complains much because it's safer to score in the dark.

But someone might come out of the bar, or the club across the street. One swipe and she's down. Her blood's all over him. The fucking blood's got to be all over him.

He takes her umbrella. An impulse, or maybe for a shield. Walks away, fast. Not to the subway. He's covered with blood. Even around here, somebody would notice.

She covered two blocks in either direction, then covered them again, questioning anyone who was loitering on the street. Most of the responses were shrugs, angry eyes. Cops weren't popular on the West End.

She watched a street hawker, who she suspected was pushing more than fashion beads and feathers, skim around the corner on motor skates. She scowled after him.

"You been round here before."

Eve glanced over. The woman was so white she was next to invisible. Her face was like bleached putty, her hair cropped so close it showed her bone-white scalp, and her eyes were colorless down to the pinprick pupil.

Funky junkie, Eve thought. They popped the white tablet that kept the mind misted and pigments bleached.

"Yeah, I've been around."

"Cop." The junkie jerked forward, stiff jointed, like a droid coming up on maintenance. A sign she was low on a fix. "Seen you talking with Crack a while ago. He's some dude."

"Yeah, he's some dude. Were you around the night that woman got whacked down the street?"

"Fancy lady, rich, fancy lady. Caught it on the screen in detox."

Eve bit back an oath, stopped, and backtracked. "If you were in detox, how'd you see me talking to Crack?"

"Went in that day. Maybe the next day. Time's relative, right?"

"Maybe you saw the rich, fancy lady before you caught her on the screen."

"Nope." The albino sucked her finger. "Didn't."

Eve scanned the building behind the junkie, gauged the view. "Is this where you live?"

"I live here, I live there. Got me a crash flop upstairs."

"You were there the night the lady got slashed?"

"Probably. Got a credit problem." She flashed tiny, round teeth in a smile. And her breath was awesome. "Not much fun on the street when you ain't got a credit."

"It was raining," Eve prompted.

"Oh yeah. I like the rain." Her muscles continued to jerk, but her eyes went dreamy. "I watch it out the window."

"Did you see anything else out the window?"

"People come, people go," she said in a singsong voice. "Sometimes you can hear the music from down the street. But not that night. Rain's too loud. People running to get out of it. Like they'd melt or something."

"You saw someone running in the rain."

The colorless eyes sharpened. "Maybe. What's it worth?"

Eve dug into her pocket. She had enough loose credit tokens for a quick, small score. The junkie's eyes rolled and her hand jerked out.

"What did you see?" Eve said slowly, snatching the credits out of reach.

"A guy pissing in the alley over there." She shrugged, her

eyes focused on the credits. "Maybe jerking off. Hard to tell."

"Did he have anything with him? Was he carrying anything?"

"Just his dick." She laughed uproariously at that and nearly tumbled. Her eyes were beginning to water heavily. "He just walked away in the rain. Hardly anybody out that night. Guy got in a car."

"Same guy?"

"Nah, another guy, had it parked over there." She gestured vaguely. "Not from 'round here."

"Why?"

"Car had a shine to it. Nobody got a car with a shine to it 'round here. If they got a car. Now Crack, he's got one, and that pissant Reeve down the hall from me. But they don't shine."

"Tell me about the guy who got in the car."

"Got in the car, drove away."

"What time was it?"

"Hey, I look like a clock. Ticktock." She snorted another laugh. "It was nighttime. Nighttime's the best. My eyes hurt in daytime," she whined. "Lost my sunshields."

Eve dragged a pair of eye protectors out of her pocket. She never remembered to wear the damn things, anyway. She shoved them at the albino, who hooked them on.

"Cheap. Cop issue. Shit."

"What was he wearing? The guy who got in the car."

"Hell, I don't know." The junkie toyed with the sunglasses. Her eyes didn't burn quite so much behind the treated lenses. "A coat maybe. Dark coat, flapped around. Yeah, it flapped around when he was closing the umbrella."

Eve felt a jolt, like a punch in the stomach. "He had an umbrella?"

"Hey, it was raining. Some people don't like getting wet. Pretty," she said, dreaming again. "Bright."

"What color was it?"

"Bright," she repeated. "You going to give me those credits?"

"Yeah, you're going to get them." But Eve took her arm, led her to the broken steps of the building, and sat her down. "But let's talk about this a little more first."

"The uniforms missed her." Eve paced her office while Feeney lolled in her chair. "She went into detox the day after the first murder. I checked it. She got out a week ago."

"You got an albino addict," Feeney put in.

"She saw him, Feeney. She saw him get in a car, she saw the umbrella."

"You know what a funky junkie's vision's like, Dallas. In the dark, in the rain, from across the street?"

"She gave me the umbrella. Goddamn it, nobody knew about the umbrella."

"And the color was, I quote, *bright.*" He held up both hands before Eve could snap at him. "I'm just trying to save you some grief. You got an idea of putting the Angelinis in a lineup for a funky junkie, their lawyers are going to whip your little ass, kid."

She had thought of it. And she, too, had rejected it. "She wouldn't hold up on direct ID. I'm not stupid. But it was a man, she's damn sure of that. He drove away. He had the umbrella. He was wearing a long coat, dark."

"Which jibes with David Angelini's statement."

"It was a new car. I juggled that out of her. Shiny, bright."

"Back with bright."

"So, they don't see colors well," she snarled. "The guy was alone, and the car was a small, personal vehicle. The driver's side door opened up, not to the side, and he had to swivel down to get in."

"Could be a Rocket, a Midas, or a Spur. Maybe a Midget, if it's a late model."

"She said new, and she's got a thing for cars. Likes to watch them."

"Okay, I'll run it." He gave a sour smile. "Any idea how many of those models been sold in the last two years in the five boroughs alone? Now, if she'd come up with an ID plate, even a partial—"

"Quit bitching. I've been back over Metcalf's. There's a couple dozen bright new cars in the garage there."

"Oh joy."

"Possibility he's a neighbor," Eve said with a shrug. It was a very low possibility. "Wherever he lives, he has to be able to get in and out without being noticed. Or where people don't notice. Maybe he leaves the coat in the car, or he puts it in something to get it inside and clean it up. There's going to be blood in that car, Feeney, and on that coat, no matter how much he's scrubbed and sprayed. I've got to get over to Channel 75."

"Are you crazy?"

"I need to talk to Nadine. She's dodging me."

"Jesus, talk about the lion's den."

"Oh, I'll be fine." She smiled viciously. "I'm taking Roarke with me. They're scared of him."

"It's so sweet of you to ask for my company." Roarke pulled his car into the visitors' lot at Channel 75 and beamed at her. "I'm touched."

"All right, I owe you." The man never let her get away with anything, Eve thought in disgust as she climbed out of the car.

"I'll collect." He caught her arm. "You can start paying off by telling me why you want me along."

"I told you, it'll save time, since you want to go to this opera thing."

Very slowly, very thoroughly, he scanned over her dusty trousers and battered boots. "Darling Eve, though you always look perfect to me, you're not going to the opera dressed like that. So we're going to have to go home to change, anyway. Come clean."

"Maybe I don't want to go to the opera."

"So you've already said. Several times, I believe. But we had a deal."

She lowered her brows, toyed with one of the buttons of his shirt. "It's just singing."

"I've agreed to sit through two sets at the Blue Squirrel, with the idea of helping Mavis into a recording contract. And no one—no one with ears—would consider that singing of any kind."

She huffed out a breath. A deal was, after all, a deal. "Okay, fine. I said I'm going."

"Now that you've managed to avoid the question, I'll repeat it. Why am I here?"

She looked up from his button, into his face. It was always hell for her to admit she could use help. "Feeney's got to dig into the E-work. He can't be spared right now. I want another pair of eyes, ears, another impression."

His lips curved. "So, I'm your second choice."

"You're my first civilian choice. You read people well."

"I'm flattered. And perhaps, while I'm here, I could break Morse's face for you."

Her grin came quickly. "I like you, Roarke. I really like you."

"I like you, too. Is that a yes? I'd enjoy it very much."

She laughed, but there was a part of her that warmed foolishly over the idea of having an avenger. "It's a happy thought, Roarke, but I'd really rather break his face myself. At the right time and in the right place."

"Can I watch?"

"Sure. But for the moment, can you just be the rich and powerful Roarke, my personal trophy?"

"Ah, how sexist. I'm excited."

"Good. Hold that thought. Maybe we'll skip the opera after all."

They walked together through the main entrance, and Roarke had the pleasure of watching her shrug on the cop. She flashed her badge at security, gave him a pithy suggestion that he keep out of her face, then strode toward the ascent.

"I love to watch you work," he murmured in her ear.

"You're so . . . forceful," he decided as his hand slid down her back toward her butt.

"Cut it out."

"See what I mean?" He rubbed his gut where her elbow had jabbed. "Hit me again. I could learn to love it."

She managed, barely, to turn a chuckle into a snort. "Civilians," was all she said.

The newsroom was busy, noisy. At least half of the on-desk reporters were plugged into 'links, headsets, or computers. Screens flashed current broadcasts. A number of conversations stopped dead when Eve and Roarke stepped from the ascent. Then, like a horde of dogs with the same scent in their nostrils, reporters scrambled forward.

"Back off," Eve ordered with enough force to have one eager beaver stumbling backward and stomping on the foot of a cohort. "Nobody gets a comment. Nobody gets squat until I'm ready."

"If I do buy this place," Roarke said to Eve in a voice just loud enough to carry, "I'll have to make several staff cuts."

That created a swath wide enough to stride through. Eve zeroed in on a face she recognized. "Rigley, where's Furst?"

"Hey, Lieutenant." He was all teeth and hair and ambition. "If you'd like to step into my office," he invited, gesturing toward his console.

"Furst," she repeated, in a voice like a bullet. "Where?"

"I haven't seen her all day. I covered her morning report myself."

"She called in." Beaming smiles, Morse sauntered over. "Taking some time off," he explained, and his mobile face shifted to sober lines. "She's pretty ripped up about Louise. We all are."

"Is she at home?"

"Said she needed some time, is all I know. Management cut her a break. She's got a couple of weeks coming. I'm taking over her beat." His smile flashed again. "So, if you'd like a little airtime, Dallas. I'm your man."

"I've had plenty of your airtime, Morse."

"Well then." He dismissed her and shifted toward Roarke. His smile bumped up in wattage. "It's a pleasure to meet you. You're a difficult man to contact."

Deliberately insulting, Roarke ignored Morse's offered hand. "I only give time to people I consider interesting."

Morse lowered his hand, but kept his smile in place. "I'm sure if you spared me a few minutes, I'd find several areas of interest for you."

Roarke's smile flashed, quick and lethal. "You really are an idiot, aren't you."

"Down, boy," Eve murmured, patting Roarke's arm. "Who leaked confidential data?"

Morse was obviously struggling to recover his dignity. He veered his gaze to hers and nearly managed an arrogant sneer. "Now, now, sources are protected. Let's not forget the Constitution." Patriotically, he laid his palm over his heart. "Now, if you wish to comment on, contradict, or add to any of my information, I'd be more than happy to listen."

"Why don't we try this?" she said, shifting gears. "You found Louise Kirski's body—while it was still warm."

"That's right." He folded his mouth into grim lines. "I've given my statement."

"You were pretty upset, weren't you? Jittery. Shot your dinner in the bushes. Feeling better now?"

"It's something I'll never forget, but yes, I'm feeling better. Thanks for asking."

She stepped forward, backing him up. "You felt good enough to go on air within minutes, to make sure there was a camera out there getting a nice close-up of your dead associate."

"Immediacy is part of the business. I did what I was trained to do. That doesn't mean I didn't feel." His voice trembled and was manfully controlled. "That doesn't mean I don't see her face, her eyes, every time I try to sleep at night."

"Did you ever wonder what would have happened if you'd gotten there five minutes sooner?"

That jarred him, and though she knew it was nasty, and personal, it pleased her.

"Yes, I have," he said with dignity. "I might have seen him or stopped him. Louise might be alive if I hadn't been caught in traffic. But that doesn't change the facts. She's dead, and so are two others. And you don't have anyone in custody."

"Maybe it hasn't occurred to you that you're feeding him. That you've given him just what he wants." She took her gaze from Morse long enough to scan the room and all the people who were listening eagerly. "He must love watching all the reports, hearing all the details, the speculation. You've made him the biggest star on the screen."

"It's our responsibility to report—" Morse began.

"Morse, you don't know shit about responsibility. All you know is how to count the minutes you're on air, front and center. The more people die, the bigger your ratings. You can quote me on that one." She turned on her heel.

"Feel better?" Roarke asked her when they were outside again.

"Not a hell of a lot. Impressions?"

"The newsroom's in turmoil, too many people doing too many things. They're all jumpy. The one you talked to initially about Nadine?"

"Rigley. He's a little fish. I think they hired him for his teeth."

"He's been biting his nails. There were several others who looked ashamed when you made your little speech. They turned away, got very busy, but they weren't doing anything. Several more looked quietly pleased when you took a couple layers off Morse. I don't believe he's well liked."

"Big surprise."

"He's better than I'd thought," Roarke mused.

"Morse? At what? Slinging shit?"

"Image," Roarke corrected. "Which is often the same thing. He pulls out all those emotions. He doesn't feel any of them, but he knows how to make them play over his face, in his voice. He's in the right field and will definitely move up."

"God help us." She leaned against Roarke's car. "Do you think he knows more than he's put on air?"

"I think it's possible. Highly possible. He's enjoying stringing this out, particularly now that he's in charge of the story. And he hates your guts."

"Oh, now I'm hurt." She started to open the door, then turned back. "Hates me?"

"He'll ruin you if he can. Watch yourself."

"He can make me look foolish, but he can't ruin me." She wrenched the door open. "Where the hell is Nadine? It's not like her, Roarke. I understand how she feels about Louise, but it's not like her to take off, not to tell me, to hand a story this size to that bastard."

"People react in different ways to shock and grief."

"It's stupid. She was a target. She could still be a target. We have to find her."

"Is that your way of squirming out of the opera?"

Eve got in the car, stretched out her legs. "No, that's just a little side benefit. Let's run by her place, okay? She's on Eightieth between Second and Third."

"All right. But you have no excuse to squirm out of the cocktail party tomorrow night."

"Cocktail party? What cocktail party?"

"The one I arranged fully a month ago," he reminded her as he slipped in beside her. "To kick off the fund-raiser for the Art Institute on Station Grimaldi. Which you agreed to attend and to help host."

She remembered, all right. He'd brought home some fancy dress she was supposed to wear. "Wasn't I drunk when I agreed? The word of a drunk is worthless."

"No, you weren't." He smiled as he skimmed from the visitors' lot. "You were, however, naked, panting, and I believe very close to begging."

"Bull." Actually, she thought, folding her arms, he may have been right. The details were hazy. "Okay, okay, I'll be there, I'll be there with a stupid smile in some fancy dress that cost you too much money for too little material. Unless . . . something comes up."

"Something?"

She sighed. He only asked her to do one of his silly gigs when it was important to him. "Police business. Only if it's urgent police business. Barring that, I'll stick for the whole fussy mess."

"I don't suppose you could try to enjoy it?"

"Maybe I could." She turned her head and on impulse lifted a hand to his cheek. "A little."

chapter eighteen

No one answered the buzzer at Nadine's door. The recording requested simply that the caller leave a message, which would be returned at the earliest possible time.

"She could be in there brooding," Eve mused, rocking on her heels as she considered. "Or she could be at some tony resort. She slipped her guard plenty over the past few days. She's a slick one, our Nadine."

"And you'll feel better if you know."

"Yeah." Brow furrowed, Eve considered using her police emergency code to bypass security. She didn't have enough cause, and she balled her hands in her pockets.

"Ethics," Roarke said. "It's always an education to watch you struggle with them. Let me help you out." He took out a small pocket knife and pried open the handplate.

"Jesus, Roarke, tampering with security will get you six months house arrest."

"Um-hmm." Calmly, he studied the circuits. "I'm a bit out of practice. We make this model, you know."

"Put that damn thing back together, and don't—"

But he was already bypassing the main board, working with a speed and efficiency that made her wince.

"Out of practice, my butt," she mumbled when the lock light went from red to green.

"I always had a knack." The door slid open, and he tugged her inside.

"Security tampering, breaking and entering, private property trespass. Oh, it's just mounting up."

"But you'll wait for me, won't you?" With one hand still on Eve's arm, he studied the living area. It was clean, cool, spare in furnishings, but with an expensive minimalistic style.

"She lives well," he commented, noting the gleam on the tile floor, the few objects d'art on spearing clear pedestals. "But she doesn't come here often."

Eve knew he had a good eye, and nodded. "No, she doesn't really live here, just sleeps here sometimes. There's nothing out of place, no dents in the cushions." She walked past him toward the adjoining kitchen, punched the available menu on the AutoChef. "Doesn't keep a lot of food on hand, either. Mostly cheese and fruit."

Eve thought about her empty stomach, was tempted, but resisted. She headed out across the wide living space toward a bedroom. "Office," she stated, studying the equipment, the console, the wide screen it faced. "She lives here some. Shoes under the console, single earring by the link, empty cup, probably coffee."

The second bedroom was larger, the sheets on the unmade bed twisted as if someone had wrapped and unwrapped themselves through a particularly long night.

Eve spotted the suit Nadine had been wearing on the night of Louise's murder on the floor, kicked under a table where a vase of daisies wilted.

They were signs of pain, and they made her sorry. She walked to the closet and hit the button to open it. "Christ, how could you tell if she packed anything? She's got enough clothes for a ten-woman model troupe."

Still, she looked through them while Roarke moved to the bedside 'link and ran the record disc back to the beginning. Eve glanced over her shoulder, saw what he was up to. She only moved her shoulders.

"Might as well completely invade her privacy."

Eve continued to search for some sign that Nadine had gone off on a trip while the calls and messages played back.

She listened with some amusement to some frank sexual byplay between Nadine and some man named Ralph. There were a lot of innuendos, overt suggestions, and laughter before the transmission ended with a promise to get together when he got into town.

Other calls breezed by: work-oriented, a call to a nearby restaurant for delivery. Ordinary, everyday calls. Then it changed.

Nadine was speaking to the Kirskis the day after the last murder. All of them were weeping. Maybe there was comfort in it, Eve thought as she walked toward the viewer. Maybe sharing tears and shock helped.

I don't know if it matters right now, but the primary investigator, Dallas—Lieutenant Dallas—she won't stop until she finds out who did this to Louise. She won't stop.

"Oh, man." Eve closed her eyes as the transmission ended. There was nothing more, just blank disc, and she opened her eyes again. "Where's the call to the station?" she demanded. "Where's the call? Morse said she called in and requested time off."

"Could have done it from her car, from a portable. In person."

"Let's find out." She whipped out her communicator. "Feeney. I need make, model, and ID number on Nadine Furst's vehicle."

It didn't take long to access the data or to read the garage inventory and discover her car had been logged out the day before and hadn't been returned.

"I don't like it." Eve fretted as she sat back in Roarke's

car. "She'd have left me a message. She'd have left word. I need to talk to some brass at the station, find out who took her call." She started to key it into Roarke's car 'link, then stopped. "One other thing." Taking out her log, she requested a different number. "Kirski, Deborah and James, Portland, Maine." The number beeped on, and she transferred it to the 'link. It was answered quickly by a pale-haired woman with exhausted eyes.

"Mrs. Kirski, this is Lieutenant Dallas, NYPSD."

"Yes, Lieutenant, I remember you. Is there any news?"

"There's nothing I can tell you right now. I'm sorry." Damn it, she had to give the woman something. "We're pursuing some new information. We're hopeful, Mrs. Kirski."

"We said good-bye to Louise today." She struggled to smile. "It was a comfort to see how many people cared for her. So many of her friends from school, and there were flowers, messages from everyone she worked with in New York."

"She won't be forgotten, Mrs. Kirski. Could you tell me if Nadine Furst attended the memorial today?"

"We expected her." The swollen eyes looked lost a moment. "I'd spoken with her at her office only a few days ago to give her the date and time of the services. She said she would be here, but something must have come up."

"She didn't make it." A sour feeling spread in Eve's stomach. "You haven't heard from her?"

"No, not for a few days. She's a very busy woman, I know. She has to get on with her life, of course. What else can she do?"

Eve could offer no comfort without adding worry. "I'm sorry for your loss, Mrs. Kirski. If you have any questions or need to speak with me, please call. Anytime."

"You're very kind. Nadine said you wouldn't stop until you'd found the man who did this to my girl. You won't stop, will you, Lieutenant Dallas?"

"No, ma'am, I won't." She broke transmission, let her head fall back, closed her eyes. "I'm not kind. I didn't call her to say I was sorry, but because she might have given me an answer."

"But you were sorry." Roarke closed his hand gently over hers. "And you were kind."

"I can count the people who mean something to me without coming close to double digits. The same with the people I mean something to. If he'd have come after me, like the bastard was supposed to, I would have dealt with him. And if I hadn't—"

"Shut up." His hand vised over hers with a force that had her muffling a yelp, and his eyes were fierce and angry. "Just shut up."

Absently, she nursed her hand as he raced along the street. "You're right, I'm doing it wrong. I'm taking it in, and that doesn't help anything. Too much emotion on the case," she murmured, remembering the chief's warning. "I started out today thinking clean, and that's what I've got to keep doing. Next step is to find Nadine."

She called Dispatch and ordered an all points on the woman and her vehicle.

Calmer, with the twist of her earlier words unraveling in his gut, he slowed, glanced at her. "How many homicide victims have you stood for in your illustrious career, Lieutenant?"

"Stood for? That's an odd way of putting it." She moved her shoulders, trying to focus her mind on a man in a long, dark coat with a shiny new car. "I don't know. Hundreds. Murder never goes out of style."

"Then I'd say you're well past the double digits, on both sides. You need to eat."

She was too hungry to argue with him.

"The trouble with the cross-check is Metcalf's diary," Feeney explained. "It's full of cutesy little codes and symbols. And she changes them, so we can't work a pattern. We've got names like Sweet Face, Hot Buns, Dumb Ass. We got initials, we got stars, hearts, little smiley faces or scowly faces. It'll take time, and lots of it, to cross it with the copy of Nadine's or the prosecutor's."

"So what you're telling me is you can't do it."

"I didn't say can't." He looked insulted.

"Okay, sorry. I know you're busting your computer chips on this, but I don't know how much time we've got. He's got to go for somebody else. Until we find Nadine . . ."

"You think he snatched her." Feeney scratched his nose, his chin, reached for his bag of little candied nuts. "That breaks pattern, Dallas. And all three bodies he hit he left where someone was going to stumble over them pretty quick."

"So he's got a new pattern." She sat on the edge of the desk and immediately shifted off, too edgy for stillness. "Listen, he's pissed. He missed his target. It was all going his way, then he fucks up, downloads the wrong woman. If we go with Mira, he got plenty of attention, hours of airtime, but he failed. It's a power thing."

She wandered to her stingy window, stared out, watched as an airbus rumbled past at eye level like an awkward, overweight bird. Below, people were scattered like ants, rushing on the sidewalks, the ramps, the handy-glides to wherever their pressing business took them.

There were so many of them, Eve thought. So many targets.

"It's a power thing," Eve repeated, frowning down at the pedestrian traffic. "This woman's been getting all the attention, all the glory. His attention, his glory. When he takes them out, he gets the kick of the kill, all the publicity. The woman's gone, and that's good. She was trying to run everything her way. Now the public is focused on him. Who is he, what is he, where is he?"

"You're sounding like Mira," Feeney commented. "Without the thousand-credit words."

"Maybe she's nailed him. The what is he, anyway. She thinks male, she thinks unattached. Because women are a problem for him. Can't let them get the upper hand, like his mother did. Or the prominent female figure in his life.

He's had some success, but not enough. He can't quite get to the top. Maybe because a woman's in the way. Or women."

She narrowed her eyes, closed them. "Women who speak," she murmured. "Women who use words to wield power."

"That's a new one."

"That's mine," she said, turning back. "He cuts their throats. He doesn't rough them up, doesn't sexually assault or mutilate. It's not about sexual power, though it's about sex. If you term it as gender. There's all sorts of ways to kill, Feeney."

"Tell me about it. Somebody's always finding some new, inventive way to ditch somebody else."

"He uses a knife, and that's an extension of the body. A personal weapon. He could stab them in the heart, rip them in the gut, disembowel—"

"Okay, okay." He swallowed a nut manfully and waved a hand. "You don't have to draw a picture."

"Towers made her mark in court, her voice a powerful tool. Metcalf, the actress, dialogue. Furst, talking to viewers. Maybe that's why he didn't go after me," she murmured. "Talking isn't my source of power."

"You're doing all right now, kid."

"It doesn't really matter," she said with a shake of the head. "What we've got is an unattached male, in a career where he's unable to make a deep mark, one who had a strong, successful female influence."

"Fits David Angelini."

"Yeah, and his father if we add in the fact that his business is in trouble. Slade, too. Mirina Angelini isn't the fragile flower I thought she was. There's Hammett. He was in love with Towers but she wasn't taking him quite as seriously. That's a squeeze on the balls."

Feeney grunted, shifted.

"Or there's a couple thousand men out there, frustrated, angry, with violent tendencies." Eve hissed a breath through her teeth. "Where the hell is Nadine?"

"Look, they haven't located her vehicle. She hasn't been gone that long."

"Any record of her using credits in the last twenty-four hours?"

"No." Feeney sighed. "Still, if she decided to go off planet, it takes longer to access."

"She didn't go off planet. She'd want to stay close. Damn it, I should have known she'd do something stupid. I could see how ripped she was. I could see it in her eyes."

Frustrated, Eve dragged her hands through her hair. Then her fingers curled in, went tense. "I could see it in her eyes," she repeated slowly. "Oh my Jesus. The eyes."

"What? What?"

"The eyes. He saw her eyes." She leaped toward her 'link. "Get me Peabody," she ordered, "Field officer at the —shit, shit—what is it? The four oh two."

"What have you got, Dallas?"

"Let's wait." She rubbed her fingers over her mouth. "Let's just wait."

"Peabody." The officer's face flipped on screen, irritation showing around the mouth. There was a riot of noise on audio, voices, music.

"Christ, Peabody, where are you?"

"Crowd control." Irritation edged toward a sneer. "Parade on Lex. It's some Irish thing."

"Freedom of the Six Counties Day," Feeney said with a hint of pride. "Don't knock it."

"Can you get away from the noise?" Eve shouted.

"Sure. If I leave my post and walk three blocks crosstown." She remembered herself. "Sir."

"Hell," Eve muttered and made do. "The Kirski homicide, Peabody. I'm going to transmit a picture of the body. You take a look."

Eve called up the file, flipped through, sent the shot of Kirski sprawled in the rain.

"Is that how you found her? Exactly how you found her?" Eve demanded over audio.

"Yes, sir. Exactly."

Eve pulled the image back, left it in the bottom corner of her screen. "The hood over her face. Nobody messed with the hood?"

"No, sir. As I stated in my report, the TV crew was taking pictures. I moved them back, sealed the door. Her face was covered to just above the mouth. She had not been officially identified when I arrived on scene. The statement from the witness who found the body was fairly useless. He was hysterical. You have the record."

"Yeah, I've got the record. Thanks, Peabody."

"So," Feeney began when she ended the transmission. "What does that tell you?"

"Let's look at the record again. Morse's initial statement." Eve eased back so that Feeney could bring it up. Together they studied Morse. His face was wet with what looked like a combination of rain and sweat, possibly tears. He was white around the lips, and his eyes jittered.

"Guy's shook," Feeney commented. "Dead bodies do that to some people. Peabody's good," he added, listening. "Slow, thorough."

"Yeah, she'll move up," Eve said absently.

Then I saw it was a person. A body. God, all the blood. There was so much blood. Everywhere. And her throat . . . I got sick. You could smell—I got sick. Couldn't help it. Then I ran inside for help.

"That's the gist of it." Eve steepled her hands, tapped them against her jaw. "Okay, run through to where I talked to him after we shut down the broadcast that night."

He still looked pale, she noted, but he had that little superior smirk around his mouth. She'd run him through the details much the same as Peabody had and received basically the same responses. Calmer now. That was expected, that was usual.

Did you touch the body?
No, I don't think—no. She was just lying there, and

her throat was wide open. Her eyes. No, I didn't touch her. I got sick. You probably don't understand that, Dallas. Some people have basic human reactions. All that blood, her eyes. God.

"He said almost the same thing to me yesterday," Eve murmured. "He'd never forget her face. Her eyes."

"Dead eyes are spooky. They can stay with you."

"Yeah, hers have stayed with me." She shifted her gaze to Feeney's. "But nobody saw her face until I got there that night, Feeney. The hood had fallen over it. Nobody saw her face before I did. Except the murderer."

"Jesus, Dallas. You don't seriously think some little media creep like Morse is slicing throats in his off time. He probably added it for impact, to make himself more important."

Now her lips curved, just a little, in a smile more feral than amused. "Yeah, he likes being important, doesn't he? He likes being the focus. What do you do when you're an ambitious, unethical, second-string reporter, Feeney, and you can't find a hot story?"

He let out a low whistle. "You make one."

"Let's run his background. See where our pal comes from."

It didn't take Feeney long to pull up a basic sheet.

C. J. Morse had been born in Stamford, Connecticut, thirty-three years before. That was the first surprise. Eve would have pegged him as several years younger. His mother, deceased, had been head of computer science at Carnegie Melon, where her son had graduated with double majors in broadcasting and compuscience.

"Smart little fucker," Feeney commented. "Twentieth in his class."

"I wonder if it was good enough."

His employment record was varied. He'd bumped from station to station. One year at a small affiliate near his hometown. Six months with a satellite in Pennsylvania. Nearly two years at a top-rated channel in New Los Angeles, then a stretch in a half-baked independent in Arizona before heading back East. Another gig in Detroit before hitting New York. He'd worked on All News 60, then made the lateral transfer to Channel 75, first in the social data unit, then into hard news.

"Our boy doesn't hold down a job long. Channel 75's his record with three years. And there's no mention of his father in family data."

"Just mama," Feeney agreed. "A successful, highly positioned mama." A dead mama, she thought. They'd have to take time to check on how she died.

"Let's check criminal."

"No record," Feeney said, frowning at the screen. "A clean-living boy."

"Go into juvie. Well, well," she said, reading the data. "We've got ourselves a sealed record here, Feeney. What do you suppose our clean-living boy did in his misspent youth bad enough that somebody used an arm to have it sealed up?"

"Won't take me long to find out." He was cheering up, fingers ready to dance. "I'll want my own equipment, and a green light from the commander."

"Do it. And dig into each of those job positions. Let's see if there was any trouble. I think I'll take a swing by Channel 75, have a nice, fresh chat with our boy."

"We're going to need more to take him down than a possible match with the psych profile."

"Then we'll get it." She shrugged into her shoulder harness. "You know, if I hadn't had such a personal beef with him, I might have seen it before. Who benefited from the murders? The media." She locked in her weapon. "And the first murder took place when Nadine was conveniently off planet on assignment. Morse could step right in."

"And Metcalf?"

"The fucker was on scene almost before I was. It pissed me off, but it never clicked. He was so damn cool. And then who finds Kirski's body? Who's on air in minutes giving his personal report?"

"It doesn't make him a killer. That's what the PA's office is going to say."

"They want a connection. Ratings," she said as she headed for the door. "There's the goddamn connection."

chapter nineteen

Eve did a quick pass through the newsroom, studied the viewing screens. There was no sign of Morse, but that didn't worry her. It was a big complex. And he had no reason to hide, no reason to worry.

She wasn't going to give him one.

The plan she'd formulated on the trip over was simple. Not as satisfying as hauling him out by his camera-friendly hair and into lockup, but simpler.

She'd talk to him about Nadine, let it leak that she was worried. From there, it would be natural to steer things to Kirski. She could play good cop, for a good cause. She could sympathize with his trauma, add a war story from her first encounter with the dead to nudge him along. She could even ask him for help in broadcasting Nadine's picture, her vehicle, agree to work with him.

Not too friendly, she decided. It should be grudging, with underlying urgency. If she was right about him, he'd love the fact that she needed him, and that he could use her to pump up his own airtime.

Then again, if she was right about him, Nadine could already be dead.

Eve blocked that out. It couldn't be changed, and regrets could come later.

"Looking for something?"

Eve glanced down. The woman was so perfect, Eve might have been tempted to check for a pulse. Her face could have been carved from alabaster, her eyes painted with liquid emerald, her lips with crushed ruby. On-air talents were often known to leverage their first three years' salaries against cosmetic enhancement.

Eve figured unless this one had been born very lucky, she'd bet the first five. Her hair was gold-tipped bronze swept up and away from that staggering face. Her voice was trained to a throaty purr that transmitted competent sex.

"Gossip line, right?"

"Social information. Larinda Mars." She offered a perfect, long-fingered hand with tapered scarlet tips. "And you're Lieutenant Dallas."

"Mars. That's familiar."

"It should be." If Larinda was irked that Eve didn't place her instantly, she hid it well behind a dazzling white-toothed smile and a voice that held the faintest whiff of upper-class Brit. "I've been trying for weeks to nail down an interview with you and your fascinating companion. You haven't returned my messages."

"Bad habit of mine. Just like thinking my personal life is personal."

"When you're involved with a man like Roarke, personal life becomes public domain." Her gaze skittered down, latched like a hook on a point between Eve's breasts. "My, my, that's quite a little bauble. A gift from Roarke?"

Eve bit off an oath, closed her hand over the diamond. She'd taken to playing with it while she was thinking and had forgotten to shove it back under her shirt.

"I'm looking for Morse."

"Hmmm." Larinda had already calculated the size and value of the stone. It would make a nice side piece to her broadcast. Cop wears billionaire's ice. "I might be able to help you with that. And you'll return the favor. There's a little soiree at Roarke's tonight." She fluttered her incredible two-layer, two-toned lashes. "My invitation must have been lost."

"That's Roarke's deal. Talk to him."

"Oh." An expert on button pushing, Larinda leaned back. "So, he runs the show, does he? I suppose when a man's so used to making decisions, he wouldn't consult the little woman."

"I'm nobody's little woman," Eve shot back before she could stop herself. She took a breath for control, reevaluated the eerily beautiful face. "Nice one, Larinda."

"Yes, it was. So, how about a pass for tonight? I can save you a lot of time looking for Morse," she added, when Eve sent a new narrow-eyed stare around the room.

"Prove it, and we'll see."

"He left five minutes before you walked in." Without looking, Larinda punched the call coming in on her 'link to hold. Practically, she used a slim pointer rather than her expensive manicure. "In a hurry, I'd say, as he nearly knocked me off the ascent. He looked quite ill. Poor baby."

The venom there had Eve feeling more in tune with Larinda. "You don't like him."

"He's a puss ball," Larinda said in her melodious voice. "This is a competitive business, darling, and I'm not against stepping on someone's back now and then to get ahead. Morse is the kind who'd step on you, then sneak in a nice kick to the crotch and never break a sweat. He tried it with me when we were on the social beat together."

"And how did you handle that?"

She rolled a gorgeous shoulder. "Darling, I eat little weenies like him for breakfast. Still, he wasn't altogether bad, a whiz with research, and a good camera presence. Just thought he was too manly to scoop up gossip."

"Social information," Eve corrected with a thin smile.

"Right. Anyway, I wasn't sorry to see him shift over to hard news. You won't find that he's made many friends there, either. He's cut Nadine."

"What?" Bells rang in Eve's head.

"He wants to anchor, and he wants it solo. Every time he's on the news desk with her, he pulls little shit. Steps on her lines, adds a few seconds to his own time. Cuts her copy. Once or twice the TelePrompTer's been screwed up on her copy, too. Nobody could prove it, but Morse is the boy genius with electronics."

"Is he?"

"We all hate him," she said cheerfully. "Except upstairs. The brass think he's good ratings and appreciate his killer instinct."

"I wonder if they do," Eve murmured. "Where did he go?"

"We didn't stop to chat, but the way he looked, I'd say home and bed. He really looked sagged." She moved her curvy shoulders, sent some classy fragrance wafting up. "Maybe he's still shaking about finding Louise, and I should have more sympathy, but it's tough when it's Morse. Now, about that invitation?"

"Where's his station?"

Larinda sighed, flipped her call onto message mode and rose. "Over here." She glided through the aisles, proving that her body was every bit as impressive as her face. "Whatever you're looking for, you won't find it." She sent a wicked smile over her shoulder. "Did he do something? Did they finally pass a law making puss ball tendencies a crime?"

"I just need to talk to him. Why won't I find anything?"

Larinda paused at a corner cubicle, the console facing out so that anyone sitting behind it had his back to the wall and his eyes on the room. Nice little sign of paranoia, Eve thought.

"He never leaves anything out, not the tiniest memo, the bitsiest note. He locks down his computer if he stands up to scratch his butt. Claims somebody stole some of his research on one of his other gigs. He even uses an audio enhance, so he can whisper on calls and nobody can hear. As if we all strain to catch those golden words from his throat."

"So, how do you know he uses audio enhance?"

Larinda smiled. "Good one, Lieutenant. His console's locked, too," she added. "Discs secured." She flicked up a glance from under gold-tipped lashes. "Being a detective, you can probably figure out how I know that. Now, the invite?"

The cubicle was perfect, Eve thought. Awfully perfect for someone who had been hard at work, then had dashed out, ill. "Does he have a source at Cop Central?"

"I guess he may, though I can't imagine an actual human playing ball with Morse."

"Does he talk about it, brag about it?"

"Hey, in the gospel according to Morse, he's got top-level sources in the four corners of the universe." Her voice lost a bit of its sophistication on the dig, and whispered unmistakably of Queens. "But he never scooped Nadine. Well, until the Towers's murder, but he didn't last long on that."

Eve's heart was pounding now, strong and steady. She nodded, turned on her heel.

"Hey," Larinda called after her. "How about tonight? Tit for tat, Dallas."

"No cameras, or you're out before you're in," Eve warned and kept walking.

Because she remembered her days in uniform, and her ambition, Eve requested Peabody as her backup.

"He's going to remember your face." Eve waited impatiently as the elevator climbed to the thirty-third floor of Morse's building. "He's good with faces. I don't want you to say anything unless I give you an opening, then keep it brief, official. And look stern."

"I was born looking stern."

"Maybe toy with the hilt of your stunner now and again. You could look a little . . . anxious."

The corner of Peabody's mouth twitched. "Like I'd like to use it, but can't in the presence of a superior officer."

"You got it." She stepped off the elevator, turned left. "Feeney's still working on data, so I don't have as much as I'd like to pressure him with. The fact is, I could be wrong."

"But you don't think so."

"No, I don't think so. But I was wrong about David Angelini."

"You built a good circumstantial case, and he looked guilty as hell in interview." At Eve's casual glance, Peabody flushed. "Officers involved in a case are entitled to review all data pertaining to said case."

"I know the drill, Peabody." Very cool, very official, Eve announced herself through the entrance intercom. "You looking for a detective badge, Officer?"

Peabody squared her shoulders. "Yes, sir."

Eve merely nodded, announced herself again, and waited. "Walk down the hall, Peabody, see if the emergency exit is secure."

"Sir?"

"Walk down the hall," Eve repeated, holding Peabody's baffled gaze. "That's an order."

"Yes, sir."

The minute Peabody's back was turned, Eve took out her master code and disengaged the locks. She slid the door open a fraction and had the code back in her bag before Peabody came back.

"Secured, sir."

"Good. Doesn't look like he's home, unless . . . Well, look here, Peabody, the door isn't fully secured."

Peabody looked at the door, then back at Eve, and pursed her lips. "I would consider that unusual. We could have a break-in here, Lieutenant. Mr. Morse may be in trouble."

"You've got a point, Peabody. Let's put this on record." While Peabody engaged her recorder, Eve slid the door open, drew her weapon. "Morse? This is Lieutenant Dallas, NYPDS. The entrance is unsecured. We suspect a break-in and are entering the premises." She stepped in, signaled for Peabody to stand tight.

She slipped into the bedroom, checked closets, and skimmed a glance over the communications center that took up more room than the bed.

"No sign of an intruder," she said to Peabody, then ducked into the kitchen. "Where has our little bird flown?" she wondered. Pulling out her communicator, she contacted Feeney. "Give me everything you've got so far. I'm in his apartment, and he's not."

"I'm only about halfway there, but I think you're going to like it. First, the sealed juvie record—and I had to sweat for this one, kid. Little C. J. had a problem with his social science instructor when he was ten. She didn't give him an A on an assignment."

"Well, that bitch."

"That's what he figured, apparently. He broke into her house, wrecked the place. And killed her little doggie."

"Jesus, killed her dog?"

"Sliced its throat, Dallas. Ear to floppy ear. Ended up with mandatory therapy, probation, and community service."

"That's good." Eve felt the pieces shifting into place. "Keep going."

"Okay. I'm here to serve. Our pal drives a brand-new two-passenger Rocket."

"God bless you, Feeney."

"More," he said, preening a bit. "His first adult job was on dispatch at a little station in his own hometown. He quit when another reporter jogged ahead of him to an on-air assignment. A woman."

"Don't stop now. I think I love you."

"All the gold shields do. It's my pretty face. Got on air on the next gig, weekends only, subbing for the first and second string. Left in a huff, claiming discrimination. Assignment editor, female."

"Better and better."

"But here's the big one. Station he worked at in California. He was making it pretty good there, scrambled up from third string, got a regular spot on the midday, coanchoring."

"With a woman?"

"Yeah, but that's not the big guns, Dallas. Wait for it. Pretty little weather girl that was pulling in all the mail. Brass liked her so much they let her do some of the soft features on the midday. Ratings went up when she was on, and she started to get press of her own. Morse quit, citing he refused to work with a nonprofessional. That was just before the little weather girl got her big break, a recurring bit part in a comedy. Want to guess her name?"

Eve closed her eyes. "Tell me it's Yvonne Metcalf."

"Give the lieutenant a cigar. Metcalf had a notation about meeting the Dumb Ass from the partly sunny days. I'd say it's a good bet our boy looked her up in our fair city. Funny he never mentioned they were old pals in his reports. Would've given them such a nice shine."

"I do love you, desperately. I'm going to kiss your ugly face."

"Hey, it's lived in. That's what my wife tells me."

"Yeah, right. I need a search warrant, Feeney, and I need you here at Morse's to break down his computer."

"I've already requested the warrant. I'll have it transmitted to you as soon as it comes in. Then I'm on my way."

Sometimes the wheels moved smoothly. Eve had the warrant and Feeney within thirty minutes. She did kiss him, enthusiastically enough to have him going red as a hybrid beet.

"Secure the door, Peabody, then take the living area. Don't bother to be neat."

Eve swung into the bedroom, two steps ahead of Feeney. He was already rubbing his hands together.

"That's a beautiful system," he said. "Whatever his faults, the asshole knows his computers. It's going to be a pleasure to play with her." He sat down as Eve started to hunt through drawers.

"Obsessively trendy," she commented. "Nothing that shows too much sign of wear, nothing too expensive."

"He's putting all his money in his toys." Feeney hunched over, brows knit. "This guy respects his equipment, and he's careful. There are code blocks everywhere. Jesus, he's got a fail-safe."

"What?" Eve straightened up. "On a home unit?"

"He's got one, all right." Gingerly, Feeney eased back. "If I don't use the right code, the data's zapped. Odds are it's voice printed, too. It's not going to let me in easy, Dallas. I'm going to have to bring in some equipment, and it's going to take time."

"He's on the run. I know he's on the run. He knew we were coming after him."

Rocking back on her heels, she considered the possibilities: leaks—human—or electronic leaks.

"Call in your best man to come over here. You take the computer at the station. That's where he was when he ran."

"It's going to be a long night."

"Lieutenant." Peabody came to the door. Her face was impassive, but for the eyes. And the eyes were on fire. "I think you'd better see this."

In the living room, Peabody gestured to the blocky platform sofa. "I was giving it the once-over. Probably would have missed it, except my dad likes to build stuff. He was always putting in hidden drawers and hidey-holes. We got a kick out of it, used to play hidden treasure. I got curious when I saw the knob on the side. It looks like an ordinary decorative device that simulates old-fashioned turn bolts." She stepped around the front of the couch and gestured.

Eve could almost feel the vibrations rising from her skin.

Peabody's voice rose slightly in octave. "Hidden treasure."

Eve felt her heart kick once, hard. There in a long, wide drawer that slid from under the cushions lay a purple umbrella and a high-heeled red-and-white-striped shoe.

"Got him." Eve turned to Peabody with a fierce and powerful grin. "Officer, you've just taken one giant step toward your detective shield."

"My man says you're harassing him."

Eve scowled at Feeney's face in her communicator. "I'm simply asking him for periodic updates." She paced away from the sweepers who were scanning the living area of Morse's apartment. They had the lights on high. The sun was going down.

"And interrupting his flow. Dallas, I told you this would be slow work. Morse was an expert on compuscience. He knew all the tricks."

"He'd have written it down, Feeney. Like a fucking news report. And if he's got Nadine, that's on one of those damned discs, too."

"I'm with you on that, kid, but breathing down my man's neck isn't going to free up the data any quicker. Give us some space here, for Christ's sake. Don't you have a fancy do tonight?"

"What?" She grimaced. "Oh hell."

"Go put on your party dress and leave us alone."

"I'm not going to dress up like some brainless idiot and eat canapés while he's out there."

"He's going to be out there, whatever you're wearing. Listen up, we've got a citywide net out on him, his car. His apartment's under heavy surveillance, so's the station. You can't help us here. This part's my job."

"I can—"

"Slow up the process by making me talk to you," he snapped. "Go away, Dallas. The minute I get anything, the first byte, I'll call you in."

"We've got him, Feeney. We've got the who, the what."

"Let me try to find the where. If Nadine Furst is still alive, every minute counts."

That was what haunted her. She wanted to argue, but there was no ammunition. "Okay, I'll go, but—"

"Don't call me," Feeney interrupted. "I'll call you." He broke transmission before she could swear at him.

Eve was trying hard to understand relationships, the importance of balancing lives and obligations, the value of compromise. What she had with Roarke was still new enough to fit snugly, like a vaguely uncomfortable shoe, and lovely enough to keep wearing it until it stretched to accommodate.

So she dashed into the bedroom at a full run, saw him standing in the dressing area, and launched into the offense strategy.

"Don't give me any grief about being late. Summerset already handled that." She whipped off her harness, tossed it on a chair. Roarke finished securing a square of gold to his cuff, hands elegant, steady.

"You don't answer to Summerset." He looked at her then, a brief flick of the eyes as she tugged off her shirt. "Nor to me."

"Look, I had work." Naked from the waist up, she dropped into a chair to pull off her boots. "I said I'd be here, and I'm here. I know guests are going to be arriving in ten minutes." She heaved a boot aside as Summerset's abrasive words scraped through her head. "I'll be ready. I don't take hours to put some dress on and trowel a bunch of gunk on my face."

Boots disposed of, she arched her hips and wiggled out of her jeans. Before they hit the floor she was dashing into the adjoining bath. With a smile for the exit, Roarke followed her.

"There's no hurry, Eve. You don't clock in to a cocktail party, or get docked for tardiness."

"I said I'd be ready." She stood in the crisscrossing sprays of his shower, lathering pale green liquid into her hair. Suds dripped into her eyes. "I'll be ready."

"Fine, but no one will be offended if you come down in twenty minutes, or thirty for that matter. Do you expect me to be annoyed with you because you have another life?"

She swiped at her stinging eyes, tried to see him through suds and steam. "Maybe."

"Then you're doomed to disappointment. If you recall, I met you via that other life. And I have a number of other obligations as well." He watched her rinse her hair. It was pleasant to see the way she tilted her face back, the way water and soap sleeked down and away from her skin. "I'm not trying to box you in. I'm just trying to live with you."

She blew her wet hair out of her eyes as he opened the body dryer for her. She stepped toward it, pivoted. Then surprised him by grabbing his face in both of her hands and kissing him with a burst of enthusiasm.

"It can't be easy." She stepped into the tube and hit the power that swirled warm, dry air over her. "I can have a hard time living with myself. Sometimes I wonder why you don't just deck me when I start on you."

"It's occurred to me, but you're so often armed."

Dry and fragrant from the perfumed soap, she stepped out. "I'm not now."

He caught her by the waist, then stroked his hands down over her firm, muscled bottom. "Other things occur to me when you're naked."

"Yeah." She wrapped her arms around his neck, enjoying the fact that by rising slightly on her toes they were eye to eye, mouth to mouth. "Like what?"

With more than a little regret, he eased her back to arm's length. "Why don't you tell me why you're so revved?"

"Maybe it's because I like seeing you in a fancy shirt." She moved away, tugged a short dressing robe off a hanger. "Or maybe it's because I'm stimulated by the idea of wearing shoes that will make my arches scream for the next couple hours."

She peered into the mirror, and supposed she was obliged to put on a little of the paint Mavis was always pushing off on her. Leaning closer, she steadied the lash darkener and lengthener, closed it firmly over the lashes of her left eye, and hit the plunger.

"Just maybe," she continued glancing around, "it's because Officer Peabody found the hidden treasure."

"Good for Officer Peabody. What hidden treasure?"

Eve dealt with her right eyelashes, then blinked them experimentally. "One umbrella and one shoe."

"You've got him." Taking her shoulders, Roarke kissed her on the nape of the neck. "Congratulations."

"We've nearly got him," she corrected. She tried to remember what was next and chose lipstick. Mavis touted the virtues of lip dye, but Eve was wary of a color commitment that could last for three weeks. "We've got the evidence. The sweep confirmed his prints on the souvenirs. His and the victim's only on the umbrella. Got a few others on the shoe, but we expect salespeople or other customers. Brandnew shoes, hardly a scuff on the bottoms, and she picked up several pairs at Saks right before she died."

She went back to the bedroom, remembered the scented cream Roarke had brought back from Paris, and shrugged out of the robe to smear it on.

"The problem is, we don't have him. He got tipped somehow that I was coming and skipped. Feeney's working on his equipment now to see if we can shake loose some data that'll lead us to him. There's a net out, but he may have ditched the city. I wouldn't have made it tonight, but Feeney gave me the boot. Said I was harassing his man."

She opened the closet, pushed for revolve, and spotted the minuscule copper-colored dress. She took it out, held it in front of her. The sleeves were long and snug from a deep scooped neck. The skirt ended somewhere just south of the law.

"Am I supposed to wear anything under this?"

He reached in her top drawer, pulled out a matching colored triangle that might have laughingly been called panties. "These should do it."

She caught them from his underhand toss, wiggled in. "Jesus," she said after a quick look in the mirror. "Why bother?" Since it was too late to debate, she stepped into the dress and began to tug the clingy material up.

"It's always entertaining to watch you dress, but I'm distracted at the moment."

"I know, I know. Go on down. I'll be right there."

"No, Eve. Who?"

"Who?" She snapped the low shoulders into place. "Didn't I say?"

"No," Roarke said with admirable patience. "You didn't."

"Morse." She ducked into the closet for shoes.

"You're joking."

"C. J. Morse." She held the shoes as she might hold a weapon, and her eyes went dark and fixed. "And when I'm finished with the little son of a bitch, he's going to get more airtime than he ever dreamed of."

The in-house 'link beeped. Summerset's disapproving voice floated out. "The first guests are arriving, sir."

"Fine. Morse?" he said to Eve.

"That's right. I'll fill you in between canapés." She scooped a hand through her hair. "Told you I'd be ready. Oh, and Roarke?" She linked fingers with him as they started from the room. "I need you to pass a last-minute guest through for me. Larinda Mars."

chapter twenty

Eve supposed there could have been worse ways to wait through the last stages of an investigation. The atmosphere had it all over her cramped office at Cop Central, and the food was certainly a long leg up from the eatery.

Roarke had opened up his dome-ceilinged reception room with its glossy wood floors, mirrored walls, and sparkling lights. Long, curved tables followed the rounded walls and were artistically crowded with exotic finger foods.

Colorful bite-sized eggs harvested from the dwarf pigeons of the moon's farm colony, delicate pink shrimp from the Sea of Japan, elegant cheese swirls that melted on the tongue, pastries pumped with pâtés or creams in a menagerie of shapes, the gleam of caviar heaped on shaved ice, the richness of fresh fruit with frosty sugar coating.

There was more. The hot table across the room steamed with heat and spices. One entire area was a treasure trove for those of a vegetarian persuasion, with another, at a discreet distance, decked out for carnivores.

Roarke had opted for live music rather than simulation, and the band out on the adjoining terrace played quiet conversation-enhancing tunes. They would heat up as the night went on, to seduce dancers.

Through the swirl of color, of scent, of gleam and gloss, waiters in severe black wandered with silver trays topped with crystal flutes of champagne.

"This is so decent." Mavis popped a black button mushroom in her mouth. She'd dressed conservatively for the occasion, which meant a great deal of her skin was actually covered, and her hair was a tame medium red. Being Mavis, so were her irises. "I can't believe Roarke actually invited me."

"You're my friend."

"Yeah. Hey, you think if later on, after everybody's imbibed freely, could I ask the band to let me do a number?"

Eve scanned the rich, privileged crowd, the glint of real gold and real stones, and smiled. "I think that would be great."

"Superior." Mavis gave Eve's hand a quick squeeze. "I'm going to go talk to the band now, sort of worm my way into their hearts."

"Lieutenant."

Eve shifted her gaze from Mavis's retreating form over and up into Chief Tibble's face. "Sir."

"You're looking . . . unprofessional tonight." When she squirmed, he laughed. "That was a compliment. Roarke puts on quite a show."

"Yes, sir, he does. It's for a worthy cause." But she couldn't quite remember what that worthy cause was.

"I happen to think so. My wife is very involved." He took a flute from a passing tray and sipped. "My only regret is that these monkey suits never go out of style." With his free hand, he tugged at his collar.

It made her smile. "You should try wearing these shoes."

"There's a heavy price for fashion."

"I'd rather be dowdy and comfortable." But she resisted tugging at her butt-molding skirt.

"Well." He took her arm, eased her toward a shielding arborvitae. "Now that we've exchanged the obligatory small talk, I'd like to tell you you've done an excellent job on the investigation."

"I bumped with Angelini."

"No, you pursued a logical line, then you backtracked and found pieces others had missed."

"The albino junkie was a fluke, sir. Just luck."

"Luck counts. So does tenacity—and attention to detail. You cornered him, Dallas."

"He's still at large."

"He won't get far. His own ambition will help us find him. His face is known."

Eve was counting on it. "Sir, Officer Peabody did fine work. She has a sharp eye and good instincts."

"So you noted in your report. I won't forget it." When he glanced at his watch, she realized he was as edgy as she. "I promised Feeney a bottle of Irish whiskey if he broke it by midnight."

"If that doesn't do it, nothing will." She put on a smile. There was no use reminding the chief that they hadn't found the murder weapon in Morse's apartment. He already knew.

When she spotted Marco Angelini step into the room, her shoulders stiffened. "Excuse me, Chief Tibble. There's someone I have to speak to."

He laid a hand on her arm. "It isn't necessary, Dallas."

"Yes, sir, it is."

She knew the moment he became aware of her by the quick upward jut of his chin. He stopped, linked his hands behind his back, and waited.

"Mr. Angelini."

"Lieutenant Dallas."

"I regret the difficulties I caused you and your family during the investigation."

"Do you?" His eyes were cool, unblinking. "Accusing my

son of murder, subjecting him to terror and humiliation, bringing more grief upon already impossible grief, putting him behind bars when his only crime was witnessing violence?"

She could have justified her actions. She could have reminded him that his son had not only witnessed violence, but had turned away from it without a thought but to his own survival, and had compounded his crime by attempting to bribe his way out of involvement.

"I regret adding to your family's emotional trauma."

"I doubt if you understand the phrase." He skimmed his eyes down. "And I wonder if, had you not been so busy enjoying your companion's position, you might have caught the real murderer. It's easy enough to see what you are. You're an opportunist, a climber, a media whore."

"Marco." Roarke spoke softly as he laid a hand on Eve's shoulder.

"No." She went stiff under the touch. "Don't defend me. Let him finish."

"I can't do that. I'm willing to take your state of mind into account, Marco, as the reason you would attack Eve in her own home. You don't want to be here," he said in an undertone of steel that indicated he was taking nothing into account. "I'll show you out."

"I know the way." Marco's eyes stabbed at Eve. "We'll put our business association to an end as soon as possible, Roarke. I no longer trust your judgment."

Hands balled into fists at her side, Eve trembled with fury as Marco strode away. "Why did you do that? I could have handled it."

"You could have," Roarke agreed, and turned her to face him. "But that was personal. No one, absolutely no one comes into our home and speaks to you that way."

She tried to shrug it off. "Summerset does."

Roarke smiled, touched his lips to hers. "The exception, for reasons too complicated to explain." He rubbed away the frown line between her brows with his thumb.

"Okay. I guess I'm not going to be exchanging Christmas cards with the Angelinis."

"We'll learn to live with it. How about some champagne?"

"In a minute. I'm going to go freshen up." She touched his face. It was getting easier to do that, to touch him when they weren't alone. "I guess I ought to tell you that Mars has a recorder in her bag."

Roarke gave the dent in her chin a quick flick. "She did. I have it in mine now, after I let her crowd me at the vegetarian table."

"Very slick. You never mentioned pickpocketing as one of your skills."

"You never asked."

"Remind me to ask, and ask a lot. I'll be back."

She didn't care about freshening up. She wanted a few minutes to simmer down, and maybe a few more to call Feeney, though she imagined he'd bite her head off for interrupting his compusearch.

He still had an hour to go before he lost his bottle of Irish. She didn't think it would hurt to remind him. She was at the door to the library, preparing to code herself in, when Summerset melted out of the shadows behind her.

"Lieutenant, you have a call, termed both personal and urgent."

"Feeney?"

"He did not grant me his name," Summerset said down his nose.

"I'll take it in here." She had the small but worthy satisfaction of letting the door close smartly in his face. "Lights," she ordered and the room brightened.

She'd almost gotten used to the walls of books with leather bindings and paper pages that crackled when you leafed through. For once she didn't give them so much as a glance as she hurried to the 'link on Roarke's library desk.

She engaged, then froze.

"Surprise, surprise." Morse beamed at her. "Bet you

weren't expecting me. All dressed up for your party, I see. You look flash."

"I've been looking for you, C. J."

"Oh yeah, I know. You've been looking for a lot of things. I know this is on record, and it doesn't matter. But you listen close. You keep this between you and me, or I'm going to start slicing off little tiny pieces of a friend of yours. Say hi to Dallas, Nadine."

He reached out, and Nadine's face came on screen. Eve, who'd seen terror too many times to count, looked at it now. "Has he hurt you, Nadine?"

"I—" She whimpered when he jerked her head back by the hair, touched a long slim blade to her throat.

"Now, you tell her I've been real nice to you. Tell her." He skimmed the flat of the blade over her throat. "Bitch."

"I'm fine. I'm okay." She closed her eyes and a tear squeezed through. "I'm sorry."

"She's sorry," Morse said between pursed lips and pressed his cheek to Nadine's so both of their faces were in view. "She's sorry she was so hungry to be top bitch that she slipped the guard you put on her and fell right into my waiting arms. Isn't that right, Nadine?"

"Yes."

"And I'm going to kill you, but not quick like the others. I'm going to kill you slowly, and with a lot of pain, unless your pal the lieutenant does everything I say. Isn't that right? You tell her, Nadine."

"He's going to kill me." She pressed her lips together hard, but nothing would stop the trembling. "He's going to kill me, Dallas."

"That's right. You don't want her to die, do you, Dallas? It's your fault Louise died, yours and Nadine's fault. She didn't deserve it. She knew her place. She wasn't trying to be top cunt. It's your fault she's dead. You don't want that to happen again."

He still had the knife at Nadine's throat, and Eve could see his hand shake. "What do you want, Morse?" Calling up Mira's profile, she carefully hit the right buttons. "You're in control. You call the shots."

"That's right." His smile exploded. "Damn right. You've got my position coming up on screen by now. You see I'm at a nice quiet spot in Greenpeace Park, where nobody's going to bother us. All those nice green-lovers planted these pretty trees. It's a wonderful spot. Of course, nobody comes here after dark. Unless they're smart enough to know how to bypass the electronic field that discourages loiterers and chemi-heads. You've got exactly six minutes to get here so we can conduct our negotiations."

"Six minutes. I can barely make that at full speed. If I run into traffic—"

"Then don't," he snapped. "Six minutes from end of transmission, Dallas. Ten seconds over, ten seconds you might use to call this in, to contact anyone, to so much as blink for backup, and I start ripping Nadine. You come alone. If I smell an extra cop, I start on her. You want her to come alone, right, Nadine." As incentive, he turned the point of the blade to prick a narrow slice at the side of her throat.

"Please." She tried to arch back as the blood trickled. "Please."

"Cut her again, and I won't deal."

"You'll deal," Morse said. "Six minutes. Starting now."

The screen went blank. Eve's finger poised over the controls, thought of Dispatch, of the dozens of units that could be around the park in minutes. She thought of leaks, electronic leaks.

And she thought of the blood dribbling down Nadine's throat.

She bolted across the room and hit the elevator panel on the run. She needed her weapon.

C. J. Morse was having the time of his life. He'd begun to see that he'd sold himself short by killing quickly. There was so much more kick in courting fear, seducing it, watching it swell and climax.

He saw it in Nadine Furst's eyes. They were glassy now, the pupils huge, slick and black, with barely a rim of color at the edges. He was, he realized with great relish, literally scaring her to death.

He hadn't cut her again. Oh, he wanted to, and made sure he showed her the knife often so that she would never lose the fear that he could. But a part of him worried about the cunt cop.

Not that he couldn't handle her, Morse mused. He could handle her the only way women understood. By killing her. But he wouldn't make it fast, like the others. She'd tried to outsmart him, and that was an insult he wouldn't tolerate.

Women always tried to run the show, always got in the way, just when you were about to grab that fat brass ring. It had happened to him all of his life. All of his fucking life starting with his pushy bitch of a mother.

"You haven't done your best, C. J. Use your brains, for God's sake. You'll never get through life on looks or charm. You haven't got any. I expected more from you. If you can't be the best, you'll be nothing."

He'd taken it, hadn't he? Smiling to himself, he began to stroke Nadine's hair while she shuddered. He'd taken it for years, playing the good, devoted son, while at night he'd dreamed of ways to kill her. Wonderful dreams, sweaty and sweet, where he'd finally silenced that grating, demanding voice.

"So I did," he said conversationally, touching the tip of the knife to the pulse jerking in Nadine's throat. "And it was so easy. She was all alone in that big, important house, busy with her big, important business. And I walked right in. 'C. J.,' she said, 'what are you doing here? Don't tell me you've lost your job again. You'll never succeed in life unless you focus.' And I just smiled at her and I said, 'Shut up, Mother, shut the fuck up.' And I cut her throat."

To demonstrate, he trailed the blade over Nadine's throat, lightly, just enough to scrape the skin. "She gushed and she goggled, and she shut the fuck up. But you know, Nadine, I learned something from the old bitch. It was time

I focused. I needed a goal. And I decided that goal would be to rid the world of loudmouthed, pushy women, the ball breakers of the world. Like Towers and Metcalf. Like you, Nadine." He leaned over, kissed her dead center of the forehead. "Just like you."

She was reduced to whimpers. Her mind had frozen. She'd stopped trying to twist her wrists out of the restraints, stopped trying anything. She sat docile as a doll, with the occasional quiver breaking her stillness.

"You kept trying to shove me aside. You even went to management to try to get me off the news desk. You told them I was a . . ." He tapped the blade against her throat for emphasis. "Pain in the ass. You know that bitch Towers wouldn't even give me an interview. She embarrassed me, Nadine. Wouldn't even acknowledge me at press conferences. But I fixed her. A good reporter digs, right Nadine? And I dug, and I got a nice juicy story about her darling daughter's idiot lover. Oh, I sat on it, and sat on it, while the happy mother of the bride to be made all her wedding plans. I could have blackmailed her, but that wasn't the goal, was it? She was so ticked when I called her that night, when I dumped it all in her face."

His eyes narrowed. They gleamed. "She was going to talk to me then, Nadine. Oh, you bet she was going to talk. She'd have tried to ruin me, even though I was only going to report the facts. But Towers was a big fucking deal, and she would have tried to squash me like a bug. That's exactly what she said over the 'link. But she did exactly what she was told. And when I walked toward her on that nasty little street, she sneered at me. The bitch sneered at me and she said, 'You're late. Now, you little bastard, we're going to set things straight.' "

He laughed so hard he had to press a hand to his stomach. "Oh, I set her straight. Gush and goggle, just like my dear old mother."

He gave Nadine a quick slap on the top of the head, rose, and faced the camera he had set up. "This is C. J. Morse reporting. As the clock ticks away the seconds, it appears that the heroic Lieutenant Cunt will not arrive in time to save her fellow bitch from execution. Though it has long been considered a sexist cliché, this experiment has proven that women are always late."

He laughed uproariously and gave Nadine a careless backhanded slap that knocked her back on the bench where he'd put her. After one last, high-pitched giggle, he controlled himself and frowned soberly into the lens.

"The public broadcasting of executions was banned in this country in 2012, five years before the Supreme Court once again ruled that capital punishment was unconstitutional. Of course, the court was forced into that decision by five idiot, bigmouthed women, so this reporter deems that ruling null and void."

He took a small pocket beam out of his jacket before turning to Nadine. "I'm going to key into the station now, Nadine. On air in twenty." Thoughtfully, he tilted his head. "You know, you could use a little makeup. It's a pity there isn't time. I'm sure you'd want to look your best for your final broadcast."

He walked to her, laid the length of the knife at her throat, and faced the camera. "In ten, nine, eight . . ." He glanced over at the sound of rushing feet on the crushed stone path. "Well, well, here she is now. And with seconds to spare."

Eve skidded to a halt on the path and stared. She'd seen a great deal in her decade on the force. Plenty that she often wished could be erased from her memory. But she'd never seen anything to compare with this.

She'd followed the light, the single light that beamed a circle around the tableau. The park bench where Nadine sat passively, blood drying on her skin, a knife at her throat. C. J. Morse behind her, dressed nattily in a round-collared shirt and color-coordinated jacket, facing a camera on a slim tripod. Its red light beamed as steadily as judgment's eye.

"What the hell are you doing, Morse?"

"Live stand up," he said cheerfully. "Please, step into the light, Lieutenant, so our viewers can see you."

Keeping her eyes on his, Eve stepped into the circle.

She'd been gone too long, Roarke thought and found himself irritated by the party chat. Obviously, she'd been more upset than he'd realized, and he regretted not dealing with Angelini more effectively.

Damn if he'd let her brood or take on blame. The only way to make sure she didn't was to amuse or annoy the mood out of her. He slipped quietly from the room, away from the lights and music and voices. The house was too big to search, but he could pinpoint her location with one question.

"Eve," he said, the moment Summerset stepped from a room to the right.

"She's gone."

"What do you mean gone? Gone where?"

Because discussing the woman always put Summerset's back up, he lifted his shoulders. "I couldn't say, she simply ran out of the house, got into her vehicle, and drove off. She did not deign to inform me of her plans."

The nasty twisting in Roarke's gut sharpened his voice. "Don't fuck with me, Summerset. Why did she leave?"

Insulted, Summerset tightened his jaw. "Perhaps it was due to the call she received a few moments ago. She took it in the library."

Turning on his heel, Roarke strode to the library door, uncoded it. With Summerset at his heels, he stepped up to the table. "Replay, last call."

As he watched, listened, the twisting in his gut turned to a burning that was fear. "Christ Jesus, she's gone for him. She's gone alone."

He was out of the door and moving fast, the order shot over his shoulder like a laser. "Relay that information to Chief Tibble—privately."

• • •

"Though our time is short, Lieutenant, I'm sure our viewers would be fascinated by the investigative process." Morse kept the pleasant, camera smile on his face, the knife at Nadine's throat. "You did pursue a false lead for a time, and were, I believe, on the point of charging an innocent man."

"Why did you kill them, Morse?"

"Oh, I've documented that extensively, for future broadcast. Let's talk about you."

"You must have felt terrible when you realized you'd killed Louise Kirski instead of Nadine."

"I felt very bad about that, sickened. Louise was a nice, quiet woman with an appropriate attitude. But it wasn't my fault. It was yours and Nadine's for trying to bait me."

"You wanted exposure." She flicked a glance toward the camera. "You're certainly getting it now. But this is putting you in a spot, Morse. You won't get out of this park now."

"Oh, I have a plan, don't worry about me. And we have just a few minutes left before we have to end this. The public has a right to know. I want them to see this execution. But I wanted you to see it in person. To witness what you caused."

She looked at Nadine. No help there, she noted. The woman was in deep shock, possibly drugged. "I won't be as easy to take."

"You'll be more fun."

"How did you take Nadine?" Eve stepped closer, keeping her eyes on his and her hands in sight. "You had to be clever."

"I'm very clever. People—women in particular—don't give me enough credit. I just leaked a tip to her about the murders. A message from a frightened witness who wanted to speak to her, alone. I knew she'd ditch her guard, an ambitious woman after the big story. I got her in the parking garage. Just as simple as that. Gave her a dose of a deep tranq, loaded her in her own trunk, and drove off. Left her and the car in a little rent space zone way downtown."

"You were smart." She stepped closer, stopping when he

lifted his brows and pressed the knife more firmly. "Really smart," she said, lifting her hands up. "You knew I was coming for you. How did you know?"

"You think your wrinkled pal Feeney knows everything about computers? Hell, I can run rings around that hacker. I've been keyed in to your system for weeks. Every transmission, every plan, every step you took. I was always ahead of you, Dallas."

"Yeah, you were ahead of me. You don't want to kill her, Morse. You want me. I'm the one who ragged on you, gave you all the grief. Why don't you let her go? She's zoned, anyway. Take me on."

He flashed his quick, boyish smile. "Why don't I kill her first, then you?"

Eve lifted a shoulder. "I thought you liked a challenge. Guess I was wrong. Towers was a challenge. You had to do a lot of fast talking to get her where you wanted her. But Metcalf was nothing."

"Are you serious? She thought I was puss." He bared his teeth, hissed through them. "She'd still be doing weather if she hadn't had tits, and they were giving her my airtime. My fucking airtime! I had to pretend I was a big fan, tell her I was going to do a twenty-minute feature on her. Just her. Told her we had a shot at international satellite, and she bit good."

"So she met you that night on the patio."

"Yeah, she got herself all slicked up, was all smiles and no hard feelings. Tried to tell me she was glad I'd found my niche. My goddamn niche. Well, I shut her up."

"You did. I guess you were pretty smart with her, too. But Nadine, she's not saying anything. She can't even think right now. She won't know you're paying her back."

"I'll know. Time's up. You might want to stand to the side, Dallas, or you're going to get blood all over your party dress."

"Wait." She took a step and, feinting to the side and reaching a hand to the small of her back, she whipped out her weapon. "Blink, you bastard, and I'll fry you."

He did blink, several times. It seemed to him the weapon had come from nowhere. "You use that, my hand's going to jerk. She'll be dead before I am."

"Maybe," Eve said steadily. "Maybe not. You're dead, either way. Drop the knife, Morse, step away from her, or your nervous system's going to go on fast overload."

"Bitch. You think you're going to beat me." He jerked Nadine to her feet, shielding himself from a clean shot, then shoved her forward.

Eve caught Nadine with one arm while she aimed with her weapon hand, but he was already into the trees. Seeing no choice, Eve slapped Nadine hard, front handed, then back. "Snap out of it. Goddamn it."

"He's killing me." Nadine's eyes rolled back, then forward when Eve hit her again.

"Get moving, do you hear me? You get moving, call this in. Now."

"Call it in."

"That way." Eve gave Nadine a shove toward the path, hoped she'd stay on her feet, and dashed toward the trees.

He'd said he had a plan, and she didn't doubt it. Even if he managed to get out of the park, they'd bring him in, eventually. But he was primed to kill now—some woman walking her dog on the sidewalk, or someone coming home from a late date.

He'd use the knife on anyone now because he'd failed again.

She stopped in the shadows, ears straining for sound, breath rigidly controlled. Dimly, she could hear the sounds of street and air traffic, could see the lights of the city beyond the thick border of trees.

A dozen paths spread out before her that would wind through the glade and the gardens so lovingly planted, so carefully designed.

She heard something. Perhaps a footstep, perhaps a bush rustled by some small animal. With her weapon blinking ready, she stepped deeper into the shadows.

There was a fountain, its waters silent in the dark. A

small children's playground, with glide swings, twisty slides, the foamy jungle gym that prevented little climbers from bruising shins and elbows.

She scanned the area, cursing herself for not grabbing a search beam out of her car. There was too much dark pouring dangerously out of the trees. Too much silence hanging on the air like a shroud.

Then she heard the scream.

He'd circled back, she thought. *The bastard has circled back and gone for Nadine after all.* Eve spun around, and her instinct to protect saved her life.

The knife caught her on the collarbone, a long, shallow cut that stung ridiculously. She blocked with her elbow, connected with his jaw, spoiled his aim. But the blade flew out, slicing her just above the wrist. Her weapon spun uselessly out of her wounded hand.

"You thought I was going to run." His eyes glowed sickly in the dark as he circled her. "Women always underestimate me, Dallas. I'm going to cut you to pieces. I'm going to rip your throat." He jabbed, sending her back a step. "I'm going to rip your guts." He swung again, and she felt the wind from the blade. "I'm in charge now, aren't I?"

"Like hell." Her kick was well aimed, a woman's ultimate defense. He went down, air bursting through his lips like a popped balloon. The knife clattered on stone. And she was on him.

He fought like what he was—a madman. His fingers tore at her, his teeth snapped as they sought flesh to sink into. Her wounded arm was slick with blood, and slipped off him as she struggled to find the point under his jaw that would immobilize him.

They rolled over the crushed stone and trimmed sod, viciously silent but for grunts and labored breathing. His hand dug along the path for the hilt of the knife, hers clawing after it. Then stars exploded in her head as he pumped his fist into her face.

She was dazed for only an instant, but she knew she was

dead. She saw the knife, and her fate, and sucked in her breath to meet it.

Later she would think it had sounded like a wolf, that howl of rage, a blood cry. Morse's weight was off of her, his body spinning away. She rolled to her hands and knees, shaking her head.

The knife, she thought frantically, the goddamn knife. But she couldn't find it, and crawled toward the dull gleam of her weapon.

It was in her hand, poised, when her mind cleared enough to understand. Two men were fighting, grappling like dogs in the pretty playground. And one of them was Roarke.

"Get away from him." She scrambled to her feet, teetered, braced. "Get away from him so I can get a shot."

They rolled again, end over end. Roarke's hand gripped Morse's, but Morse's held the knife. Through the rage, the duty, the instinct, came a titanic, jittering fear.

Weak, still losing blood, she leaned back on the padded bars of the gym, steadied her weapon hand with the other. In the dappled moonlight she could see Roarke's fist plunge, hear the crack of bone on bone. The knife strained, the blade angling.

Then she watched it plunge, watched it quiver as it found its home in Morse's throat.

Someone was praying. When Roarke got to his feet, she realized it was herself. She stared at him, let her weapon lower. His face was fierce, his eyes hot enough to burn. There was blood soaking his elegant dinner jacket.

"You're a goddamn mess," she managed.

"You should look at yourself." His breathing was labored, and he knew from experience that he would feel every miserable bruise and scrape later. "Don't you know it's rude to leave a party without making your excuses?"

Legs trembling with reaction, she took a step toward him, then stopped, swallowing the sob that was bubbled in her throat. "Sorry. I'm sorry. God, are you hurt?"

She launched herself at him, all but burrowing when he

caught her close. "Did he cut you? Are you cut?" She yanked back, began to fumble at his clothes.

"Eve." He jerked her chin up, steadied it. "You're bleeding badly."

"He caught me a couple times." She swiped a hand under her nose. "It's not bad." But Roarke was already using a square of Irish linen from his pocket to staunch and wrap the arm wound. "And it's my job." She took a deep breath, felt the black edges around her vision creeping back until she could see clearly. "Where are you cut?"

"It's his blood," Roarke said calmly. "Not mine."

"His blood." She nearly wobbled again, forced her knees to lock. "You're not hurt?"

"Nothing major." Concerned, he angled her head back to examine the shallow slice along her collarbone, the rapidly swelling eye. "You need a medic, Lieutenant."

"In a minute. Let me ask you something."

"Ask away." Having nothing else, he tore part of his ripped sleeve to dab at the blood on her shoulder.

"Do I come charging into one of your board rooms when you're having trouble with a business deal?"

His eyes flicked to hers. Some of the fierceness died out of them into what was almost a smile. "No, Eve, you don't. I don't know what got into me."

"It's okay." Since there was nowhere else to put it, she jabbed her weapon onto her lower back where she'd fixed it with adhesive. "This once," she murmured and caught his face in her hands, "it's okay. It's okay. I was scared when I couldn't get past you for a shot. I thought he would kill you before I could stop him."

"Then you should understand the feeling." Giving her a supporting arm around the waist, they began to limp off. After a moment, Eve realized she was limping primarily because she'd lost a shoe. Hardly breaking stride, she stepped out of the other. Then she spotted lights up ahead.

"Cops?"

"I imagine. I ran into Nadine as she was stumbling along the path toward the main gate. He'd given her a pretty rough time, but she'd pulled it together enough to tell me which direction you'd gone off in."

"I could probably have dealt with the bastard on my own," Eve murmured, recovered enough to worry about it. "But you sure handled yourself, Roarke. You got a real knack for hand to hand."

Neither of them mentioned how the knife had come to be planted in Morse's throat.

She saw Feeney in the circle of light, near the camera, with a dozen other cops. He merely shook his head and signaled for the medteam. Nadine was already on a stretcher, pale as wax.

"Dallas." She lifted a hand, let it fall. "I blew it."

Eve leaned over as one of the medics dispensed with Roarke's first aid on her arm and began his own. "He pumped you full of chemicals."

"I blew it," Nadine repeated, as the stretcher lifted toward a medunit. "Thanks for the rest of my life."

"Yeah." She turned away, sat heavily on the cushioned support in the triage area. "You got something for my eye?" she asked. "It's throbbing bad."

"Going to be black," she was told cheerfully as an ice gel was laid over it.

"There's good news. No hospitals," she said, firm. The medic just clucked his tongue and began work on cleaning and closing her wounds.

"Sorry about the dress." She smiled up at Roarke and fingered a tattered sleeve. "It didn't hold up very well." Getting to her feet, she brushed the fussing medic aside. "I'm going to need to go back and change, then go in to file my report." She looked steadily into his eyes. "It's too bad Morse rolled on his knife. The PA's office would have loved to bring him to trial." She held out a hand, then examined the raw knuckles of Roarke's and shook her head. "Did you howl?"

"I beg your pardon?"

She chuckled, leaned on him as they headed out of the park. "All in all, it was a hell of a party."

"Hmm. We'll have others. But there's one thing."

"Hmm?" She flexed her fingers, relieved that they seemed to be back in full working order. The MTs knew their stuff.

"I want you to marry me."

"Uh-huh. Well, we'll—" She stopped, nearly stumbled, then gaped at him with her good eye. "You want what?"

"I want you to marry me."

He had a bruise on his jaw, blood on his coat, and a gleam in his eye. She wondered if he'd lost his mind. "We're standing here, beat to shit, walking away from a crime scene where either or both of us could have bought it, and you're asking me to marry you?"

He tucked his arm around her waist again, nudged her forward. "Perfect timing."

JUDGMENT IN DEATH

She stood in Purgatory and studied death. The blood and the gore of it, the ferocity of its glee. It had come to this place with the willful temper of a child, full of heat and passion and careless brutality.

Murder was rarely a tidy business. Whether it was craftily calculated or wildly impulsive, it tended to leave a mess for others to clean up.

It was her job to wade through the debris of murder, to pick up the pieces, see where they fit, and put together a picture of the life that had been stolen. And through that picture to find the image of a killer.

Now, in the early hours of morning, in the hesitant spring of 2059, her boots crunched over a jagged sea of broken glass. Her eyes, brown and cool, scanned the scene: shattered mirrors, broken bottles, splintered wood. Wall screens were smashed, privacy booths scarred and dented. Pricey leather and cloth that had covered stools or the plusher seating areas had been ripped to colorful shreds.

What had once been an upscale strip club was now a jumbled pile of expensive garbage.

What had once been a man lay behind the wide curve of the bar. Now a victim, sprawled in his own blood.

Lieutenant Eve Dallas crouched beside him. She was a cop, and that made him hers.

"Male. Black. Late thirties. Massive trauma, head and body. Multiple broken bones." She took a gauge from her field kit to take the body and ambient temperatures. "Looks like the fractured skull would have done the job, but it didn't stop there."

"He was beaten to pieces."

Eve acknowledged her aide's comment with a grunt. She was looking at what was left of a well-built man in his prime, a good six-two and two hundred and thirty pounds of what had been toned muscle.

"What do you see, Peabody?"

Automatically, Peabody shifted her stance, focused her vision. "The victim . . . well, it appears the victim was struck from behind. The first blow probably took him down, or at least dazed him. The killer followed through, with repeated strikes. From the pattern of the blood splatter, and brain matter, he was taken out with head shots, then beaten while down, likely unconscious. Some of the injuries were certainly delivered postmortem. The metal bat is the probable murder weapon and was used by someone of considerable strength, possibly chemically induced, as the scene indicates excessive violence often demonstrated by users of Zeus."

"Time of death, oh four hundred," Eve stated, then turned her head to look up at Peabody.

Her aide was starched and pressed and as official as they came, with her uniform cap set precisely on her dark chin-length hair. She had good eyes, Eve thought, clear and dark. And though the sheer vileness of the scene had leached some of the color from her cheeks, she was holding.

"Motive?" Eve asked.

"It appears to be robbery, Lieutenant."

"Why?"

"The cash drawer's open and empty. The credit machine's broken."

"Mmm-hmm. Snazzy place like this would be heavier in credits, but they'd do some cash business."

"Zeus addicts kill for spare change."

"True enough. But what would our victim have been doing alone, in a closed club, with an addict? Why would he let anyone hopped on Zeus behind the bar? And . . ." With her sealed fingers she picked up a small silver credit chip from the river of blood. "Why would our addict leave these behind? A number of them are scattered here around the body."

"He could have dropped them." But Peabody began to think she wasn't seeing something Eve did.

"Could have."

She counted the coins as she picked them up, thirty in all, sealed them in an evidence bag, and handed it to Peabody. Then she picked up the bat. It was fouled with blood and brain. About two feet in length, she judged, and weighted to mean business.

Mean business.

"It's good, solid metal, not something an addict would pick up in some abandoned building. We're going to find this belonged here, behind the bar. We're going to find, Peabody, that our victim knew his killer. Maybe they were having an after-hours drink."

Her eyes narrowed as she pictured it. "Maybe they had words, and the words escalated. More likely, our killer already had an edge on. He knew where the bat was. Came behind the bar. Something he'd done before, so our friend here doesn't think anything of it. He's not concerned, doesn't worry about turning his back."

She did so herself, measuring the position of the body, of the splatter. "The first blow rams him face first into the glass on the back wall. Look at the cuts on his face. Those aren't nicks from flying glass. They're too long, too deep. He manages to turn, and that's where the killer takes the next swing here, across the jaw. That spins him around again. He grabs the shelves there, brings them down. Bottles crashing. That's when he took the killing blow. This one that cracked his skull like an egg."

She crouched again, sat back on her heels. "After that, the killer just beat the hell out of him, then wrecked the place. Maybe in temper, maybe as cover. But he had enough control to come back here, to look at his handiwork before he left. He dropped the bat here when he was done."

"He wanted it to look like a robbery? Like an illegals overkill?"

"Yeah. Or our victim was a moron and I'm giving him too much credit. You got the body and immediate scene recorded? All angles?"

"Yes, sir."

"Let's turn him over."

The shattered bones shifted like a sack of broken crockery as Eve turned the body. "Goddamn it. Oh, goddamn it."

She reached down to lift the smeared ID from the cool, congealing pool of blood. With her sealed thumb, she wiped at the photo and the shield. "He was on the job."

"He was a cop?" Peabody stepped forward. She heard the sudden silence. The crime scene team and the sweepers working on the other side of the bar stopped talking. Stopped moving.

A half dozen faces turned. Waited.

"Kohli, Detective Taj." Eve's face was grim as she got to her feet. "He was one of us."

Peabody crossed the littered floor to where Eve stood watching the remains of Detective Taj Kohli being bagged for transferal to the morgue. "I got his basics, Dallas. He's out of the One-twenty-eight, assigned to Illegals. Been on the job for eight years. Came out of the military. He was thirty-seven. Married. Two kids."

"Anything pop on his record?"

"No, sir. It's clean."

"Let's find out if he was working under cover here or just moonlighting. Elliott? I want those security discs."

"There aren't any." One of the crime scene team hurried over. His face was folded into angry lines. "Cleaned out. Every one of them. The place had full scope, and this son of a bitch snagged every one. We got nothing."

"Covered his tracks." With her hands on her hips, Eve turned a circle. The club was triple-leveled, with a stage on the main, dance floors on one and two. Privacy rooms ringed the top. For full scope, she estimated it would need a dozen cameras, probably more. To snag all the record discs would have taken time and care.

"He knew the place," she decided. "Or he's a fucking security whiz. Window dressing," she muttered. "All this destruction's just window dressing. He knew what he was doing. He had control. Peabody, find out who owns the place, who runs it. I want to know everybody who works here. I want to know the set up."

"Lieutenant?" A harassed-looking sweeper trudged through the chaos. "There's a civilian outside."

"There are a lot of civilians outside. Let's keep them there."

"Yes, sir, but this one insists on speaking to you. He says this is his place. And, ah . . ."

" 'And, ah' what?"

"And that you're his wife."

"Roarke Entertainment," Peabody announced as she read off the data from her palm PC. She sent Eve a cautious smile. "Guess who owns Purgatory?"

"I should've figured it." Resigned, Eve strode to the entrance door.

He looked very much as he'd looked two hours before when they'd parted ways to go about their individual business. Sleek and gorgeous. The light topcoat he wore over his dark suit fluttered a bit in the breeze. The same breeze that tugged at the mane of black hair that framed his poetically sinful face. The dark glasses he wore against the glare of the sun only added to the look of slick elegance.

And when he slipped them off as she stepped out, the brilliant blue of his eyes met hers. He tucked the glasses in his pocket, lifted an eyebrow.

"Good morning, Lieutenant."

"I had a bad feeling when I walked in here. It's just your kind of place, isn't it? Why do you have to own every damn thing?"

"It was a boyhood dream." His voice cruised over Ireland, picked up the music of it. He glanced past her to the police seal. "It appears we've both been inconvenienced."

"Did you have to tell the sweeper I was your wife?"

"You are my wife," he said easily and shifted his gaze back to her face. "A fact which pleases me daily." He took her hand, rubbing his thumb over her wedding ring before she could tug it free again.

"No touching," she hissed at him, which made him smile.

"That's not what you said a few hours ago. In fact—"

"Shut up, Roarke." She glanced around, though none of the cops working the scene was outside or close enough to hear. "This is a police investigation."

"So I'm told."

"And who told you?"

"The head of the maintenance team who found the body. He did call the police first," he pointed out. "But it's natural he'd report the incident to me. What happened?"

There was no point in griping because his business had tangled around hers. Again. She tried to console herself that he could and would help her cut through some of the muck of paperwork.

"Do you have a bartender by the name of Kohli? Taj Kohli?"

"I have no idea. But I can find out." He took a slim memo

book out of his breast pocket, keyed in a request for data. "Is he dead?"

"As dead gets."

"Yes, he was mine," Roarke confirmed, and the Irish in his voice had taken on a cold note. "For the past three months. Part time. Four nights a week. He had a family."

"Yes, I know." Such things mattered to him, and it always touched her heart. "He was a cop," Eve said. This time her brows lifted. "Didn't have that data in your little scan, did you?"

"No. It seems my personnel director was careless. That will be fixed. Am I allowed inside?"

"Yeah, in a minute. How long have you owned the place?"

"Four years, more or less."

"How many employees, full and part-time?"

"I'll get you all the data, Lieutenant, and answer all pertinent questions." Annoyance gleamed in his eyes as he reached for the door himself. "But now, I'd like to see my place."

He pushed inside, scanned the destruction, then focused in on the thick black bag being loaded on what the death attendants called a stroller.

"How was he killed?"

"Thoroughly," Eve said, then sighed when Roarke simply turned and stared at her. "It was ugly, okay? Metal bat." She watched Roarke look toward the bar and the spray of blood sparkling on glass like an incomprehensible painting. "After the first few hits, he wouldn't have felt anything."

"Ever had a bat laid into you? I have," he said before she could answer. "It's not pleasant. It seems far-fetched to think it's robbery, even one that got well out of hand."

"Why?"

"There'd have been enough prime liquor, easily fenced, to keep anyone cozily fixed for some time. Why break the bottles when you could sell them? If you hit a place like this, it's not for the bit of cash that might be copped, but for the inventory and perhaps some of the equipment."

"Is that the voice of experience?"

She teased a grin out of him. "Naturally. My experience, that is, as a property owner and a law-abiding citizen."

"Right."

"Security discs?"

"Gone. He got all of them."

"Then it follows he'd cased the place carefully before-hand."

"How many cameras?"

Once again, Roarke took out his pad, checked data. "Eighteen. Nine on this floor, six on two, and the other two on the top level for full scope. Before you ask, closing is at three, which would have staff out by half past. The last show, and we've live ones here, ends at two. The musicians and the entertainers—"

"Strippers."

"As you like," he said mildly. "They clock off at that time. I'll have names and schedules for you within the hour."

"Appreciate it. Why Purgatory?"

"The name?" The ghost of a smile flirted with his mouth. "I liked it. The priests will tell you Purgatory's a place for atonement, rehabilitation perhaps. A bit like prison. I've always seen it as a last chance to be human," he decided. "Before you strap on your wings and halo or face the fire."

"Which would you rather?" she wondered. "The wings or the fire?"

"That's the point, you see. I prefer being human." As the stroller wheeled by, he ran a hand over her short brown hair. "I'm sorry for this."

"So am I. Any reason a New York City detective would have been working under cover in Purgatory?"

"I couldn't say. It's certainly likely that some of the clien-tele might dabble in areas not strictly approved by the NYPSD, but I've not been informed of anything overt. Some illegals might change hands in privacy rooms or under tables, but there's been no large transactions here. I would have known. The strippers don't turn tricks unless they're licensed, which some are. No one under age is allowed through the doors—as client or staff. I have my own standards, Lieutenant, such as they are."

"I'm not coming down on you. I need a picture."

"You're pissed that I'm here at all."

She waited a minute, her short, choppy hair disordered from its dance outside in the early breeze. As the morgue techs opened the door to transfer Kohli, the sounds of the day punched into the club.

Traffic was already thickening. Cars crammed irritably on the street, air commuters swarmed the skies. She heard the call of an early-bird glide-cart operator call to the techs and ask: "What da fuck?"

"Okay, I'm pissed that you're here at all. I'll get over it. When's the last time you were in here?"

"Months. It ran well and didn't need my direct attention."

"Who manages it for you?"

"Rue MacLean. I'll get her information to you as well."

"Sooner than later. Do you want to go through the place now?"

"No point in it until I've refreshed myself on how it was. I'll want to be let back in once I've done that."

"I'll take care of it. Yes, Peabody?" she said, turning as her aide inched forward and cleared her throat.

"Sorry, sir, but I thought you'd want to know I reached the victim's squad captain. They're sending a member of his unit and a counselor to inform next of kin. They need to know if they should wait for you or see the wife alone."

"Tell them to wait. We'll head over now and meet them. I have to go," she said to Roarke.

"I don't envy you your job, Lieutenant." Because he needed it, he took her hand, linked their fingers firmly. "But I'll let you get back to it. I'll have the information you wanted to you as soon as I can."

"Roarke?" she called as he started for the door. "I'm sorry about your place."

"Wood and glass. There's plenty more," he replied as he looked at her over his shoulder.

"He doesn't mean it," Eve murmured when he'd shut the door behind him.

"Sir?"

"They messed with him. He won't let it go." Eve heaved out a breath. "Come on, Peabody, let's go see the wife and get this particular hell over with."

The Kohlis lived in a decent, midlevel building on the East Side. The kind of place, Eve mused, where you found young families and older retired couples. Not hip enough for the single crowd, not cheap enough for the struggling.

It was a simple multiunit, pleasantly if not elegantly rehabbed post–Urban Wars.

Door security was a basic code entry.

Eve spotted the cops before she'd double-parked and flipped her On Duty light to active.

The woman was well turned out, with gilt-edged hair that curved up to her cheeks in two stiletto points. She wore sun shades and an inexpensive business suit in navy. The shoes with their thin, two-inch heels told Eve she worked a desk.

Brass. Eve was sure of it.

The man had good shoulders and a bit of pudge at the middle. He'd let his hair go gray, and there was a lot of it. Currently, it was dancing in the breeze around his quiet, composed face. He wore cop shoes—hard-soled and buffed to a gleam. His suit jacket was a little small in the body and starting to fray at the cuffs.

A long-timer, Eve judged, who'd moved from beat to street to desk.

"Lieutenant Dallas." The woman stepped forward but didn't offer her hand for a polite shake. "I recognized you.

You get a lot of play in the media." It wasn't said with rebuke, but there was a hint of it in the air, nonetheless. "I'm Captain Roth, from the One twenty-eight. This is Sergeant Clooney out of my house. He's here as grief counselor."

"Thanks for waiting. Officer Peabody, my aide."

"What is the status of your investigation, Lieutenant?"

"Detective Kohli's body is with the ME and will have priority. My report will be written and filed subsequent to notification of next of kin."

She paused to avoid shouting over the sudden blast of a maxibus that pulled to the curb half a block down.

"At this point, Captain Roth, I have a dead police officer who was the apparent victim of a particularly brutal beating in the early hours of this morning while he was in a club, after hours. A club where he was employed as a part-time bartender."

"Robbery?"

"Unlikely."

"Then what is the motive, in your opinion?"

A little seed of resentment planted itself in Eve's gut. It would, she knew, fester there if she wasn't careful. "I've formed no opinion as to motive at this stage of my investigation. Captain Roth, do you want to stand on the street and question me, or would you prefer to read my report when it's filed?"

Roth opened her mouth, then sucked in a breath. "Point taken, Lieutenant. Detective Kohli worked under me for five years. I'll be straight with you. I want this investigation handled out of my house."

"I appreciate your feelings in this matter, Captain Roth. I can only assure you that as long as I'm primary, the investigation into the death of Detective Kohli will receive my complete focus."

Take off the damn shades, Eve thought. *I want to see your eyes.* "You can request the transfer of authority," Eve continued. "But I'll be straight with you. I won't give it up easy. I stood over him this morning. I saw what was done to him. You couldn't want his killer any more than I do."

"Captain." Clooney stepped forward, laying a hand lightly on Roth's arm at the elbow. There were lines fanning out from his pale blue eyes. They made him look tired and somehow trustworthy. "Lieutenant. Emotions are running pretty high right now. For all of us. But we've got a job to do here and now."

He glanced up, homing in on a window four stories above. "Whatever we're feeling doesn't come close to what's going to be felt upstairs."

"You're right. You're right, Art. Let's get this done."

Roth turned to the entrance, bypassed the code with her master.

"Lieutenant?" Clooney hung back. "I know you'll want to question Patsy, Taj's wife. I have to ask if you could go a little easy just now. I know what she's about to go through. I lost a son in the line of duty a few months back. It rips a hole in you."

"I'm not going to kick her while she's down, Clooney." Eve shoved though the doors, caught herself, turned back. "I didn't know him," she said more calmly, "but he was murdered, and he was a cop. That's enough for me. Okay?"

"Yeah. Yeah, okay."

"Christ, I hate this." She followed Roth to the elevator. "How do you do it?" she asked Clooney. "The counseling thing. How do you stand it?"

"To tell you the truth, they tapped me for it because I have a way with keeping the peace. Mediation," he added with a quick smile. "I agreed to survivor counseling, to give it a try, and found I could do some good. You know what they feel— every stage of it."

He pressed his lips together as they stepped onto the elevator. The smile was long gone. "You stand it because maybe you can help . . . just a little. It makes a difference if the counselor's a cop. And I've discovered in the last few months it makes a bigger one if the counselor's a cop who experienced a loss. You ever lose a family member, Lieutenant?"

Eve flashed on a dingy room, the bloody husk of a man, and the child she'd been, huddled broken in a corner. "I don't have any family."

"Well . . ." was all Clooney said as they stepped off on the fourth floor.

She would know, and they were all aware of it. A cop's spouse would know the minute she opened the door. How the words were spoken varied little, and it didn't matter a damn. The minute the door opened, lives were irrevocably changed.

They didn't have the chance to knock before it began.

Patsy Kohli was a pretty woman with smooth, ebony skin and a closely cropped thatch of black curls. She was dressed to go out, a baby sling strapped across her breasts. The small boy at her side had his hand clasped in hers as he danced frantically in place.

"Let's go swing! Let's go swing!"

But his mother had frozen in place, the laughter that had been in her eyes dying away. She lifted one hand, pressing it to the baby, and the baby to her heart.

"Taj."

Roth had taken off her sunshades. Her eyes were coldly blue, rigidly blank. "Patsy. We need to come in."

"Taj." Patsy stood where she was, slowly shaking her head. "Taj."

"Here now, Patsy." Clooney moved in, sliding an arm around her shoulders. "Why don't we sit down?"

"No. No. No."

The little boy began to cry, wailing yelps as he tugged on his mother's unresponsive hand. Both Roth and Eve looked down at him with stares of sheer, hot panic.

Peabody eased inside, crouched down to his level.

"Hi, pal."

"Going swing," he said pitifully, while great tears spilled down his chubby cheeks.

"Yeah. Lieutenant, why don't I take the boy out?"

"Good idea. Good thinking." Her stomach was busily tying itself into knots at the rising sobs. "Mrs. Kohli, with your permission, my officer will take your son outside for awhile. I think that would be best."

"Chad." Patsy stared down as if coming out of a dream. "We're going to the park. Two blocks over. The swings."

"I'll take him, Mrs. Kohli. We'll be fine." With an ease that had Eve frowning, Peabody lifted the boy, set him on her hip. "Hey, Chad, you like soy dogs?"

"Patsy, why don't you give me your little girl there." Gently, Clooney unhooked the sling, slipped the baby free. Then, to Eve's shock, he passed the bundle to her.

"Oh listen, I can't—"

But Clooney was already guiding Patsy to the sofa, and Eve was left holding the bag. Or so she thought of it. Wincing, she looked down, and when big, black eyes stared curiously up at her, her palms went damp.

And when the baby said, "Coo" she lost all the spit in her mouth.

She searched the room for help. Clooney and Roth were already flanking Patsy, and Clooney's voice was a quiet murmur. The room was small and lived-in, with a scatter of toys on the rug and a scent—one she didn't recognize—that was talc and crayons and sugar. The scent of children.

But she spotted a basket of neatly folded laundry on the floor by a chair. Perfect, she decided and, with the care of a woman handling a homemade boomer, laid the baby on top.

"Stay." she whispered, awkwardly patting the dark, downy head.

And started to breathe again.

She tuned back into the room, saw the woman on the sofa gathered into herself, rocking, rocking, with her hands gripped in Clooney's. She made no sound, and her tears fell like rain.

Eve stayed out of the way, watched Clooney work,

watched the unity of support stand on either side of the widow. *This,* she thought, *was family. For what it was worth. And in times like this, it was all there could be.*

Grief settled into the room like fog. It would, she knew, be a long time before it burned away again.

"It's my fault. It's my fault." They were the first words Patsy spoke since she'd sat on the sofa.

"No." Clooney squeezed her hands until she lifted her head. They needed to look in your eyes, he knew. To believe you, to take comfort, they needed to see it all in your eyes. "Of course it's not."

"He'd never have been working there if not for me. I didn't want to go back to work after Jilly was born. I wanted to stay home. The money, the professional mother's salary was so much less than—"

"Patsy, Taj was happy you were content to stay home with the children. He was so proud of them and of you."

"I can't—Chad." She pulled her hands free, pressed them to her face. "How can I tell him? How can we live without Taj? Where is he?" She dropped her hands, looked around blindly. "I have to go see him. Maybe there's a mistake."

It was, Eve, knew, her time. "I'm sorry, Mrs. Kohli, there's no mistake. I'm Lieutenant Dallas. I'm in charge of the investigation."

"You saw Taj." Patsy got shakily to her feet.

"Yes. I'm sorry, very sorry for your loss. Can you talk to me, Mrs. Kohli? Help me find the person who did this?"

"Lieutenant Dallas," Roth began, but Patsy shook her head.

"No, no. I want to talk. Taj would want me to. He'd want . . . Where's Jilly? Where's my baby?"

"I, ah . . ." Feeling sticky again, Eve gestured to the hamper.

"Oh." Patsy wiped tears from her face, smiled. "She's so good. Such a love. She hardly ever cries. I should put her in her crib."

"I'll do that for you, Patsy." Clooney rose. "You talk to the lieutenant." He gave Eve a quiet look, full of sorrow and understanding. "That's what Taj would want. Do you want us to call someone for you? Your sister?"

"Yes." Patsy drew in a breath. "Yes, please. If you'd call Carla for me."

"Captain Roth will do that for you, won't you, Captain? While I put the baby down."

Roth struggled, set her teeth. It didn't surprise Eve to see the annoyance. Clooney had essentially taken over, gently. And this wasn't a woman who liked taking orders from her sergeant.

"Yes, of course." With a final warning look at Eve, she walked into the next room.

"Are you with Taj's squad?"

"No, I'm not."

"No, no, of course." Patsy rubbed her temple. "You'd be with Homicide." She started to break, the sound coming through her lips like a whimper. And Eve watched with admiration as she toughened up. "What do you want to know?"

"Your husband didn't come home this morning. You weren't concerned?"

"No." She reached back, braced a hand on the arm of the couch, and lowered herself down. "He'd told me he'd probably go into the station from the club. He sometimes did that. And he said he was meeting someone after closing."

"Who?"

"He didn't say, just that he had someone to see after closing."

"Do you know of anyone who wished him harm, Mrs. Kohli?"

"He was a cop," she said simply. "Do you know anyone who wishes you harm, Lieutenant?"

Fair enough, Eve thought and nodded. "Anyone specific? Someone he mentioned to you."

"No. Taj didn't bring work home. It was a point of honor

for him, I think. He didn't want anything to touch his family. I don't even know what cases he was working on. He didn't like to talk about it. But he was worried."

She folded her hands tightly in her lap, stared down at them. Stared, Eve noted, at the gold band on her finger. "I could tell he was worried about something. I asked him about it, but he brushed it off. That was Taj," she managed with a trembling smile. "He had, well some people would say it was a male dominant thing, but it was just Taj. He was old-fashioned about some things. He was a good man. A wonderful father. He loved his job."

She pressed her lips together. "He would have been proud to die in the line of duty. But not like this. Not like this. Whoever did this to him took that away from him. Took him away from me and from his babies. How can that be? Lieutenant, how can that be?"

And as there was no answer to it; all Eve could do was ask more questions.

Ready to find
your next great read?

Let us help.

Visit prh.com/nextread

Penguin
Random
House